BROKEN FIELD

Also by Jeff Hull:

Pale Morning Done:
A Novel (2005)

Streams of Consciousness:
Hip-Deep Dispatches from the River of Life (2007)

BROKEN FIELD

A Novel

Jeff Hull

Arcade Publishing

Arcade Publishing books may be purchased in bulk at special discounts for sales promotion, corporate gifts, fund-raising, or educational purposes. Special editions can also be created to specifications. For details, contact the Special Sales Department, Arcade Publishing, 307 West 36th Street, 11th Floor, New York, NY 10018 or arcade@skyhorsepublishing.com.

Arcade Publishing® is a registered trademark of Skyhorse Publishing, Inc.®, a Delaware corporation.

Visit our website at www.arcadepub.com.

10 9 8 7 6 5 4 3 2 1

Library of Congress Cataloging-in-Publication Data is available on file.

Print ISBN: 978-1-62872-978-8
Ebook ISBN: 978-1-62872-982-5

Printed in the United States of America

ACKNOWLEDGMENTS

MOST OF THIS NOVEL WAS WRITTEN in a one-room cabin with no running water, electricity or internet connection, somewhere between Hingham, Montana, and Canada. What it lacks in amenities the place makes up for with sweeping views of the Hi Line's austere beauty and an incredible sense of space and peace. It is a place with no directions and no demands, an immersion for the imagination. The Lookout was built by Craig Sterry so that writers, painters, musicians—artists of any kind—can work uninterrupted and inspired by the depth and breadth of the land and unbroken sky. To Craig and his wife Vonnie, I owe endless gratitude. They gave me a place. They read what I wrote there. They brought me farm-fresh eggs, tomatoes, corn and other treats. Their generosity and insights had everything to do with how this book happened.

I would like to thank my other friends in North-Central Montana. Over the years, Ray and Amy Sibra have provided me shelter and stories and so much of my introduction to life on the northern plains. I borrowed some names from people I know in that part of the world and some I don't—because why make up names when there are perfectly good ones walking around all over? The characters attached to these names are in no way meant to represent the character of actual people. The story is completely fictional, too, and all likeness to actual people or events is coincidental—though, sadly, similar occurrences seem to happen every year, all over the country. These happenings are certainly not specific to rural places, and, though I may have created a few unsavory imaginary people, they do not reflect the experiences I have had with the many wonderful real people of Big Sandy, Chinook, Fort Benton, Hingham, Inverness, Chester and other small, Northern Montana towns.

I must thank Tony Lyons, and also Charlie and Nick Lyons, for setting in motion the coincidences that led to this book being published by Skyhorse. Lilly Golden was again, as her name suggests, an incredibly valuable contributor to the way this book turned out. Thanks to David Cates and Liliana Silver, who read early drafts and helped shape the end result, and Dan Bennett and Peter Dodd, who helped with some of the football pieces.

My parents have been endlessly supportive over the years and deserve much credit and gratitude.

Most of all, I want to thank Kim Baron for her love, her support, her understanding, her kindness, her wisdom and her talent for making everything I do better always, all ways.

This work is dedicated to my son Rowan, and to the memory of Chris Hull.

BROKEN FIELD

August

WHEN SHE SAW THE CAR—A DARK, low-slung Chevy sedan, its vinyl roof tattered and flaked—Josie thought of it only as a possible way out of her situation. She was a sixteen-year-old girl alone on a vast landscape, standing beside a broken down grain truck on a long and empty gravel road, miles from help or houses or a cell signal. This, Josie felt, was just another trial of harvest. The dark car slowed quickly, seemed to fishtail a little, as if the driver had not intended to stop, and then suddenly changed his mind. The tires, Josie noticed right away, were too bald for driving gravel.

A long crack in the windshield read like the map of some twisted journey across a confined world. Josie Frehse wasn't naïve. She knew that sometimes trouble came from Havre or Lewistown or over the border from Medicine Hat or from the Fort Miles reservation and sometimes it came in cars like this one. But she didn't feel trouble. Josie had been driving a grain truck since she was fourteen.

She'd been riding along in one since she was five. This was the life she knew, and she knew what to expect from it: big red diesel-burning International Harvester combines in a staggered line chugging over a wheat field, powerhouses against the land and sky; chaff suspended in wafted layers, coloring the setting sun. The thickness of it in her nose, the chewing thrum of the engines.

A hawk racing low across the horizon. Bluish-green humps of mountains beneath bluish-white piles of clouds, the tawny gold and green squares stretching from her, the dips and curves of crop lines, black crescents of dirt under her fingernails. Grit on her fingertips, her jeans sweaty in the seat, the truck steering wheel trembling and jerking as she bounced along beside the combine, trying to keep the bucket under the gout of grain pouring into it.

A ballad blasted through her tinny phone speaker. Her father drove one of the combines. Her brother Jared drove another one. Her boyfriend Matt drove one. Matt was about to turn eighteen, and Jared already had. Josie was sixteen going on seventeen, and she had ideas about how fast that should happen and how much faster the rest should come, but felt still uncertain about whether those ideas made any sense. For days now, she had been steering her grain truck down the rows of the field, feeling the bumps bouncing her in her seat, wrestling the steering wheel, singing the good lines with the country singers, careful to maintain an exact distance while the combine poured its load out. And then she had honked and waved and peeled off across the field, headed for the elevator in Chinook.

Like she had a hundred times before. In Chinook, she would wait while the auger sucked the grain from the truck's hold, each load tens of thousands of dollars' worth of hard, bouncy kernels, her family's whole year of life—cereal, shampoo, jeans, home heating fuel, tampons, trash bags, books, everything they would have in their house—augered into the fat, shiny silos along the railroad tracks.

The seeds would trundle down the parallel bend of railroad tracks to Seattle, then cross a sea she'd never seen to Korea to become steamed buns. The Koreans got very precise about moisture and protein content in their wheat, and these days the farmlands around Dumont were producing exactly what they wanted. Only this time, she broke down.

It was nothing she could fix. It wasn't oil, wasn't coolant. It wasn't the steering column, which she'd helped her father disassemble and repair the year before. This felt like transmission. This felt like the truck was twenty-seven or thirty-two- years old—who knew exactly?—and it was done. It had just stopped going. Josie could step on the gas, hear the engine ring, but the truck rolled to a stop.

She strong-armed it to the side of the road. She got out, got under the carriage, looked at the transfer case, saw the little glimmery metal slivers shining in the viscous liquid, didn't feel good about the truck going any further. They would have to get another truck here and transfer the loads. It would cost them time. There was nothing she could do about it.

Breakdowns come and breakdowns go. Breakdowns sometimes meant trusting strangers. Strangers were not ominous. Even if you were broken down all by yourself on a stretch of gravel road miles from the nearest house and beyond cell range. In this country living was hard, and no matter how self-reliant you were, trusting your neighbors was a part of getting through.

Nobody made it alone. What she was worried about—the only thing she had been worried about when she saw the dark sedan slowing to pull over—was time. The late August sun blazed and the sky seemed to ache blue with the effort of holding all the light above her. In every direction the land raced away forever, horizon and sky pinching the edges of distance down.

Standing in the middle of it all, nowhere near where she wanted to be, even the big grain truck looked tiny on the ground. Somebody, she'd thought while she waited on the gravel road, would come along. It might take hours, but someone would come. And then somebody did.

It was not somebody she expected. It was a man, she could tell, a man driving alone. Instead of pulling over behind her truck, the driver let the car creep up to where she stood beside her cab. Josie saw feathers hanging from the rearview—hawk feathers or eagle feathers. The car stopped, and she saw that it wasn't really a man driving; he was a boy. A teenager, someone close to her own age. He wasn't wearing a shirt, just jeans and no shoes.

He looked Indian, maybe from the Fort Miles reservation. His face looked sharp, his eyes dark. His black hair held a tousled sheen, like it had been blowing in the open windows while he drove down the highway. It was longish and unkempt, like a '70s rodeo star. Josie felt a twitch of shame, because something about his seediness affected her in a physical way.

She didn't like her response. He seemed unclean in a raw sense. He was lithe and lank, his jeans loose and low, the band of black underwear apparent above their waist. He rested one arm on the top of the steering wheel, wrist bent, hand dangling. Josie noticed the smell coming from the car. Cigarettes.

Some pot, maybe. When she met his eyes for the first time, she felt exposed. Hunger, she thought. That's what she was reacting to. His naked hunger. Josie was a good-looking girl. She always caught boys—and, if she was being honest, some men—looking at her a certain way. They mostly laughed it off or looked embarrassed about being caught.

They almost always did something to soften what they'd been doing. This boy didn't. Josie wondered if she should tell him she was fine, didn't need help. That her people were on their way. She had pepper spray in the truck, a canister her father had bought her when they'd gone hiking in Glacier Park for grizzly bears. She thought about how close she was to the bear spray. A long scrape ran down the passenger side of the car, dented and scraped of paint. The fake leather on the boy's passenger seat was torn.

The yellow sponge guts of the car prolapsed from the rupture in the surface. He didn't say anything. He just looked at her across the empty passenger seat like he was waiting for her to tell him why he'd stopped. The sky looked so bright, the gravel white on the road, the grass in the borrow pit a green supersaturated with sunlight. Inside the car was a purple shadow. She saw the twenty-four-ounce can of Icehouse beer in his drink holder. Lots of people she knew had a beer while they drove.

And here was someone who might save her time. She and her family spent hours and days racing a clock they couldn't see the face of, the clock that ran until the next heavy rain. Working until midnight, working until two in the morning, working through the night when the bruisy thunderheaded clouds lined up in the west and started marching across the horizon, sleeping in the truck to be ready at first light, racing the rain.

Rain could make the difference between a million dollars and a year of eating off insurance. Everybody in this part of the world was doing the same thing. The men, the boys, they started harvest each year with such high spirits, heroes in their own cabs, but by the end their eyes grew unfocused from too many hours inside their own heads, too much jostle and vibration, too many miles of rows, and they swore quickly and quietly and always. Only her brother Jared stayed smiling—though Josie knew that was because his face was shaped in a grin, even when he wasn't anything but just walking around.

Though he was the one most likely to have a real smile for her when she peeled away from his combine. His smile came a lot like the hawks, swift and pure and never when you were thinking about them. She wished she could be that way. She wished she didn't have to think about so many things. Boys didn't have to think about so much. Sometimes when it was Jared and Matt and their friends, Jared would describe himself as "165 pounds of bone and sinew and cock," and that wasn't all wrong. Boys could act, do, clean up later. Working the harvest was this way.

You drove your truck, you could think anything. Josie planned her wedding driving the truck, though the ceremony—party, let's call it a party, she always thought—didn't necessarily feature Matt Brunner. She re-lost her virginity dozens of times driving the truck, in ways she wished it had actually happened, and wondered if it was bad that Matt wasn't always the guy she imagined being with. She made new friends she'd never met. She wandered pieces of Italy, though knowing nothing about Italy she patched together museums and cliffside villages and bike rides and enormous meals featuring little round pieces of cheese and skinny slices of meat.

Josie had a child in the truck. Some days she made the women's basketball team at Stanford, took heroic shots with the clock winding down. She won several important games. Sitting behind the wheel, she rethought and repositioned herself, imagining exactly where her feet would land, the precise extent of her shoulder fake, how the ball moved.

The flip of her wrist that sent the ball airbound, the rotation of the seams. Josie imagined whole lives in the truck, lives of her friends, lives of her family. She would get so bored she imagined her crazily vague distant future, a family she might have, a little boy, and she named him Rowan, and she let Rowan's bone-blonde hair grow long and fine over his shoulders, and she brushed it. Sometimes Matt Brunner was the star of her future.

Sometimes there were boys she didn't know yet. She sang the good songs on her playlists, loud, hitting every decrescendo, every bit of tremolo. When the light was low and fading and just right, the songs could mean so much. Josie loved harvest. She loved late summer, mass meals, sweat, ball caps on grimy hair, and thirty-two-ounce bottles of Diet Pepsi. She loved the sweet dry smell of cut wheat and the sweet nostalgia of a season not quite over, and she loved the approaching school year that would snap some order onto the long, shapeless days of summer on the northern plains. Most of all, she loved the time alone in her own head, the space it gave her.

She loved the doing. The not having to worry about next. Worrying was like praying for bad things to happen, her mother always said. Next made her queasy.

"I broke down," she said to the boy in the car, because she didn't feel comfortable not saying anything.

"Need a ride?" he asked.

"Are you from around here?" she asked. In the islands of paint where the finish on the car was not faded and matted, the high sun sparkled the way it did on deep water.

"I just moved," he said. His tongue slowly tapped each word. "You from here?"

"Yeah," she said.

"I can give you a ride," he said.

"There's another truck coming right behind me," she said. It wasn't a wish. One would be coming, but she didn't know when.

"Okay," he said. "But if you need a ride before then."

"Where are you going?" she asked.

"I'm not going anywhere," he said and laughed like the idea of going somewhere was funny. "I'm just driving."

Josie thought *what the hell—he's a kid.* And this was something different. Not much different happened in her life, not much changed from day to day or year to year. This kid was different, not like Matt, not like the farm boys she had grown up with. It could, she thought, go badly—though she had no real-life understanding of how badly, simply because it's impossible to imagine the reach of pain you haven't felt yet. But the alternative was sitting on the side of the road for—an hour? Three hours? However long it took the next vehicle to come along. And here was a boy she shouldn't want anything to do with, with a car she didn't want to get into and a big beer in his drink holder.

"Yeah, okay," she said. "I gotta go back this way. It's about forty-five minutes back . . ."

"I got nothing but time," he said. "Time ain't no big deal."

"Let me get my phone," she said. "Maybe we can just drive down the road until we get service and make a plan then."

"Sure," he said. "Get in."

The door hinge shrieked at her when she opened it. She expected the car's dark interior to be cool, but it was only a closer sort of heat. She hadn't fetched her bear spray, hadn't locked the truck. She sat down, aware that her T-shirt was damp with sweat.

She unlocked her phone screen, brought up the dial pad and crooked her thumb over it, as if she was a touch away from finding other help. The boy barely waited until she'd sat before stomping on the gas. Josie heard gravel pinging all over the undercarriage. She could hear the engine deepen its throat, could hear it suck more gas. He lifted his twenty-four-ounce beer can, the aluminum shining on both sides of his fist, toward her. "Want some?"

"No thanks."

"I got another can."

"I'm good," she said.

He drove with the fingers of one hand wrapped tightly to the wheel, slouching, the wind blowing ribbons of his hair around his face. It seemed his chosen form of oblivion. He twisted the radio knob and rap music she knew nothing about battered the tin-can speakers buried in the dashboard, the bass cracked and fuzzed. Josie spent her whole life around men and boys and their love for engines and machines.

She lived in what everybody called Next Year Country. Dryland wheat farms were a race against time and weather and the market. You almost never got it right. You almost always went into winter saying, "Next year we'll hit it right." And when you did hit it, when you got a Next Year, when the profits came in long numbers, the first thing that happened was the men bought bigger trucks and combines and attachments.

This boy and his love for going fast in his beater car was nothing new to her. What was different was the way he held off speaking to her.

As if he had something to show her first. They tore across the gravel road. Josie knew how fast was safe; this boy wasn't being safe. There had been something about him from the first glance that had told her he wouldn't be safe. But she had wanted to come with him.

Over every rise, Josie felt the lift in the her seat before the heavy sedan stomped on its springs coming down. The car slid in the loose gravel, and she could smell the chalky dust they raised. He tilted the beer can at her again. She waved it off.

"What's your name?" he finally asked, not looking at her.

"Josie," she said. She had to yell over the roar of wind through both open windows and the rabble of the tires racing over gravel. "What's yours?"

"LaValle," he said.

"What?" she yelled.

"LaValle."

"That's your first name?"

"No."

Sitting next to this boy she should not be in a car with, they raced across the landscape she had known her whole life. Every second she was getting closer to where she was supposed to be.

* * *

Saturday, November

BEFORE IT ALL STARTED, TOM WARNER stared down at his foot in a black Nike cleat. He coached in cleats because sidelines got muddy and slick and because it made him feel closer to the game, made him feel like he'd felt when he played. A guy had damned few occasions to wear cleats in his early forties.

He loved the way they gripped the earth. He looked down at his cleat, toe planted on the mostly dead grass, heel resting in the white chalk of the sideline, and everything else fell away. Tom felt his weight on that foot. Thousands of steps a day without a thought, then comes one deliberate move, a plant, a push-off, a shift that alters direction. Without thinking, his eyes followed the point of his foot on the grass toward the goal line.

As if he might run there. And then his attention opened to take everything else back in, the low autumn bronze and blue light, slanted all day this late in November, the Canadian chill edging the air. A ring of ranch trucks surrounded the rectangle of planted grass. Beyond them, the grasslands flowed toward an unbroken horizon, dolloped with tiny swirls of sage and small hills.

All the lines raced under the sky far into the distance. Tom turned to see the ranchers and farmers and mothers and sisters behind him talking in cheery tones, expecting something. He heard the frayed chords of his players, their trying-to-be-husky voices resonating with the stakes of the moment. There was a lot going on at the field.

Everybody there was excited. Twenty or thirty people, mostly the opponents, Plentywood high school and junior high kids, sat in a tiny stand of homemade, home-team wooden bleachers at mid-field. Mothers and grandmothers brought lawn chairs and sat back from the sidelines with wool blankets over their legs. Ranchers and farmers stood in clusters, wearing feeding caps and irrigating boots, rocked back on their heels. Or they sat in their ranch rigs parked pointing at the field, spitting globs of tobacco-streaked saliva out rolled-down windows, ready to pop on headlights to illuminate the action if the game dragged too long into the short northern after-noon.

It was just a moment, this taking in the swirl of the day, some-thing he liked to do, and then his focus sharpened onto the field and his boys. Then came a crescendo he'd known his whole life as his boys chased their kick-off down the field, the action and sound leaping by him, the huffs of boys running as hard as they could, sidelines cheering, the clack and clatter of colliding pads. Teenaged boys from two tiny towns threw themselves at each other and clashed and bashed and shoved and drove. Tom Warner took in the grunts of effort, the smell of torn-up grass and soil, clots of mud flying from cleats.

There was nothing else like it. Except in moments of extraor-dinary uncertainty, when Dumont was on defense, Tom let his assistant, Slab Rideg, do the coaching. Slab knew what he was doing and the autonomy kept him invested, and when he felt invested he coached with his hair on fire. On the first two plays, Tom stood on the sideline and quietly appreciated his team's containment of the Plentywood offense. In eight-man football, the beginning was always a dance, jabs and pokes, probing and prodding, teams trying to figure out where the big weaknesses lay.

When you only fielded eight boys on a side, there were always weaknesses. This early in a game, Tom liked to assess which of his boys had shown up to play—having their heads in the game had been Dumont's big weakness in the past two seasons. Then the third play unfolded, and Tom had a clear cool sense of what was going to happen for the rest of the game. He watched the Plentywood quarterback take the snap and scurry down the line. The Plentywood quarterback was slight, even by Class C standards, but fleet.

He was a wizard with ball fakes. A tailback trailed behind the quarterback and swung out toward the corner to set up the option. Tom saw everything happening from the first steps, saw the threads and seams and vectors. He watched his defensive end, six-foot-three, 180-pound Waylon Edwards, shuttle step to find the perfect angle and lower his shoulder to level the tight end assigned to block him, thudding the boy onto his butt. Tom glimpsed the instant of panic on the Plentywood quarterback's face as Waylon Edwards appeared not only where he wasn't supposed to be, but charged with a full head of steam.

And then Waylon rammed most of himself into the quarterback's chest, hacking his arm to guillotine the desperation pitch. Tom could hear the gut-crushed *oooffff* of air expel from the Plentywood boy's lungs, saw the boy's head whiplash as he flopped backward in a sudden heap. A plastic mouthguard spun through a sky bright blue, mottled with tiny white morsels of cloud. A helmet skipped and rolled ten yards back.

Then it was hell among the yearlings. Tom could have closed his eyes and known exactly what was happening, just from the barking cheer of the Dumont sideline when the kids saw the football fly free, the somewhat meaner roar of the Dumont fans, adults who had driven five hours to witness this kind of unbridled aggression from their children and the children of their friends and neighbors. Tom did not judge them in the least.

He loved the pure vicious intent of the play. A totally clean hit, but Waylon Edwards was announcing to all the people gathered around that little field that he'd taken the five-hour bus ride to Plentywood to blow people up. The ball twirled into the air, then fell and nose-tumbled through the backfield. The Plentywood tail-back, trailing the quarterback, found himself wrong-footed, unable to shift quickly enough to dive on the errant pitch. Then he found himself thumped to the turf by a broadside blow from Dumont's safety, Jared Frehse.

A second wave of jacked-up cheers surged from the Wolfpack bench, resonating in the deeper-chested ranchers and farmers who'd sacrificed a day of fencing or tractor repair or winter wheat seeding or any number of chores that needed completing before the snow started flying to make a six-hundred-mile round-trip so they could shout about their boys outmuscling some other boys. Despite the energy he'd jolted into the Plentywood quarterback, Waylon Edwards remained upright and hyper-aware of the ball, which he chased, scooped up, stumbling to keep his feet under him as he rambled twenty-six yards untouched for Dumont's first score.

Part of Tom thought, *woo-hoo and god T. damn!* And for a good piece of a moment he felt alive, sizzling with the energy of that play. He fought hard to hold off what he knew was coming, fought to hang on to the joy of the boys, their savage woofing and adrenal-ized high-steps. But always, always, at the end of these things, it got hard to make more of what it was than what it was.

Tom had coached Class C football in Montana for sixteen years, small schools, eight players on a team, eighty-yard fields.

He knew there were tricks and peculiarities, but lots of games came down to who out-athleted whom. His job insisted he believe that you could coach will, you could coach teamwork, you could coach sustained effort.

He had to think he could coach up those other guys, the average players and the small, slow, inexperienced boys, so that one of them might throw a block that would spring a run, read a coverage, jump a route—make a play nobody expected them to make—or else why would he be coaching? But a lot of it kept coming down to who the big guys were, who the fast guys were, who controlled their bodies in athletic ways and who didn't. Who made mistakes and who didn't.

Who wanted it more. And then there was this team. The seniors he had on the field should have already won at least one state championship. If Tom were better at what he did, he thought, they would have won two. He had already won two, with two different teams from two different towns, and knew how it could be done. His Dumont team, far more athletic, far more skilled than any he'd ever coached, should be slathered in glory, or at least hungry to be. Sometimes they were.

But sometimes they weren't. It visited him every day that maybe it was his fault. Could anyone really coach the hunger, the want-to? Could he? When he'd played, he believed his coaches ratcheted up the want-to in him. When he started coaching, he believed one hundred percent he could inspire kids to want to run through walls, like they talked about on NFL broadcasts when the games were slow.

Now, with sixteen years of experience and two state titles to his name, he honestly didn't know. Sometimes he saw it. Today. Tom knew, before his somewhat famous offense ever took a snap, what was going to happen on this day on this field. Three plays in, and he knew the parents of Plentywood players and the longtime Plentywood boosters standing around the home field or sitting in their pickups alongside it were going to have to wake up in the morning viewing their team the way Tom viewed the prairie they all tried to live on: something capable of a surprise now and then, but most often the home of shrunken enthusiasm you should have seen coming.

The Plentywood people were going to have to start reconciling how this game, and the bright season that led up to it, affected their sense of scope and emotional memory. That's how sports were in the small towns scattered across the vast sweep of Montana's high plains. Winning football mattered in a way that weddings and births and twenty bushels per acre and hundred-dollar beef and three-dollar wheat mattered—happy party times, points of focus for the collective memory of a group of people who independently arrived at decisions to occupy roughly the same space on a landscape that didn't give one chilly shit about them.

He knew that his own people were looking to plant a flag in the terra incognita of time, to fly a banner named "Dumont Wolfpack, State Champions" in future dialogues, a standard against years when rains don't fall and equipment breaks down and disappointment at home threatens to elevate bitterness into a hegemony. The Dumont people wanted some personal mythology, and it was his job to goddamn deliver it.

He caught Slab Rideg's eye as his assistant coach stomped back to the sidelines after meeting the defensive players coming to the sideline, smacking their helmets, swatting their asses, screaming in their faces. A twenty-six-year old former Dumont defensive lineman who had come by his nickname during fitter days, Slab in so much motion always made Tom a little queasy. The kids now called him Flab behind his back.

"You feel that?" Slab shouted at Tom. "That's what we're doin' here!" Slab was lost in a how-do-you-like-me-now rage of enthusiasm, fodder for the boys.

Tom watched his players come off the field after scoring the extra points—they always went for two—and watched white steam pour from their heads into the cool November afternoon when they pried their helmets off, saw in their smiles the real adolescent pride in being able to do what they thought they were supposed to be doing. He doubted they knew why they loved it—none of them would truly know why they loved it until years later, when it was all gone. The kids clapped high fives and barked, firing each other up. Across the field the boys on the other sideline were also hard-scrabble ranch boys who bulldogged and castrated calves, slopped hogs and bucked bales, boys for whom physical strength and work shaped every day of their lives.

Tom surveyed the Dumont fans who'd driven the five hours to watch the game. He saw Mike Latshaw, whose father had died when he put a car up on a lift and the lift collapsed, pinning the man against an air compressor. The valve had punctured him and injected forced air until he couldn't keep living. He saw Ethan Miller, wiry in glasses and a black T-shirt and a brown Carhartt, Ethan who one night came in late from plowing and picked up a stray cat with a collar on at his front door, wondering what a cat could be doing miles from any other homes, only to have his wife point out that he was cradling a skunk with a canning ring stuck around its neck.

And Katie DeSoto, shriveled and sunburned with barely enough muscle to move her joints, an old drunk who once, when her husband hid her car keys to keep her from going to town for booze, stole his ancient Farmall tractor and drove it twenty-seven miles overland to the nearest bar—then sold it to an Indian for $500 more than it was worth. He was surprised to see Jenny Calhoun— who had children in the school, but none of football-playing age— and also not surprised.

Her long sandy hair hung loose for a change, luffing in the breeze. And then he was back into the game, watching Slab coach the defense to a three-and-out. Half of his boys played both ways, but they came to the sideline, lingering for an extra squirt of water. Tom found his quarterback and saw something on the boy's face, a sneer of his short upper lip, a little too much light in the boy's bright blue eyes.

He snatched Matt Brunner's jersey in his fist and thrust his face up against the boy's facemask. He recognized in Brunner's eyes an enervated sizzle.

"Matt! Core offense," Tom said. "If it breaks down, go to the next play. No hero. Okay? No hero."

"I feel you, Coach," Brunner said. Tom could smell the onions from the burger Matt had eaten for lunch. Also, he knew Matt hadn't really heard him.

"Listen to me!" Tom hissed quickly. He jerked Matt's facemask so close it bashed his own nose. Tom could feel the cut.

He saw Matt's eyes focus on the blood that welled quickly on the bridge of his nose, teetered and spilled to one side onto his cheek. Then Matt's focus came back to his eyes. "Core offense," Tom said. "You play smart, we win. No hero. You play smart, we win."

The novelty of Tom's bleeding nose had burned off. Cool-boy recklessness smeared a grin on Matt's face. He said, "We gonna huck it?"

"Trust me," Tom said. He pointed the facemask toward the field and let it go. "Go play like you know how." He whacked Matt on the butt and the quarterback loped onto the field.

Tom wheeled and yelled, "Frehse! Where's Frehse?"

Jared Frehse, already jogging toward the huddle, spun back and sprinted to his coach.

Tom put his hands on his hips, looked at Frehse, looked at the field, looked back at Frehse, and tilted his head. He turned a bit away from the field, making Jared step with him and creating the sense of a private conversation.

"Look around," Tom said. "See that other team?"

"Yes, sir."

"See those fans on the other side?"

"Yes, sir."

"What do you see?"

"They don't look happy, Coach."

"They are not happy," Tom said. "And your job is to make them stay not happy today."

Jared looked up at Tom and said, "What happened to your nose, Coach?"

"You know what I'm worried about?" Tom asked.

"No hero," Jared said, because this was not a new conversation.

With even, deliberate spacing, Tom said, "Go win the game."

Jared's smile faded and his mouth shrank into a small dash on his face. He nodded once, pivoted, and ran onto the field in steps that seemed to barely use the ground.

Tom called three consecutive option plays and Jared Frehse—whose last name and ability to make defensive players look like they were standing still had long ago prompted the nickname "Mister Freeze"—skittered and scattered for seven or eight yards each play. Even as Tom heard the Plentywood coaches screaming for their defensive backs not to crowd the line, to watch for the pass, he saw the safeties cheating up, focusing on Jared Frehse. So on the fourth play of the drive, Tom let Matt Brunner fake a pitch to Jared, bootleg opposite field and gun the ball down the sidelines to Alex Martin. Brunner threw a beautiful ball and Martin, who was embarrassingly alone out there, sprinted under it, then gamboled down the sidelines for Dumont's second score.

The Dumont fans and bench erupted again. A few players on the field bumped chests or slapped helmets, but his team was already coming back, getting ready to play defense. They were in it today.

When they were in it, there were maybe two teams in the entire state of Montana that could stay on the field with them. Plentywood wasn't one of them. Plentywood managed a first down on the next series, then Matt Brunner intercepted an ill-advised crossing route. Back on offense, Tom called a quarterback draw, watched Matt grin from the huddle, then watched him dig up the middle for thirty yards.

Jared scored again on the next play, finding a seam at the line, and making the safety stumble so badly he had to put his hands down on the grass to stay upright. Jared cruised into the end zone with his head tilted back. The few boys who didn't play both ways clustered near Tom on the sidelines, sweat streaking the dirt that covered their bare arms.

Tom saw in their eyes an adrenaline stoke he knew from experience you could only legally find on a football field, the primal thrill of physically imposing your will on another person. Tom loved football more than any other form of competition, and the fast and feral Class C eight-man game more than any other kind of football. The placement of a contest so squarely amid the open land and sky he had grown up in always brought it all home.

By halftime, the Dumont Wolfpack had built a thirty-five-point lead. It would have been mindbendingly difficult to blow such a lead, but Tom had seen his team do mindbendingly stupid things—the meltdown in last year's state semifinal a thoroughly discussed example among Dumont's chattering and drinking class, which comprised about everybody—and so on their first offensive play of the second half, Tom sent in a play he called at least once every game.

Every Class C coach he faced knew he'd run it. Sometimes he ran it over and over, with slight variations, daring the other team to stop it. He understood that he had built the play into something bigger than it was, a personal touchstone of sorts. In the Dumont playbook, the play was called 85 Look Left Veer Option Right.

The boys just called it "Six." Six was Jared Frehse's number, and six points was how the play often ended. At the snap, Matt Brunner took two steps to his left. Behind him Frehse did exactly the same thing. The entire defense, their anger and shame pricked by a halftime scalding from their coaches, poured in that direction. Then Matt Brunner planted his left foot, pivoted to the inside, and pitched the ball back to Jared, who had also planted and reversed direction, heading right.

Frehse caught the pitch in mid-stride. From there his job was to out-sprint the defense around the right corner. Tom waited for Jared to plant his right foot and make the corner because, in that physical gesture, no other boy he'd seen in over two decades of playing and coaching football had ever reminded him so much of his own son. For a brief moment, Tom could be transported to another wind-scraped town where sun and winter peeled paint from the boxy little houses, watching another young boy race along a sideline like he might run all the way to the never-ending horizon. None of the fans standing around this field in Plentywood, not the home team nor his Dumont people, knew anything about Derek Warner, but by the time Derek had turned thirteen, Tom understood that his boy had been gifted with physical talent far greater than any Tom had ever possessed.

By the time Derek was fourteen, he was gone. Now, Tom watched Jared Frehse fly across the backfield, then plant a flicker-quick right foot and launch upfield, slapping away the grasping hands of an overpursuing linebacker. Tom had never coached a better broken field runner.

Jared's hips tucked under him, the ball cradled and pumping back and forth in his arm, the helmet leading forward, his legs blurring. Tom squinted his eyes so he could see another boy, and for a moment felt a sweet jag of connection to a past that was nowhere as wrecked as his present. After Jared scored, even the least athletic of his two dozen players saw action—even twiggy little Wyatt Aarstad, who could barely fill his uniform, ran onto the field, where he was run over by someone on every play. But, Tom noticed with a snippet of pride, Wyatt got up every time with something to say.

That the kid got his ass beat play after play but still seemed excited to be on the field seemed like as much a success as any score. As the teams walked toward their locker rooms after the game, Tom jogged ahead of them, feeling a twinge of guilt for not lingering to enjoy the congratulations of Dumont fans who had come so far to watch the show. He knew he should say something to Jenny Calhoun and maybe even wanted to. But he retreated to the locker room with Slab Rideg—whose actual name was Bill—and watched to make sure none of his players were disguising injuries, or faking them. He tried to talk to his team, tried to manage egos, tried to tell them that beating Plentywood 56–13 did not mean they'd played their best.

It was clear they did not exactly believe him. They were teenagers in cut-off T-shirts and Under Armour compression shorts and they were, at times like these, undeniable. Waiting for the boys to dress, Slab held onto the bill of his ball cap and moved it around on his head, which Tom knew meant he wanted to talk.

"Undefeated," Slab said.

"Lot of teams been undefeated before the last game," Tom said.

"Undefeated and number one, Tommy."

"Number one on our side of the bracket," Tom said.

"Lot of Dumont people out there," Slab said. "This team means a lot to them. Would it kill you to be a little happy about it?"

"I'm happy. I said I am."

"Shit, everybody was here," Slab said. "Be a good time to go on a crime spree back in Dumont."

"What would you steal?"

"Carrie Ann came over," Slab said, and that was where this was going. Slab had married Carrie Ann, an enormously exuberant woman, three weeks before. And now she had driven five hours just to stand on the grass and watch her brand-new husband coach eight kids playing defense for an hour and a half.

"Why don't you ride back with her," Tom said, certain this was Slab's hope all along and that it also included a detour down through Billings or at least Lewistown, trying to snatch a little honeymoon activity in a hotel that had a pool and a salad bar and slushy pre-mixed cocktails like pina coladas or strawberry daiquiris. Tom didn't want to think more about it than that. He liked Slab fine, admired his ardor and dedication as a coach, but did not want to imagine him smiling goofily across a table at his recent bride after a drink too many.

"What about the bus?" Slab asked.

It was against school policy to have only Tom and the bus driver as adults on the bus. But Dumont was the kind of town where policies were more suggestions until things went really wrong. Tom said, "Krock O' and I can handle it. Go. Have a time."

* * *

There were things worth knowing about her history and things not worth knowing. Josie Frehse lay on the foot of a bed in a hotel room in Havre. Her mother sat propped up against the headboard of the bed. For most of the season, the volleyball team traveled with the football team, played a game wherever the boys played, saved money on transportation. But now football had shifted into playoffs and volleyball had turned to the district tournament, which put Josie in Havre with her mother, while her father had gone to Plentywood to watch Jared play. Why Josie found herself in her mother's hotel room after dinner thinking about discussing sex was less explicable.

"Anything you want to tell me, you know you can, right?" Judy Frehse had just said out of the blue. The tournament was in Chinook, but there was only one hotel in Chinook and eight teams traveling there. So the Dumont girls drove two and a half hours to Chinook, played their games, then traveled the twenty miles to Havre for the night. They had lost the day before and then lost again in the play-back round.

They'd go home the next day and start thinking about basketball season. Judy Frehse sat against the headboard, legs stretched on the bed, facing the TV but tilted toward Josie. She wore jeans and a plaid blouse and a button-up cardigan. At her feet on the bed was an open pizza box. Josie reclined on her back, knees up and apart, absently scrolling through her phone, still in sweats from the game.

First her mother had said, "Your dad called. The boys won big time, 56–13. Jared had four touchdowns."

"Matt?"

"Threw for two and ran for one. Or threw for three. He did good."

And that made Josie happy. The girls' volleyball team losing made her unhappy, but the football team losing was a bad time for everyone. It had only happened three times since Jared and Matt and Alex Martin started playing together as freshmen. They'd lost to Malta in the first round of the playoffs that first season. They lost to Wibaux in the state quarterfinals their sophomore year.

And Wibaux had beaten them again last year in the semifinals. All three losses had been awful for days. It meant a sullen big brother and an upset father and a moody boyfriend and everybody at school pretending there was nothing to be excited about for at least a week.

And then her mother said, "How are things with you and Matt?"

What her mother was really asking was, *Are you and Matt having sex? Is he going to make you pregnant?*

Which was funny, because she'd gone to her mother's hotel room in the first place partly because she was wanting to talk about Matt. Normally she would be with her teammates, her girls, Snapchatting, texting boys with probing if not outright flirtatious exchanges, taking endless selfies until they captured the look they most wanted to project to the world. Josie wouldn't necessarily be doing all of that, but she'd be there to support it.

Josie was in what, by all high school standards, was a serious relationship. She might throw the occasional selfie on Instagram, but never directed at anybody specific, except Matt. The other girls on her team were considerably more reckless. They'd all grown up in Dumont, gone to school with the boys in their class since the time they were in kindergarten. Hardly anybody dated anybody in the old-school sense. You were always somebody's little sister.

Or the cute boys were your cousins. New boys were rare—this year there was one, but he was the strange and silent half-Indian boy who had given her a ride when her grain truck broke down, and he didn't do sports, so nobody knew yet where he was going to fit in. Or if he would at all. But Josie had the quarterback. The guy everybody wanted. He'd not been afraid to make his feelings for her clear, even though her brother was one of his best friends.

Which made her feel lucky. That she didn't have to take preening, duck-faced selfie or shots of her legs from the bikini bottoms down and send them to boys in Hingham or Glasgow or Whitewater—boys she'd maybe met at a basketball camp in Bozeman or a track meet in Great Falls—made her feel luckier. Last year, a senior girl had invited as a prom date a boy she'd met who lived in Alaska! They Skyped and Facetimed and Snapchatted for months after meeting, and his parents had flown him down so they could dance in Dumont's tiny gymnasium and make out in her daddy's borrowed pickup truck parked in a wheat field and rocked by the wind.

And that girl had moved to Alaska after she graduated and lived there with him today. Matt Brunner was a lot more perfect than other options. Matt's father was a wheat farmer, although not as successful as hers, and that maybe wasn't fair because her dad and his brothers owned several of the biggest farms in northern Montana, pieces of land put together by four generations of leather-soled homesteaders and their resilient offspring and held together by luck and lack of imagination through the Dust Bowl and the eighties farm crisis and other impossible times for dryland farmers.

And they teamed up, worked together, her father and his two brothers, to improve economies of scale. That's how her dad always explained how they managed to come out ahead so often. Josie didn't always love how her dad talked about Matt's dad, as if Gary Brunner just wasn't lucky, or didn't have something it takes to be a good farmer. Her dad liked Matt enough, though, or liked the certainty of Matt in his daughter's life.

For a long time, Josie had liked that, too. Sunrise, sunset, Josie and Matt. Except for when she felt contained by Josie and Matt, contained by the expectations that other people seemed to have for her. More and more she chafed when her friends spoke with certainty about her following Matt to college.

She hated when her mother's friends hinted about some eventual marriage, as if that was something she should race toward before she got pregnant and became an unwed mother. Which was exactly what her mother was talking about now, in her absolute but vague way. And what was funny was that Josie and Matt had been having sex for over a year now. After a certain while with him, after enough long drives down dirt roads that ended in abandoned farmsteads, homesteader shacks leaning and bending toward the earth in a slow surrender to frost heaves and wind, after enough ardent tomfoolery in the backseats of extra-cab pickups while the sunset tangled in the branches of Russian olive shelterbelts, after enough handholding on the four-block walk between the high school and Pep's bar, where the kids sometimes met after school for cheese fries and the special pizza with jalapeno, peanut butter, and pepperoni, after enough lap-sitting at parties and—she guessed this was really it—after figuring out that the whole business of being a couple wasn't just fooling around, sex had seemed sort of inevitable.

There had been a time—too short, in retrospect—where she signaled Matt to convince her, but she'd gone into it resigned to the notion that she would be convinced. It seemed like something everybody did. Josie still believed that her mother couldn't know anything about that. Her mother had grown up in the eighties, which in Dumont was like the fifties, getting malts at Mo's diner with their boyfriends, riding in big groups to dances in other towns and coming back home in big groups. Goodnight kisses and waiting until marriage. That was the life she imagined for her mom. Her mom couldn't know that Britnee Mattoon had sex even before Josie had—she'd done oral with several different guys and the full thing with at least two.

Ainsley Martin had also done oral if not the actual intercourse, but had engaged in behaviors far more lurid, to Josie's thinking, prancing around in front of the computer screen bare-breasted in lace and animal print underwear she bought at Victoria's Secret in the Missoula mall for some guy in Spokane she'd met on Tinder. Josie had toyed with the notion of remaining a virgin until college, but then thought, what would be the point? It was such an arbitrary deadline. Why not have her first experience with someone she knew well and trusted? Matt, for all his failings, was reliable. Or predictable.

She knew what she was getting. He wasn't going to stray. He wasn't going to pick up a venereal disease. He wasn't going to get some other girl pregnant. He wasn't going to—what was the phrase Britnee had used? Hump and dump. He didn't take off after she gave in. Josie kept her face turned to her phone, but peeked at her mom trying to make a casual move out of picking up another piece of pizza, then, as if it were nothing, saying, "You know you can talk to me anything, right, Jos?"

"I know, Mom."

"Is everything going okay?" her mom asked, now watching the local news on the TV. The weather report was on. Nobody watched the weather like farm families. Josie tapped on her phone, liking a Snapchat video Britnee Mattoon had just posted. Britnee was a cheerleader and had gone to the Plentywood football game. They must be passing through somewhere with reception for her to post the snap. The video was her running onto the field after the boys won. Josie could see Jared—because Britnee had a hell of a crush on Jared, though it always got her nowhere—and then Matt.

The boys with their helmets lifted over their heads, roaming around the field, looking for the next person to tell them how great they were. Josie always though they looked stupid doing that. Win and walk away. Unless it was something big. Unless it was the state championship. Because that's what this team should win.

"How did you know?"

"What?" her mom asked.

"How did you know that Daddy was the one?"

"The one for what?"

Oh god, Josie thought, the sex preoccupation. Her mother feared pregnancy with the active vigor that other people feared terrorists or hippies. Maybe she should just tell her mom and get that over with.

"That you wanted to be with him," she said instead. "Like, forever."

"Well," Judy Frehse said, and then she thought for a little while. "You know when I was a kid we didn't have Facebook and all those things. You only knew who you knew."

"Uh-huh," Josie said, hoping her mother wasn't about to say that she didn't have many choices.

"And your dad came from a big family that was really close. I liked that, how close they all were. And everybody knew them. You know. We weren't like you and Matt. He was older, and he went away and did his military service and when he came back he just made it pretty clear that I was the one he wanted. I was senior in high school and that's what you did then when you graduated high school. You got married and had a family. You were considered lucky if you did that."

"Couldn't you have married anybody? Why Daddy?"

"Well, your dad back then, he was a really handsome guy. And he was funny and charming. I know you probably don't see that in him now. But he was. He made us all laugh. He and his brothers and they ran around with Hal Hartack, who was a big sports star, and your dad was the funny one. And he was a great dancer. And he had this souped-up Camaro he used to drive around. We all thought that was the coolest thing ever, because, you know, it wasn't a farm truck. Meanwhile, his dad liked to kill him when he bought it, but we didn't know that. All we knew was he liked to drive fast and play loud music and have a good time and to us . . . I mean, he was a catch, your dad was."

Because you didn't have many choices. It was him or his brothers or cow-faced Hal Hartack.

"Are you worried about something with Matt, Jos?"

"I don't know," Josie said. She sat up, swung her legs over the edge of the bed so she was sitting and facing her mother, the heels of her hands pressing into the mattress beside her. "I should probably go back to my room."

"What are you worried about?"

"I don't know. It's just . . . hard to know. How do you know? I don't know."

"What don't you know? You've been with Matt a long time. Has something changed?"

"I don't know. Matt's going to go off somewhere next year. I'm still here."

Her mother allowed an indulgent chuckle. "It wouldn't kill a girl to be faithful to her boyfriend for a year. You'll get to go to college, too. Probably you can go where he goes if you want."

It was the laugh that told Josie how much her mother had missed the point. "What if I don't want?"

"Why would you not want to?"

"I don't know. That's the thing. Matt's the only boyfriend I've ever had. What if, just say hypothetically, I meet somebody better for me in college?"

"Well," her mom said, eyebrows raised as if to say, there's the risk you run. "Josie, a whole lot of girls out there would give a lot to have the kind of relationship you've had with Matt."

Now, Josie thought, you're talking about yourself. "It was different for you, Mom. You knew. I don't know if I know. And I see all these people out there, and what if one of them is really cool and really perfect for me? What if that's who I'm supposed to be with?"

"I do think it's hard for you kids living in this world with all your Snapchats and those apps. When you spend so much time thinking about how things could be, it's hard to see how they really are. I think that's how your dad and I have gotten along so well. We didn't go into it with a bunch of big ideas we read from people we didn't know about how things should be."

"But there's a difference between how things should be and how things could be," Josie said. *What is versus what if.* The new paradox she liked to spend time thinking about.

Her mother held silent for a moment. Maybe they had had about as much grown-up talk as either one of them could handle for this one time. Because what came next was her mother putting a ribbon on it.

"All I know . . ." and when Judy Frehse started a sentence with *All I know,* you knew you were approaching bottom line territory. So Josie stood up. "All I know," Judy said, "is the world is stocked full of other things. You can spend every moment thinking about all those other things. Happiness is wanting what you have."

Josie made a nod and said, "Breakfast at seven tomorrow? Bus rolls at eight."

"Have fun with your friends. You guys played hard today."

Josie said, "Thanks, Mom." But she was already out the door.

* * *

When he would think about it later, Tom, who was no believer in fate, would think that you could point to that moment, right there when he let Slab Rideg go, as the start of how things got so crooked and crossed. He could pick a lot of other spots, too—the day his son died, the day his wife left him, the day he moved to Dumont, the way he'd treated this team the previous year when they'd lost a playoff game they should have won by four touchdowns.

He'd opted for tough love, and maybe that had been wrong. What happened next, after the Plentywood win, was that Tom became dreamy, a curse he'd always borne. Hours after the game, deep in the night, on a yellow school bus as it rolled down the dark two-lane, exhausted from coaching a big win, exhausted from coaching a whole season and managing the egos and emotions of twenty-four teenaged boys, exhausted from knowing that the most exacting coaching was now to come—the quarterfinals, the expectations of the boys but also of a whole town—exhausted and unguarded, Tom let dreaminess infest him.

He always sat behind and across the bus from the driver, his team all behind him. Tom let his head fall against the window, feeling the cool glass plane on his forehead—a clear delineation between an endlessly stretching November night on the endless unseen plains outside and himself, enclosed in a metal box with a collection of excited and excitable teenaged boys. Sometimes on these longer return trips, the boys would tire late in the night, watch DVDs, play games on their smart phones, the talk simmering down to girls in school, or women on TV, or girls they'd never actually met but knew from social networks and webcams.

The bus tires hissed on the narrow highway like a continual unpeeling of tape. While he rested his head against the window, Tom thought again about the son he once had, the way he ran, his beautiful stride. Which led him to think of Sophie. Sometimes Tom allowed a waking dream of Sophie to run through his imagination. It often started with something that had actually happened, though pretty quickly he invented events the way he wished they might have gone. And then, seeking a perfection that never existed, if he thought of a better way for the imaginary sequence to unfold, he backed up and started all over from the beginning.

Sometimes this led to sleep. A couple hours into the bus ride, he was nearing the imaginary perfection of a moment that had started as a snatch of remembered dialogue:

Sophie: This goddamned wind . . .
Tom: It's the same old wind it always is.
Sophie: I'm starting to feel like it's coming right through the walls.
Tom: Good reason to roll a little closer.

In real life, most of what had come before the snatch of dialogue about the wind had been the cracklings of a long-smoldering fight. In this sense, imagination was only a swift feint, a juke he let himself bite on. Still, in his semiconscious state, he found himself tweaking and tuning, plugging in other segments from a past in which he and Sophie spoke adoringly to each other—as if what they had said might still shape the way their lives were now. The net effect was that Tom found himself drawing deliciously close to again feeling what he had loved about Sophie.

The scene in his mind now—the dark bedroom, the minor-key moan of the wind, the rumpled ridgelines of covers, her moon-lit blue cheekbones and forehead—felt so close. But then he fell asleep. He woke to the grainy grind of the bus's brake drums and the artificial haze of the gas station, the vapid fluorescent light etching a bubble of clarity in the endless sea of dark.

The bus door hissed open and Jimmy Krock, the driver, called into his rearview mirror, "You got fifteen minutes here, boys. Take a whiz and get your fizz. Fifteen minutes, or we'll leave you here for the Indians to boil you for dinner. They don't waste any part of the carcass."

Had he been paying closer attention, Tom would have noted the slight hitch in the flow of sound from the boys in the back of the bus. Instead, he winced at Krock's comment, a reference to the Fort Miles reservation that stretched, unseen in the darkness, for hundreds of square miles to the south. Nothing seemed to spook boys who grew up in Montana's small prairie towns like evocations of reservation Indians—catchall bugaboos propagating the worst of racial stereotypes. Tom, still groggy and trying to bookmark where he'd lost control of his Sophie dream stood and addressed the boys already jostling to file forward. "This is a fine town, full of fine people, but be back on the bus in fifteen minutes."

He shot a glance at Krock, who reflected a *who the fuck you kidding* grin. This was an ongoing skirmish. Tom stood and ducked down the bus steps, feeling the cool slap of wind on his face, its rippled vectors fingering through his hair. He could taste soil, dulcet and dusty in the air, blowing from the cut hay fields that lay invisible under the night all around them, a comforting odor to him, even mixed with the rancid stench of gasoline. A Chevy Suburban pulled into the station behind the bus, carrying the cheerleaders. The girls bounced out of the rig.

Some climbed the steps up onto the bus, where several of the boys remained. Tom walked across the pavement into the convenience store, the fluorescent light striking his eyes like a whiff of ammonia. He hurried his purchase of a Diet Pepsi, poured a coffee, and took it outside to Krock, who huddled around the corner of the building just outside the wash of light, sensitive that the kids might see him smoking, even though they all knew he did.

Everybody called him Krock O', even the kids. Now in his seventies, he had been the school's maintenance man since sometime in the 1980s. He loved to drive, knew the roads, and Tom was happy to have him behind the wheel. The chitchat was fine as long as they could veer away from ingrown and festering xenophobia.

"My parents grew up not far from here," Krock O' said. "By Canada. North Country."

"Really?" Tom said.

"Yeah. Out to hell and gone. Shit, the stories they told," Krock O' said. "Plowing hundreds of acres behind mules, then the hail would wipe out their crops and they'd eat oats and potatoes all winter. Drinking water came from a little reservoir that the cows shit in. It's a wonder any of them lived. My granddad's brother shot his own wife through the neck because she wanted to go to town for a dance."

"Are you kidding?" Tom asked.

"Not even a little."

"What happened?"

"Everybody was so goddamned tough back then," Krock O' said, flicking an ash that skidded and sparked red against the asphalt. "She turned out fine. He skeedaddled. My people never saw him again, but they heard he holed up in the Bear Paws for a while, stealing horses."

"I'll be damned," Tom said. He sniffed the air and considered his social life, a Saturday night at a gas station in the middle of nowhere, he and a septuagenarian bus driver huddled beside the cinderblock building, hours from home and scoured by wind.

Then the boys on the bus engineered some teenage triumph that sent underclassmen whooping and scurrying into the convenience store to be the first to spread the news to their shopping teammates. Tom stood with Krock O' in the darkness and said, "That sound bad to you?"

"How the hell would you tell?" Krock O' replied.

Tom grunted. "How's the driving?"

"Nothing to it but the wind," Krock O' said. "You took a little snooze."

"Naw," Tom said.

"About an hour."

"Really? Wow."

Krock O' shrugged. He couldn't imagine much meaning less to him.

"Anything happen?" Tom asked.

"Oh, shit, who knows? If it ain't coming up in my side mirror, everything behind me is yours," Krock O' said.

"That's a wildly irresponsible philosophy," Tom said.

"My gift," Krock O' said and shrugged.

The parent who drove the cheerleaders' vehicle, Brad Martin, shuffled over and hunched to spark a cigarette of his own. Brad's daughter Ainsley was on the cheer squad; his son Alex, a senior, a wide receiver and cornerback. Brad Martin had injected himself into his children's academic career by, among other things, getting himself elected to the school board, and he never missed an athletic contest involving either of his kids. His willingness to drive meaningless hours over the vastness of the Montana pains to see Alex play football meant the Dumont Wolfpack always had cheerleaders, and that Tom didn't have to put up with the girls riding on the bus, being wooed and harassed, often in consecutive moments, by his hormone-addled football players. This allowed Tom to sometimes see Brad Martin as a minor hero. Though that burnish often dulled once Brad started talking out loud.

"Solid W," said Brad, a man who seemed to lean into everyone, inspiring everyone he had a conversation with to take a step back. He shook his head and pursed out a tight smile meant to let Tom know that nobody was surprised by this, or Tom's integral role in it, or expected any less. "Boy, but I want to grab that Hansen kid and kick his ass around until he throws a decent block."

Tom considered a collection of replies he could have deployed, then shrugged. First of all, his guess was that, had Brad grabbed the Hansen kid, he'd find himself flat on his own back, staring at the sky and breathing in careful, round breaths. Just to not be provocative, Tom issued a *could be* sort of shrug. The Hansen boy had played neither particularly well nor particularly badly for a kid who, until the summer before, had spent most of his young life driving tractors and grain trucks and pushing cows around. He was big and strong and good with his hands and relatively light on his feet and wanted to learn and was having a good time trying.

Effort was not his downfall. But the culture of small-town athletics often drove parents to fits of incivility far more than actual in-game performance merited.

"He cannot play that sloppy in the quarters," Brad said.

Tom tried to neither express concern nor dismiss Brad's. Dumont had just opened the playoffs by winning a game by forty-three points, and the following weekend they would enter the quarter-finals as the prohibitive favorite to blow out whichever team they faced. Any given kid probably *could* play sloppy in the playoffs.

On this team, they historically had at inopportune times. A shout pealed from the bus, then a group hushing. Tom wondered if he should walk back to the bus and check what was going on. Brad Martin kept talking about players and how they had performed or failed to. He liked his son's blocking, but felt Alex had struggled with the ball and yards-after-catch.

"No surprise," Brad said, "He never gets in rhythm."

This hardly veiled criticism of Tom's play-calling never surprised Tom but couldn't make him give a shit, either. Fortunately Brad found valor in his son's defense, which, he opined, had been rock solid.

"That side of the ball," Brad said, "is where the boy's going to make a living."

Tom didn't have the heart to tell Brad, leaning against a wall at this particular gas station in the middle of so much nothing, that his son was not going to make a living on either side of the ball. He was, truly, a fine Class C wide receiver and decent defensive back, but Tom himself had been an outstanding Class C player, and had received no scholarship offers, had been forced to walk on at 1-AA University of Montana, and on the first day of practice understood with a startling clarity just why: outstanding as he had been against farm boys, day one revealed how much less athletic he was than every single other player on the Montana team. Truly hard work could sometimes carve out a niche for a player, but hard work was not Alex Martin's strategy of choice.

Alex was almost certainly going to make his living working at Brad's family's implement dealership. Or maybe he'd flee to a city where there were things like restaurants and bars and theaters and lots of other young people that he could meet and drink with and make out with and make love to and marry. As a policy, Tom tried to be candid with parents concerning expectations of their children's athletic futures, but only when forced into a corner about it.

Beside him, Krock O' pinched the coal from his cigarette, tossed the filter onto the ground, and, without a word, leaned into the wind and started stiff-legging his way to the store for his habitual pee-before-driving-again. Tom used this as a signal to check the convenience store. He swept through the restrooms to make sure they were empty. Brad Martin stood just outside the store door as if Tom had asked him to wait there. They walked in the direction of the vehicles.

"Wanna swap?" Brad asked, smiling his put-upon smile as he hesitated before committing to the Suburban. Tom couldn't see any harm in allowing Brad to believe that riding several hours with a busload of high school football players would be more meaningful or less stupefying than the same trip with high school cheerleaders.

"That'd be about the end of me," Tom said, which was enough to let Brad peel off toward his vehicle feeling vindicated.

As Tom drew near the bus door, just as he was lifting a foot up onto the first step, a fluttering of activity spooked him. Two girls scurried from the bus practically right underfoot. They broke into laughter when they hit the pavement and began running toward Brad Martin's Suburban.

Well, Tom thought, his heart momentarily thumping, a little shocked by how much they'd surprised him. He would come to always remember this moment, remember those two girls, Ainsley Martin and Britnee Mattoon, as the sorts of ciphers that arise in and around moments that matter in a life, obtuse actors that elude attempts to assign cause and effect and yet remain embedded in eventual outcomes.

Then Krock O' climbed aboard and slid into his seat and the bus engine coughed up and the bus turned onto the highway and the wheels slipped deeper into their long kiss with the asphalt. Tom tried to return to the fantasy he had been cooking up before he'd fallen asleep: the wind, Sophie, the bedroom, blue night. He tried to start again at the beginning and remember all the altered responses that had infused him with such fondness, tried to remember the pretend words he had assigned to Sophie, mixed with real memories of the glint of her eyes, the way she held her mouth, her upper lip peaked and crested in a sort of sexual challenge.

He tried again to pretend that after he had said, "Good reason to roll closer," Sophie had not said, "Good reason to move to San Diego."

And that he had not bristled and sulked. And that the air had not come to feel close and rancid so that he welcomed the wind and its metaphoric rinsing of invisible foul particles from around him.

He tried instead to see her again, moonlight from their one bedroom window lighting her raised edges, leaving most of her washed in curved pools of shadow.

* * *

Tom woke as always at 5:30 a.m., a bit woozy, still strung out from the bus ride. He felt he could eventually have creaked out a hundred push-ups and two hundred sit-ups, like he used to do every morning, but walking across the room to make his morning coffee seemed like a wobbly proposition.

Also, he felt a burble of misgiving about something that had happened the night before, something he'd missed, something that was going to affect his boys. These seniors—Frehse, Brunner, and Martin—had, since their freshmen year, starred on teams more talented than almost every opponent they'd faced, and still they lacked coherence. Confidence they did not lack. It was the follow-through to confidence that seemed absent, the thing that turned confidence into results in combination with other players.

Determination, maybe, was what that was. Waylon Edwards had it—and he was the junior, the one player from the group Tom would get another chance with. Jared Frehse had it sometimes, but dropped into inexplicable lapses. Brunner and Martin . . . they seemed to believe that if they showed up, things should go their way. He had been unable to solve the puzzle and knew this was his failure.

You can't coach speed or strength, but you can coach antidotes to complacency, some means of directing cockiness. These thoughts plagued him early Sunday morning as he waited in the doorway for his dog Scout to do her business. Then he stood at his kitchen counter and bent back the crinkled foil on a pumpkin pie that Jenny Calhoun had brought to him after school the Friday before, walking it across the parking lot to the field where he had stood discussing formations with Slab Rideg.

Jenny had started bringing him good-luck pies weekly since the first game of the season, though he doubted she meant them to comprise his complete Sunday morning breakfast fare. She was courting him, or inviting him to court her, however that worked. Tom found it convenient to pretend he didn't know that. But Jenny—with her tall, erect spine and a bosom exactly as ample as you'd expect to find on a woman raised on the plains and raising two children—was hard to ignore in his world.

Tom wished he could fall in love with Jenny, because she was on so many levels the kind of person he long ago believed he could spend his life with—until he had met Sophie and her urban slinkiness, her intense interest in appearance and reaction, her worldview piercing far beyond Montana's high plains. Separated from his wife for five years, divorced for the last four of those, Tom was, in theory, not averse to starting to love someone like Jenny Calhoun. He saw her as sweet and pretty from the ground up, with smooth features that were lovely in their very plainness, and he felt comfortable admiring her sturdiness.

It was what he had come back to. After his divorce, he'd had sex with a few women. His first outing had been with a younger woman who wore fishnet stockings at a bar in Great Falls, a woman who sank her teeth deeply enough into his shoulder to leave mirrored blue archipelagos of contusions. He had felt alive at the time, because she made him feel something toward a woman he hadn't felt since Sophie had left, something sharp and vivid that wasn't anger.

There had been a woman he liked, a pretty woman who worked in a flower shop in Havre. She wore jeans and a flimsy top over barely harnessed breasts and had the word "peace" tattooed on her left wrist. She felt straightforward and heartfelt on the first two dates, to the point that he started to not want to have sex with her before he ever did, afraid to come too close too soon to something so genuine.

But she convinced him it was something she needed. After making love to her on their third meeting, he had gone into the bathroom of the hotel room and wept as quietly as possible, because she was wonderful but not the one person he wanted her to be. After that, Tom had gone without sex, made it one of those things you don't have—love, money, a new four-wheeler, a double-barreled shotgun, the attention of your parents, sex. Things you could pretend to not crave as you moved along, though you could live without them, as many people proved.

When he wanted to feel emotions that approximated the feelings love could spark off, he spoiled his dog or reduced himself to recycled imagination of a love long lost, like his waking dream on the bus. It wasn't like he had an abundance of choices. Dumont was Dumont. Any amorous activity he might fire up would likely happen in Great Falls or Billings or Havre or Missoula.

Until Jenny Calhoun got divorced and spent some time alone and decided she didn't want to be alone anymore. In Dumont, Tom was the available man, and she was the available woman in the thirty-five-and-up age bracket. Only she was also a real person with feelings and real life involving real children and, almost certainly, some leftover dreams.

Also she knew everybody who knew him. They both taught at Dumont High, he history, she English. His excuse to not engage with her in recent weeks had been the time-suck of football season, a not-disingenuous assertion to make to oneself. But the pies kept coming every Friday. Delicious as they were, the pies required no immediate reciprocity—even if there was a lingering taste of attachment in every bite. He coached, and tried to treat the pies like the same kind of thing everybody in town did for the football team. Wolfpack players got free ice cream and pizza at Pep's, free sodas from Hannah Alderdice at the IGA, where they also could have free movie rentals. The Booster's Club grilled a steak dinner for the boys at the high school on Friday evenings. Pearl Aarstad and her sister Ida prepared box lunches for the team's bus rides to away games.

Everybody in town, it seemed, wanted to keep the boys wallowing in boosterism and starchy carbohydrates. Which made Tom look down his chest at his gut while giving it an exploratory pat. There was too much to slap there. He tried to imagine what a woman might think of him naked, and didn't like what sprang to mind. He was going to have to step up his workouts, start running outside of practice, maybe go back to the sit-ups and push-ups. Today he might walk five or six miles, and that might burn some of the pie breakfast. He pulled his shotgun from the closet and slipped into his hunting coat.

Scout, his three-year-old springer spaniel, whined and whined and spun in tight circles, threatening to break her ankles off. Just after he loaded her into the truck, but before he climbed into the driver's side, Tom heard his house phone ringing, a highly unlikely event at 7:00 a.m. on a Sunday morning. He had no intention of answering it, but did walk back to the house, opened the door to listen if a message was being left. One was.

"Coach Warner? This is Marilyn Mattoon? My daughter Britnee is a cheerleader? Anyway, she took the school camera to the game yesterday because she's also on yearbook? Mrs. Calhoun—oh, I guess it's Ms. Calhoun, although that's not really right either, is it? Anyway, Jenny lets the yearbook kids take the camera to school events. Anyway, this morning I was just sort of looking through the pictures, which I do a lot of times because I can't make it to the games? I think you're going to want to see some of these pictures, Coach Warner. I wonder if something really, um, inappropriate might have happened on the bus."

Although he recognized his responsibility as high school teacher and football coach to respond to certain concerns, Tom suspected a lot of inappropriate pictures got taken on buses heading home from football games across the state. Whatever Marilyn Mattoon found so inappropriate could wait until Tom had a chance to make his head right. He drove the nine miles to town and then on through it: past the high school, then through the one-block downtown.

Two bars faced off across the street from each other. The grocery store and Wells Fargo bank squatted on opposite corners, anchors of commerce. The town hall—a former double-wide added onto and opened up to create space for the sheriff's office—was the only building with lights on. He passed one other vehicle. On the far side of town in the onslaught of empty countryside, he listened to the crunch of gravel popping under his tires and the occasional ping of rocks ricocheting off the truck's undercarriage.

He liked it when he could feel the wheels swim a little in the loose stuff piled around the occasional ninety-degree turns necessitated by the old section roads running into someone's broader holdings. Usually during this time he did not think for a moment about his team, or wonder where the boys were, or what they had done after the bus spilled them into the parking lot in front of the school late the night before. Usually he didn't worry about whether they were contemplating backside containment, or whether they were thinking about beating up a kid who looked at a particular girlfriend for too long.

He didn't care, for this brief period, if they were being respectful to their elders or nursing hangovers. Or he did, but he didn't make himself think about it. He allowed himself this break, every Sunday, and it usually held until at least noon. Eventually wonderings would creep in like roaches, unobtrusive at first, lingering while they tickled some appendage, until he noticed them and they became skittle-quick, scurrying for deeper cover.

Today they were already all over his mind. Tom drove until the road dipped down into a broad coulee, then pulled off onto a tractor path and parked in front of a barbed wire gate, an almost silly barrier set against the scope of so much grassland beyond it. The dog began a frenzied dash around the interior of the pickups' cab. Tom had long since quit trying to calm her and instead reached across and punched the passenger side door open, allowing Scout's kinetic energy to eject her into the daylight. Tom stepped into the brisk air of a late fall morning before sunrise on the plains, when a gray wash filled the sky and the flatness made the landscape seem manageable.

Once sunlight flooded the scene, it would accentuate the world with shadow and contour and the aching hallmarks of distance. The wheatfields and grasslands visible at the far edge of the horizon would seem to spin, a vertigo caused by the shortcomings of parallax in the face of such vast stretches of open land.

Your eyes would need to be a mile apart for any meaningful grasp of this sort of expanse. Tom followed his dog across a field until the earth tilted steeply down and they dropped into the coulee bottom, land owned by the family of a boy who had played for him two seasons before, on which he had a standing invitation to hunt. They walked thick, tangled buckbrush and rosehip patches, dense in the oxbows of a dried-up stream.

The coulee snaked between the breaks hemming it on either side, wrapping against declines eroded into scooped walls. Scout ran fast and furious, nose scribbling across the grass in front of her, sketching a map of where birds used to be. Her stubby tail wiggled on her butt. When Tom saw her nose begin to jerk her head around while she ran, he quickened his pace, and within a few dozen yards a hen pheasant blew up from the brush in front of her. The dog quick-footed like she was being hauled to the birds by scent, her paws scrambling to keep up.

More pheasants burst from cover, hens, their frantic wings a staccato chatter in decrescendo from the moment they leapt into the air. Scout started running in circles, doubling back on the scent of all the birds that were no longer hidden in the grass. Tom watched her carefully and moments later heard the whistling chatter of a rooster bursting toward the refuge of the open sky and he shot it. They worked up the coulee for a couple of hours. Tom shot another rooster that Scout almost ran over before it went airborne.

He knocked a Hungarian partridge out of a covey that leapt into the air in front of him like a flock of exclamation points. Then Tom hiked up the steep slope of the coulee onto the flat wheat fields for the long walk back to the truck, and that's when his mind began to stick on the phone call. Sure, farmers rose early, but why would anybody be so upset by photos from a bus that they would call him before 7:00 a.m.?

The walk was long, and Tom quickly started to ignore Scout, who kept thinking she was hunting, while he let anxiety start eating into his gut. What had his boys done? There was always enough to feel bad about within easy reach, if he let his attention turn that way. The boys on his team—on all the teams he'd ever coached in his career—comprised a swirling pastiche of emotional states. Sometimes it was simple pimply adolescent anxiety. Some kids experienced the profound, ongoing effects of physical and emotional abuse and neglect.

Some suffered the lingering ravages of a century of inbreeding and the attitudes it creates. All of them had the potential to be affected by the sort of insular depression that plagued small towns in huge, unforgiving landscapes. And they also had the potential to be bright and hopeful and helpful and championship-caliber young men.

They were day to day. Every season the ramifications erupted in a sort of rhythm, like the boiling of a viscous liquid, the burn rate of which determined how much he enjoyed his work. Tom loved to win and hated to lose, but he felt far more satisfied when, at the end of the season, he'd done something to help each of the boys be more prepared for the practice of life than they had been coming in.

He wanted to believe he had shown each of them a way of thinking they had not considered before. Which was why this team disconcerted him so. Tom was, when he cared to parse through it all, alone in the world and, as he grew older, a bit of a crank: divorced, survivor of a deceased son, three years past forty. He had chosen a career in which job security was as solid as the weekly performance of hormone-addled teenagers, the least consistent people on the planet. And so sometimes he went to the bar.

As a social strategy it was far superior to drinking alone. He realized that's where he was heading next. Pep's bar was the least likely place for him to escape thinking about this new pressing concern.

But rolling his ankles over the frozen clods of plowed dirt on the long walk back through the stubble field, by the time he reached his truck, a cold beer had grown to near mythic proportions in his mind. He drove back through town to drop Scout off at home, and while he was in the house, he dialed Marilyn Mattoon's number. The call went to voice mail. He drove again to town, thinking he would swing by the Mattoon farm after getting a beer and some lunch. Tom stuck to Pep's because they served the kind of sandwiches you could find in more civilized portions of the state, and some of the best pizza he'd ever had.

He avoided the Longbranch, where the less fastidious drunks hung out, and tried to confine his Pep's visits to Sunday afternoons, when HDTV and NFL games could be trotted out as excuses. Tom allowed himself to characterize these appearances as a sort of deliberate penance—or the small-town equivalent of a press conference.

It kept him humble, appearing before his collected critics once a week, absorbing their best shots face to face—although he was not so foolish as to assume that any of them saved their best shots for his face. This year so far it had been a relatively easy ride. Occasionally someone griped about the play-calling. More regularly he heard about this or that boy not getting enough playing time.

But when the team was 10–0 and averaging a double-digit margin of victory, even the most focused critics had their busywork cut out for them. It was just after noon by the time Tom pulled up in front of Pep's. The moment he swung open the heavy door, the acrid stench of stale cigarettes and diesel oil and the funk of unclean clothes blanched all the morning's fresh air from his nose. It took his eyes longer to adjust from the vast brightness of the wheatfields to the murk of the bar. The room's brown linoleum floor and dark wood wall panels soaked light from the atmosphere.

The extravagant glory of the back bar, carved in the day when cattle was king and the people who ran cattle periodically exploded in inexplicable fits of fanciness, importing finely crafted objects of beauty by railroad, was muted by not enough light to distinguish its filigrees from its curlicues—that and a draping of soft porn beer posters covering leaded glass cupboards, along with mimeographed quipperies like "We don't have a town drunk, we just take turns" and the display tree of blaze orange camo Pep's ball caps, gallon jars of pickled eggs, and racks of Ruffles potato chips rising in front of it.

A dozen people sat at or stood near the bar in loose collections, all of them men. Brad Martin and Jimmy Krock sat next to each other where the bar made a graceful, inverted L swoop, and Tom, feeling like he needed a goal, stepped amid them.

Krock O' looked at him and asked, "Get any?"

"A couple roosters and a Hun down on Danreuther's place."

Neither Krock O' nor Martin—nor, for that matter, anybody else in the bar—cared. Nobody who still worked on a farm would admit to having the time to walk around the fields shooting at birds. Carrying a rifle on the combine to knock over some pale-faced antelope or mule deer you happened to bump into, maybe. Bird hunting bordered on uppity-ness.

"That dog of yours turning out any good?" Krock O' asked.

"She's a genius," Tom said.

"I had a good dog once. Got hit by a car and broke its leg," Krock O' said. "He must have figured it was just one of those crazy goddamned things that happen, because no sooner than he healed up, he wandered right back out in the road and got killed."

"I had a dog," one of the farmers at the end of the bar piped up "I trained it not to eat. Almost got it trained up, then the damn thing died."

Nobody laughed, on purpose.

"See the films yet?" Brad Martin asked.

Tom could have pointed out that it would be virtually impossible to arrive home at one a.m. Saturday night/Sunday morning, hunt until noon Sunday, walk into Pep's just after noon, and somehow squeeze three or four hours of breaking down game film into his day.

"No," he said, instead.

"When you do, count how many passes Hovland drops," Brad said. "That kid couldn't catch the clap in Reno."

Tom said he'd make a note of that, but he didn't need to watch film to recall that Carson Hovland had dropped two passes— exactly how many Alex Martin, Brad's son, had dropped in the same game. Then he noticed that Carson Hovland's father, Greg, sat four stools down with a pile of paper money on the bar in front of him to signal that he planned on being there a while.

"Why, I hope you fall through your own asshole and break your neck," Greg Hovland said to Brad. He always made Tom happy. Greg Hovland knew nothing about football. Tom doubted he knew how many games were in the playoffs. But his son, an only boy among four daughters, had gone out for football, and now Greg was trying to pay attention.

Consequently, he was thrilled by any good thing that happened, and had to be convinced when something bad had. So far this was all friendly banter, everybody chuckling, but Tom sensed inside its warm bubble some searing edges. None of the men in this bar were afraid of swallowing too much beer or whiskey and getting on the fight. Tom overheard Greg Hovland say, "I got Coach," and then Hal Hartack, the bartender who also owned the joint, arrived with a bottle of beer.

"We'd give you the keys to the town after that win Saturday," Hartack said, "but it ain't really the kind of place you lock."

Tom smiled and nodded at the beer. "Finally," he said to Hal. "I was wondering what I'd done to piss you off."

Hal forced a hard little grin to indicate he found Tom cute, but not funny. "If you could get a beer here every time you wanted one," he said, "I'd feel bad about myself. Nice game yesterday."

Tom knew Hal hadn't seen it, had no idea whether the game had been nice or not and really meant, "nice *win* yesterday." A one-man wrecking crew when he had played fullback and line- backer on the fabled 1989 team—Dumont's one and only state

championship squad—Hal doubled as a sort of quality control offi-
cer and unofficial keeper of the myths.

Hal lingered in front of Tom. "You going to keep starting that
Hansen kid?" he asked.

"He's doing fine," Tom said, knowing that this was more ribbing
than criticism. Dave Hansen had, the previous week in front of the
home crowd, been beaten a couple of times by a very good defensive end from Scobey, and Matt Brunner had been spectacularly
crushed on a couple of those failures. But Brunner had bounced
right back up, patted Hansen on the butt, barked at him to pick it
up a bit, and Dave had done his best.

"He plays his guts out," Tom said.

"Sure looks like he's got plenty of gut left over," Brad Martin
said.

"He could hit the weight room," Tom conceded.

"He could hit just about anybody on the other team, make me
happy," Brad said.

"We gonna beat Wibaux this year?" Greg Hovland called down
the bar.

"We're going to take them one at a time," Tom said, in a tone
that indicated it was ridiculous he should even have to say it. "If
that's okay with everybody."

Silence followed. A few heads turned to Hal.

"I don't know," Greg Hovland said, "I always try drinkin' em all
one at a time, and that often turns out badly."

The truth was, Tom wished they would talk to him about anything but football. He had grown up in a town very much like this
one, albeit nearly 250 miles away, and though he understood it
might be perverse to imagine that he wanted to sit in a bar and
have grimy, unwashed men in overalls make disparaging comments
about his wife leaving him—as opposed to his football team—that
was, in fact, at the heart of it what he hoped might happen here
on any given Sunday. There was something validating in knowing
nobody was holding back anymore.

In three years, it had yet to happen, and this Sunday wouldn't break the stretch. When Tom finally made it home, the light on his answering machine blinked a menacing semaphore. The message said, "Coach Warner, this is Marilyn Mattoon again. I called this morning? I really think you should come look at these photos."

Although the parents of his students would not appreciate intoxicated phone calls from school staff, he felt like he could fake it enough to call her back.

"Mrs. Mattoon," he said when she answered. "I'm sorry. I got your call this morning when I got back from some bird hunting, and I tried to call you back. Would have been about noon, one o'clock, somewhere in there."

"That's right, I had to run to the grocery."

"What the, uh, what's bothering you?"

"Somebody's got to see these pictures from the bus ride last night," Marilyn Mattoon said. Tom was trying to remember if she was always such a scold, but realized he didn't have much experience with her.

"It's a little late tonight. I've got . . . things I have to do."

"I don't know if I should show these to you or straight to the superintendent."

That lit a bulb in Tom's mind. "Okay, look I'll come over . . . half hour be okay?"

"I'll be here," Marilyn Mattoon said.

Tom headed for the bathroom to find a bottle of Scope.

* * *

By the end of first period Monday morning, Josie Frehse—rhymes with "breeze," she liked to say, as in "Call me the . . ." which she knew from the Lynyrd Skynyrd LPs her dad sometimes played on his still-viable turntable, although the boys, when they were feeling mean, just called her "Frigid"—had heard four different things had happened to Wyatt Aarstad on the bus on the way home from the game Saturday night. Any one of them gave her reason to do some thinking.

She might, at long last, have to make a move she'd been thinking about for a while. Her brother Jared had told her that one, it was all a big goof. Coach Warner had fallen asleep and Wyatt Aarstad had agreed to let the guys tape his arms with athletic tape. Then, when the bus stopped for gas, they were going to quickly tape him to the overhead rack where all the pads and helmets and shoes and other equipment was stowed for the drive. They thought this would be a funny picture for the yearbook. But, Jared had said, things got a little out of hand. Jared had bailed and gone into the convenience store—and that fact alone told her something not good had happened.

When she pressed him, he said, "Ask your boyfriend." Later, Josie had heard that Wyatt had, two, been taped, hung from the rack, but then had his pants stripped to his ankles, and that Ainsley Martin and Britnee Mattoon had taken turns posing for pics, smiling by his naked butt cheeks—which, Josie thought . . . *yick*. The third thing she heard—told to her by Britnee Mattoon herself, who'd after all been there on the bus for part of it and had heard the story firsthand for other parts—was that, while she personally had done no such yicky things, some yicky things had, in fact, happened to Wyatt Aarstad.

Some of the guys had stood on a seat in front of him while Ainsley Martin swung Wyatt back and forth, forcing his face into the boys' crotches. This one deeply puzzled Josie. She could not understand why simulation of gay oral sex would make football players feel more manly than they already felt after beating up another football team all day.

The fourth thing she heard had happened—and this she lumped together as the fourth thing, but it actually came in flurries of texts and chats throughout the afternoon and evening Sunday and several variations and possibilities were brought to light so that she couldn't point to one thing and say, *Okay, this was fourth,* but rather thought of the underlying horribleness of the basic act that was revealed to her as the fourth thing and the variations as endless and non-verifiable—was that different portions of what she'd already heard were true, but that additionally either (a) a broomstick (sort of unlikely on a school bus) or (b) a stick (possible), or (c) a pen (most probably, in Josie's opinion) or (d) a candy bar (really?) was actually poked into Wyatt's anus by either 1, some senior football players (though nobody was taking credit) or 2, a couple cheerleaders (which could include Ainsley Martin and Britnee Mattoon, one of whom denied it), all of which, it did not escape Josie's immediate opinion, was sort of like rape.

"Isn't that, like, rape?" she said to Britnee Mattoon, standing huddled in the hallway with a clutch of girls discussing the situation in hushed but rapid tones before the next class period bell rang.

"It's not rape," Britnee said. "I mean, guys can't get raped?"

"What about in prison?" Josie said.

"That's different," Britnee said, her frown a dismissal. "They were just goofing. It wasn't, like, rape. It wasn't, like, serious."

"I don't think it matters," Josie said. "If someone put a candy bar in you . . . ?"

"It's different," Britnee said.

"How, really?" Josie asked.

"Who knows if it even happened?" Britnee said.

"Well, you were there."

"I didn't put no candy bar nowhere," Britnee said. "What happened before I got there or after I left I don't know about."

Josie felt less sanguine. *Poor Wyatt Aarstad*, was all she had been able to think about it all so far; that and who were the shitsuckers responsible? Or, more to the point, was her shitsucker boyfriend Matt Brunner involved in some major way, and if so, would this be the thing that finally caused her to make the break and walk away? Was today the day she would have to make that decision and end the part of her life—the last two years, essentially, the only two that really had mattered much—in which she and Matt were a couple? She thought about it in those sweeping, dramatic terms: the end of her life so far. She had been thinking about what a breakup with Matt might mean for a while now.

On the one hand, in a place like Dumont, there were not many Matt Brunners—quarterback, power forward, handsome in his way, well-liked by adults. And all by themselves, Matt and his friends, including her brother, were perfectly normal human beings capable of singing country songs and holding someone's hand and rubbing a dog's belly. But put two or three of them in a group and they could grow dangerously stupid and talk too much about things they didn't even really know if they wanted, like certain rifles and anal sex. That was even more true when one of the two was Matt.

Put any one of them with Matt, and stupidity was always the Third Musketeer. That could be fun when it was cliff-diving at the reservoir, or hooky-bobbing, or making a campfire lively and full of entertainment. When you were with Matt, everybody was paying attention to you—everybody except, usually, Matt. To get Matt to pay attention it was most convenient to cause some sort of pissed-off drama or to wind up semi-naked at the end of the evening. She had to admit that when she and Matt were alone together, it was not the sort of romance she had envisioned for herself.

She found herself talking about things she had to work hard to feign an interest in—shotguns and video games and jokes that were funny or not funny and sometimes downright disturbing. She found herself listening to talk about coyotes in traps, or virulent strains of antipathy toward Indians from Fort Miles, the latter particularly disappointing since, to her knowledge, Matt had never actually made the attempt to engage any one of these people in a conversation (*How could you*, was his retort, *they're always too drunk to walk, let alone talk*). Not that he was incapable of sweetness.

Not that he didn't occasionally flash glimpses of vulnerability. And that's what kept her in it, at this stage of the game, those moments when he admitted fear and doubt—when he told her he vomited before calculus tests; or that his knees literally went weak when he walked into his house after he'd had a bad game, for fear of what his father was going to say; or that, early on, he'd felt butterflies in his stomach, like pre-game jitters, every time he'd wanted to kiss her. Those confessions allowed Josie to hold out hope that he would keep revealing more and more of his tender places.

Matt would go to UM or MSU and play football or basketball, and she would go to one or the other and play basketball, and one day he would leave behind the foolishness of team sports and feats of pickup truck derring-do and eventually most of what they did together would be to take care of each other. The boy would grow up.

He would almost have to. *Didn't everyone?* She felt like she was growing up every day, even when she didn't want to. So she would stay levelheaded here. None of her information so far had specifically implicated Matt in whatever had really happened on the bus, and the information had flowed liberally, given that basically everybody in school was pouring it out liberally, whether they knew any facts about it or not.

Which made her think *poor Wyatt Aarstad* even more acutely. Josie promised herself she was going to spend some time thinking about how Matt was involved as soon as things settled out and some sort of consistent story emerged. The thing was, it mattered. This seemed like the kind of thing over which you had absolutely no control, but that could change your life completely.

This at a time when Josie had already embarked on another secret mission involving Matt and his propensity to make people feel like shit. In fact, during second period on Monday, enervated by the jangle of news about Matt and the others, Josie found herself seated in Coach Warner's American history class, working on a note. A note-note. Not a text or a DM or a post.

Handwritten. Trying to assemble the note dispelled her usual sluggishness—fatigue from the weekend's volleyball tourney, early chores this morning—most notably because she couldn't let any-body see her writing it. She started the note by writing "Matt," surrounded by lots of hearts-and-clouds doodles on the top margin. She traced Matt's name over several times, and surrounded it with an outward pointing halo of rays meant to simulate the sun or some radiance. But she had every intention of tearing that top section off before delivering the note to its actual recipient.

* * *

After school, Tom walked out to the field to tell Slab Rideg to run practice—just the usual conditioning, basic plays, nothing new, nothing fancy—and then meet him to look at film for the upcoming Absarokee game. The winds plowed up by the weekend's low front had settled. It was something he first sensed—the way the magpies flew in straight arcs instead of rowing up and down roller-coaster trajectories; the pasty smell of wet clay allowed to build in his nose; clouds hovering in the pale blue sky as if they had been painted there; the fieldgrass standing upright, no undulant sway—and then understood.

A huge flock of geese floated high overhead, rearranging them-selves like a drifting musical score, black notes on blue. Instead of the violent leaning of the wind, Tom felt upright as the gravel crunched under his shoes. The high school stood almost empty, an aftermath scene, Tom felt, in the absence of the streaming of students who had just coursed it. He reentered the school's side door, into the gymnasium, and immediately smelled athletics: the antiseptic used to clean the locker rooms, the wax on the basket-ball floor, the lingering odor of decades of sweat.

He had always loved these smells. His footsteps echoed as he crossed the gym, making him feel suddenly larger than he was. From the ceiling hung three banners announcing Dumont's Class C basketball state runner-up finishes in 1954, 1967, and 1988, and the big framed crimson and blue banner trumpeting the football state championship of 1989. He could add another one, and that thought should have comforted him, but instead he felt sick— yesterday's beer like a cold wire coiled in his stomach on top of roiling dread.

He went to his classroom, checked his personal email account on his laptop, saw the name in the inbox: Sophie Warner. SoLo he had called her for so long. There was a time when he had loved seeing that name pop up. Now he cringed. He stared at the bold font and thought for a long while. *Nobody*, he thought, *is who they want to be after a divorce*. He clicked on the email.

> Heard you're still undefeated! I know that means a lot to you, so con-
> gratulations. I hope you're happy. I wish we could just talk. I feel bad
> about so many things.

Tom closed the email and looked away from the screen, thinking that a life is full of options and interests and they're not always the same thing. The exclamation point bothered him more than anything. Tom had the gift of pouring trust into people who didn't deserve it—as his football team was demonstrating—which cre- ated a sort of pissed-off optimism that he struggled to avoid. He battled not to confuse the profound with the abstract, but this email smeared all the lines and landed him flat on his ass.

Sophie, of course, could not have known what was happening. She probably thought she was catching him on a high, the end of a winning season, and might be genuinely congratulating him. He wanted to believe, despite mountains of evidence to the contrary, in her best self. He wanted to believe she had grown past bitterness and fear and left that terrible island of aloneness he had admittedly stranded her on—the only hope that kept her in the world of his mind. Maybe she had wanted to be in touch all fall, but had har- nessed the impulse until there was the landmark, an undefeated season, a big playoff win. Maybe she was that sweet, waiting for something to praise him about.

Maybe a thing he'd been thinking for a while could be true: maybe there was a difference between hypocrisy and unresolved contradiction. Outside of her relationship with her son, Sophie never had been able to handle prolonged emotional interaction. Sophie needed the mundane, chased the stupid sexy sidelong glance, anything to cheapen the notion that in loving something genuinely she might lose. Then, of course, she had. Tom gathered his papers and walked down the hall to the office of the high school principal, David Cates, who also happened to be the school's superintendent.

He had brought the camera here at the start of the day, on the way to his first class, and he knew Cates would be waiting for him. He rapped on the doorframe, ducking his head into the office. Cates nodded him in. The camera sat on the desk in front of him. Tom already knew the images on it, couldn't get them out of his mind. There had been several of young, skinny Wyatt Aarstad, wrists and ankles taped to the rack that ran above the bus seats for storing books and backpacks. Wyatt, a scrawny freshman boy, proved a mystery to Tom, exerting concentrated effort on the field, though he seemed to expect defeat.

And still he was mouthy as the day is long. In the first few images, Wyatt clowned, laughing, making faces. There followed a series of photos of naked buttocks, separated from context, suspended in imagination. A few seemed to be Wyatt's, as evidenced by the suspended nature of the body and glimpses of the white athletic tape they'd used to secure him. In others, at least some boys had stood on the bus seats and held their own dropped-trouser asses to Wyatt's face.

In one photo, something brown protruded from buttock cheeks that must have been Wyatt's, forever altering Tom's reaction to the brand "Butterfinger." In another, a boy stood in front of Wyatt with his pants unzipped in the front. Tom could see the base of a penis. There were more.

After he collected the camera from Marilyn Mattoon the night before, he had thought about deleting the pictures. He could tell Mrs. Mattoon the boys had been pranking, had been mooning each other. Boys did that sometimes in the locker room. It didn't seem crippling. She had told him she'd not taken a very close look at the photos—once she'd seen what they were, she'd turned the camera off, disgusted, and called him. But a drearier reality dulled that impulse.

But letting this go might mean that somebody else—maybe a teammate, maybe a classmate, maybe years from now a wife or a small child—would one day pay more dearly than Wyatt Aarstad. Bullying started young and rarely planed out. How serious was this case? The complicating factor was Wyatt himself, a kid who just wanted to fit in and thought braying like a mule would be the ticket.

How could the laughing, goofing Wyatt in the early pictures reconcile with the few face shots from the later images—those *Jackass* movie looks of disgust, maybe, but certainly not surprise? Tom walked into Dave Cates's office and sat down. A man whose once-black hair had gone silver and gained swept-back waves, Cates sat straight up behind his desk, doing his best to appear tall. Cates had never been an athlete. Like Tom, he had moved to Dumont from somewhere else in Montana.

"Comes now the conquering hero," he said, his voice nasal and in a high register. "Have the city fathers approached you yet about erecting a likeness in the center of Broadway? We're thinking of calling it 'Man, Unvanquished.' Just you with that third-down scowl on your face, twelve feet tall against the sky."

"That was a Saturday idea. It's a different Monday now."

Cates's sigh telegraphed a slight disappointment that they were cutting straight to the chase. "The big thing," Cates said, "is that it's the school's camera. That and Bill Rideg not being on that bus."

"Both my fault," Tom said, and then made a statement that had been tangled in his mind since he'd seen the pictures but that he dreaded pushing past his lips. "I think I might have to submit my resignation."

"Quarterfinal game this Saturday," Cates said. It sounded close to a question.

"I didn't pick the timing," Tom said, a protest to head off a protest. "I'm not trying to tell you your job, but if it were me, I might be firing me. I mean, I wouldn't blame you for sending a strong message here."

"Resigning from the team—this team, at this time—sends a pretty strong message," Cates said. He seemed impressed with it, although not in a particularly copacetic way. "Some people would want a piece of you for quitting."

The two men looked at each other for a moment. Tom felt as if each were trying to understand what the other was going to struggle with. He didn't think he needed anything from Cates, no permission or approval. He supposed if he were being completely honest he wouldn't mind some underlying empathy.

Or sympathy. He'd gotten himself so twisted he'd confused the two. Should he really resign? Would Cates even accept the resignation? That would put Tom in a pickle. What if he offered and Cates forced him to honor his contract and they ran through the state championship game, knowing a few things he wished he didn't know? He didn't know if he had enough boys-will-be-boys in him, or if there was enough victory champagne—more likely Miller, the champagne of beers—to flush the bad taste away.

He could ride the momentum to another coaching job at a bigger school—Class C championships at three different schools had never been accomplished in Montana football history; job offers would come—and leave the memories of this place to languish in the mean wind and the dust of his wake. Sometimes he did think like that, although he didn't always like it later.

"I'm sorry, Dave," he said. "I really am. Christ, I got off the bus to stretch my legs, talked to Krock O' like I always do. Went inside to check the restrooms like I always do. Brad Martin was there going on and on and we stayed out a little longer than usual maybe—I remember thinking Krock O' could probably use a little longer break. It was a long drive and late. But I just had no idea. When it comes down to brass tacks, I just . . . I have no defense. Slab was there, one of us would have stayed on the bus or got back on earlier."

"Tom, you know you don't have to explain yourself to me," Cates said. "But I think we should hold onto horses here. Let's start by you telling me what you know and when you knew it."

Tom did, starting with how he had fallen asleep, then got off the bus, got back aboard, what he had seen, what he failed to see. Cates listened without interruption, a feat he was known for. Then Cates spent a pensive few moments of silence steepling his fingers against his lips. He wriggled and restacked his spine in a perfect upright posture, before speaking.

"I think," Cates said, "this could blow over if we wanted to let it."

That caught Tom by surprise. "Do you want to let it?"

"It's . . . delicate. Obviously," Cates said, creaking out a smile. "The Aarstad boy hasn't complained to anyone. There's a certain willingness, I think, to see a certain level of misbehavior as youthful indiscretion. We were all young once, and we all made mistakes . . ."

"I never did anything like this," Tom said.

Cates indulged the interruption with a nod, then continued, "But you knew people who did, and you didn't hate them for it, and you didn't ruin their future athletic and academic careers over it." Cates raised eyebrows, inviting Tom to challenge that version.

"This might be a first time for you, but it's not for me," Cates went on. "At any school in any year, kids make mistakes that could have serious impacts, but don't, because somebody decided not to let youthful indiscretion ruin young lives." He took a strategic pause, coming from a new start. "You know, ultimately, this school belongs to the town.

"What I don't want is some emotional brawl that makes my students, and their parents and people in town, stake out sides. What I do want to do is sit tight at this moment. We don't know enough yet. If we've got some jacks to stuff back in their boxes, I'd like to spend a little time getting a feel for which way the wind is blowing in town. If you're comfortable with that."

Tom was not, but didn't feel like he'd actually been asked a question. He wanted this part to be over, wanted to blunder into the next bit of drama with at least the roles clearly defined: him, poor supervisor of out-of-control athletic powerhouse, shoddy character builder, failed father figure to a group of hapless teenagers, falling on his sword. But so little in his life seemed to proceed the way he expected it to.

When, he wondered, was that going to change? He'd thought he'd been making good choices, moving to Dumont alone, getting away from Winnett—where professionally he'd reached his greatest triumph and personally everything had gone wrong. He'd thought he had been thinking things through. He'd thought he had been starting over by building a strong foundation, trying to make connections in the community.

He'd thought he'd been trying to assemble a solid football program that featured what he thought of as his hallmark, the teaching of teenaged boys to harness their aggression, to focus it on very specific situations on the football field, to leave it there. He'd thought he had been teaching kids to remain levelheaded in emotional situations. He'd thought he was pretty fucking good at it.

Now this. He left Cates's office feeling like a dog lunging against a short leash, just wanting off though not particularly sanguine about which way he wanted to run. Tom viewed his own coaching as a crusade to teach small-town boys to be decent human beings first and accountable teammates second. Only after he'd managed good progress on these two fronts did he endeavor to sharpen their athletic skills and talk about hard work and dedication.

Now he felt disloyal to his own rhetoric. Before going to the practice field, Tom went to his classroom and sat at his place in the front. He looked at the empty desks before him. He liked teaching in the classroom as much as he liked it on the field. He liked teaching history, subscribing to the old view of history as first tragedy and then farce. Witnessing the opening of a young mind was one of the most powerful experiences he had ever known, and he got to see it happen every year.

That several of the minds he faced in any given year seemed impermeable at a premature age was a fact he found neither daunting nor discouraging. Depressing sometimes, yes. But sometimes he could stick a shim in even the most seamless blockheads, could find a hairline fracture that the right sliver of knowledge might pry into. Sometimes the victories were merely temporary, but which ones weren't, in the grand scheme of things?

The challenge of the hunt alone was worth the chance of failing. If he resigned his football job and turned out to be only a history teacher, well, there were worse things. Tom felt he should not go to practice today, should let Slab run things. Slab might need to get used to that.

Walking out of his classroom, Tom saw Josie Frehse in her volleyball practice gear, lingering in the hallway, talking to a tall, lean kid Tom didn't recognize. Then he did—Mike LaValle, new kid in school. He was in Tom's American history. Josie talked to everybody; Tom liked that about her. She didn't hold herself above anyone.

Jared was the same way. Tom wondered about this Mike, what he was like. He couldn't tell much about the kid as a student, though truth be told, he usually honed in on his students a little more once football season was over. LaValle did his work on time, but didn't do anything extra. He sat silent in class. Josie looked over her shoulder, saw Tom approaching, and her posture changed. There was something furtive in her stance. The conversation ended before Tom reached them and Josie loped down the hall and into the gym. Mike LaValle watched Tom walk past.

"Mike," Tom said.

"Coach," Mike said.

Nothing more. And then Tom was pushing through the door and back out into the day.

* * *

The voice that severed Caroline Jensen's reverie early Tuesday morning was a usual one, her coworker and nominal boss, Pearl Aarstad. "You got that sauce going yet?"

Caroline had already opened four massive cans of acrid tomato sauce and poured them into the vat squatting atop the blackened industrial stove. She had drained the canned sliced mushrooms and plopped them into the soupy red liquid, and was now dicing and adding a dozen onions. Caroline couldn't imagine that Pearl wasn't smelling the greasy brown odor that streamed from the platter-size frying pan filled with sizzling ground beef, and therefore known that Caroline had started the sauce, but Caroline wasn't convinced Pearl's question was for her anyway. So many of Pearl's voicings were mental notes, which she apparently possessed no mechanism for fencing into her own skull.

"We've got lunch in two hours and fifteen minutes," Pearl sang out. "Get that sauce going and the green beans on. I'll start setting up desserts."

Pearl passed by her, looking geriatric and hygienic at the same time—stooped over a stained apron, hair hidden in plastic netting.

"What are you hearing about your nephew?" Caroline asked.

"I've got seventeen nephews, Caroline," Pearl said. "Which one do you want?"

Caroline made a nervous titter. "Wyatt," she said. She didn't say, *Which one do you think?*

"I don't know what to think about that," Pearl said.

"I hope he'll come over soon," Caroline said. "I could make him some dinner. Mikie said he's keeping to himself."

Caroline had always imagined that's what having friends would be like for her son, and for her—making dinner for Mikie and some boys who sat around in his room pretending to do homework, maybe eavesdropping to learn a little teen-boy scuttlebutt. It had never happened.

In Great Falls, Mikie LaValle's friends had hung out on street corners with skateboards and graduated quickly to tattoos and piercings, just a few criminal skills away from meth habits. Most of them had carried knives, though that had seemed elaborate at the time. Which was why Caroline had moved to Dumont.

Since they'd moved earlier that summer, almost all of Mikie's friends were, in fact, invisible, part of some online "community" in bedrooms around the country and world, kids who threw themselves for hours into disturbing role-playing quest games.

Pearl said, "I don't know why my nephew Wyatt does or doesn't do anything. I know he usually asks for what he gets."

Though she didn't know exactly what had happened, Caroline felt sad for Wyatt Aarstad. She felt sad for her son, who seemed to be Wyatt's only real friend. She was not allowed to call her son "Mikie" to his face in the school building. For years she had, just for fun and a little projection of her hopes for him, called him Mighty Mike.

Mighty Mike LaValle. She had given him his father's surname, back during the hopeful six-month period before Mighty Mike's father took off in a car with two other men and a woman in a red tube top and a thong showing from her too-low jeans and never come back. Mighty Mike had seemed cute when he was a little boy, but few teenagers inspire notions of might—least of all a gangly kid with such searing eyes and a mop of raven-black hair all raked into his bony face, one who insisted on wearing black jeans and motorcycle boots to school every day and some piece of metal in his nostril.

And so she'd altered her pet name, told herself it wasn't a sad day when she understood that Mighty Mike had become Mikie LaValle. In the high school, she'd recently found out, the boys called him Mikie LaVagina, among other things. Proximity to the reservation hadn't brought the succor, either, that Caroline had imagined just looking at a map. Which made her realize—without irony or judgment—that she was a dumb white woman for thinking it would. She had hoped Dumont, scraping up against the Fort Miles reservation, might harbor other kids with mixed Indian blood, which she had hoped might ease Mikie's late adolescence identity issues.

Dumont, meanwhile, could hardly be more white. The only Indians in town straggled in from the rez to the bars, where they sat in huddled clusters, blowing smoke in the air like sour breath they wanted to get rid of. Even when the Indians felt confident and loud, when they won at Keno or danced and had fun in Pep's—they almost never ventured into the Longbranch, where it was made obvious they weren't welcome—the Dumont patrons did their level best to imagine that no Indians were sharing the room with them.

On top of that, Caroline had not been steeped in tribal dynamics when she found herself steeped in Mikie's father. He had been from Browning, a jarringly handsome wolf-eyed Blackfeet man—at least Caroline had thought so when he swept up to a backyard barbecue in Great Falls in his battered green pickup and she had first laid eyes and, regrettably quickly, hands on his lanky form on the bench seat of that pickup parked in the lot behind the La Quinta hotel—which meant that in addition to being looked down upon by the whites in Dumont, Mikie, half-Blackfeet, was shunned by the Assiniboine or Gros Ventre kids he might encounter from the Fort Miles rez. She didn't talk to Pearl about the boys again for a while.

Later, as the lunch crowd breached the cafeteria doors, Pearl worked the vegetables and garlic bread. Caroline felt a subdued mood permeating the room today, not the usual febrile shedding of morning energy. Mikie stood in line with the only kid besides Wyatt Aarstad she had ever seen him eat with—Arlen Alderdice, a sophomore boy as skinny and purposely unkempt as her son. The boys from the football team, Matt Brunner and Jared Frehse, Waylon Edwards, and Alex Martin, always first through, had filled their trays and were looping back against the line, moving to their regular table, closest to the food window to minimize effort when they invariably came back for seconds. They would pass by Mikie, as they did every day.

As she did every day, Caroline hoped that passage occurred without incident. Sometimes Matt Brunner stopped at Mikie, fronting him close enough that his tray might bump Mikie's chest, and he would say things. Caroline had no idea what Brunner said—she couldn't hear, and Mikie would never tell her. But they clearly caused her son shame, a crimson blush that flooded his face with such vividness she could almost feel the heat on her own skin.

When Mikie came through the line today, Caroline spoke softly to him. It was his rule that she not address him too overtly in front of his schoolmates.

"How's your morning?" she asked, a ritual question.

"Fine," he answered, the most profound thing he'd ever said about his morning. His stringy hair draped his face, obscuring his eyes.

"Hey Mike," she said, alerting him that next she was going to transcend their usual exchange. His head jerked up and his eyes, now shimmery pale blue, leapt to hers, filled, she saw, with raging paranoia about how she might humiliate him. She kept her voice low. "Why don't you guys sit over there with Wyatt today?"

"Right," Mikie said, bundled with a look close to pure spite, discolored only by a hint of confusion at how an adult person could be so stupid. He checked the students on either side of him in the line, making sure nobody was paying attention to this.

"There's an empty seat."

"You really have no idea how this cafeteria works," Mikie shot back. He pulled out of line, failed to have green beans or garlic bread slopped onto his plate. Mikie rushed in a shuffle across the floor, headed for the far corner of the room, where he and Arlen Alderdice—and sometimes Wyatt—sat in near-exile every single day. But Caroline saw that, coincidentally, Matt Brunner rose from the table where he sat with his teammates. She knew something was going to happen when, as Brunner stood, she noticed the Frehse boy deliberately look out the window and gently shake his head. Brunner headed toward the service window as if he'd forgotten something. Caroline wanted to call out to Mikie, whose path Brunner seemed on a collision course with. She wanted to warn him just to get his head out of his ass, to step to the side.

She wanted to shout *Dodge!* But it was Brunner who, at the last minute, dodged, pivoted, lifting his arms as if he were the one trying to avoid contact. In doing so, he tapped the bottom of Mikie's tray from underneath with such a quick, casual stroke that a plateful of spaghetti splattered her son and the floor in equal measure. Once the plate was done clattering against the linoleum, Mikie stood looking down at the mess like a dog that knows what comes next.

"Damn, boy!" Matt said. He stood with his palms open and arms hung in victim's span. "You ruined my shirt."

Caroline wanted to vault the counter, grab that prick by the hair, and swat his face back and forth until she got tired of it—it took every effort to stand silently, her heart knocking at her epiglottis, her head bowed as if she could, honestly, be just glancing up momentarily from her work. She scanned the room, hoping David Cates, the principal, who usually ate his own lunch during this period, would arrive on the scene and arbitrate quick justice. Cates was nowhere to be seen today. The teachers hadn't come in from smoking outside yet, and Pearl only glanced up briefly to locate the source of the disturbance, then headed for the mop.

"I'm sorry," Mikie was saying when Caroline looked back. Kids in the lunchroom brought food to their mouths without taking their eyes from the drama playing out before them.

"What was that?" Matt asked, hands down around hip level but no less outstretched. "Was that a pip I heard squeaking?"

"Is this really the best time to be a jerk, Matt?" a girl's voice said.

Mikie said, "I said I'm sorry, man."

Matt pointed a long, burly finger at him. "You better watch yourself, *man*. I'm about done letting you slide."

Mikie bent to collect his splatter and, in what seemed an oddly inappropriate move to Caroline, Matt stepped closer, glowered down at her son. Then another boy from the football player's table, the Edwards kid, stood and moved to Matt and looped an arm around his shoulders, talked in a low voice into his ear. Matt made a bluster of not wanting to go, but whatever Edwards kept saying to him allowed Matt to be drawn back to his table, where he and his friends continued glaring at Mikie while several of the other boys whispered intensely at him.

Then a glaring sort of laughter broke out. Mikie weathered the stares of his collected peers by pretending to ignore them, though tinges of disgust turned the corners of his mouth in. Caroline noticed his friend, Arlen, had managed to scurry as far from Mikie as was possible in the geometry of the room, and now settled quietly down at their usual table, lowering himself to the chair as if too much weight too soon might detonate a bomb.

* * *

Walking briskly across the parking lot at the end of the school day, Tom's ability to compartmentalize had completely disintegrated. Sophie's email from the day before: *I feel badly about so many things.* What could that have possibly meant? Didn't they both stagger around under the enormous weight of things to feel bad about? In a way it was nice to know that Sophie did feel bad, that she didn't feel as self-righteous as she had left him believing she felt.

But why circle back to it now? Tom noticed Jimmy Krock emerging from the bus garage, wiping his hands on a greasy rag.

He didn't want to talk to anybody, but could see Krock O' heading for him. Tom supposed he'd be a popular destination around town for the next little while. He nodded at Krock.

"How's your seat?" Jimmy asked.

Tom thought about the right answer. "Hotter than a five-dollar pistol."

"Bet it is," Jimmy said.

Tom could see Jimmy was feeling a kindred spirit. Why was it, Tom wondered, that when things went badly, people contrived their most direct possible connection to whatever went wrong? You saw it in car accidents all the time: *My cousin was driving by there and saw the glass on the road. Said it must have been a bad one.* Or: *My sister knows the wife's sister. They say the wife's just all tore up. Can't sleep or anything.* It seemed like a habit of accessing misfortune so you could become an authority on it. Or maybe it was as simple as an inherent tendency to embrace the inevitable and get a head start on wrapping your head around the notion that everybody was bound for bad times in the end.

"Imagine folks are talking," Tom said.

"Oh, it's the feature story around town. I heard someone say they cornholed the kid," Krock O' said.

"Funny how things get around."

"Heard you're quitting," Krock O' said.

"It's being discussed," Tom said.

"Sure that's best? Seems to me these kids need someone to set an example for them. Someone with some integrity."

"That's why it's being discussed."

Krock O' snorted. Tom knew he was disappointing the other man, and wished he cared more. He didn't have time for a soul search in the parking lot, just wanted to be outside the school building for a moment. Normally Tom used his lunch break to drive home and let the dog out, give her some food, watch her stub of a tail vibrate while she ate. The truth was he treated the dog as a touchstone.

He'd truly understood his singlehood had become permanent the day he realized he'd quit picking dog hairs from his home cooking. But on this day, Cates had asked Tom to not leave the premises. By lunch, rumors were milled, spilled, and thrilling the student body. The teachers and staff were no better, huddling between classes, whispering furtively what they knew or thought they did. Tom had sat in the teacher's lounge and stuffed spaghetti from the cafeteria into his mouth, tasting the acidic tomato sauce.

His teeth found bits of soybean and grit in the meat. Nobody had called for him. In the football office, Tom found a note from Cates. He went straight to Cates's office and knocked. Cates looked like he'd been working in a sweatshop. His hair had finger tracks plowed through it, and his eyes bore evidence of vigorous rubbing.

"How are you feeling?" Cates asked.

"My goddamned stomach's churning, and I've got terrible pains that just zing in and disappear," Tom said. "It's either a physical manifestation of the stress and anxiety I'm feeling or just gas from that spaghetti."

Cates wanted to smile, Tom could tell. "Better have Slab run your practice again tonight," Cates said. "Let's get the boys in here one by one."

Tom saw that coming. He'd thought about it. "You talked to that attorney?"

"She'll be over tomorrow."

"Let me tell Slab to run them through some drills. Maybe we can soften them up a little. He can send them in one at a time."

Tom told Rideg to run the boys until they were sick. Build up to it with a couple-mile jog, then start them on sprints. No plays today. No contact. Just physical exhaustion. Tom had a list of names in a specific order. He gave it to Slab, then went inside the school building to Cates's office. Two hours later, Tom had talked to several of his players and was taking a look at the boy sitting in front of him and Cates, Waylon Edwards.

Even quivering with muscular exhaustion, Waylon projected the sense that he was one step ahead of you and sneaking around to kick you in the ass. It was a neat trick, and unsettling in a kid who was already six-three and blessed with an intimidating physical prowess. Tom could smell the vomit on Waylon's breath.

"Coach, all I saw was what you already knew," Waylon said. Tom found something hinky about the tense of that last verb.

"You've got nothing else to add?" Tom asked.

"Just everybody helping to tape Wyatt up," he said. Less question than confirmation.

"Everybody."

"Pretty much as far as I could tell. We did it, like, in advance because we knew we had to get him up on the rack quick. We knew we wouldn't have much time when we stopped for gas, for you to be off the bus. It took a group effort. I don't remember exactly who did what."

Tom had learned early in his exposure to Waylon that the boy was inordinately smart in a town where it was not cool to be smart, so had found acceptable outlets to exercise his intelligence— mainly smart-assing. He probably understood the consequences of Saturday night's folly better than his teammates did.

Waylon probably guessed that the school officials would be looking to suspend some players. He probably furthermore guessed that the Wolfpack wasn't going to win a quarterfinal game without the players school officials were thinking about suspending. He knew who they were. Waylon may have taken solace in the notion that, as a junior, he had the following year to make an impression on college scouts, but he must surely have understood that he wouldn't have Matt and Jared and Alex on the field with him the following year.

Tom, too, had all next year to figure out how he felt about Waylon Edwards, but right at the moment he didn't like the feeling he was being jerked around by the kid. At the moment he had a feeling, a sharp pinch in his brain, like a sliver he could see in his skin but couldn't get the tweezers on. The sliver was Matt Brunner.

"None of the photos on the camera are of you?" Cates asked.

"I don't know anything about what those pictures are," Waylon said. The adults sat in silence, which Waylon couldn't stand.

"It was just a joke," Waylon said. "We just thought it would make a funny picture for the yearbook."

"By stripping him and exposing yourselves?" Cates asked.

"Do you realize how stupid that sounds?" Tom asked Waylon.

"Wyatt was totally down with it. He went for it."

"And did he go for it when somebody put their naked buttocks and genitalia in his face?" Cates asked.

Waylon made a conciliatory squint, but said nothing.

"Tell me about the candy bar."

"I don't know anything about that candy bar," Waylon said.

"Waylon . . ." Tom said.

"I don't know anything about that candy bar. I don't. I do not."

"Get out of here," Tom told Edwards.

Next he'd send for his quarterback, but he wanted to let Matt suffer a little bit longer outside. Tom had no delusions about breaking the kid, had coached him long enough to know that a little extracurricular workout couldn't ding the shine of Matt's bravado. Tom suspected Matt rather liked the trappings of suffering in front of his peers. As much as he knew they'd used Waylon Edward's easy brawn, Tom simply couldn't imagine the taping of Wyatt Aarstad happening without Matt's involvement, without his ringleading.

Cates pushed himself back from his desk. "It's amazing how people lie," he said. "They just sit and lie right to your face. I never understood how people can do that. I tried it a couple times when I was younger, but I got all tied up and embarrassed. I could never pull it off. Some of these kids, even after we tell them what we already know, they try to cover."

"It's a teenager's job to lie," Tom said.

"Right," said Cates, after thinking about that for a moment. "To their parents. Not to the world, though."

"Well, they never believe you already know what happened," Tom said. "They always think you're trying to trick them."

Silence settled between the two men, until Cates broke it. "I should tell you that, unless Mr. Brunner drops some kind of bomb, this keeps looking more and more like horsing around. I don't see any criminal intent. What they did was stupid, to be sure, but the Aarstad boy seems at least complicit. I just don't see any clear lines."

"I think we don't see it the same way," Tom said.

Cates leaned back in his chair, pressed his lips together, looked at Tom. They were going to be frank now. "Think of the big picture. This football team means a lot to this town. You, of all people, should appreciate that. And the accomplishment you personally are on the verge of?"

"I appreciate it," Tom said, "but that doesn't make it an excuse."

"I'm at pains to understand why you seem so resigned toward resigning," Cates said.

Tom thought for a moment. It was a good question. Did he really not want to win a second state championship? What was his problem with the boys on this team? He said, "I think there are right things to do."

"Well," Cates said, "we're doing some. You should know that I've talked to the members of the school board. There's been a meeting called for tomorrow night. Let's let things play out, let others weigh in. Let the town decide. It is their school." As if to end further discussion, he checked his watch and said, "Let's get Brunner in here."

"Let me talk first," Tom said. He rose and walked down the hall and stepped outside the side door, caught Slab's attention. Tom yelled "Number twelve" and went back into Dave's office. From the office window, they could watch Matt head for the lockers at a run, not about to admit that the sprints had taken a toll, although his stride appeared crazy-legged. In a few minutes, the boy knocked on the door, still wearing practice sweats and a T-shirt, although he had shed the pads and cleats.

"Yes, sir—sirs?"

Oh, this. Tom told him to have a seat and then they went through a little drama wherein Tom told him that some of the boys had already broken the code and told things they had all agreed to stay silent about, and so Matt should not hold back and be caught lying. Matt's role in the drama was to nod calmly and peep a touch of smile to indicate it was his opinion that Tom was blowing smoke. Then Tom told the boy his team was in a bit of trouble.

What they needed was for someone to start acting honorably before the whole season collapsed into nothing. Tom said that he was looking to Matt for that, didn't expect it much from the rest of them. Tom said that what he prized most in Matt was his decision-making capability.

It was why he was such a leader. Matt seemed attentive. His breath had settled down to a steady rattle. Tom stared out the window at the practice field, short dead lawn carved from a horizon of longer dead field grass. Without looking at Matt, he said, "How many hours you reckon you've spent out there?"

"Well, we've had nine weeks of practice—eleven if you count the two before our first game. That's . . ."

When he saw Matt was intending to do math, Tom interrupted. "Your whole life, Matt? How many hours in your life have you spent preparing to play football?"

"God, I don't know, Coach."

"Hundreds? Hundreds, at least, just in formal practices. Thousands when you count all the pickup games and weight sessions?" Tom said. He turned and let his gaze fall heavily on the boy. "What's it worth to you?"

"I don't know," Matt replied without thinking.

"What are your plans? Do you plan on going on, playing college ball somewhere?"

"Football or basketball," Matt said.

"Do you know how it works for Class C players? I mean, recruiters are not exactly driving up and down Route Two, hunting for five-foot eleven-inch quarterbacks."

"I'm six-foot," Matt said.

Tom shrugged. "Northern, they know who's around, but that's small potatoes for you. Carroll, Dickinson keep an ear to the ground out here. But the Bozeman, Missoula coaches, anyone from out of state?" Tom could see Matt had no idea where he was going with this. He said, "Here's how college coaches recruit Class C players: they call me. Every year, they call me and say, 'You got anybody you think can play?' If I do, which is not most years, I say, 'You know, this kid or that kid might be a good fit for your system.' They say, 'Send me some film.' Then they ask me, 'He a good kid?'"

Tom stopped, let Matt feel that. When he saw the light come on in the boy's eyes, he picked up his spiel again. "When they call me this year, Matt, I'll tell them I have some guys I think can play. I'll tell them about your arm and your feet and about your ability to recognize defenses, and about your timing. Mechanics. Those are the easy questions. But when they start asking me about your character—and they will, because you're a marginal recruit at best and they'll need the intangibles to believe. Colleges can't waste scholarships on knuckleheads who are going to get themselves thrown off the team two semesters in.

"So when they ask, 'Is he a good kid?' Am I going to tell them, 'Matt's as honest as the day is long, I could trust him with my life?' Or am I going to have to say, 'To be honest, he's kind of a jack-off. Makes poor choices off the field, sneaks around, lies to his coaches, sticks candy bars up teammates' asses . . . ?'"

Tom expected a long quiet, but Matt came right back with, "I guess you'll tell them what you want to tell them." He was obviously offended by the question. "I hope the first thing."

Tom let some time simmer away, sat staring again at the field, then at Matt. "Mr. Cates is going to ask you some questions now," Tom said. "Before you answer, I want you to think about how much time you've spent playing ball, practicing for ball, thinking about ball. I want you to think about making some good decisions. Because your answers right here are going to determine how I answer those recruiters." Tom arched his eyebrows, trying to convince Matt that he knew more than he did, perhaps even the answer to the forthcoming questions. He nodded to Cates.

"Did you take that boy's pants off?" Cates asked.

Matt was shiver-quick. "Not me. No, sir."

Just as quickly, Tom knew he'd done it.

"Are we looking at you in any of these photos?" Cates asked, fanning out the printed copies.

"No, sir," Matt said, "you're not."

"This belt doesn't look exactly like the one you wore to school today?" Cates asked, pointing to a photo of a naked ass with the pants still visible in the frame. The belt was a broad, tooled leather belt that Tom knew Matt wore with a Big Bud buckle the size of a dessert plate.

"Lots of guys have leather belts." Matt shrugged. "Look, Mr. Cates, to be honest, there's no way we can win out if I get suspended. Coach knows it."

Cates's eyes opened wide, as if this were his brand-new thought for the moment. He jerked a glance at Tom, as if beseeching him to consider the concept. Then he pressed the bridge between his thumb and forefinger into his brow and shook his head. When he seemed to have rubbed this most recent experience from his forehead, he said, "Matt, you're going to get the chance to answer these questions again in the next couple days, in front of the school's attorney. Maybe in front of the sheriff. I hope you do a better job. I want you to think about what we know and what you know and how you want to answer to your team and your school and your parents and your community. And to yourself. Why don't you take off that team gear and go home and think about it."

* * *

That evening, at a small blue double-wide home plopped atop a rise like a thumb in the wind, Mikie LaValle stormed through the door and blew through the kitchen without a word, heading straight to his room. Caroline let him stew for an hour, then called him for dinner. Mikie opened the door and began to emerge, a wary squint in his eyes.

"Crunchy tuna casserole," she sang, standing outside his bedroom door, dangling a favorite she had scrambled to throw together, running to the store for the Grape Nuts he liked to have sprinkled on top.

"Don't be nice to me," Mikie said.

"Mikie," Caroline said. "Come out here and help me eat this."

Mikie stood beside the table. He picked up his spoon and pried it into a hunk of tuna casserole.

"Tell me why you won't sit with Wyatt Aarstad," Caroline said.

"Christ, Mom, it's not my choice."

"Why can't you just—"

"You're doing the third degree," Mikie said. He picked up his plate and run-walked down the hall to his room, making the door slam a highlight of his retreat.

"Mikie," Caroline said, regrouped, patience buttressing her voice. She rapped her knuckles against the door. She had yet to hear the blanking surge of indefinable music, so knew he had not gone to ground yet. She could still reach him. She rapped again. "Mikie . . ."

"What do you want?" he whined through the door.

"We're going to talk, Mikie. Now or in an hour or tomorrow. Might as well get it over with so the rest of your night can be pleasant."

"You don't listen when we talk."

"I can't listen through the door."

"You don't listen when we're face to face. Your ears are on inside out."

Caroline almost chuckled. "I'll listen. I'm all right-side-in ears."

The door cracked open. Mikie filled the vertical space, a cartoon boy as narrow as the stripe of space he stood in

"Can I come in?" she asked. Always the negotiation over space. It felt important, to Caroline, to be someplace where he could throw no barriers between them. It obviously felt important to him to maintain a certain distance. The bedroom might prove too confining.

"No," he said.

"All right, then, will you come out?"

"Where?"

"I don't care, Mike. I want to see your face when I talk to you. Why don't you come into the kitchen."

"No," he said, firmly. Because that was her territory.

"Then let's go in the front room." Those were pretty much the two options when it came to two people trying to sit and talk in their house.

"The hallway," Mikie said.

Caroline could see this was going to be a test. She asked, "This hallway?"

"Yeah."

"Okay," she said, thinking: *close to the rabbit hole.* "You come out in the hallway with me."

Caroline slid down the wall and sat on the floor, crosslegged. Mikie pulled the door open enough to slip through the space he created. He stood against the wall, arms crossed, watching the toe of his sock, worn nearly through, Caroline noticed, slide against the carpet.

"You gonna sit?" she asked.

"I'm fine," he said. "I like this better."

"Looks pretty stupid, me sitting here and you standing way up there," Caroline pointed out. "Mikie, I'm on your side, baby. Sit down here with me."

"You're not on my side, Mom. You're going to try to get me to tell you a bunch of stuff I can't tell you."

"Why can't you tell me?"

"Because I don't know," Mikie said, seemingly exasperated by the inanity of the question.

"What don't you know?"

"How can I know what I don't know?" These answers seemed to physically pain the boy.

"You don't know or you can't tell?"

"I can't tell what I don't know," Mikie said. "And I don't know what I can't tell."

"Okay," Caroline said, feeling like a new direction might improve the quality of communication, "why is Matt Brunner so mean to you?"

"I just bumped into him. It pissed him off. That's all."

"You just bumped into him?" But, Caroline remembered, Matt had said, *I'm just about done letting you slide,* as if there were some process in play. "Is it because you're friends with Wyatt?"

"It was an accident."

"I saw what happened, Mikie."

"It was an accident, Mom, all right? I spilled shit on him and he got mad."

Caroline let Mikie struggle under the weight of that big fat lie for a few moments. "Why's he so mean to you, Mike?"

Mikie glared at her. "Are you, like, new or something? He's mean to whoever he wants to be mean to."

"He's a bully," Caroline conceded, "but lately he seems focused on you. Why is that?"

Mikie took a long moment and glanced around at the hallway, as if the answer might be painted on the walls, or floating beyond them, in some great free wide-open space outside the stricture of the hallway. Then he said, "I don't know. Because I'm new here. I don't have any friends. Because you took me out of the school where I had friends and had fun and dragged me to this hellhole." Instead of that last coming as withering accusation, it seemed to exhaust Mikie, and he slid down the wall until he, too, was sitting on the floor of the hallway, his long legs stretched parallel to her.

"Yeah," she said, "I know." They'd gone round and round on this, and she retreated to rote phrases in something close to a sing-song delivery to sum it up. "I thought it would be good for you. I understand that you don't see that now, but I thought it would be the best for you. Did you ever do anything that Matt might think is a reason to be especially mean to you?" She was thinking now of the girl's voice: *Is this really the best time to be a jerk, Matt?* Not *Stop it, Matt.* Not *Back off, Matt.*

"Oh sure, Mom, blame me. That's great. Fucking great."

"Don't you talk to me like that."

"Don't *you* talk to *me* like that. The one person who claims to be on my side and you're blaming me for that prick being a prick. That's beautiful." Mikie made a lavish production out of "beautiful," a telltale that the conversation was over. He lumbered to his feet and disappeared through the door slam.

Caroline felt the slamming sound blast tension from her body. As if by slightly delayed reaction she toppled over, lying on her side on the carpet, which, she couldn't help noticing from this close vantage point, was filthy. Another way she'd failed to manage even the simplest sort of life that other people seemed to lead with ease. Caroline wanted badly to sob, but felt too stunned and suddenly empty. She knew she could lie on the floor for the rest of the evening and Mikie would never peek out the door to notice, but she knew that to do so would be trading in just the sort of defeat he expected of their life together. So she stayed only a little while longer, trying to imagine how it had happened that her every little failure should have such ringing resonance.

* * *

Finished with volleyball practice, showered and feeling refreshed, Josie Frehse was home alone, trying to digest enough American history to complete the two-page study guide Coach Warner had sent home with them and resisting the twin lures of satellite television and the dinging text tone of her cell phone. Her father was gone, helping to excavate an irrigation dam for someone over sixty miles away.

Her mom had gone to her sister's house, "visiting," a ritual Josie couldn't wait to avoid—sitting around people you've seen nearly every week for seventeen whole years, listening to them talking about people you've also known your whole life, telling you things you've heard six times already. "Ruby went over to Spokane to see her niece last month," followed by a long discussion about which of her siblings' daughters that might be. "Mason's hand got all stove up in the harvester," followed by a litany of previous injuries Mason had incurred around the farm.

"Harold drove his pickup off the Cow Creek road," followed by a long familiar list of trucks slipping off gravel berms, and the relative damage caused by each. Josie much preferred to stay home and read a book, to have someone she'd never met tell her things she never knew. So she had begged off with homework. Her brother was in his room, and then suddenly wasn't.

He was walking down the hall and into the kitchen, where she sat at the table. With a lot of metallic clatter, he wrangled a soup pot from the cupboard, then filled it with scoops of barley from a burlap sack in the pantry. He added water and generous stream of salt and turned on the stove.

"That seems like a lot," Josie said.

"Just pre-salting my bacon," he said, turning to lean against the counter and look at her.

"You'll never do it," Josie said.

Jared took in a deep breath, sighed. "I'm gonna have to," he said.

"Nah."

"Dad'll make me."

"Dad's totally in love with them."

"I know," Jared said. Josie always joked that his resting bitch face was a smile, but now a real grin stretched it further. "He likes to pretend they're a pain in his ass, but I catch him out there feeding them treats."

"He bought them apples in town the other day!" Josie said.

Jared had, the previous spring, begged permission from their parents to acquire a pair of piglets. His pitch was successful largely because, on his own initiative, he had staked out a piece of the barn and built an indoor-outdoor pen. Matt Brunner had come to help place the posts and Josie had pitched in with them, holding rails in place while Jared bolted them to the posts. "Bolts?" Josie remembered Matt saying. "Fancy."

It had been a fun project, time with her boyfriend and her brother, laughing and making fun of Jared and building something together. Jared engineered an automatic watering system, which Matt helped him build.

Cal Frehse had scotched the pig idea initially. "We're wheat farmers," he said. "We don't do livestock." But watching all the industry happening among the kids, their father had allowed himself to be convinced. Jared originally sold the idea of just one pig, but when he and Josie and Matt had driven to Willow Creek to pick it out, the farmer who was selling them mentioned how social pigs were.

"You'd better get two," Matt had said. "You can't have lonely piggies."

Jared had waffled, his grin growing comical. "One would be sad."

"Last thing you want," Matt said. "Nobody wants sad bacon."

Jared had named the pink little female Carnitas and her brown mottled male littermate Chops. The idea he had pitched to their parents revolved around fattening the pigs all summer and fall and slaughtering them at the beginning of winter. Both the pigs were in excess of 130 pounds now. Whenever Jared was working around the yard, he let them roam free. They were getting obnoxious in their demands for attention and, if she didn't see them coming, could knock Josie over when they leaned on her legs, angling for a head scratching.

She sometimes found Jared sitting in the pen, the pigs lying beside him, one's snout on his lap. Now that fall was tilting toward winter, Jared had taken to cooking hot meals for them. There was no way he was going to slaughter them. His latest strategy had been talk of breeding them, which always caused their father to lift an eyebrow. Jared stirred the pot on the stove.

"What do you think's going to happen?" Josie asked. "With the team."

"Well, they're not going to kick Matt off," Jared said. He moved to the refrigerator, opened the door, and started rooting through the shelves and drawers. He pulled some carrots from the crisper. "Not now."

"Why do you think?"

"If they kick Matt off, they have to kick Alex and Waylon off, and then there's just no way we can win." He held them up, showed Josie how soft and bendy they were. She shrugged. He tossed the carrots into the pot of barley, greens and all.

"Why would they have to kick off all three?"

"Oh, just from what I heard. They all, like, did stuff."

"Maybe some did more stuff than others?"

"Hey, Jos," he said, raising the steaming ladle from the pot as he held both hands up in a surrender, "you know the deal—if you want to know something Matt did, get it from Matt. You can't put me in the middle."

"You'd tell me if he did stuff that was really bad, though."

"He did stuff," Jared said, raising his hands even higher, more denial of responsibility. "Whether it's really bad isn't for me to say."

"Well that's not true, because you didn't do that stuff, so you must have had an opinion about it. You didn't even stick around to watch."

"I had to pee," Jared said, which was also not true—or at least, she was pretty sure, not the reason he got off the bus. "And now I have to feed the piggies."

He stepped into the mudroom and grabbed a Carhartt coat and some heavy cowhide work gloves. Then he lifted the steaming pot from the stove and started out the door with it.

"Don't play with your food," Josie said, meaning the pigs.

He smiled, then said, "I'm heading over to hang at the Martins'. Waylon should be there. I'll try to find out what the latest scoop is."

And then Josie was back at the books, with the house to herself. When Matt texted her a half hour later, he wrote, "practice sucked ass today the worst ever"

"How come?" she tapped back, wondering if this meant he wouldn't want to come over.

"coach pissed about wyatt. punished us"

"Y did u do that?" Josie texted.

"I didn't Y the big deal everybody pranks"

Josie believed generally that when you wanted to find something out, you asked directly about it, but she didn't want to launch a big discussion over text. Boys did things she didn't understand the need to do all the time. She'd already told Matt during school that she'd probably be home alone this evening, which meant if things held to form, he was going to come over, suss out the situation, and want to have sex.

Originally she had wanted him to come over so she could pin him down about what had happened on the bus. If anybody should know, she should, as close to all the people involved as she was. Jared was never going to say a word about it to her, because she was his little sister and he didn't have to tell her anything. But she ought to be one of the people that other people could come to for the straight skinny.

But then the bullshit Matt had pulled in the cafeteria at lunch spurred her to make an impulsive choice that had set something in motion. Now she didn't want Matt stopping over, or at least not for very long. Josie wasn't sure she wanted to have sex with him, given the fact that she might be breaking up with him any day now, depending on what she found out about what had happened on the bus. But even if she *had* felt like it was okay to have sex with him, now she didn't want that kind of togetherness.

She just wanted to be alone, to have some time to think about how she felt without somebody feeling her. When Matt knew her parents weren't expected home for some while and he wanted to stop by, she knew that directly saying no would make him want yes. So Josie had texted, "Okay. Maybe we can watch *Ghost*?"

Josie though *Ghost* was a truly stupid movie. But she knew that the best way to make Matt scarce was to offer him pretty much what he wanted, only on terms somewhat unpalatable to him. Watching Matt eat, for instance, gave her cramps. But she sometimes offered to cook for him when she didn't actually want to see him, because he didn't like any of the things she knew how to cook. It almost always worked. Her phone rang. It was him.

"I'm pretty beat from practice," Matt said. "I'll stop over, but I don't know about a movie."

Josie banged out most of the study guide answers in the next twenty minutes. Then Matt walked through the door without knocking, a standard practice. Josie had seen his pickup rumbling down the dirt road for almost a mile. She'd opened the console beneath the TV, as if readying the DVD player. She'd put a pot of water on the stove to boil, pasta and rice being her two culinary achievements to date.

"Hey," she said when he came through the back door and into the kitchen. "How's my big sexy?"

"Burning with cramps." He grimaced while he reached down to remove his shoes before stepping into the room. "Coach damn near killed us."

Matt limped to the kitchen table and sat on a wooden chair there, his legs stretched out in front of him.

"Why don't you go lie down on the couch, and let me rub your legs a little. I bet I can get you feeling better," she said.

Josie crossed the room and sat on his lap—or his upper thighs, which were sloped with the stretch of his legs—facing him. His hand wrapped around her butt to keep her from sliding down.

"They can't do anything to me," he said, as if she had asked him that question. "Are you kidding? They'll probably suspend Alex and Waylon for a game. But there's no way they're gonna kick me off. Not now. Not if they want to win."

Josie let her fingertips rest on his chest.

"Why do you guys do such mean stuff to each other?"

"It's nothing. God, it's so nothing. You can't even understand unless you had it done to you. It's like tradition. Makes the team tighter. Builds character."

Josie wondered, *Whose?* Now she felt his hand begin to rub her buttocks, an almost involuntary act any time his fingers were near her. Tonight it felt mechanical, although she couldn't say whether because of something in him or her.

"Then why'd you knock Mikie LaValle's tray out of his hands at lunch?" she asked.

"That was a totally accidental thing." He pulled his head away to get a wider perspective on how that was playing.

She frowned, allowed a serious disappointment to ripple over her face. "I saw it, Matt."

The movement on her butt ceased. Matt grew sullen and spoke down at his chest. "Why do you give a shit?"

"What did he ever do to you?" she asked.

"What did he ever do to *you?*"

"Nothing," Josie said. She pulled from his lap and stood. "He didn't do anything *to* me or *with* me. God, Matt."

"You're the one who's all the time talking to him," Matt argued.

"I talk to everybody. I'm not a jock snob."

"Yeah, but you know he wants to get with you, and when you keep talking to him all the time, you let him think something might happen."

"Stop it. Just . . . stop," she said quickly recognizing a potential shortcut to his departure. "I don't even want to talk to you when you're being this stupid. Why don't you just"—she made a wipe-the-slate-clean sweep—"go home, and rest and feel better and call me when you're not so dumb."

"I'm not—" He was whining, which signaled her opportunity to drive her momentum.

"You're tired and sore and worn out, so you have an excuse. But you're being stupid," she said. "You know I would never *get with* someone else."

"It's not you I'm worried about."

"It's me who makes decisions about who I talk to and who I don't and what I do. You know I'm not your property and you don't have to defend me, and I'm not going to talk about it again. Ever. That's the deal." He looked beaten and baleful, not even energetic enough to be defensive, and she felt genuinely sorry for him. "I think you're just really tired."

"But we have the place to ourselves," he said.

"You know what? My mom and dad are going to Great Falls Thursday night and they won't be back until really late. I'm supposed to go but I'll just tell them I have to study." She knew she was safe there. Matt never had sex that close to a big game. *I'm not superstitious*, he had told her once, *just kind of stitious*. That was when he had been charming a lot of the time.

"That's two nights before the quarterfinals," Matt said

"You'll be fine by Saturday, big boy." Might as well ride it. "I'll go easy on you."

"Promises, promises," he said. His attempt at a hungry grin made him look goofy and sad.

"Go on home tonight and rest, and start thinking about what you want to do on Thursday . . ."

He reached up and cupped her left breast, but she pushed his hand away slowly.

"Come on," he said. "Just a little taste."

"Save it. It'll be worth the wait."

She won the reprieve and within minutes had struggled through a few long sloppy tongue kisses and some more half-hearted fondling, an indication of how truly exhausted he was. And then Matt was gone, a full hour before she thought she could realistically get him to leave. She waited until the twin red dots of his rig taillights winked out in the darkness, knowing he'd be far down the road and not turning back, then she snatched her car keys from the key rack and slipped out the back door, letting herself feel lost in the night. She was alone enough in the house, but too surrounded by other lives.

When Josie felt this way, she wanted to be off by herself, wanted the possibilities of space, that sense she had driving the grain truck during harvest. Her first order of business was music. She scrolled through her playlists until she found Big and Rich and clicked on "Save a Horse, Ride a Cowboy," which she played at inadvisable volume as she drove down the quarter mile of driveway to the county road. A low moonrise pressed an edge of yellow onto a hanging line of soft clouds and, beneath it, silhouetted the crenellations of the Bear Paw mountain range to the southwest. She felt the wind jostle her truck when she got up to speed on the county road.

When the Big and Rich song was over, she switched to Dave Matthews's "Where Are You Going?" and sang as loud as the music. She wanted the noise, because soon she would be quiet. She wanted stimulation—her brain burbling with the music, her body rocking the beat—because next she would be blank. She spotted the two-track where it met the gravel road and turned onto it. She could hear the tall, dead grass stems whisking against the undercarriage of her truck.

The two-track was rutted and crawled over rocks. Her truck lunged and swayed over a low rise and then the reservoir spread out before her, a pan of dark water streaked by moonlight. The wind, the dark water, the mountains beneath the moonlight— here she had found a place to be with just herself. Except tonight she saw another vehicle, a car. As she drew closer, she recognized the torn vinyl roof of the dark sedan. She could see him sitting on the hood of the vehicle, the glowing coal of a cigarette red on his inhalation. She pulled up beside him and stopped.

He didn't acknowledge that she was there. She couldn't see much more of his face, itself inhaled by the black Quicksilver hoodie. There was something bad and wrong about this boy. Maybe it was the things she knew she was not supposed to like about him that made her want to find out more. He was not traditionally good looking—more like a fortress comprised of unexpected angles— but there was some surprising strength to that, and she could not deny that she just liked looking at him. Josie pulled up beside his car, turned off her engine, sat for a moment, thinking, *What in the hell is he doing here?*

Then, *Well, just trying to help.* Though she knew there was a lie in there. She got out of the truck, feeling the wind rush into her legs, and walked around the front of her pickup, stood a few feet from him.

He had one hip up on the hood of the car, one foot on the ground.

Across the reservoir moonlight reflected off the water on the cliffs in wobbling rectangles. Mikie LaValle lifted his head so just the prominent points of his face, his long nose and sharp chin, pierced the silhouette of his hoodie. He flicked the cigarette into the grass and turned to look at her.

"Thought that might be you when I saw the truck on the county road," he said. "Wasn't sure."

"You can tell my truck from that far away?"

"Moon's bright. I know trucks."

"I didn't know you came here," she said.

"I go lots of places."

"I come here," she said.

"Just here?"

"When I want to be alone."

"Sorry."

"I didn't mean it like that." Josie's mood felt fluid. She was still disappointed to not be alone. But there was something nice in the surprise of finding a friend here. "Do you come here . . . I mean, I've never seen you here before."

He shrugged. "Why here? What for?"

"When I want to think about things," she said. "Get away from stuff."

"What stuff do you have to get away from, Golden Girl?"

"Golden Girl?" Josie said, not peeved. More like, *Is that the best you've got?* "What are you trying to get away from, Indian Boy?"

She could see his eyes in the moonlight snap to her face and glare. Then his long mouth split a dull white slit in the darkness, a smile. He said, "Blackfeet Boy."

Josie nodded. She been afraid, after she said that, of how he might take it.

"Everything," he said.

"Everything what?"

"I come here to get away from everything. My mom. My history. My life." A pause. "Your boyfriend."

"Your mom seems nice to me," Josie said.

"Cuz she's not your mom. You don't live with her."

"Nobody's mom is easy to live with," Josie said.

"Family's like the horizon, man," Mikie said. "It looks pretty much the same to everyone, but there's a lot of shit between here and there."

"Deep thoughts," Josie said.

Mikie turned his hands palms up, like he'd been caught at something. "I don't know. When I'm outside like this I feel more like myself. More like who I'm supposed to be."

He turned and stared out over the water again. Josie felt a wave of wind push against her face, work through her hair. She was out of things to say. She peeked at his face, dark beneath the hoodie. The moon, the cool colors of night, shaded all his angles. Softened, he could be a handsome kid. Unwound, he was different looking, not for everyone, but there was something exotic about the way his eyes tilted toward each other, something a little thrilling in the edges of his nose and cheekbones. A wildness around his mouth.

"I don't have any great ideas," she said. "About Matt. I don't like what happens. What he does sometimes."

"He's a douche."

"Well . . ." Josie said, by way of bookmarking a protest to be named later.

"Guys like him get everything they want but it's never enough," Mikie said. "They take things other people don't have."

"It's not like that. You don't really know him. Things are hard for him, too."

"He's a douche."

"You're definitely going to want to keep that opinion to yourself."

"Yeah?" he took a long drag from his cigarette, then flicked it, a twirling red coal into the night. Smoke poured from his nose and mouth. "You think I couldn't hurt your big boyfriend?"

Josie toed the dirt beneath the windblown dead grass. They had been having a nice conversation and then suddenly they weren't. Just as quickly, she wasn't sure she was happy to be here anymore. Mikie seemed so quick to shift moods. She wondered if he could be dangerous to her at a time like this. But when she looked at him, she saw this . . . *boy.*

"Come," she said. Because Josie knew a thing or two about boys. She held an arm behind her and crooked a finger and said, "Come."

She sat on a large rock at the water's edge, knowing he would sit beside her, and in a few moments he did. She looked at his face. "Look, I don't know if you have Asperger's or some serious social-izing problems, but I'm just trying to be a friend and defuse a situation that could get someone hurt. And by someone I mean you."

Mikie made a noise that sounded like a long lead into the word "shit."

Josie let her head drift left and right. "I'm trying to help, Mike. I'm trying to be a friend."

"Help away," Mikie said.

"The thing about Matt . . ." Josie tried.

"Maybe he's just stupid," Mikie said.

"He's not stupid. He's actually pretty smart. You can't really be a stupid and be a quarterback. Ignorant on purpose maybe, but not stupid."

"How come every time I talk to you we talk about your boyfriend?"

"Okay," she said. "Try talking about something else. What's Wyatt saying about what happened?"

His eyes flashed to her. "You thought I'd tell you something you don't know?"

"Never mind," Josie said. But that's exactly what she'd wanted. "Talk about something else."

"Okay," he said.

And then they didn't. They sat on the rock and watched the wind ripple the reservoir, spangled with moonlight. What seemed like a long time ensued, during which Josie thought about things she could talk to him about. He seemed to need someone to talk to, but she was shy on appropriate subjects. Sports was clearly a non-starter. Nobody talked about wheat except in terms of readiness or lack of readiness or money or lack of money. Wildlife? She could talk about the hawks in the summer. At some point, Josie knew, she was going to have to deal with the question of just what she was doing out here in the night, trying to think of things to talk to this boy about.

Mikie sat on the edge of the same rock she sat on. When he looked over the water, she could only see his nose, pale and sharp, jutting from the profile of the black hood. When she leaned back she could see his boxers protruding from the waistband of his jeans, blousing over his butt. He was nearly sitting on the jeans' belt loops.

"If you could go anywhere in the world, where would you go?" Mikie asked.

"Who would I be going with?" Josie asked.

"By yourself," he said. His emphasis told her he'd never considered another possibility.

"I don't know," she said. "Seattle, maybe. Depends on who I went with."

"Why?"

"If I went with friends I might want to go to someplace like Seattle. If I went with my family, I'd like to go to California."

"What about if you went with your boyfriend?"

She shrugged and shook her head. "We've never gone anywhere together. Not like that."

"So that's it? Seattle?"

"Maybe Korea," she said. "I'd go with my dad to Korea so we could see where all the wheat goes. They make it into these buns. I'd like to take my dad, and eat some of those buns."

"You like your dad?"

"I love my dad," she said.

"What do you like about him?"

"He's always there," she said. "He always encourages me. And he's a hard worker, and he's fair and nice to people."

Mikie rubbed his chin as if contemplating the validity of those criteria for successful father figures.

"You talk to him a lot?"

"Yeah. We don't, like, talk talk. I mean, he's my dad. We just talk about stuff. But not, like, personal stuff. We talk about things we see on the farm, or basketball."

"Hm," Mikie said. And then he didn't say anything, and the moon burned in the sky and the wind puffed and gusted and fingered through Josie's hair.

"What about you?" she said. "Where would you go if you could go anywhere?"

"I'd go to Iceland," Mikie said, his voice slow and a little dreamy, as if describing some long-held vision. "Or New Guinea." Josie had never imagined either Iceland or New Guinea. She couldn't imagine what they might have in common beyond their sheer foreignness. "Or maybe Croatia. I think I have some ancestors from Croatia. Mom's ancestors."

Josie had no idea where Croatia really was. New Guinea sounded like Africa. Iceland must have been in the north. Croatia was in that mess of countries that clotted the map between Europe and Asia. But she didn't understand where these lands lay in her own imagination. They seemed to occupy a rich and vital niche in his. What filled that part of her mind?

"If you could meet anybody in the world—alive or dead—who would it be?" Josie tried.

"My dad," Mikie said.

And that stopped her. Mikie shifted on the rock and as he twisted toward her she watched to see if he would reach out and place a hand on her knee. The surprising thing was she understood that part of her wanted him to. His hand was coming around. Wavelets slapped at the rocks below them in a dissonant, rhythmless chop. Up where they sat, the rocks were dry, but the dense smell of muddy water permeated the air.

The moon shone weakly, and a cold breeze made Josie want to pull her own hoodie over her head. She wanted this strange boy to put his hand on her knee because she wanted to find out how she felt about it. She wondered how long she would leave it there before she made him take it off.

"If you caught terrorists, would you kill them?" Mikie was asking as he twisted. She watched his hand still coming around. She felt like it hovered over her knee, and she could feel the place where it would touch her, the weight of it sealing the denim of her jeans onto her skin. The hand dropped, kept dropping, fell to the side and planted on the rock beside her. For a moment she stared at it, in disbelief.

He missed. Should she have scooted her leg to catch it? And now she was staring at his hand, but she couldn't keep doing that without drawing attention to the fact that she was staring at it, which might alert him to something on her mind, which she absolutely didn't want him to find out about from her. She re-heard the question.

"Don't they kill themselves?"

"What if you caught the guys who planned 9/11?"

"I don't know," she said.

It hung between them while Josie glanced at the fingers that had so narrowly missed her knee. Even with only moonlight, she could see nicotine stains thick on the nail of his thumb, spread like iodine on the skin around it. His nails were ruins chewed to their bed rims. His cuticles featured scythes of salmon-colored skin, exposed flesh and tiny puckered scabs. She could get him to stop that.

That would be an early priority. As if he'd forgotten he'd asked her the question, he asked another one. "What makes people want to blow up the world?" He wasn't expecting her to answer. It was like a question from a song.

"They hate us," she said, though.

"Ever wonder why?"

"I don't know. They don't like our religion, I guess," Josie said.

"Your religion," he said.

"They don't like the way we live," she said.

"And the way we jam it down everybody's throat. That's why I want to go to, like, New Guinea and Iceland some day. We don't have any power there. They've probably never even heard of us."

"They're crazy," she said. "You can't rationalize with them."

"That sounds like something parents say," Mikie said.

Which stung her. It was something she'd heard from her parents—her dad—which didn't make it wrong. Which was also not what stung. Josie had the distinct sense that Mikie disdained secondhand opinions, particularly when they were handed down from adults.

"You wanna get high?" he asked then, and Josie felt the careful little bridge they'd been building start collapsing between them, starting with the footings at her end.

"I don't get high," she said. That came out more harshly than she intended. "Totally cool if you do. I'm not, like, a prude or any-thing. It's just . . . not my thing."

"Ever try it?"

"Nope," she said. She'd worked this one through and knew where she stood on it. Fine for anybody else; not her bag.

"I'm gonna get you so folded," he said, and his mouth opened in a shiny grin. His teeth were not fangs at all, she could not help but see now, but instead looked a bit too small for a mouth wearing this wide of a smile.

"No you're not," she said. This felt less like statement-making than it did teasing. A little bit of teasing.

"Before it's all over, I'm gonna get you so high your eyeballs'll pour right out of your head."

"That sounds sooo appealing," she said, able to laugh at him. But what she was thinking was: *Before what's all over?*

* * *

Tom had driven home feeling battered by the day—not side-swiped or body-blocked, but rather as if he'd endured a thousand slaps since he'd awakened that morning, and had never known when the next one was coming. And that email from the day before: *I feel bad about so many things.* He was going to have a worse tomorrow, wondering what had gone on in Sophie's head to make her type that and click "send" as a function of how he should reply.

The past, he'd learned, was nothing like it used to be. He paid little attention to where he was driving, having done so for so many years, until he noticed a clump on the side of the road. Dead pheasants, skunks, coyotes, antelope—the roads around Dumont were littered with the collisions between a human society racing into the future and an animal world firmly rooted in travelogues divorced from time.

Tom braked, pulled over, stepped from the truck. The air felt chilly, and the end of the day sat in a powdery purple band along the horizon, pink on top of that. There was no high light, so every-thing felt close at hand. He walked around the truck. It was the white fur that threw him. A fox, belly up, its red coat down on the pavement, as dead as a fox could get. Tom went on home.

Sitting in his house later, Scout fed and walked, Tom had three or four beers. He was, he felt, entering a moment of weakness, or at least that's what he told himself when he picked up the phone to call Jenny Calhoun. He had no idea what he wanted to talk to her about. She was still up.

"It's a little late," she said, "but if you really need an ear."

Tom held onto enough of his sense of remove to try to talk her into eating out with him. But she said, "The only place that's still serving is pizza at Pep's. I can't leave the kids. Why don't you come over here?"

He proposed picking up a pizza at Pep's on the way over, then added, "We can just eat it and then I'll go." Which sounded stupid as soon as he'd said it. She offered to "whip something up" for him.

"Let me bring a pizza. I'm already inconveniencing you. What do you like on it?" he asked.

"Oh, I ate with the kids a long time ago."

"Humor me."

"Anything but olives. And sausage. I don't like their sausage. It's too gritty."

He loved olives and she was probably the wrong person to take this out on, but the prospect of a night alone with droopy-eyed Scout seemed too daunting. Tom felt a depression coming on, like the cold fronts that sometimes moved across the autumn sky, a density of purple-gray cloud as far as you could see, slowly closing out the light. There was no way to flee out from under it. He needed to be with someone, and Jenny was the person who seemed most interested in talking to him about things in his life. Well, the only one.

"This thing going on about the bus, it's a mess," Tom said, when they sat at the oak harvest table in her kitchen. He had never been in her house before, but felt like he had, felt like the timeworn furniture and practical functionality of everything in the kitchen was exactly what he expected, the dishtowels folded neatly, the appliances tucked away, the cleared counter space. Her six-year old son and eight-year old daughter were both in bed by the time he arrived, and he and Jenny talked in hushed voices, adding a façade of gravity to a situation that Tom secretly felt was already more grave than a lot of people knew. He had started in on his first piece of pizza and relished the way the still-warm but not flesh-burning cheese felt against the roof of his mouth.

"Did anybody get hurt?" Jenny asked.

Tom thought about that while he chewed. "I think somebody always gets hurt in these situations," Tom said.

"How bad?"

"Maybe not go-to-the-hospital bad. Maybe down-the-road bad. Although, I hear people talking and there seems to be a whole bunch of folks who think not a damned thing happened worth worrying about."

He finished the piece of pizza and began prospecting the box, looking for the next candidate. He had no idea he had been so hungry. "I'm thinking I'll offer my resignation."

"I heard that," she said. Jenny drained her wine glass, which drew his attention to her. He could tell she wanted more details but wouldn't push for anything he didn't feel comfortable volunteering. She never did. "I just want you to know I'm pretty good at keeping my mouth shut about private things. I managed not to tell anyone for two whole years that my husband was sleeping with a cocktail waitress in Lewistown," she said and smiled, so he did, too. Then the levity evaporated like cold steam and his eyes fell.

"There were some girls involved, too. Cheerleaders who were on the bus when we stopped to get gas."

"Cheerleaders are a bit more aggressive than we were in my day," Jenny said.

"You were a cheerleader?"

"Crimson and blue, all over you," she said, moving her fists in a parody of tiny cheer pumps.

"But not aggressive?"

She pressed her lips together. "Way too self-conscious. I just did it because I thought that's what the cool kids did."

"Wasn't it?"

"Not really. The really cool kids, I found out later, were at home helping their folks around the farm. Or they were in the library reading Paul Bowles and Jack Kerouac."

"You know, I never liked Jack Kerouac," Tom said. He wanted that third piece of pizza, but didn't want to sit and feed like a hog. He wanted to ask her to have a piece, but now found himself in a conversation for the first time, he realized, in—what? Years?

"He wrote about football," Jenny floated.

"He wrote about Neal Cassady, not so much about football. He never got it about football, which made me realize he didn't get it about a lot of things. It was really all just his filter that people bought up."

"Football can mean different things to different people."

"Sure."

"I think I could have guessed you wouldn't be a big Kerouac fan. Though, true confession: I used to fantasize about that Neal Cassady." She seemed to make herself blush a touch. "When I was a lot younger." She watched him looking at her. "Well, come on, Tom, there wasn't a lot for teenaged girls in Dumont to fantasize about."

For a moment Tom felt a different portion of his brain stimulated. He felt sly and clever, as if he were a lot younger and flirting with a pretty girl, a girl who seemed to be telling him something about herself that she wanted him to know for a reason.

"You can't imagine a jock who reads, huh?"

"That's not it at all," she said. "Some of our best students play sports. I just didn't pick you for someone who read a lot of Kerouac. You don't seem the type."

"Assignments in college. Back in the day . . ."

"Back in the day," she said, too.

"Funny thing, back in the day something like this thing that happened, probably nobody says anything about it."

"Oh, a lot of bad things happened back in the day didn't get talked about," she said. "Domestic violence. Sexual assault. Child abuse. There are really good reasons those days are on their way out. It's important to keep them shuffling out the door."

"Yeah," he said and nodded, then felt dumb sitting there nodding. He wondered how many people in dusty little towns like Dumont were trying to forget things that happened to them twenty or forty years before, things so awful they told only one person or nobody about, things they knew nobody would want to listen to them talk about.

"I think people should talk about this one," Tom said.

"So you're going to make them?" Jenny asked. She kept looking at him and when he had no answer she said, "I'm not arguing. I just want to know if you've thought through how it's going to go. Might get a little rough."

"Oh, you know . . . shit. I mean, look at my life," he said, but this seemed to bother her. So he said, "I can make my life be okay one way or the other. This kid . . . he's just a kid. He didn't get to choose."

"You're not giving him a choice now, either. He's going to be humiliated when this is all over town."

"It's all over town now."

"Not the way it's going to be. Not out in the open where Mom and Grandma and Aunt Pearl know all the clinical details."

"What happened to keeping those days shuffling out the door?" Tom asked.

"You wanted someone to talk to. I assumed you meant 'to' and not 'at.'"

"I did."

She reached over and rubbed her palm against the knob of muscle on his shoulder. She let the hand rest there, which made him look at it, until she dipped her head so he'd look at her eyes. "I'm not on a side," she said. "I'm just trying to be here in the middle, with you. Feel what it's like."

Her hand still rested on his arm, and he could not ignore the weight of her warmth. He knew he could, if he could concentrate, identify a reason she would want to touch him like that, but it felt beyond his reach at the moment. He wondered if this was what it felt like to have a nervous breakdown, this detachment from things you knew you could pin down, if only you could funnel the appropriate amount of attention to them. But getting a handle on the attention was like trying to tackle an imaginary friend. When he asked, the sound coming from his throat felt empty in the middle. "Why?"

She took a moment to form a response. "I think you're a good man in a bad spot. And I think you could use a friend."

A *friend*, he thought. Was that what he needed? Tom couldn't remember the last time he'd made a new friend. He had plenty of pals, but friends? It made him again try to switch his focus, which was disappointing, because for a moment there, for the first time in a very long time, he had thought that what he truly needed was a woman, a compassionate figure of flesh and languid movement, a throat to confide his dry lips on, the curve of a waist to rest his stiff, weary hands along.

A woman other than his fantasy conjurings of his former wife. Of course, Jenny had been right. Desire was not an appropriate driver in this moment—or if it was, any attempt at follow-through would end in comedy, not romance. A *friend*, she had said. Maybe he had misread the pies all along. Maybe they were part of football fever. Or its tradition, its form. She had never encouraged him to come to her house—or anything else for that matter. Her reputation as a good listener and a kind person to others in her community was well established. He had probably read all of this wrong, perhaps subverted her motivations to fit his subconscious needs. At this moment, complicating his life with desire was a bad idea, anyway. But who plans these things?

Who has such a firm handle on what they want? Not Tom Warner, not sitting in Jenny Calhoun's kitchen and feeling the blue gaze of her eyes, feeling the warmth of her palm on his shoulder, not when he felt like the rest of his world was losing its familiar shape. He reached for her, leaned across the table to do it, dragging his shirt through the pizza box, in a move that looked more lurch than love. He cupped his hand behind her head and pulled her face to his, probably with more urgency than he should have. His lips pressed against hers, found them feeling lush against his, pliant even, but not eagerly anticipating his arrival.

Not exactly matching his ardor. He kissed her for a moment, waiting for her to catch on, but she didn't and then he noticed that her head maintained its pressure against his hand—she wasn't pulling back, but she sat in the same posture she had when he'd made his move, only she had stiffened a bit. He dropped back in his seat.

"Aw, damnit all. I'm sorry," he said. "I . . . I got carried away. Misread . . ."

"So sudden," she mumbled, her fingers lightly combing hair back into place.

"I shouldn't have. I didn't mean to . . ."

After an awkward pause she said, "No. I just . . . really didn't expect . . . tonight, like that . . . that's not how I expected it to happen."

"That was inappropriate, I'm sorry," Tom said. Jenny was the kind of woman who expected to be courted a bit, he suddenly understood, and the clarity of that realization hit home because he'd just treated her like some woman he'd met in a bar. Show up half drunk with a pizza. She had kids in the house. "Overwhelming. I didn't mean to be overwhelming. That's not how I am. I don't want you to think that's how I am." There followed a long awkward pause. To Tom, Jenny seemed confused and suddenly inaccessible. She sat and stared at the doorway with her eyebrows arched, one of her wrists turned so her half open palm was up. She looked like she was hoping an explanation might drop into it.

"I should maybe go," Tom said. "I'm going to go."

Though of course he wanted her to argue and stop him from leaving, Tom saw her sitting up straight in her chair, looking disheveled and a touch puzzled, and it was too much for him. "I'm really, really sorry," he said.

"No," she said. "You don't have to go."

But he did have to go, now. He'd convinced himself. He needed to escape his embarrassment, and there was no way that could happen in this kitchen. He found himself caught in one of those momentary internal debates about irrelevant details: should he take the rest of the pizza home with him or leave it for her and the kids? It was his pizza and he was still hungry, had only eaten the two pieces.

"I don't know what got into me."

So many things to feel bad about. The urge to flee overcame all feeding concerns and he left, his last glimpse of Jenny revealing a woman staring at his pizza with a small baffled smile on her face. Tom hurried to his vehicle and let the engine rev while absent-mindedly leaving his foot on the gas pedal.

He failed to cool the rpms down and the vehicle jerked when he dropped it into reverse. His drive home took him through downtown, where the lights of Pep's bar still glowed. Horrified by the prospect of lying in his bed, staring at the ceiling, his heart kicking, his body still awash in a throbbing cocktail of lust and shame, he pulled in. He barged through the door and ordered a whiskey ditch, saw Hal Hartack's eyebrows arch, then remembered the alkalinity of the Dumont water supply.

He changed it to a straight shot, upped it to a double, and asked for a beer back. Hal poured the drinks without comment, moved on down the empty bar a ways, and pretended to polish beer mugs with the dish towel always draped from his waist. Two Aarstads Tom barely knew sat at the other end of the bar, talking loudly to each other, although Tom didn't tune in.

Hal waited until Tom had choked back the shot and taken a long soothing swallow of the beer, then said, "See that Monday night game?"

Tom glared at him, then understood the question. He shook his head.

"Doozy. Packers won right at the end. That goddamned Rogers, he can throw a tomato through a brick wall."

Tom let Hal talk to him about the game for a while. Then a second shot glass came and went and a second beer and he started to lose track of the story of the game. The tension and frailty he'd felt coiling around him all day began to unwind, and he found himself perversely enjoying the sensation of a true falling apart. This, he thought, must be the way the dissolute drunks do it. He was looking at all sorts of hell to pay in the morning, but couldn't imagine how that would be any different if he let himself go tonight. He skipped the third whiskey but had another beer.

"Odd night for a bender," Hal said. "You don't seem the type."

"You're the second person tonight to suggest I don't seem the type," Tom said.

"It's an insightful town," Hal said.

"Or a judgmental one," Tom said.

"We've just been here a while," Hal said, grinning.

Tom wondered how much that mattered. He suspected they knew how they were, all six hundred or so of them having grown up together, continually under each other's influence and sidelong eye. And yet there were always surprises. The autumn before he had been driving around the spare tablelands, looking for places to hunt birds, when he'd pulled into a farm yard and met a rancher who'd named his dogs Biko and Biafra. Tom had assumed the references were to musicians, but the rancher, a man almost exactly his age, who had attended the University of Montana during the same period Tom had and remembered him from the football team—a stunner in itself, since Tom had hardly played and nobody remembered his presence—told him that while music had drawn his attention, the dogs were named in honor of a man and a struggle.

Though he admitted that he let his kids call the second dog, simply, Bia. And there was Jenny with her Neal Cassady fantasies.

Tom liked to believe a guy like Hal knew hardly anything at all about him, even if he had grown up in a plains town even smaller than Dumont.

Hal wouldn't suspect his predilection for chai tea, or Spanish goat milk cheese you could get in Missoula, or, probably, that his favorite books were by Richard Ford and Alice Munro, because both writers seemed able to vitalize the significance of small moments in the wide-open bleakness of life on the vast rural plains. He doubted Hal would know under what circumstances he intended to use the fake punt he'd been practicing with the team.

"I suppose," Tom said, because everybody seemed to know these things, "you heard I'm quitting."

"The hell you say," Hal said, moving down the bar to grab the whiskey bottle again. Coming back now. "Whatever those boys got up to, that shit goes on every year on every team in every town."

"It doesn't. It happens in some places and not others. Why do you think that is, I wonder?"

Hal didn't look like he wanted to think about that. He looked like he wanted to grab Tom by the collar. He sort of swaggered to stop in front of Tom. "We did some horsing around when I played," Hal said. "I don't remember any big tragedies because of it."

"This got a little out of hand, Hal."

"Things do get a little out of hand from time to time," he said. "That's why they call it 'life' instead of 'the part where everything is always in hand.' That don't mean you quit. You pull your team together and tough it through. You don't let it ruin the whole season for all those boys."

"You sure you're not talking about ruining the whole season for somebody else?" Tom was thinking: *like you.*

Hal seemed to take stock for a moment, then leaned his forearms on the bar so he was closer to Tom's face. Anybody watching might find the gesture casual, even friendly. When he spoke, Hal's tone was tight and contained, some surprising blend of confession and thoughtful, if unsolicited, advice.

"The truth is a slippery fish, Tom. I'll tell you something— people think I care about how the football team does, think it's a big deal to me. And it doesn't hurt me any to play along. But hell, I'm sixty-seven years old. I got a boy that died just like yours did. Mine was twenty. Got in a highway accident. Never got to know him as a man. My daughters gave me four grandchildren. They're what I live for. Football doesn't mean shit to me.

"But I do care about this town. You said I might be thinking of someone else you'd ruin the season for, and you're not wrong. I think about those boys on the team and how this might be their one shot at something like glory, ever, in their whole lives. Look at me. You think my life got a lot more glamorous after winning that state championship? It's a Tuesday night, and I'm sitting around talking to a dumbass quitter."

Hal slapped his palm lightly on the bar, then closed a fist and wrapped his knuckles on it. "So yeah, all those little old ladies baking the boys pies, and the divorced gal down the street from me who never went to a football game in her life since high school, but she's got a crimson and blue flag flying in her front yard this fall. Pearl Aarstad, who wouldn't set foot inside this bar, but she corners me whenever I see her at the grocery and wants to talk about how the boys are doing, do I think they're going to win this Saturday. You should see the light in that woman's eyes. Yeah, I am thinking about what it might ruin for some folks. Maybe you should. Maybe you should think yourself clear, and make sure you're not using one little incident as an excuse to punish some-body else."

"Punish who?" Tom asked, offended.

"I don't know, Tom. Some folks seem to think you've had a bit of a chip on your shoulder since you got here. Maybe you want to punish us all. Maybe we don't measure up to what you expected. Or maybe we remind you too much of where you came from. Maybe you want to punish yourself for all the things that never happened the way you wanted them to."

Tom waved him off. Psychobabble was the last thing he expected from Hal Hartack. He wanted another drink, but he didn't want to have to ask Hal for anything, not now.

"Think long and hard about what you're doing, Tommy," Hal said. "A lot of people are going to care. Not just about whether our undefeated team has a coach—I'm talking about that other situation, too, with the Aarstad boy." He glanced conspicuously down the bar at the two men who were in some way related to Wyatt. "Things like that, they get misinterpreted, they can tear things up."

"How would you define misinterpreted?" Tom asked. He kept trying to latch onto reasons to be angry at what Hal said, though Hal did not seem to be angry at him.

"I'm just saying sometimes a thing can be two things at once. These little football games, they're all stories about who we really are in this town. You man up and do what's best for those boys. Right now they need guidance," Hal said, then straightened, lifted his forearms from the bar, gestured at Tom's beer and the twenty-dollar bill on the bar beside it. "This was all on me if you cut yourself off and go on home."

Hal backed away, careful not to appear abrupt, and wandered down to the other end where his other two patrons sat. Reverting to jovial form, Hal called out to the men, "You dumbfucks figure out which side of your asses you sit on yet?"

Tom drove home. On his way out of town, he passed the Sportsman Motel, where he did a double take. Two news vans were parked in the driveway, one a Havre station and the other out of Great Falls. He'd never seen a news crew in Dumont before. Suddenly Tom felt blood in the streets of his heart.

* * *

"Gabriel Dumont was a Metis. Does anybody know what that means?"

Silence. Tom never let that bother him.

"The Metis were mixed-blood descendants of Canadian Indians and French fur trappers. Like most native people, they lived off the land, trapping, hunting buffalo and other animals. In the late 1800s, after a series of skirmishes and battles in which he and a rag-tag army completely outmaneuvered and defeated Canadian government troops, Gabriel Dumont and Louis Riel, who were the first nationalistic leaders of the Metis people, formed a government that was recognized by the Canadian government in 1870," Tom said.

"Canada realized it was safer and beneficial to have peace on the frontier and a stable nation to deal with and so they ceded what is now most of Manitoba to the Metis people as sovereign territory.

"Of course, in the way these things tended to go, nearly as soon as they gave the Metis Manitoba, they found reasons to take it back, and arrest warrant was issued for Riel. But Riel and Dumont were tough, clever men. Even with a likely death sentence hanging over him, Riel managed to disguise himself and sneak into a meeting of the Canadian Parliament and sign in as a representative of Manitoba. He had to flee immediately, never got to vote on any legislation. Meanwhile, Canada opened Manitoba for white settlers, who, of course, claimed all the most productive farmlands and relegated the Metis to poverty."

Tom could see that his reading of history had an effect on certain students. His version poisoned their cowboys and Indians childhoods, and nobody wanted to have to reimagine those memories of innocent slaughter. Some of the boys managed to create poses that transmitted their disgust, slouching and slinging their hips forward, legs sprawling, chins tucked down to chests, hands splayed so that their inactivity could hardly be missed. Waylon Edwards chose to appear obviously staring out the window, so dismissively thinking about something else that he occasionally smiled and frowned about whatever went on in his head.

Some of the girls stared at him to let him know they were paying attention because this might be on the test, but they were holding it against him for making them know this stuff that they would never care about. Well, but people should know who their town was named after, was Tom's thinking. And he noticed a few heads were turned up. Josie Frehse was trying to pay attention without appearing too eager, because that wouldn't be cool.

Mikie LaValle watched Tom talk in a way that made him know the boy had questions he wouldn't ask out loud. But maybe he'd come around later. So Tom plowed ahead.

"Riel fled to the US, and Dumont moved westward to Saskatchewan with a large group of Metis. Riel wound up living not far from here for a while, while Dumont and his people scattered and settled across the Saskatchewan territory. They lived there for years, believing they had outrun their troubles, until— white settlers started encroaching again, with the tacit approval of the Canadian government.

"By then, some people think that Riel had begun to lose his mind a little. He began to speak of himself in messianic terms. You know what that means?" Tom asked.

"Like he was a chosen one, or something?" Josie answered.

"Yeah. He started to talk about himself like he was a messiah, come to save the Metis people. Like he was almost godlike. But people still believed in him and they sure believed in Gabriel Dumont's ability to fight. So Dumont left his peaceful farming life and came to Montana to talk Riel into leading the people again. Together they went to the plains of Alberta and Saskatchewan and started organizing another resistance.

"In Canada, this movement was called the Northwest Rebellion. Gabriel Dumont was brilliant again as a military strategist. They fought a battle at a place called Duck Lake and they crushed the Canadian forces against them, even though they were completely out-armed and outnumbered. In Manitoba and in the Northwest Rebellion, Dumont just beat the federal forces time and again."

"Kind of like us and Drummond." The voice startled Tom. It was Waylon Edwards, who apparently had been listening enough to draw a parallel.

"What's that?"

"Well, Drummond has more guys on their team, and they have better facilities and more money in their school. They always win state. And when we play them, we're going to have fewer warriors, but we're going to beat them in battle after battle until we win the game," Waylon said. He was proud of himself.

Whereas Tom felt patronized. He knew exactly how smart Waylon was, knew Waylon was comparing the football team to an underdog army as a suck-up to the football coach/teacher. But his tone had a "cool story, bro" condescension to it. Too, Tom knew how the parallel went askew.

"You might want to rethink that when you hear what happened in a battle at a town in Saskatchewan called Batoche. That's where the rebel army was completely overrun by the Royal Canadian Mounties. The Metis fought well for three days, but were finally outmanned. Riel was captured and hanged."

"What happened to Dumont?" Waylon asked.

"Well, Gabriel Dumont managed to slip away with a few other rebels and escape. They crossed back over the border and came here, settled right in this area. The Metis rebellion ended at Batoche. Dumont ended up in Buffalo Bill's Wild West show, traveling to New York City and Paris. His family put down roots in our place. And at least one Montana town was named for him. The town of Dumont was originally part of the Fort Miles reservation. Although later, the reservation shrank as settlers and homesteaders wanted the rich bottomlands around here, so the town eventually slipped outside the reservation borders."

* * *

Later, when she went home, Josie would consider how fascinated she must truly have been, to be at all distracted on a day that the sheriff and the school attorney had been parked in the principal's office, interviewing students—not coincidentally her boyfriend— all day long. There was a tension in the house when she came in, her mother sitting at the table with her brother, neither speaking.

Her dad's truck was in the yard, so he was around and likely the source of what nobody seemed to be talking about. Tension was the last thing she wanted to dive into. Jared lifted his glance to catch her eye and hold it for a moment.

Josie looked a question at him, but he gave her nothing. She went right to her room and closed the door. Why had nobody ever told her that her town was named after a mixed-blood rebel? She had, of course, never bothered to ask anybody how Dumont got its name, but this was, to her, the kind of surprise that left you mis-understanding everything. She knew several of the Hi-Line towns were allegedly named back when the Great Northern railroad was laying out towns and its hucksters were shilling real estate. The story went that a company employee spun a globe and stuck his finger on it to produce town names like Malta, Havre and Glasgow.

Every other town she knew was named for military or govern-ment officials—Fort Peck, Fort Miles, Fort Benton—or trappers, settlers, or railroad officials—Wibaux, Shelby, Jordan, Sidney, Scobey—all, she had long ago noted, white people. In fact, in a region famous for its Indian inhabitants, every town she knew was named for or by a white person.

Except Chinook, which was named for the wind. When she had been very young and played cowboys and Indians with her brother and the boys, she was always an Indian. The boys—Jared and Alex and her cousins—thought it was because she was a girl and they, as boys, got to be the cowboys. But she would have chosen to be an Indian anyway. Josie hated the way people treated the Gros Ventre and Assiniboine people from the Fort Miles reservation who sometimes came to town. If they weren't overly friendly to white people, Josie thought, well, it wasn't as if we hadn't given them two hundred years' worth of reasons.

And now come to find out, she was living in the only town in the northern Montana named after a man most noted for his Indian blood and his anti-government leanings. She felt particularly outraged by Coach Warner's eventual assertion—voiced in the exchange that followed with Waylon—that, had he lived today, Gabriel Dumont would have been labeled a terrorist. She found herself aswim in the history. *Batoche.* The word repeated in her head, obsessively. *Batoche.* It all fell apart in Batoche. Gabriel Dumont sounded like an angel's name, and she imagined him at the battle of Batoche, playing a shining brass trumpet to signal a charge, smoke and dust swirling around him. And they had almost won.

They had almost pulled it off. Josie had never heard of the Northwest Rebellion, Gabriel Dumont, Louis Riel, the Metis, none of it. She knew about Sitting Bull and Crazy Horse. She knew some stories about the Blackfeet, Sioux, Cheyenne, and Nez Perce because she'd read about them on her own. She knew about the Fort Baker massacre, whiskey and the blankets full of smallpox. She knew a lot about the fur trappers, the railroad, the homesteaders, the Dust Bowl, but she'd never, in eleven years of education, read a word about the Metis. That seemed criminal.

Her sense of outrage kept her engaged in the subject even while Coach Warner and Waylon jabbed back and forth. She wondered if the Metis people looked like Mikie LaValle. She wondered what tribe Mikie's Indian side came from, and thought to ask him, but then worried that it might be impolite. Mikie was not a polite boy, but Josie thought he was edgy and mean sheerly as a reflexive mechanism. She felt at all moments coming from him a palpable fear of being hurt. She doubted he'd trust anybody anytime soon, but she'd bet she could teach him to trust her.

If that's what she chose to do. Josie had never bothered to censor her thoughts about boys who weren't Matt. This wasn't the first time she'd had them, and it wouldn't be the last. She'd never cheated on Matt, but she often thought about boys she saw fleetingly when she traveled to other towns for basketball or football games, remembered the way they stood, the cut of their hair, how jeans hung on their hips. She thought about the nameless, faceless college boys to come, wondering how they would be different than Matt, what things she would talk about with them, how they would hold her in a way that made her feel more loved than desired. It did occur to her that Mikie was not one of her usual types.

He was odd, dark and sharp. She wouldn't call him handsome in any of the usual ways. Fierce maybe, but that was something he was trying to show. Fierce and so afraid. Behind it, she was starting to realize, lived a mind consumed with dreamy escapist things he'd never done and probably would always be too afraid to try.

Or maybe he would. Maybe he'd be one of those rare kids who leave Dumont after graduation and never come back. You heard stories of them, going off to New York City, or joining the army and living in Germany. She had been at the grocery store with her dad once, a year ago, when a young man who had joined the military walked out of Pep's and recognized her father. They had talked briefly and the young man told her father where he had been. Guam, he said. Korea. Panama. Those were ones she remembered.

She had looked them up in the atlas when she got home to see where they were. Standing there, on the sidewalk outside the IGA, she could almost smell the faraway places on that guy. He wore different jeans than everybody she knew, and a shirt that looked Italian, or like Italians she had seen in movies like the Godfather or the Sopranos might wear. His skin was weathered, bronze, as if he had been tanned by a different sun than theirs. Maybe Mikie would be like that one day, coming home confident and full of views from the world. For a moment she entertained the notion of imagining herself heading abroad with him, but then thought, no.

She couldn't, in fact, convince herself that her interest in Mikie was at all romantic. It certainly hadn't started out that way. She had been protective of him, then curious about him, and now was curious about herself. He might, she realized, allow her to find some things out about herself. She had a note from him in her pocket, for instance, asking her to call him tonight. It was so charming, getting handwritten notes when everybody else sent texts. It reminded her of something her parents might have done when they were in high school.

She wondered if she would call him. Josie felt hungry, wondered if the kitchen was a safe zone yet. She decided to pretend nothing was wrong, emerged from her room with a rattling of her door handle and a snippet of song coming from her mouth, then swung down the hall, humming. Jared sat at the table, bent over some homework. He saw her, looked toward the mudroom, where Josie could hear the washing machine running. When his eyes came back to her, she the sadness in them stopped her humming.

"Dad wants me to slaughter the pigs," Jared said.

* * *

Caroline Jensen had been in town late working her second job, the evening shift at the IGA, and came home after dark to the faint aroma of pot. She knew Mikie smoked, had caught him a couple of times and tried grounding him for it, but how could you ground a kid when you couldn't be home to make sure he didn't go anywhere? She didn't want him to smoke pot, but was less enthusiastic in her protests than she could be, because she didn't mind lighting up a spleef every now and then and found it less offensive and a better outlet for Mikie than the other teenage drug of choice, heavy drinking. Mikie's father had succumbed to bouts of heroic alcohol indulgence that devolved into bouts of domestic violence.

She'd ended that after a few severe beatings, but still lived with a tiny but steady enough trickle of fear that he might show up again one day out of the blue and kill her. It was easy to blame the booze. Caroline didn't want Mikie to fall into drink. She felt his Indian genetics made him vulnerable to it. So she used that to excuse the pot as an acceptable way of taking the edge off the angst every teenager felt.

But she also felt she couldn't come off as too lenient, so she'd drawn a line at smoking in the house. Now Mikie sat at the kitchen table, eating a bowl of Captain Crunch and reading a book. Earbuds dripped black tentacles along his cheeks. His head bobbed to a rhythm in sync with his chewing. She signaled for him to turn the music down.

"What'd you learn in school today?" she asked. This was a standard question, asked every day.

"Nothing," he said, the standard answer.

"They ought a burn that school down and build a monster truck arena," she said. "Never teach the kids a thing. Total waste of my taxes."

Mikie cocked an eye her way as if to say, *now you're talking*.

"Seriously," Caroline said. This, too, was rote. She asked, he said nothing, she pushed, he sometimes told her a thing or two about school. "Tell me one thing you learned."

Mikie pushed his lower lip out, obviously decided something. He sat up straighter in his chair, but shrugged lest she get the impression he was displaying enthusiasm. "I learned who this town is named after."

"Who's that?" Caroline asked.

"You don't know?" Mikie asked, a bit smugly.

"I guess I don't. I guess I never thought about it."

"Gabriel Dumont," Mikie said, nodding up a big deal.

"And he is . . ."

"Half-breed," Mikie said, "Like me."

"Don't use that word," she said, but not with anything behind it, because she thought he was so damned cute when he thought he knew something. And Mikie was into this, moving his hands to represents nations and slabs of geography and, later, skirmish lines.

"He was. Metis. There's a whole nation of people who are half-breeds and they're called Metis. They're French and Indian, like in that war, and they're from Canada, around Minnesota and they have, like, their own culture. Dumont, though. Dumont, though, was badass. He was the leader of the warriors. The Canadian army had more guns and more soldiers and better horses but Dumont, though. He was like, I got this. He was too fierce. And too smart. He'd lay ambushes and, like, pretend to be retreating but really he was just luring the army into a trap. He fought a whole rebellion and beat the army at first, though later they lost, but so Canada had to give the Metis a whole country to be all theirs. That's what Manitoba is. But then they took it back."

"Who took it back?"

"Canada," Mikie said, his mood tripping toward annoyed by her lack of understanding.

"OK, Mikie, just tell the story clearly. You know how. First things first, then the next thing. Don't get impatient."

"Sorry," he said, which meant roughly, she had come to understand, *whatever.*

Mikie went back to talking in what amounted, for him, to a rush. "Canada gave Manitoba to the Metis, but then they took it back—"

"How come?"

"I dunno. They made up some reason."

"That doesn't sound fair."

"It's history, dude. It's not about fair. So anyway, Gabriel Dumont came out here and lived down in the breaks, kind of hiding out because he was a rebel and there was a price on his head."

"Here?"

"In *Canada.*"

"Don't be impatient."

"Could you not tell me what to do?"

They had hit an impasse, a fairly usual one. Caroline knew her way around it, but let things sit for a moment, thinking of it as letting her message sink in. "Okay, there's rice in his bed in Canada."

Mikie conceded a snort of laughter, one quick bolt. "He came out here and was just living his life, farming and stuff, when he saw the same thing happening again."

"What same thing?"

"Oh, the usual—whitey stealing the land."

Caroline shuffled a warning look his way.

"So he got another army together and they tried to win again and get their own country in Saskatchewan. And he was, like, this brilliant, bad mo-fo general. They were totally outnumbered, but he kept beating the Canada army, bashing their brains in. But they lost and he escaped across the border into Montana and lived right around here."

"That's quite a story," she said. "You make it up?"

"I learned it in history class."

"All right, okay," Caroline said. She jacked a cigarette out of her pack and lit it, took a deep hit. "I'm impressed. What do you think of that other big story at school?"

"That . . . woooo. That's some nasty, gnarly stuff, man." He almost laughed when he said it. "But I don't put nothin' past those guys."

"Anything," his mother said, and let it fall. "Do you see now why I wanted you to make an effort to reach out to Wyatt Aarstad?"

"Uh, no." The *are you crazy?* conjugation.

"Wyatt could use a friend, Mikie. I bet he feels really lonely. I bet he can't believe those guys would do something like that to him." Then she let that fall away, too. She knew Mikie felt intense embarrassment over the way certain factions at school treated him and, though part of her thought it might be nice for him to be able to talk about it, she feared that talking to her about it would only intensify the shame. Caroline went about emptying the two plastic bags she had brought from work, canned vegetables and tuna, a box of spaghetti, a head of iceberg lettuce. "That your dinner?" she asked, meaning the cereal.

He didn't answer, so she kept putting things away.

"Was my dad good looking?" Mikie asked.

This was as different as the gushing about history. She said, "About the best-looking man I ever laid eyes on."

"So I must of got my looks from you."

Caroline sat back, perplexed. In one sentence her son had managed to gut-punch her with the full fore of his insecurity. *Kids.* "You're a very good-looking young man," she said.

"Said his mom."

"You are. Of course you are. You've got those nice high cheekbones"— she reached across the table and squeezed his face in her fingertips, shook it back and forth a couple of times, —"those deep, dark eyes." She lowered her tone, falling into voice-over. "The beautiful girl peered into his deep, dark eyes. 'I love you, too, Mikie,' she said . . ."

He pulled his head away. "God, Mom, you're setting new records for gross parental abuse."

"I love it when you call me God Mom."

They stared at each other and then Mikie couldn't meet her eye and Caroline suddenly understood what was going on. "Mikie," she said, "do you have a girlfriend?"

"No." She might have been asking if he'd worn her underwear to school.

"You. Do," she said. "Who is it?"

"You're a dork, Mom. You have no idea what you're talking about."

"C'mon, spill it. Give it up. Who's the chickie?"

"There's no *chickie.*" Mikie got up from the table, carrying his cereal bowl to the sink. Caroline watched him walk away from her, saw his skinny hips and bony shoulders and thought, *I'll be goddamned—there's a man in there.*

"Well," Caroline said, "your momma has one piece of advice."

"Mother." He clattered the bowl in the sink and turned to leave the kitchen. Caroline cut him off, hands on his shoulders to square him up.

"You respect her, Mike LaValle," Caroline said. "Whoever this girl is, you respect her and listen to what she says."

"That was two," Mikie said.

"I thought maybe you could use the extra," Caroline said. Something about her son entering the misery of teenaged love made her feel giddy. "Don't be impatient with her. Respect her. And listen to her."

"Now that's three."

"A woman knows what a woman wants." She held up a take-note finger.

"I don't think they do," Mikie said. "I don't frankly think they have any fucking idea what they want. You don't."

Caroline whipped her head quickly, as if trying to see something zipping around the room. "See that?" she asked. "Bounced right off."

"God, are you a fifth-level *dork*," Mikie said, using his hands to knock hers off his shoulders and twisting away. "I got homework to do."

"You have homework to do."

"That's what I'm telling you."

"Not in my native tongue," she countered.

"In mine," he said. "Metis."

And then he was gone, squirming down the short hall toward his room. Behind him, Caroline started swishing around the kitchen, singing to the Ricki Lee Jones tune, "Mikie's in love . . ."

* * *

Wednesday evening, Tom ran a half-hearted practice. He saw Matt Brunner eyeing him warily. At one moment he caught Alex Martin standing, hands on hips, staring at him with barely contained impatience. The players jogged through drills. He stuck it out, called the plays, but spent more time watching the blue-black line of clouds coming from the west—a hundred miles off but visible as one long low rampart stretching the entire horizon.

Cold air filled the wind and seemed to suck his breath away when he exhaled. Standing on the sidelines, whistle clenched between his teeth, he thought he should feel worse about what was happening.

But there was no emotion. It was just a line he realized he had crossed. He remembered Sophie's email: *I feel bad about so many things.* After the team left the field, Tom stopped in the film room, gathered some thumb drives, and drove home. He let the dog out, fed her, turned on the TV for background sound, then settled in with his laptop and popped in a thumb drive with film of last year's semifinal game against Wibaux.

But before he could click on the file, he caught a splash of the Havre news channel on the TV. He didn't want to watch long, and didn't have to before he felt an awful recognition about the establishing shot. There stood a young blonde reporter in front of the high school in Dumont, desperately seeking the proper angle to point her face so that her hair blew clear of it. The reporter—she couldn't have been much older than the kids who went to his school, Tom thought, twenty-two, twenty-three at the most—gestured at the school behind her.

"Getting the real story is difficult here, in this small, close-knit farming community," she said, "but what we do know is that, during a hazing incident that took place on a school bus on the way home from a high school football game last Saturday, a young boy was humiliated and, some sources say, sexually assaulted."

Sexually assaulted? Who told her that? Unfortunately the reporter, who had the impossibly unlikely name of Penny Meriwether, wasn't going to fill him in. The screen filled instead with the face of Jon Aarstad, a particularly broken-down version of that clan and Wyatt's father. Jon's teeth jostled the front of his lower jaw, even while they gapped on the upper. One eye seemed higher on his cheekbones than the other. His pallor lent the appearance of someone who had chain-smoked their entire life, from birth.

"Those boys assaulted my son on that bus," Aarstad was saying, his mouth hooked in a snarl of disgust. "That wasn't no kind of hazing, it was an assault. They held him down and they did things to him that were obscene. They humiliated him. They humiliated me, just being related to it. They ought to go off to jail."

Tom watched as the reporter proceeded to wheedle five "no comments" out of Dave Cates. Next she waylaid a sequence of teenagers trickling out of school at the end of the day. Most of them said they didn't know anything about it. The reporter asked one girl what she thought of hazing and the girl replied, "It's, like, whatever, you know? It happens, but it's not, like, an epidemic or anything." The girl laughed at the end.

The next student Penny Meriwether stuck the mic in front of was Mikie LaValle. Mikie glanced around as he replied and produced the overall impression that he wasn't sure if he should be saying any of this out loud. He said, "It sucks, man. Some people can get away with anything in this school."

"Which people do you mean?" Penny Meriwether asked.

"Football players," Mikie said. "Athletes." He was already starting to lean out of the frame, ready to bolt the moment he had a chance. The reporter put her hand on his upper arm and pulled in closer to him.

"Is hazing a significant problem at Dumont?" she asked.

An editor muted the *Hell* that began the next sentence, so Mikie LaValle's lips started moving before he spoke, "—yes. There's all the time stuff going on with the jocks. If you're not in the right crowd, life can be . . ." and the editor muted a *shit*.

In its way, it was remarkable work. Penny Meriwether had managed, in very brief period, to portray his football team as a wilding pack of vicious rogues, his school as an enterprise fraught with peril, and his town as primarily the home of feral idiots. He wanted to call someone in the hopes of being assured that it hadn't been as bad as he thought it was. Dave Cates was the right candidate, but Tom wanted not to talk to Cates for a while.

The person he did want to talk to was Jenny. He thought he shouldn't call her, though. She might want some distance from him right now, or he wanted it from the embarrassment in her kitchen the night before. She'd certainly not been in touch, and he'd been too ashamed. So instead he switched over to the laptop and started the game film. He fast-forwarded and slowed only to watch play after play of Jared Frehse running, the way he leaned into his speed, the way he pumped his arm with the ball. Tom loved when Jared made the cuts that left defenders grasping air.

He loved the fleet footwork, the flutter of steps that let Jared's body move from one place to another only inches away, but out of reach. Tom's son could do that when he was only ten—the spin move that whirled him a yard to the right and left a linebacker lunging at nothing but his own momentum. The plays Tom watched and rewatched were the speed moves, the moments when Jared outran everybody to a spot, then cut upfield and outran everybody to the end zone.

There was nothing simpler in sports than that—one player faster than all the others, understanding angles and using them in combination with his innate awareness of his own velocity. Watching the film, Tom felt odd about his place in the world, how suddenly it had all changed. He had had a son, a good boy who he had wanted to teach things to. A boy with his own remarkable velocity and preternatural control over his own body. Everything had centered around that boy.

Tom's life had tilted, pointed in a specific direction. And then, suddenly, that was all gone, leaving everything in front of him blank. He had an ex-wife more alive to him in dreams than she'd ever been in real life. He had an email on his computer that he still hadn't answered. He didn't know if he was a football coach anymore—he'd find that out later in the evening. Down the road in town, there was a woman he'd tried to kiss the night before, a woman he'd thought had wanted him to kiss her, and now had no idea about. He flicked off the television.

Scout lay curled on the floor, bored. It was time to go to town, to the school board meeting, and find out what was going to happen to him. He looked around his little home, just an old beat-up farmhouse that he liked because it sat in the middle of thousands of acres of wheat fields. It held no stories about him or his life.

If he wasn't going to be the Dumont football coach, chances were the house wouldn't even be home for much longer. Tom left Scout inside, using his foot to block the door to her when he left to drive to town.

* * *

When Marlo Stark had left Great Falls that afternoon, the blizzard was just getting underway there, blanking out the distance and churning up the sky with slashing white snow. She had hoped to leave town hours before and beat the weather. Then the day ran away from her and her best bet became a race against accumulation. Fifteen minutes outside of town, she felt in it for the long haul. Chet had seemed genuinely unhappy about her leaving for the night, which warmed her heart and cranked up a little guilt. She didn't want to spend the night in Dumont, by any means, but she still felt a little guilty about dropping it on Chet so suddenly. But it was her job, and he had to deal with that. She made a pretty little penny representing school boards around the state—a niche practice that only a couple other attorneys occupied and none to the degree Marlo did.

She wasn't going to give that up for Chet or anybody else, no matter how inconvenient it could sometimes be. Ah, Chet. What was she going to do with sweet, handsome, adorable-like-a-Labrador-retriever Chet? Marry him, she guessed, since she was engaged to him—although the only way she'd managed to stay engaged so long was to allow herself to believe, every day, that before the wedding day something would happen to blow the whole thing up. Until then she would be good to him, and love him, because she did love him. But she already wondered if, eventually, she would not be faithful to him.

She'd never been faithful in a relationship, ever. She'd never loved anybody the way she loved Chet, either. So maybe there was hope. She could hold onto that. Or maybe, when she knew she had to step outside the bounds of the marriage, she could manage it in such a way that he would not be hurt. Marlo spent a lot of time thinking about this as she drove through the snow without even the benefit of a horizon line to aim for.

She wondered what was wrong with her, why she couldn't be happy with one person, but consoled herself by thinking that knowing something so important about herself was better than pretending she didn't know it, and inviting disaster to explode at unexpected moments. She could manage it, she told herself again. Her hands hurt from gripping the wheel. The radio stations fizzled quite early, long before Big Sandy, and she didn't pick up new ones until she was almost to Havre.

The weather was too dicey to text and drive. Instead, she sang loudly to old Indigo Girls songs played on her phone as the only viable option for staying distracted from the snow, which came at her windshield like the stars on the old Star Trek programs when they shifted the *Enterprise* into warp speed. She stopped in Havre for a tuna sandwich at the Subway, and discovered that her hands were curved in an arthritic arc. Three hours later, woozy from staring at snow in her headlights, Marlo pointed her car off the road and into the parking lot of the Sportsman Motel in Dumont. A sign on the door said, "No gutting animals inside."

She had planned to arrive in plenty of time to review the case and ready herself for the meeting, but a late start and the heavy snow cost her hours, and now she dumped her belongings in her room and stalked a few steps across the dirty carpet to duck into the cramped bathroom. She started to splash some water on her face, to wash the stress lines out after the drive, but the stench of alkalinity rose from the sink and drew her attention to the white deposit crusting the faucet.

She didn't need to check the showerhead to know that each individual nozzle bore its own white buildup. Deciding against using tap water to rinse her face, she wondered if people who showered daily in the alkaline water had tiny white deposits ringing their hair follicles. She had brought bottled water for drinking—a necessity she had learned long ago on her trips to eastern Montana—but she cracked the cap on a bottle and splashed some on her face, then smacked her cheeks with her palms and gave them a little pinch.

Back in her car, now saturated with the reek of stale tuna from the leftover half of the sandwich, Marlo drove the four residential blocks of Dumont to the downtown modular unit that housed the sheriff's and mayor's offices and the conference room used for most civic meetings.

She felt strung out and harried and entirely unprepared for the night. Then she noticed the trucks. Her previous visits to Dumont had taught her that, at night, the downtown block never saw more than a knot of three or four outfits parked outside Pep's and another four or so across the street outside the Longbranch. Marlo was not prepared for the welter of pickups swelling the streetside. She parked against the already deep ridges of snow that had been plowed against the berm.

This meeting had all the important hallmarks of a very bad idea. When David Cates had called her and described the hazing incident, she recognized immediately the potential for sexual assault implications and the lawsuit that would inevitably follow. Her advice had been to accept the coach's resignation, reassign him to classroom duties, suspend the boys involved, let the sheriff's office investigate any criminal wrongdoing, and just sit back and see what happened—in effect, the legal thinking was to force anybody who wanted to file a suit to make the first move, rather than provide ammunition. She had also advised Dave to submit his own resignation to the board.

Put it in their hands. Calling a public meeting to discuss the incident without first knowing the investigative facts was volatile and not-thought-through, and she had told Cates so. But people in town wanted to get to the bottom of things, and they put the kind of pressure on the school board members that only small towns can exert. Marlo had had no time to even conduct rudimentary phone interviews with the involved parties. She knew virtually nothing about what had happened until she spoke a second time with Dave Cates, and felt fuzzy even then. Dave and the coach clearly hadn't understood the legal subtleties that could have guided their questioning of the boys.

They hadn't, for instance, talked with any of them in the presence of their parents. But Marlo's job was to legally facilitate what the board wanted to do, or tell them it wasn't possible. She was an "advisor," which, in her experience, served the same role as a lighter fluid-soaked piece of newspaper in getting a fire started. It lit the blaze, but was gone in seconds, had no determining outcome on where the fire might spread to, and nobody could tell you anything about it afterward. Marlo was forced to park two blocks away from the Sportsman and walked in a short, shuffling strides through the snow, pelted by wind-driven pellets all the way. A clot of people spilled out of the double-wide-sized prefab municipal building and into the street.

Most wore feeding caps and Carhartt jackets and didn't seem as bothered by the snow as she was. The school board's special meeting, meant to "discuss incidents on school property and personnel issues" according to the 8½ by 11 posters placed, to accommodate state law, in prominent public places, quickly became one of the best attended non-sporting events in Dumont history, a feat made even more remarkable in the face of plunging temperatures and a snowstorm that blanked out the stars and moon.

Parents arrived from farmsteads thirty miles outside of town, knowing they would have to grapple their way home through temperatures approaching zero and a wind-driven ground blizzard. People made way for Marlo, recognizing her perhaps not as the school board attorney, but as someone from out of town carrying a briefcase. She pushed into the corridor of the municipal building and then into the meeting room, which was stuffed with humanity.

Every chair was occupied and onlookers ringed the room along the walls. Two pairs of cameramen and glossy TV reporters staked out competing positions and flooded the room with too much light. Marlo recognized a reporter from the *Great Falls Tribune*. The individual voices she caught were held to a level below that of normal conversation, but the sound of so many created a roaring murmur. Most disconcerting was the overwhelming reek of alcohol spewing into the air.

"Ms. Stark," Dave Cates said, rising to lever up a handshake when she reached the table where the five school board members and the superintendent sat. "Or I guess it'll be Mrs. soon. Mrs. what again?"

"Hi, Dave," Marlo said, using the handshake to pull him into a light hug. She had been told, by a senior partner, that her hugs were not exactly the image of professionalism the firm wished to convey, about which she thought: *Bonk that.* And why did she hate people—men, specifically—knowing that she was engaged, mentioning it out loud, waving it in her face? "It would be Crawford, if I was changing my name. But I'm sticking with Stark." She made her eyes round and wide open. "Big night."

"No hyphen?"

"Pretentious, don't you think?" Marlo said. "I've made too much money as a Stark to gamble on earning out as a Crawford."

"It *is* a big night," Dave said.

"Is this everybody?" she asked.

"I think we were waiting for you."

"I mean, is this everybody in town?"

Dave laughed and said, "Pretty near."

From their first interaction, several years before, she could tell Cates got a kick out of her, and that gave her a certain charge, too. She knew herself, knew she enjoyed her effect on men, wouldn't deny herself that. Maybe she reminded Dave of his single, college days. He made a big deal of the fact that they both were educated in Missoula—he an undergrad at the university, she at the law school. Dave smiled, tighter this time. Marlo glanced around the room and thought, *There is nothing quite so charming as a room full of farmers who imagine they're fit for public consumption.*

She particularly liked the festive turquoise or white kerchiefs that wrapped so many throats. Hardly anybody in the urban centers wore kerchiefs around their necks anymore, but several men in the audience sported what were obviously clean and special ones, blossoming from their shirtfronts at their Adam's apples.

"You know we can't do this, right?" Marlo said.

"Can't do what?" Dave asked.

"Your sign says the meeting will discuss personnel issues. You can't discuss personnel issues at a public meeting," Marlo said. "You can decide them, but you can't discuss them. Privacy laws."

"Well, I'll be," Cates said. "See, the board wants to clear the air. Act firmly and decisively."

"Sticky wicket, Dave," Marlo said. "This is all well-intentioned bad thinking. We need to know some things before we have a public meeting. When you say the board, who's the driver?"

"Brad Martin."

"Remind me."

"Board chair. Ultra-booster. Boy a senior on the football team. Daughter a sophomore cheerleader and track star. Big in the community. Runs the implement dealership. Ties to everyone. Big supporter of the school and the town."

Jesus, Marlo thought. "Well, let's start thinking."

"Be pretty hard to undo this," Dave said, holding open hands to suggest the entirety of the collection around him. "Can't tell everyone to go home."

"Let's figure something out," Marlo said. "First thing, there's not enough room in here. You can distract the crowd by suggesting a new venue—the high school gym would be my suggestion. While they're reassembling, maybe we can squeeze in a quick closed-door executive meeting with the board and the coach."

"I guess that's why we pay you the big bucks?"

"Sure," Marlo said, thinking, *that's as good a reason as any.*

* * *

When he saw the volume of traffic in town, Tom had parked his rig at the high school and walked the three blocks down to the town hall meeting room. He didn't push his way through the crowd, but he knew he'd have to be in the room where everything was happening, and so he excused himself as he struggled through the clogged hallway. Heads turned, people saw who he was.

"Happy?" one of his player's parents said as he squirmed past. They were closing ranks.

He was, he understood, already an outsider. He had not even made the main room when he heard a raised voice, identified it as Brad Martin's, then registered the groan of disapproval. The mass of backs before him suddenly became bellies and faces and the crowd emptied out of the building. Tom was washed back into the sharp, cold night. His eyes watered, going from the humid press of so many people to the frigid air.

He heard people telling other people the meeting had been moved to the high school. Up and down the street, pickup engines started, white headlights blinked on, and red brake lights flared as people prepared to drive the three blocks to the school.

Tom lingered, hoping to catch David Cates, and then, when the surge had ebbed, saw Dave, the five school board members, and an attractive woman in a wool skirt emerging from the town hall. Cates's eye lit on Tom. "Perfect," he said. "Here he is. Let's get this done."

Dave grabbed Tom's shoulder, said, "Come with us," and pointed him down the street. Two doors down, they all filed into Pep's bar.

"Really bad idea," the tall woman in the city skirt, who Tom noticed had a luxuriant fall of long dark hair heavy enough to lay mostly straight even in the windy night, protested as Dave held the bar door open.

"You'd rather face the wolf pack?" Dave said.

"There's got to be a law against this," the woman said.

School lawyer, Tom realized. During the short walk, he had overheard her lean into Dave and whisper, "Is it my imagination, or are most of the board members already glazed?"

"They may have gathered at the bar before the meeting. Row their ducks. Hardly unusual. They're adults," Dave had said back, not bothering to whisper.

They filed into the bar, several board members going straight for a stool before the attorney stood by a long table and loudly cleared her throat. Except for Hal Hartack, Pep's was empty—everybody in town willing to brave the weather had gone to the high school gym. As the board members milled about and sorted out seats, Dave Cates placed a hand on Tom's back, moving him into a position at the end of the table.

"Marlo, this is our coach, Tom Warner. Tom, Marlo Stark, the school district's attorney."

Tom nodded, held out his hand, and saw Marlo Stark take him in. Her hand felt cold, but strong in his. He said, "Pleased to meet you, ma'am," which seemed to not make her happy.

"Did you see that news report?" Brad Martin asked Tom.

"I did," Tom said.

"Couldn't really have been much worse, could it?" Dave said.

"Short of trotting out some ACLU lawyer, or Jesse Jackson, no," Brad said. "I see she's here."

"Who?"

"That same reporter from Havre. I'd like to get her alone in a room for a little while."

"Mr. Martin, try really hard not to say that kind of stuff out loud, okay?" Marlo Stark said.

"You need to understand that this whole thing is ridiculous," Brad said. "Absolutely everybody involved is overreacting."

"Well we need to get to the bottom of it, don't we?" Dotty Lantner, a farm wife in her mid-fifties with a tight brassy hairdo to match equally tight Wrangler jeans, said.

Brad scoffed. "Dotty, you know as well as I do that every class did harmless little hazing rituals, and they did way more than what happened on that bus. I saw a lot worse than this when I played."

"Well, Brad, that might be kind of sick," Dotty said. She watched herself torch up an Ultra Slim, inhaled, and then angled her mouth to shoot a plume of smoke over her shoulder.

"You're a woman, Dotty, so you can't understand," Brad said. "This is a rite of manhood. Been going on for generations. It's ridiculous to make a federal case out of it now. It's the same god-damned thing that always happens when you start making everything politically correct."

Dotty Lantner sent her eyebrows on a little vault, letting everybody know she didn't want to be pinned down with political correctness.

"Here's the thing: if anything close to a sexual assault happened on that bus," Marlo said, "we have legal exposure."

"I know what happened on the bus," Brad said, his voice escalating. "My boy was there. Jesus Christ, it wasn't some kind of sex crime. It was just high school boys goofing off, plain and simple."

"That's what we're all here to find out, Brad," Dotty Lantner said. She looked at Marlo. "Right?"

"Well, people want to know what happened," one of the men said. His name, Tom knew, was Nathan Merrill, and he had kids coming into the system, including one with potential as an offensive lineman. Merrill farmed and ranched north of town. A huge man who made everything he wore look too small, he always seemed soft-spoken and smart. "You see how many people showed up tonight. They want to know what happened. Isn't it our duty to find out what happened on our school property?"

The lawyer responded quickly. "You're going to have an angry crowd waiting for you at the school. We need to do our business here quickly. Mr. Martin, you need to officially open an executive meeting and then you all need to decide what you're going to try to decide and from whom you need to hear to make your decisions."

Tom watched Brad Martin stare at the lawyer.

"I'd like to hear from Hal Hartack," Dotty said, "about drinks."

"Okay, let's try to stick with reality, because that's what we're doing tonight," Marlo said, which seemed to sting Dotty.

"We're in a damned bar," Dotty said.

Hal Hartack seemed to have heard and wandered out from behind the bar. "Bring anybody anything?"

Everybody ordered drinks except Marlo, who had water, and Tom, who went for a Diet Coke. Impatiently waiting until everyone had ordered, Marlo said, "You have to decide whether Mr. Warner and Mr. Cates should stay in their current positions."

"I'm offering my resignation," Tom said. He could see Hal Hartack's head turn as he walked back toward the bar. The table sucked into its own silence. "I think it's the right thing to do."

"You have to decide whether or not to accept Coach Warner's resignation. I think you also have to decide whether Mr. Cates should stay in his position."

Beside Tom, Dave Cates's cheeks flushed, and he looked at Marlo with astonished eyes.

"I'm sorry, Dave. If the board finds the coach negligent enough to accept his resignation, legally you're next in line. They need to decide your disposition, either formally supporting you, suspending you, or letting you go." To the rest of the group, she said, "What factors are going to help you decide these issues?"

"We're not accepting any goddamned resignations," Brad said.

"To be perfectly honest, I'd love to shitcan Warner," Dotty Lantner said, then seemed to remember he was sitting at the table. "Sorry, Tom. I think you're a nice fellow, but it's how I feel."

"Oh for Christ's sakes," Brad said, "she's pissed off because her nephew never got on the field last season. Be reasonable, Dotty. Why don't you shitcan your personal agenda and think about what's best for the team. What's best for the town."

"Maybe some of us don't feel like letting football players do whatever they want is best for the town," Dotty said. "Maybe some of us are sick of that attitude, and sick of crap these kids get away with and everybody thinking this Warner walks on water just because they win some games."

"They're going to win the state championship, Dotty," Brad said. "Do you have any idea what that could mean to a kid? Do you have any idea what that could mean to this town? Of course you don't. But it's something to be proud of. Something the whole town can be proud of. Like we were when Hal and the boys won the championship. Do you remember that? It matters to people. It matters to people in this town."

Coincidentally, Hal Hartack arrived with the drinks as his glory was being burnished.

"The ones who are living in the past," Dotty said.

"Well, here's our chance to live—to live large—in the present," Brad argued.

"You're not actually on the team, Brad," Hal Hartack said, which silenced everyone.

Until Marlo said, "How are you going to make this decision?"

The group stayed silent.

"Something tells me you have some ideas," Nathan Merrill said.

Tom could almost hear the unspoken "Thank you" in Marlo's nod. "Here's what you have to decide," Marlo said. "One, did Coach Warner break school district rules on the ride home from the game? Two, was the coach negligent in his supervision of his team? Three, was anybody harmed due to his negligence? Four, could the harm have been avoided had procedures been followed? As to question three, that's going to be your liability—it's not something that's really easy to decide. But the other three questions are pretty cut and dried. Now, what do you need to hear to answer those?"

"When you say liability . . . ?" Merrill asked.

"I can tell you right now that there's the makings of a civil suit in this incident," Marlo said, and Tom found himself rapt by how she had taken control of the board, how they all sat around the table ke little chicks waiting to be fed, big eyes blinking. Marlo turned to Merrill, which allowed Tom to observe her openly and have his first impression—that she was beautiful even without the intelligence—reinforced. "You want to know liability? When a case like this gets to the courts, juries are totally unpredictable. You could be on the hook for millions. I didn't have time to review your budget or insurance policies, but I'm guessing you can't afford that."

Brad Martin leaned forward and said, "Are you kidding me?"

"Mr. Martin, juries don't always think like you do."

Brad fell back forcefully, as if this were preposterous.

"Coach Warner?" Marlo asked.

Startled to find himself addressed, even though he knew that's why he was there, Tom hesitated before saying, "Yes?"

"Where were you when the alleged incident occurred?" Marlo asked.

"Well, I'm not sure, because I'm not sure when the incident started," Tom said. He thought he caught a look from her. "I'm not trying to be difficult. I was sitting up front where I always sit and I guess, sometime during the ride, some boys in the back started taping Wyatt Aarstad's legs and arms. I don't know exactly when that happened.

"And then when we stopped for gas, I got out to stretch my legs and to monitor the convenience store, make sure everybody left the bathrooms and nobody was horsing around in there."

"Do you think most of this happened while you were off the bus?"

Tom sat with his eyes dumped in his lap, communicating to Marlo that he hadn't thought things through that much and now seemed puzzled by the seeming impossibility of it all. He said, "Some of it had to have. I would have seen some of that stuff."

"Didn't you fall asleep on the bus?"

"Yeah, but . . ." Tom stopped. His sigh hissed. "It's a long day. We met at the school at 5:30 in the morning, drove five hours, played a game, which is exhausting all by itself. Then there's that long bus ride home. I may drift in and out."

"So it could have happened anywhere?

"I'd think Krock O' . . . Jim Krock, the driver, he would have seen a kid hanging from the book rack."

"Isn't it district policy to have another adult on the bus with you?"

"Yes. It is."

"And presumably that person would stay on the bus with any students while you stretched your legs, or used the facilities."

"Well, just being honest, sometimes we both would get off at gas stops at the same time for a little bit. But yeah, he would have gone back to check on things or I would have. That's how we usually did it."

"Why was that person not with you on this trip?"

"I gave him permission to ride home with his wife. She made the long drive . . ."

"He's a newlywed," Dave Cates interrupted. "The wife drove five hours to watch him coach. You can't begrudge him that."

"Begrudge, no," Marlo said. "David, you don't seem to understand. I don't begrudge anything. I'm trying to keep your school from going bankrupt." To Tom, she said, "Do you know of other instances where your players engaged in what could be interpreted as hazing?"

"I don't," Tom said, speaking like he knew his explanations were inadequate. "At the beginning of the season we make them sign a form. By signing the form they acknowledge that they know what hazing is and they pledge not to do it. And they knew that hazing would get them kicked off the team."

"Why?" Marlo asked.

Tom looked at her quizzically.

"I'm asking, Coach Warner, because the very act of having them sign that form would indicate that you might have some prior knowledge of hazing events or of some predilection toward hazing. Is that the case?"

"In the high school I went to, there was a lot of hazing. I remember that and remember it was destructive to the team, and I didn't want to see that happen here. When I came in here, I heard—well, I saw—that there was a bit of that tradition here. I didn't want it interfering with the team chemistry I was trying to build."

"If I might," Dave interrupted again, "Tom came to me with the idea for the form at the beginning of his first season with us. I was aware of other incidents around the state, and I thought the form was an excellent idea, even though at the time I was not aware of any hazing activity going on in Dumont high school or on our sports teams."

"That's not what my nephew says," Dotty Lantner said, as if talking to Amy Sibra seated beside her, but speaking loud enough for all to hear. "Or your buddy, Brad."

"Look, the man clearly wasn't aware of any wrongdoing," Brad Martin said. "Why punish him for something he was completely unaware was happening?"

Even Tom looked askance at him.

"The issue here is negligent supervision," Marlo said. Seeing Warner's reaction, she quickly said to him, "If the school district regulations say there must be two supervising adult on the bus and you failed to have two supervising adults on the bus—*and* you fell asleep—I don't care if you're riding with Mary Poppins and her kid sister, it's negligent supervision. I mean, how can parents legitimately feel it's safe for their kids to get on a bus for a sports trip when you're the supervisor?"

"So I think she's telling us we pretty much *have* to fire him," Dotty said.

"My capacity is strictly advisory," Marlo said, "but I can tell you that when something happens to a student who's under the supervision of a school system employee, the school system has legal exposure. Without acting, you're a sitting duck for civil liability. And if it looks like you tried to cover anything up"—this last said while meeting Brad's eyes—"you'll be killed in court."

She held Brad's glare. His jaw worked in what Tom assumed were gurgling responses, none of which he could find a convincing form for. The writing was pretty much all over the wall—Tom was already convinced he needed to be punished, and he was dragging Dave down with him—and everybody but Brad knew it. Or Brad knew too, but felt he could overcome reality with a force of will.

He seemed to be assessing the four other board members, two men and two women. Tom tried to guess which board members Brad thought were his. Dotty Lantner was clear in her position. Nathan Merrill seemed willing to be led by Marlo Stark. The other man, Josh Danreuther, a truck driver who had once played football at Dumont High, seemed likely to fall toward Brad. Amy Sibra seemed distraught, a wild card.

After a long silence Tom asked, "Am I done with questions?"

The lawyer said, "Does anybody else have any questions for the coach?"

Nobody answered. She shrugged. "The formal vote will take place in the public forum."

"Okay," Tom said. He stood and moved to the bar. There seemed no reason not to.

*   *   *

Marlo found herself tracking the coach as he walked to the bar— admiring the cords of muscles and tendon swinging beneath the rolled-up sleeves of his shirt, his broad tanned hands—and then shocked by the slap of Brad Martin's hand on the table. Brad was beseeching Josh the truck driver. "Josh, you played football. You now what it's like," Brad said.

"He's right. It's funny," Josh said and laughed in a way that nowledged a lot of people wouldn't find it funny. "You should seen some of the things we did. We probably hurt some of kids back then."

'y difference is there weren't any cameras around," Brad ' cameras were exactly the root of the evil here.

"So you think we should encourage that?" Dotty Lantner said. Her drink was empty and she had become less judicious about where she spouted her smoke streams.

"I think these boys probably had some of it done to them, and so they thought it was just what you do," Josh said. "Tradition."

"That sounds like so much happy horseshit to me," Dotty said.

"You don't have to be mean, Dotty," Josh said. "I'm just telling you what I think."

Marlo knew she had to turn this, head them off at the pass and focus them on David Cates. They would have a firestorm waiting for them at the high school. For the record, Marlo led Dave through a series of questions meant to establish what he knew when. He'd had the opportunity and responsibility to act before anybody else, and hadn't—aside from questioning the players. Marlo had been Dumont's school lawyer for over a decade, and she liked Dave fine, but now realized just how ineffectual he planned to be. Her questions laid a legal blueprint for everybody present to follow, though she knew they might not.

"I'll tell you something between you me and the fencepost," Marlo said, when she was done asking Dave questions. "If it turns out that what happened to that boy was anything that could be interpreted as a sexual assault, be prepared to hand over the keys to the bank vault." Marlo's entire legal practice comprised school board dynamics, and a majority of it consisted of far-flung rural towns. She knew how to appeal to the fiscal sensibility of hard-nut farmers and ranchers. "So, from here, you need to deliberate," she said. "Then you need to go down to the gym and announce your findings."

"What should we do?" Nathan Merrill asked.

"That's up to us," Brad said.

"Lawyer lady?" Dotty Lantner said. She held her cigarette near her cheek and Marlo felt herself sized up. She knew Martin hated her for being a woman with as much power as he had, but also understood how rural women sometimes hated her for having the nerve to upstage their men. She didn't get that from Dotty, though there was a separate and equal disdain.

"From a strictly legal perspective," Marlo said, making sure she caught Dave Cates's eye, "and you have to remember I'm only here to advise the school board on their legal position and not to defend any one person, but I would recommend that, at a minimum, you reassign Coach Warner to classroom-only activities. He clearly violated district procedures, so that's a no-brainer.

"But I would also recommend that you strongly consider suspending him and Mr. Cates without pay, pending formal review. As to the students on the team, I don't even know who they are yet, but I will be happy to interview students tomorrow to help you decide how to handle their cases." She gave them her hard news frown. "If what I learn confirms what we think we know so far, I'm probably going to recommend suspending the primary actors from extracurricular activities for the rest of the year. And I would allow the sheriff's department to handle the formal investigation."

"Sheriff will take weeks, " Dotty Lantner said. "I want to know what happened on that bus. As the body that operates the school, I think we deserve to know what happens on our property."

"That," Marlo said, "is perfectly within your purview. But you have no investigatory experience, which is why I recommend allowing the sheriff to handle it."

"You know how to investigate, don't you?" Dotty shot back.

Marlo nodded.

"Then you do it."

Amy Sibra finally spoke. "The sheriff's only going to be asking about criminal stuff, right? Don't we need to be able to make judgments about moral issues?"

"We're not in charge of morals in this town," Brad said.

"We're the goddamned school board," Dotty said. "That's exactly what we're in charge of."

"Look, we don't have time for all that," Brad argued. He was working up to a storm. "These kids have a future at stake. They'll have marks on their school records. They have to know if they can get back in school and get on with their lives. You should all know," Brad said, staring down Marlo, "that I've spoken to a group of parents prepared to go to court over this."

Marlo scanned the room to gauge how that went over. A silence ensued in which the board seemed locked in visibly displaying their exhaustion to—and with—one another. Dotty Lantner let her head drop back and blew outward, straight into the air. Marlo could smell the exhaled booze.

And the worst was yet to come. When they gathered themselves to leave and face the crowd at the high school, Marlo noticed that Dave Cates was not quite so eager to walk close beside her as had been earlier. She swung over to the bar where the football coach sat.

"Coming to the show?" she asked.

He shook his head.

She waited until he swung his face toward hers. "It's nothing personal. You know that, right?" she said, making sure he was meeting her eyes.

"Yeah, I know."

"I'd like to talk more . . ."

"I bet you can find me here when the other thing is over. Or . . ." He waved a hand. "I'm not too hard to find."

And Marlo knew again, looking at this rough, handsome man—a man whose career she might ruin, who yet seemed so unconcerned— that she would never be faithful to her husband-to-be.

* * *

Josie came with her parents and Jared. Matt arrived with his parents. The two families gravitated toward each other and found themselves clumped in the bleachers along the gym, waiting for something to start. And Josie let Matt hold her hand. A long time had passed, and she tried to glean from the people around her what was happening. She also tried not to talk, felt this was an occasion when she was best silent. But what was going on? The gym was more crowded than she'd ever seen it—if a quarter of these people came to one of her basketball games, she'd have been thrilled.

Josie had seen the way her parents sat at their kitchen table with Jared an hour before, an untouched glass of water in front of each of them, the light bright overhead, the conversation not a conversation at all but a sputtering series of declarations.

"This is your future, son."

"I can't remember anything like this happening before in my whole life."

"I don't know what's going to happen if you get suspended."

"Could be the end of a lot of dreams."

"Things seem funny at the time when they're really not."

Jared had clearly had no idea how to respond to any of it. He had started with proclaiming relative innocence—he didn't do any of the things the other guys did, he said—then glommed on to the "everybody always does this stuff; it's not a crime" party line. But Josie's parents were pragmatists, not moralists.

Whether it was right or wrong, they focused on what would happen next, how to reconcile fact with future. Jared and Josie had never been told that they would have to win scholarships to go to college, but early on both of them set along that trail athletically and academically—both of them had 4.0 GPAs—and assumptions started to follow. When they walked into the packed gymnasium, Jared was clearly bowed. He and Matt were used to being looked at in a crowd, and Jared was a kid whose face, in repose, fell into a broad smile shape.

Josie thought it was an idiot grin, but she witnessed over the years how it made people react to Jared with warmth. It helped that his eyes were bright and people said they twinkled. Whereas Matt stood more aloof. He let people approach him, but there was always that sense of obeisance in the transaction. Even with adults, there was always a sense Matt was doing you a favor by letting you into his glow. That served him well tonight. The noise in the gym ratcheted steadily up.

On the gym floor, two news camera crews had set up and were interviewing anybody who was willing to stand under the lights. Between interviews, the reporter combed the crowd, saying hello in the stiffly polite way that meant she had no business being here. What kind of guts did it take to be a stranger and come into this gym amid so much hostility and do your job? Josie couldn't really see it now, but wondered if something would happen to her in college that would give her that kind of courage. If she did, she would certainly have a better hair outfit when she did it. That frumpy silk blouse and huge gold square-linked necklace?

Porn stars wore better accessories. Josie was both anxious for the meeting to start and anxious about it starting. She worried about Matt's father and what kind of scene he might make if things went badly. Though to all outward appearances he seemed to like and approve of her, Matt's father scared Josie. She knew things Matt had told her, things that happened when nobody else was around. And she sensed Matt's same anger simmering beneath his father's skin, boiling behind his eyes.

She'd seen it in Matt on a couple of occasions, almost always when he was drunk. This was, she knew even as it was happening, one of the first big moments of her life. She knew she was sitting in a moment that would change a lot of things she had taken for granted about how the world worked. An hour later, her father said, projecting several rows around them, "To hell with this. If they don't start soon, I'm leaving." Josie had already noticed people leaving, though some came back. She suspected they were going to the bar and sneaking drinks. Or just smoking outside. She doubted her father would leave.

"This is seven colors of bullshit," Gary Brunner said. By then the rumor had already rippled through the crowd that the school board was meeting in private before the public performance. "What the hell takes so long to cover up?"

But then Brad Martin walked into the gym, head high, lips pressed together, gazing at the crowd as if they were all assembled to witness some performance he had planned. He gave his head a little shake, as if to say, *By damn, I did my best.* And just from that one look, Josie's sense of the evening soured. Matt's hand interlocked with hers, dropped between her knees, and she squeezed it. He looked down at her, and she looked up and smiled and hoped he understood how much she cared, right this moment, about what happened to him.

And then things happened quickly. Later, Josie would think of it as a movie or a play, the way things just started spinning by. The room seemed even brighter than before, as if someone had found extra lights to turn on. Josie watched the TV reporter break off in mid-interview, turn and say something to the camera, then move to the front of the room. Scattered hoots and catcalls popped from the bleachers; others attempted to hush the malcontents.

One voice yelled, "Star chamber!" which Josie didn't understand. The board members hadn't even settled their fannies in their seats before Wyatt's father, Jon Aarstad, was up on the gym floor, striding toward the row of chairs where they sat, an arm raised and a finger scanning to point inclusively at the group of them. He stopped a few feet in front of the microphone that had been set up for public comment. There his arm-sweeping turned to jabs on the more emphatic points of what he said: "You people *cannot* meet in some secret, behind-the-doors *meeting* to decide *what's going to happen here.* Not in the America I live in."

He went on while Brad Martin stood and said, without the aid of a microphone, "Mr. Aarstad . . ."

"Who do you think you *are?*" Aarstad said.

"Jon, please . . ."

"This is a *public* school. These students are *our* sons and daughters . . ."

"Jon, if you would settle down, please, we'll . . ."

"I am *not* going to settle down until *you* tell me *what the hell is going on* . . ."

". . . try to get started with the public discussion . . ."

". . . You can't lock parents out when you're talking about our kids."

"We will have a public discussion period for everybody to participate in, Jon. Jon . . ."

Brad quit arguing, his body language slumping to announce defeat in every way save literally throwing his hands up. His retreat left a silence that Jon Aarstad's voice filled with, "My boy was assaulted on that bus. *Which one of you is going to make that up to us?*"

Aarstad, sensing that he had commanded the floor and thundered that last line free from refutation, seemed pleased with himself. He stood and nodded to people on both sides of the bleachers as if he had expected applause. But he saw a sheriff's deputy take a couple steps off the wall behind the school board members, and Aarstad walked to the nearest bleacher and, before anybody could scoot to make room, sat on the bench's corner.

"Could somebody perhaps," Dave Cates said to the silenced board, "move to open the public portion of the meeting?"

Somebody did and Brad stepped up and grabbed the microphone, taking it back to his seat with him. "Now, if the audience would let us, I mean, if that's the way you plan on behaving tonight, we can pack this thing up and do it another time," Brad said, his tone petulant. "Okay, if you'll let us, we're going to open a discussion concerning the resignation of Tom Warner as football coach for Dumont High. The board has already convened an executive meeting and heard from Coach Warner and our legal counsel. We'd now like to open the meeting up to public comment. Anybody who has anything to say about the matter should approach the board."

"What happened on the bus?" an audience member called, provoking spontaneous approval and applause.

A confusion of disapproval burned through the crowd. Brad Martin again raised the mic to his mouth and said, "I'm going to have to ask you all to speak in turn or be removed from the gym."

Then a silence settled in. Martin started again. "We are still actively investigating the events that occurred on the Dumont High School bus on the way back from the Plentywood game last Saturday. We know you want answers. But come on. We all know each other. We all know we're doing our best. There's a process that has to play out and we have to let it.

"Now, there is something we have to settle tonight. We all know something happened on that school bus and some of us think one way about it and some of us think another way, but whatever we think, we know that it was serious enough that we're forced to examine people's roles. School district has a clear policy that any school bus used for extracurricular transportation requires two adults on board at all time. Coach Warner, by his own admission, dismissed his assistant coach to ride home with his wife. Which, according to technical, legal definitions, is maybe a problem. That's according to our legal counsel."

Brad turned and held an arm out toward the woman seated beside Principal Cates, and Josie's attention suddenly focused on her. Josie liked the way she dressed, a charcoal calf-length skirt. She looked smart, the way her eyes and face moved, taking everything in, undaunted by the surroundings. Josie wondered what it would feel like to be a woman like that. Again, she thought about college, how that must be the thing that changes people from girls in small towns, or even wives in small towns, to people who go and do things in the world. Then the mic was opened to the public. Principal Cates took the first turn, talking about how much faith he had in Coach Warner.

"Coach Warner is a builder of men. I know that if Coach Warner knew what happened on the bus that night, he would have stopped it in its tracks," he said.

A few football players' parents followed. A sophomore on the team took the mic and said he had wanted to play for Coach Warner for years, that it meant a lot to him. Cody McClain said that for a hundred goddamned years boys had been horsing around—which earned him a warning from David Cates about language—and that it was natural and normal and how they sorted things out and how they learned to work as a team and it was about the stupidest god . . . and he caught himself before finishing by saying about the stupidest thing he'd about ever heard of to fire a coach and shut down a team for boys horsing around and just doing what teenaged boys do.

Krist Hager stood and said, "I don't know if anybody realizes this, but our team is about to play for the state championship. Do we really want to bench our coach when these kids have a chance to do something that special?"

But Mrs. Labuta got up and said, "I got an eighth-grader. You're telling me I should let him get on that football bus next year after what I know happened last weekend? I don't think so."

And then Charlie Warzel said, "Now listen, we're not going to take away these kids' opportunity to do something that hasn't been done here since 1994. We're not. It's stupid to even think so." He glared at the school board. "Am I right?"

And Josie felt he really was. It was just the way he said it. She'd gone back and forth all night, and then she felt like it had been settled for her. So when Brad Martin cut the process off and said they had to vote or they'd be there all night, and then board quickly voted 3–2 in favor of reassigning Tom Warner to classroom-only duties, Josie was shocked. No more coaching this year.

Only Josh Danreuther had voted with Brad Martin. Then the discussion about Dave Cates took everybody by surprise, which meant only a few people were prepared to come to his defense. The board voted the same way, 3–2 in favor of suspending him without pay pending further investigation. Brad Martin led a hoop-jump during which the board formally decided to allow Marlo Stark to investigate any wrongdoings on the bus, in order to determine disciplinary action. The board would reconvene in two days to announce their decision. Then Brad said, "Regarding the suspension of players . . ." and Josie felt Matt's hand flex in hers. She saw Jared's head tilt up.

"Principal Cates and Coach Warner have presented evidence to the board that four Dumont football players and two cheerleaders were primarily involved in the incident on the bus last Saturday. Now, again, we don't know what happened. And the sheriff and our legal counsel will continue to investigate. But our legal counsel has advised us that we need to decide about any short-term action against any of these players."

"What's the evidence?" Gary Brunner bellowed. Josie had been feeling his frustration boiling, itching, and sensed some sort of outburst was inevitable. *Not so bad*, she thought. *A fair question, at least.*

Brad looked up toward Gary Brunner and laughed a short, funny-you-asked chortle. "Well, about that"—again he swept a hand toward the attorney—"we are not allowed right now to say what's in that report, because our legal counsel says . . . she will be doing more investigating. So we're going to have some interviews and have that meeting on Friday and we'll let you know what we learn."

Boos spattered the crowd as they began to understand they were not going to learn what they had come to find out. Gary Brunner booed and then put his hands beside his mouth and yelled, "What about the playoffs?"

Dotty Lantner, a woman Josie had always thought of as sort of gross in the way she tried to be overtly—there was no other way to say it—sexy at an age beyond that kind of display, said, "Law and morality don't care about the playoffs."

Dotty Lantner sat looking at Brad Martin with a burlesque of ridicule. The thing was that while it was hard to disagree with what Mrs. Lantner said, Josie did.

* * *

Three or four beers in, Tom could let his focus go soft and still see the images from the film he had watched before he came to the meeting. Well, the bar. He could close his eyes and see the players converging like a moil of insects locked in some tiny struggle, an occasional leg waving loose. And then a figure in crimson and blue breaking free, reeling along the top of the screen, faster than the other images now drawn in behind it. Jared Frehse popping loose on another of his gallops down the sideline, making an open field cut—the quickest little stepover, but enough to thump the safety down on his ass—and remembered how athletic competition purified the beauty of small moments. He could see it in his head when he watched Jared Frehse in mid-stride swiveling his hips, crossing his right foot over his left, and, without the slightest loss of momentum, angling anew, alone on the field with nothing but grass in front of him: *That's how Derek would look if he were still . . . if he were, still.*

Tom could see the little boy in baggy pants with a helmet that made his head threaten to topple over. He remembered the first time a bigger boy ran right through his son, Derek flattened, the crying after. He missed that comforting, and then the instruction, how to dip in the knees, how to tilt a shoulder, how to meet velocity with vector. He had started to teach Derek those things and now nobody would ever teach Derek those things.

Derek's light had gone out so quickly. A blown bulb. For Tom, the lights had dimmed in a long slow tease. He had been a big star linebacker and fullback on an eight-man team in the middle of nowhere. He had heard people talk about him, seen people look at him. Adults who paid no attention to his friends walked across gravel parking lots to speak to him.

Tom's scholarship offers came from regional Division II schools, and he had taken the shot at the University of Montana, a quality program that was consistently ranked and always pointed toward the national playoffs. Players from the Grizzlies made the NFL; it happened every year. But Tom realized when he got to the first practices what he was up against. Everybody on the field was faster, bigger, stronger. After the first days of contact practice, he was beaten, a physical wreck. He was nowhere near fast enough to play in the offensive backfield and knew he would have to make the team as a linebacker.

He wasn't that big. He would have to outwork all the other line-backers to play. So the lights dimmed a little. They didn't shine on him as a player his freshman year, but the team played in the national title game, and that light burnished them all. He was part of something amazing, a flight to Chattanooga—Tom had never been in a plane. He had never been outside of Montana's borders except for the interstate game between high school all-stars from Montana and North Dakota. In Chattanooga there were reporters with microphones at their practices, the crowd screaming for them and at them, the ESPN cameras on the sidelines.

They had not won, but just being in those moments seemed like more than he had ever hoped for. Tom's sophomore year he worked hard, lifted hard, ran hard, played hard on the scout team, but never played in a game. That year the team went back to Chattanooga and this time they won the national title. The light was brighter yet, warm and glowing enough for all of them. Two of his teammates were drafted into the NFL and two others joined pro teams as free agents. On campus, girls he didn't even know wanted to drink shots of tequila with him, because he played for the Griz.

Some of them went home with him and did things he didn't know real girls would do. That off-season Tom worked even harder, gut-busted every sprint, studied film for hours. Now the Grizzlies had recruited even faster, stronger young men in the wake of two championship appearances. He knew he would have to outsmart them and out-gut them. By his junior fall, Tom sweated his way onto the field for short yardage situations.

He collected twelve and a half tackles on the season, and made a few plays that he still remembered in his nerve endings. He made a clean stick of a rolling Northern Arizona quarterback for a loss

on a second and goal. He collided with a Montana State ball car-
rier to cause a fumble. In a playoff game, he separated a receiver
coming over the middle from the ball he'd just caught on a critical
third down. He could hear that one, could feel the crack of pads,
remembered how the back of his hand smacked against receiver's
shoulder pads and hurt for four days.

All three of those plays had brought crowds of 18,000 people
to a full-throated roar. Those moments—the crowd thundering,
the band playing, his screaming teammates whacking his back and
shoulder pads and helmet—allowed him to forget the two years
of knowing that he was in over his head. His senior season Tom
started at outside linebacker. He made a few nice plays during the
first two games, but then he got hurt—the stupidest thing, a turf
toe, but he was already slower than everybody else, and the injury
dragged him enough that the coaches began to sub in another
player, a transfer from a juco in Texas named Jason Jackson, a big
kid with running back speed.

Jackson was hungry for the lights and the cheers, too, and
worked hard and played hard and, soon, Tom was back to coming in for short yardage downs. He nursed his toe, making it hurt
more than it did, giving himself an excuse to be on the bench,
but the truth was, the other kid was just better. Up and down
better in almost every aspect of the position. The coaching staff
let Tom start the last home game of his senior year, against the
Bobcats. By the second series, though, Jackson was on the field.
Tom traveled for the playoff game, but didn't play. The Grizzlies
lost in the first round.

And that's how it was over. The clocked ticked down to all zeros
and everything he had thought was important for so many years
was, in the space between 00:01 and 00:00, over. Tom's attention came briefly back to the bar. He wondered when Hal Hartack
would come and lecture him about character or something.

But Hal ignored him. Other people had come into the bar, and
they ignored him too. Jared Frehse, that cut. Derek. Derek. Derek.

The Wibaux playoff game from last year. Tom recalled, then, the week after the Wibaux loss, a dinner with Dave and Liz Cates and Jenny Calhoun. He had been pretending for a really long time it had just been a convenience, but supposed he should admit it was the first fix-up.

Another thing that didn't seem to matter anymore. These were the thoughts that sometimes stood in the way of looking at every day with enthusiasm. The kiss he had laid on Jenny had felt inevitable yet fraught with peril even as he had leaned from his chair to start it. And then, of course, her reaction, or lack of one. When he caught himself trying to think about it, he whisked it away.

Now, sitting in the bar, fired as a football coach, he couldn't imagine how he could beat it back again. He saw Jenny's nose, not long but straight, leading down from the pools of her dark brown eyes to the mouth he had wanted to press his to. Her upper lips held a curl as if sliced on a short angle, leaving it always almost parted. He remembered wanting to see that face—wanted to see it now—melting into some expression that was not polite laughter, or gentle empathy, something more selfish and reckless at the same time. He wanted not only to see that transformation but to cause it.

He couldn't see how he ever would. But then he pulled himself around, tried to think a different way. He could do something as simple as going to her house, talking to her about what she thought now. He took his cell phone from his pocket, looked at it, thought, *Here's a bad idea.* But he couldn't imagine how it could matter, or make things worse. He tapped out her number. When she answered he said hello and listened for clues that she was pleased he had called. He spoke carefully.

"I've been meaning to call you. So much has happened the last couple days, but there was that thing with us that happened first, and I wanted to talk to you about it," he said.

"Uh . . . well, okay," she said, "Yeah, I guess we could talk about that."

"You going to be around this evening?"

"Um, sure. I'll be here."

"Can I swing by?" he asked. "Would that be okay?"

"A little bit later is better," Jenny said, "after the kids are in bed."

Tom felt, for a moment, happy. At least whatever happened between them wouldn't be because he let things go so long that the choices were made for him. And then Tom felt a hand on his shoulder. Turned to see Krock O'.

"Bad year for not drinking beer," Krock O' said. "What'd you find out?"

"Done," Tom said. Shrugged.

Tom suddenly noticed the other people in the bar. At the Keno machines he saw a woman he recognized but couldn't place and a tall, gangly boy he knew from school—Mikie LaValle, who had recently expressed what seemed like a genuine interest in academics. He had borrowed one of Tom's history books. That was the woman, he realized, Mikie's mother, the cook at the school cafeteria. He lifted a hand and smiled at her when she looked up from the machine, and thought she brightened and waved back.

Mikie's glance was too quick. Hal Hartack noticed Krock O's arrival and started making his way toward their end of the bar, stopping to set up a pair of men among the half dozen or so slumped on their stools.

"They let you quit on us?" Hal asked.

Tom pressed his lips together.

"Would it have mattered if I quit or they fired me?" Tom asked.

Hal tilted his head to one side as if he hadn't thought of that angle. He shrugged. "Not to me," he said.

"Hell, I never quit anything in my whole life," Tom said. The cool assessment in Hal's expression made Tom look around the room. Even Caroline at the Keno machine was watching.

"Divorced, aren't you?" Hal asked.

It hit Tom like a slap, and he felt his eyes flare. For a moment he felt like he might reach across the bar and smack Hal, maybe jump over the bar and keep pummeling him. But what followed the anger was a flush of shame, a dampening as thorough as anything he'd ever known. Tom just squeezed his beer more tightly, made an effort to relax the bundle his jaw muscle had bound into.

"Let me provide you with a soothing alcohol balm," Hal said.

He came back with a double whiskey and plopped it on the bar with another beer. He brought Jimmy the customary Bud Light and tended to other customers. Tom sipped the whiskey at first, but that turned to longer swallows and then it was gone. Hal caught his eye, without speaking a word asking about another shot. Tom, feeling like he now owed Hal something—at least some relief from petulance—nodded.

"You ever get so you want someone to tell you you're doing the wrong thing?" Krock O' asked after Hal dropped the next shot off.

"You trying to sign me up for a father figure?" Tom asked back. He left the edge off when he added, "I may not need the things you need."

"I'd think you'd want to be careful, telling an old man about the difference between the things you think you need and the ones you think he needs."

"You aren't that old," Tom said.

"I'm not talking about quitting, you know," Krock O' said.

Which made Tom sit back and try to figure out what Jimmy *was* talking about. He thought everything around here had been reduced to his being let go and the season coming to a halt. In fact, since last Saturday, he couldn't think of any one person talking to him about anything that wasn't on some level about it. He couldn't remember anybody even mentioning that it had snowed a foot and a half in just a few hours, for instance.

Jimmy threw him a line. "I mean going into a hole. Quitting on everything else. I'd hate to see you dig yourself so deep you can't ever come back to any of it. Don't quit on these kids."

Tom hadn't thought about any of that, really, hadn't been able to see down the road. *That's exactly what losing a child does to you,* he thought. *It takes away your feel for the future.*

And then Marlo Stark was squeezing around the heavy wooden door of the bar. He didn't recognize her at first, wondered who this woman could be, someone he didn't know, blinking in the darkness of Pep's. But she saw him and smiled and flapped up a quick wave, then tromped straight toward him, and he recognized the skirt, and then the hair, and then her face as she came closer.

"I hear this is the best pizza in Dumont," she said.

"I think that's right," Tom said. He didn't know what else to say.

"Mind if I sit down here?"

"Oh, heck, no." Tom shifted the stool in front of her, though it didn't need to be shifted. "Sit right down."

Marlo did, and she asked him what the best pizza to order was, so he told her he liked the jalapeno, but she'd probably prefer mushroom pepperoni. Hal appeared and said, "You must be the little lady that fired our football coach."

"Well," Marlo said, "that would be your school board that fired your football coach, but I'm the one who told them it would be a real good idea, legally speaking." Tom felt Marlo's hand on his shoulder, warm and humid at first, then the lightest squeeze when she said, "Sorry."

"Too bad the law and common sense always seems to butt heads these days," Hal said, "What can I get for you?"

Tom said nothing, stared into his reflection in the mirror behind the bottles of the back bar. He saw himself raise his eyebrows, purse his lips, considering, then drank from his beer. Marlo's hand fell away, leaving a sensation of coolness where it had been. Her voice assumed a different tone while she ordered a pizza with mushrooms and pepperoni and a bottle of Fat Tire. "You'll eat some of my pizza, won't you?" she said to Tom and Krock O'. "There's no way I can eat all of it."

"No, no," Tom said, "I have to get home here pretty quick to feed my dog." Now he was sorry he had drunk whiskey. He felt fuzzed and heavy-headed. He didn't know Marlo at all, only that Dave thought highly of her. Earlier she had made Tom feel out-smarted, which made him uncomfortable even when there wasn't an oily layer of booze on top of everything else. Tom struggled to assemble sentences that sounded civil and friendly and polite.

"Know Jimmy?" he asked.

She had not been introduced to Krock O', so he did that. Neither seemed likely to follow up.

"So you're still here," Tom said.

Marlo made big nods. "I'm going to be here for a little while, I think. Interviewing players tomorrow. It's too much driving to go all the way to Great Falls and then turn around and come back here a day later. Especially with the snow. I can just work in my hotel room over the weekend."

"Oh heck, you don't want to be stuck in your room all week-end," Tom said.

"Well, the upside is I make vacation pay. It'll be lucrative."

"At our school board's expense," Tom said, just for commen-tary, although he then thought it was a stupid thing to have said. Beside him, Jimmy Krock was pushing back from the bar. Tom didn't want to lose Krock O'. They'd been talking about serious stuff and now there was this woman who made him nervous on the other side of him. But Krock O' was rolling his shoulders to bring his coat forward so he could zip it.

"Hey don't go," Tom said. "I owe you a round."

"I'm pushing off," Jimmy said. Tom was thinking Krock O' was bailing out. Jimmy didn't have a real destination, he was going to stumble across the street to the Longbranch and plop down there for several more hours. But Jimmy was gone before Tom could muster any sort of reasonable objections, leaving him sit-ting with the lawyer lady from Great Falls. He looked at her hand, saw her engagement ring, realized he'd seen it before, realized he'd checked, actually, the first time he'd seen her. "Your fella gonna come out for the weekend?"

Marlo pursed her lips and shook her head in a tight waggle. "I don't think so."

"Heck, tell him to come out. He a hunter? I'll take him bird hunting." Tom realized he was doing a thing he hated, a holdover from football—filling space just because he'd spotted the gap. But if history was any judge, once he started in with nervous jabber, his hopes for curtailing it exceeded all known evidence of his ability to do so.

Marlo said, "Not really a bird hunter type."

Is there a bird hunter type? he wondered. *Is that a bad thing?*

"What type is he?"

She smiled. "The handsome businessman type. The don't-get-your-new-shoes-dirty type. Don't get me wrong, I love the socks off the guy. He's just not a stomp-around-in-the-dirt kind of boy."

"Huh," Tom said, unable to avoid contemplating whether or not he'd just been insulted. He thought probably not, but then why did it feel so much like it? He mulled it over for a while and Hal brought a pizza and slid it on the bar in front of them. It looked so good Tom wanted to rub his face in it. He wanted to taste each individual piece. Tom began to feel an inexplicable rise of something like panic, keyed by the notion that he'd been quiet for too long.

"Dave said you went to UM Law School," Tom said.

She nodded with her mouth full of pizza.

He said, "I went to school in Missoula too."

She swallowed enough to speak. "Really? When?"

"Oh, hell, when the dinosaurs were still there," he said.

"Fun town," Marlo said, and bit into more pizza.

"Sure was. Boy, I had a ball there. Used to hang out over at the Rhino bar a lot."

"The law students always hung out at Sean Kelley's," Marlo said.

"That wasn't there when I was there," Tom said. "Missoula, gee, Missoula was a whole new world for me. I came from a place where

I could walk five miles and still be on my dad's land. My aunt ran the only restaurant for fifty miles in any direction. The mayor refereed high school basketball games. You could watch your dog run away for three days. Missoula felt like the big time."

"Did you just say 'gee'?"

"I think I did," Tom said.

Marlo lightly pressed her fingertips on his forearm to tell him, "I came there from Boston, so it wasn't so gee. But I fell in love with the place."

Tom tried hard not to look at where her fingertips had just left his arm. "Huh. Well, yeah. I'll bet it was. Different like that."

"Eat some of this," Marlo said, and gestured with a wedge of pizza toward the rest of the pie. "There's no way I can finish all that."

"Don't you want to save some for tomorrow?"

"I'm not eating anything that spent the night in the Sportsman Motel," Marlo said.

"Fair enough," Tom said, and reached for a piece of the pizza.

Another beer went by and Tom felt like he had settled down during a long exchange of stories concerning things they liked about Missoula. Marlo started comparing Missoula to other places she'd lived in or been to—Madison, Wisconsin; Austin, Texas—which then launched her on a long list of places she loved—Mystic, Connecticut; Yachats, Oregon; Cortina in Italy—none of which he'd been to and most of which he'd never heard of.

"Paris doesn't have a thing on Fort Miles," someone said, and Tom looked past Marlo to see Caroline Jensen leaning against the bar. She put her cigarette to her mouth and squinted while she took a quick huff, then laughed a smoky exhalation. Her voice was rimed with smoking.

Tom smiled, genuinely amused at Marlo's reaction, which was to be taken aback, followed by an immediate playing along. Marlo said, "Fort Miles almost certainly has less dog shit."

"Marlo, Caroline," Tom said. "She works in the . . . at the school."

"Are you a teacher?" Marlo asked her.

"I could teach folks a few things," Caroline said. She twisted her mouth and shot a long stream of smoke out the side, away from Marlo. She was leaning on the bar with one elbow. "But no."

"Oh," Marlo said.

"Bummer about what happened, Coach," Caroline said.

Tom let both hands fall open. "Something had to give."

"Fair enough," she said.

Tom didn't know what to say next, but Caroline didn't seem to be leaving. She seemed a bit drunk. Then her son, Mikie, strode over and said, "C'mon, Mom. We gotta go home."

"Just came in to get a pizza," Caroline said. "Play a little Keno. The kid loves the Keno."

"Right," Mikie said. He wouldn't look at Tom, kept his face turned to his mother and his back angled to the others. "I got homework."

"Really?" Caroline said. "You're concerned with homework now?"

"Mom."

"All right, Mighty Mike, you're the boss man." She dug into her jeans pockets with one hand, sinking it to the wrist.

"Mother."

Caroline held out a jangling set of car keys. "Go warm her up for your momma. Don't want my bones to get cold." After Mikie had stalked out, she leaned in and said, "He loves your class. Always talking about history and Dumont and all kinds of things he learns in there."

"That's nice to hear," Tom said.

"He's a good kid. A really good kid. Well, he's mine."

Mikie was back and dragging his mother out of the bar by a belt loop. She laughed. "He's a funny goddamned kid, isn't he?"

She laughed harder. Marlo held her eyebrows in a high arc while pursing her lips, then fell back to eating. Tom had more pizza until it was mostly gone. He guessed it soaked up some of the alcohol in his system so he didn't feel so swimmy. He remembered that he was supposed to talk to Jenny Calhoun now, and that bolt of recall was softened by the following thought that it would be better to talk to her with food in his belly, a less drastic sense of swirl in his head. Then remembering Jenny made him think of Scout.

"Oh hell, I'm going to have to go, too" he said, rolling his hip to slide up his wallet and then thumbing bills from it. "Hey, it was really great getting to talk with you."

"You, too," Marlo said. She flipped over the bill for the pizza and started digging in her purse. "Here, I'll walk out with you."

Outside the cold air stabbed right into the bottom of his lungs and he coughed, but then breathed deeper. The snow squeaked underfoot. Tom walked to his truck and Marlo tagged along, heading to the Subaru parked on the other side of him. But in looking at her vehicle his eye caught something odd about his, and he spent a long moment examining the truck before he realized what it was. All four tires were flat. He knelt beside the closest one, and saw the slit. He didn't need to look at the rest.

"Wow, that's shitty," Marlo said behind him.

"I'll be go to heck," Tom half-whispered. What he meant was, *I'd like to wring some little fucker's neck* . . . To Marlo he said, "Think you can give me a ride?"

"Sure. What else do I have to do?"

"Let me report this to the sheriff."

He walked down the block to the municipal building.

* * *

When the meeting broke up, Matt and Josie had walked out together, Matt holding Josie's hand. She noticed how he seemed unable to meet anybody's eye, how he kept his own eyes looking at his feet, head ducked and angled like he was walking through wind. As soon as they cleared the building and stepped out into the still-driving snow, Matt had said to Josie, "Come with me."

Josie thought both of them had arrived with their parents and couldn't imagine what vehicle they would drive. She said, "What do you mean?"

Matt had tightened his grip on her hand. "Don't say no to me right now."

So she hadn't. "I have to tell my parents," she said.

It turned out he had his truck, and they drove from town and talked briefly about where to go. He drove her to his house, ten miles west of town. He swung off the paved road and drove between two quarter-mile-long shelter belts of stunted Russian olive trees. The headlights shone on the lime-green clapboard walls of the house. But Matt didn't park there, instead wheeled past a long green Quonset building. His father had plowed the snow already before coming to the meeting, so there was a lane leading to a combine, tractor, and three grain trucks, all three dusty looking even in the snow, parked behind the Quonset. They had spent a great deal of time in this pickup parked in this very spot, a sort of no-go zone that Matt's parents let them have.

Josie had lost her virginity in the pickup's back seat here the spring before. Matt doused his headlights, but left the truck engine running so they could have heat. He cradled the steering wheel, staring out at the white streaks of snow lasering continually across the windshield in the dark, then looked at her. Stared at her. His eyes looked big, sad. She knew better than to look away.

"It's going to be okay," she said, though she wasn't sure that was true.

"How is it going to be okay, Josie?"

"Things will work out," Josie said. "They always do."

"I'm gonna get totally fucked," Matt muttered. He picked at a flaw on the leather wrap on his steering wheel.

The radio played classic country songs, Loretta Lynn now, and the dashboard lights glowed greenish on Matt's face. Josie heard the sound of the fan pumping heat from the engine and tried to imagine how she would say something to make Matt feel better. She couldn't think of a thing.

"You guys are getting made an example of," Josie said. She was not sure she believed this, either. Her palm made long strokes on his thigh. "It's not fair."

Matt was silent for a long time, his arms cradling the steering wheel, his chin close to resting on it. Josie could see tears welling in his eyes. Then he said, "I'm done, Josie. I'm done. What am I gonna do?"

"You're not done," Josie said. "Nothing's been decided yet. And even if . . . I mean, there's basketball. There's college."

Matt's face swung toward her. "Goddamn, Josie, how can you be so blue skies and butterflies?"

"A lot of people go to college without sports," Josie said.

"With my grades? Where?"

"You can go to Northern . . ." she said. She held one of his hands in one of hers, and rapidly stroked the back of it with her other fingers.

"Are you going to go to Northern?" Matt asked.

"Matt, sweetie, even if all the worst things happen, you have the farm. There's always that," Josie said.

Matt's hand jumped from hers. "Are you fucking kidding me?" he said. "The farm?"

"I just mean . . ."

"Jesus, Josie. Jesus."

"Matt," Josie said. "You can do so many things. You have options. That's all I meant."

"How many of them include you?"

Josie didn't like what she was going to say next, but she had said it so many times before that it must in some way be true. "Wherever I go there's a place for you. You know that." She had probably even meant it, for a while.

Matt turned from her, looked out at the snow. Josie sat with her hands pressed between her legs, not sure what to do next. Johnny

Cash sang "I Still Miss Someone." *Well, I never got over those blue eyes* . . . sounded like a message sent back from a future she couldn't imagine.

Then Matt said, "You don't know what it's like to be me."

"I know it's hard for you," Josie said.

"I'm, like, a public figure in this town."

I'm not? Josie thought. She was an athlete as much as he was. And everybody knew her business. But she knew better to say any of it. Instead she said, meaning to suggest they all labored under a common curse, "We're in the fishbowl."

Matt stared through the windshield now, and Josie had the sense that he was voicing dialogue he'd turned over in his head many times, but never had the opportunity to say out loud to somebody who might be predisposed to feeling sorry for him. "You're sweet, Josie," Matt said, and Josie couldn't help hearing it as though that might not be the best thing to be. "With you, everybody likes you 'cause you're sweet. With me, everybody likes me because of what I do. On the field, on the court.

"People don't like me for me. There are guys who graduated a couple years ago who want to fight me. I've never done anything to them. They just want to fight me to show me something. Put me in my place. That's what my life is like. I make one mistake, and everybody wants to jump on it."

"I know," Josie said, though she did not know. He seemed a little grandiose, but his sense of himself had always scaled differently.

Then Matt shifted in the seat, opened his hips more toward her, leaned back against the driver's side door, and started talking to her through hooded eyes, which, Josie could see, were full of tears.

"Do you know what it's like to fail in front of him?" Though his head was against the window, he rolled it quickly to indicate the direction of the house, unseen in the blowing snow.

"I know that part is hard," Josie said.

"You think you do."

"I know what I see and what you tell me."

"I remember the one time in my entire life that he hugged me," Matt said.

"That can't be," Josie said. She hadn't meant to say it out loud.

"It was a hot day in the summer. I was seven. I was playing out here, by the shed, just on the other side." He lifted his chin in the direction. "All of a sudden I turned around and there was this big fucking rattlesnake, all coiled and ready to hit me. I have no idea where it came from. I just froze. Panicked. Couldn't move. I was pinned against the shed and this big goddamned snake just flicked his tongue out and rattled his rattle, and I was so scared.

"I started to cry. Then all of a sudden my dad—I don't even know where he was or where he came from—he boots the snake away and grabs me up and carries me away. And he hugged me." Matt stopped and made sure she was seeing him, then spoke slowly. "He hugged me. I could feel his arms around me, tighter than they needed to be just to carry me. He was hugging me. I still remember how good that felt." Matt's head tilted like he wanted to hear something in his own voice. "I've been waiting for it ever since. But that was the one and only time."

Josie looked at the big, rugged boy she'd spent her entire first love on, and she felt something deeper for him, something more stirring than what they had been calling love. "I'm so sorry, Matt," she said. She reached out to grab his hands and try to pull him closer to her. "Come here."

But Matt held back.

"Some people just aren't very good about showing people how they feel," Josie said, thinking—and not liking that she was thinking it—*like you.*

"You don't even know." Matt sat up straight and leaned toward her. Josie pulled his head to her breast. She held onto his head while she felt him shudder and cry. He cried hard, then, let go, heaving sobs, and she held him tight. For a while his hands felt like anchors in her flesh, seeking anything to gain purchase, but his breathing became more regular and his hands changed. She felt his fingers flex, felt them move, felt them on her breasts, reaching for her ass.

"Oh, God," Matt sobbed. He had shifted toward her, leaned into her, tilting her back against the passenger door. She tried to hold his head, run her fingers through his hair. She tried to do nothing to seem sexual, but Matt's fingers dug into her wherever he grabbed, like he might tear a piece of her off. His head raised and his eyes, teary and bloodshot, held inches from hers. He looked right at her while his hands went to the fly of her jeans, lowered the zipper and unhooked the button. His palm pressed against her belly as his fingers pointed down.

"Matt," she said.

"Don't say no to me tonight. I can't hear you say no to me tonight." His words were ragged and full of holes, like wind through the shelter belts.

And so Josie didn't say no. She lay back and hardly moved while he exercised what seemed to be some extreme need. It was over quickly, but in those short moments, Josie began to understand with a new, sharper clarity that whatever she had once dreamed about Matt and their life together was not what it was going to be like.

* * *

Marlo drove and, once they were outside of town, the snow glistened in her headlights like tiny diamonds brought to a boil. Even with the heater blasting, she felt aware of the cold surrounding the thin metal skin of the car. She sensed the greenish glow from her dashboard, could see it on Tom's face. She thought, *isn't this the little adventure.* She said, "I can't believe someone would slit your tires. This town's a little, uh, well, some rabble's been roused."

"Most people in town—and when I say 'most people' I mean most people who aren't cretins—are probably okay with how things are being handled," Tom said. "There's just always a few who have to stir things up, and those people, when they reach their wit's end, it's been a short trip."

Clear enough, Marlo thought. It was quite easy to sit in her office in Great Falls and feel critical about people who would support kids making bad decisions. But even her short time in Dumont had illustrated exactly how few the outlets for interpersonal expressions were here. Farming was an essentially solitary business, drawing usually from a family-based labor pool. The few merchants in town provided focal points for interactions.

There was the bar. And then there was the school, and the kids who went there. She knew it was facile for her to zip into town for a few days, make a group of judgments, and then leave. For Tom and Dave Cates, the rest of the school year was going to be long. Tom seemed down now. He had been cute in the bar, a little flustered, a little motor-mouthed. Nerves, which Marlo had felt flattered enough to assume was about her. He was not a man who took her breath away, but he seemed raw and powerful, a bare person who didn't shrink from the lack of cover. His kept his hair sheared in a short part that was obviously not one of his major concerns.

His gesture was moving forward. He looked, in all the right ways to her, like a man. Just after checking in with the sheriff, Tom had made a phone call. It had been quick and quiet and, Marlo knew, it was to a woman. This made her reassess Tom, largely because she had not spent much time assessing him in the first place. She had, on first glance, assumed he'd be the married type, with a squad of kids being raised to eat up yardage and answer in prompt "yes sirs." When she found out he was divorced, she assumed the size of the town, the dearth of age-appropriate single women, would mean he was not in a relationship. In her work, she'd run across plenty of small-town high school staff who wound up married to former students, but he didn't seem that type. It was his isolation that clued her in, the tangible sense he exuded of being closed around the edges, drawn inward. Some divorced guys did that. Some went hog wild. You just never knew.

"Girlfriend?" Marlo had asked, when Tom had flipped the cell phone closed.

"I don't have a girlfriend," he'd said, and then he'd kept his trap shut.

Marlo didn't know about that. These little towns were a blighted sort of gold mine for single women in the sense that the odds were good but the goods were odd.

She drove with him past a row of dead cottonwood trees, trunks ghostly white and scarred against the snow, their leafless branches suspended overhead in frozen grasps. She had no sense of what lay beyond them as the vehicle whizzed by, only fields and fields beneath vaguely undulant sheets of snow. He told her to turn onto a snow-blown road that she could feel against the tires was gravel, and then another, until her headlights caught the reddish brown fuzz of a shelterbelt, old shrubs planted a hundred years ago, perfectly even rows on either side of a long drive. The headlights drew the house from darkness as she approached.

"Casa Tom-o, eh?" Marlo said.

Tom made a low appreciative whistle. "Spanish, Australian, and Canadian in the same sentence."

She liked that he was poking fun at her. She liked this. It felt like not being engaged, not about to be married.

"Come in, warm up before you head back to that posh hotel room?" he asked.

It was only eleven o'clock. She still felt a little lift from the two beers she'd had at Pep's. Maybe he'd offer a drink. She twisted off the ignition and stepped again into the snow.

The dog was a surprise—not that Tom had one, but the unleashing of its energy in such tight, spiraled bounds. The sounds coming from it, moans twisted into yelps by the end, made Marlo laugh. The dog was clearly chewing Tom out.

"You could go on in," he said. Awkward again, unsure of himself. He seemed to vacillate between prepossessed self-confidence and this complete inability to feel at peace inside his skin. "I have to stay out a minute until she calms down enough to do her business."

"I'll wait," Marlo said.

They stood six feet from one another and watched the dog, Scout, as she quit leaping at Tom and began scurrying around the yard, nose to the snow, huffing scent. Then, from the darkness, a warbling yodel bubbled up, stretching to high whining yelps. Marlo thought something must be dying out there, but then said, "Coyotes."

Tom nodded. "Song dogs."

"Cool. I haven't heard them in a long time."

"They'll come after her," he said, tipping his head toward Scout, who had jerked to attention, staring into the floating sound. "That's why I have to stay out with her."

"She could hold her own against a coyote, can't she?"

"But it wouldn't be just one. How they do it, one coyote kind of appears, and the dog takes off after it, chases it over a little rise, and then a pack's waiting. I've seen it."

Scout finally squatted, and Tom said, "Let's get inside."

Inside the house was as plain as it was outside. Warped pine flooring underfoot tilted her sense of security as they walked through the kitchen, where she spotted on the bare counter-tops nothing that looked edible, nor any evidence—dirty dishes, scraps—of anybody ever having eaten here. The living area consisted of a sofa, worn atop the arms, and an ancient armchair sagging beside a table with a lamp on it. A boom box with a CD player sat on the floor against a third wall beneath a handmade set of shelves that also supported the smallest flat-screen TV she'd ever seen. The fourth wall was occupied by a space heater. A low coffee table stretched in front of the sofa. Books and magazines were stacked on top of and beside it. Here she spied a few crumbs, suggesting he ate at the coffee table while watching the little TV.

"Love what you've done with the place," she said.

Tom ducked his head. He waved a hand at the two pieces of furniture, inviting her to take her choice, and said, "Anything to drink?"

"Yeah, I'll have a Marlborough Sauv Blanc. Any label's fine."

"Bud Light, then?"

Marlo smiled.

"I do have some vodka . . ."

She smiled bigger.

She chose the sofa. She hadn't felt this way in a while, but recognized it—a willingness to put herself in a situation and let things happen, suspending all the strictures and filters she mostly held herself to. It was the kind of thing that led her to smoke cigarettes, to try pot for the first time, and it had led to some incredible sex. She liked the old familiar feel of it, liked that she didn't allow an impending marriage to limit her experiences. As long as she was true to herself.

In the end, that's who she'd have to live with. Tom brought her a vodka tonic with—this surprised her—a real lime wedge, poured into a kitchen glass. He set it on the table in front of her, and then dropped into the arm chair with his own drink. They sat in the spillover glow from the kitchen. Tom's dog leapt into his lap, and he let her, encouraged her with affectionate pats and a scratch between the eyes. The dog looked at Marlo as if to say, *Don't even think about it.*

"So I'm guessing," Tom said, "you didn't go to high school in a place like Dumont."

"God no. I went to school in Boston. All-girls school."

"I didn't even know they could have those anymore."

"Sure you did. Us Catholics can get away with that stuff. Well, with the pope on our side. I actually went to the Vatican once. On a trip to Europe after college. I was so hungover I couldn't even look up at all the fabulous art. The one thing I remember is right there in the Vatican gift shop, the gal working had a little CD player and she was listening to just the most thuggish gangsta rap—Tupac rapping nasty lyrics. Right under the pope's nose."

"I've never been to Europe," Tom said.

"All the young people over there listen to rap. They have all the slang down. You're in Prague and someone starts talking to you in a heavy Eastern European accent about"— she started imitating one—"I only listen to the West Coast rappers because they are keeping it so one hundo."

"I don't know anything about rap," Tom said.

Then a silence settled in and Tom kept stroking the dog.

"We didn't have anything like this where I went to school," Marlo said. "This hazing stuff. I mean, girls were catty and awful, but nothing like this. And the guys we knew—we were sort of affiliated with an all-boys school—they never talked about this kind of stuff happening. We would have heard."

"It's not the kind of thing people keep quiet," Tom said. "When it happens, kids seem proud of it. At least to each other."

"Still, I think I can see why people in town are so angry about the season coming unraveled," she said. "I'm not saying I agree, but I imagine some of them feel robbed of a big thing they were looking forward to."

"Not a lot of other big things on the agenda," Tom agreed. He sat back with the dog in his lap and looked at her. Marlo realized she had come here thinking she might sleep with him. He was so different than anybody she'd ever been with before, and she knew she was willing if he did anything to trigger it. But sitting here in his house now, she couldn't imagine how she could fuck a guy who looked both so isolated and so content to be.

Maybe she wanted to be the person who got under that armament, pierced it, got a sense of who was really in there. But what if what she found was a disappointment and then she'd just waste all that guilt? She wondered if she could make him talk about something that would make her decision for her.

"Why'd you submit your resignation?" Marlo said. "If you don't mind me asking. I mean, why didn't you wait to see what the school would do?"

Tom made a subtle body move that encouraged the dog to slide down to the floor. He scooted to the edge of the seat cushion. With his elbows on his knees, he wrapped one fist in the other and rested his mouth against them. Then the hands dropped and he looked at her and said, "When I came here . . . well, no. Let me back up. When I started coaching I didn't know much about it. I just wanted to win, keep close to that excitement from when I was playing. Still young. My first coaching job was in Great Falls, CMR, a big high school under a guy who had some real strong ideas about how to get kids to realize their potential. He did a lot of screaming, a lot of swearing, a lot of swatting, really encouraged a lot of aggressive behavior. He liked that the other kids in the school were afraid of the football players.

"I didn't like that. I don't know if it was coming to these small schools, being a teacher, too, and seeing those other kids in the class every day and just getting to know them all and remembering how interconnected you are with your community in a place like this, even at their age . . . I don't know what it was. But when I got my first head coaching job—in a school about this size—I decided to try things a little different. And it worked, I think. We won a lot of games, and I think the kids were good kids. And then . . . things changed in my life, and I came here. And by then I just wanted to use processes that make the kids stretch without defeating them. I wanted these kids to set goals on and off the field.

"It's why I made them sign that no-hazing agreement—which also covered agreements not to drink or take drugs or get in trouble in the community. Even if they didn't reach all their goals on the field, I wanted to give them goals they could control, something they could succeed at and say they did. To me, this incident is partly about living up to your word. I know there's a whole other side to it, but that's what it came down to for me. They failed to live up to their word, but I failed to create an environment where living up to your word was more important than tormenting the freshmen kids." Tom stopped, looked at the TV as if something were happening there.

"That seems a little hard on yourself," Marlo said. "If you don't mind me saying."

"It was my job to make sure that kind of stuff didn't happen—particularly on a bus where I was in charge. I let myself down. I let Wyatt Aarstad down. I let the parents of all those kids down." He seemed ready to list more people he had disappointed, but then stopped and shrugged.

"Do you have kids?" she asked.

He nodded, his eyes glazed still from the thoughts he had started to lose himself in. "I did," he said, his voice coming in from far away. "A son."

Marlo felt something moving in her. "Is he . . . ?"

"He's gone."

"Gone?"

"He died."

"Oh, shit. I'm so sorry. How did . . . ?"

"An accident. A car accident. I was driving . . ." Tom seemed then to run out of words and rubbed his face with both hands. Then he became artificially animated. "But you're new at that marriage stuff, probably all full of enthusiasm. Ready to think about kids of your own."

"Yeah, sure." She smiled, and let herself slide into a luxurious slump on the couch. "We're coming to it a little later in life, so our expectations are appropriately tempered."

Her cell phone rang then, and Marlo instinctively dug into her purse to retrieve it. She glanced at the number glowing in the semi-darkness, then clicked it off. She saw Tom watching her and felt like telling him.

"Chet," she said, and shook her head. "My fiancé. Probably just calling to say good night."

"You don't want to answer?" Tom asked.

"Well, no," she said. "It would be a little hard to explain, don't you think—almost midnight and I'm at the football coach's house, drinking vodka?"

"Be harder to explain why you're not in your room, answering the phone," Tom said.

"I can just say I turned the phone off and went to sleep," she said. "It's no big deal."

"Why lie?" he asked, and she could see he was thinking of that as one of those questions that tells you where everybody stands.

"Why put somebody through something for no good reason? There's capital T truth, and then there's the truth that everybody can live with," Marlo said.

Tom thought about that. "The old 'If you must be honest, be beautifully honest?'" he said.

"Nice," she said, not expecting Kahlil Gibran from the coach—even if he'd mangled it a little. "It's not like I'm out banging some guy and not telling my husband because I want to stay out of trouble." She took a long—longer than usual—swig of her drink. "I'm not dishonoring Chet. But would his life be better if I answered that call and told him where I was? Would he sleep better tonight?" She let a shrug drop. "I'm living a truth I can live with, and a truth that makes Chet's life better. I don't see the condemnation."

"What if something were to happen that dishonored him?"

"Then I'd have to think about it differently." She almost added, *nothing's going to happen to dishonor Chet*, but for some perverse reason she couldn't quite stick a pin through, she stopped short of that. Instead, she said, "Do you think we'll ever reach some capital T truth about what happened on that bus?"

"Boys at that age are a mixed-up bunch of people," Tom said, and she couldn't tell if he sounded disappointed or let off the hook by the change in subject. But then he went on, "You're a coach, you see the locker room, but you don't hang around in there." Tom's voice sounded replete, as if he were on his last excuse and he wasn't sure even he believed it anymore. "They did awful things at my school, too. I never did them, but I had some done to me when I was a freshman."

"What the hell?" Marlo asked. "Why do they do that to each other?"

"Something like this happens every year. Big towns, little towns. It's the big dog humping the little dog," Tom said.

"But why?"

"Because they can," Tom said. "Because we let them."

"I know it's pervasive," Marlo said. "I represent a lot of school districts. I'll let you in on a little secret—I've dealt with maybe a dozen hazing incidents in the past year, and yours isn't even close to being the worst. One kid had a bar of soap shoved up his anus. It just didn't go public. I mean, some unbelievable stuff happens. I don't understand why boys feel like they have to do this to each other. It must be some power thing. Like you said, like dogs."

"Dominance. Control," he said. "They're pretty deeply seated impulses. Those developing psyches . . ."

"Why does it not happen in some places?"

"I think it comes down to the adults in the room."

Marlo smiled, thinking about the adults she'd been in rooms with in the past day. She felt herself step back, an imaginary shaking of her head, frustrated. If he had made any sort of move, she could have found herself reacting, and instead they'd had this long conversation about teenaged boys. She was tired now, facing another tedious day. She sat up, gathered herself.

"Time to go?" Tom asked. He seemed surprised, and she wondered if he thought he had all night.

"Yeah, sorry. Just tired. Long day and another one tomorrow," she said, then tried to turn on a little charm. "Thanks for keeping a gal company."

"It's been a long time since I talked so much to someone who was older than seventeen."

Poor lonely bugger, she thought, then, and wanted to stay again. The dog was probably in danger of getting the hair petted right off it. Marlo pressed her lips into a tough little grin. "It was interesting," she said. "I liked it. You're interesting."

Tom stood and clearly didn't know where to space himself vis a vis her. He said, "Since you're going to be around a couple days with nothing to do, if, you know, you want to do something just, uh, you could give me a call. If you want to do something. Get out. You know."

"All right," she said, chipper enough to bounce to her feet and start across the room. This was awkward, but the trick was to keep moving through it. She wasn't sure it was finished, though this installment seemed to be. She would have to not let it bother her to just keep moving across the floorboards, no matter how they felt underfoot.

* * *

In the morning the snow lay like a denial of everything that had happened before it. But that, Tom knew, was temporary. He coughed in the cold as he stepped off the porch, sputtering gouts of steam. Scout ran in bounding circles, lifting herself clear of the snow before plunging back down, her nose high. The dog seemed to be enjoying the thrill of this new surface. Tom felt the cold in his eyes making his eyelids feel too short to close. His fingers felt fat, wouldn't curl down into fists. *What*, he wondered, *had happened here last night?*

Such an odd time to be fascinated with someone new, someone from so far away. And on top of that, he had to worry about just how much of a fool he'd made of himself. But she had come out here, hadn't she? Well, she gave him a ride. And then she came in, and sat and drank and talked.

Anyway, she was about to be married, and that was enough. Meanwhile, he knew he had to talk to Jenny, which was why he was dressed and ready, once the dog did her business, to jump in his old truck—the one he kept for elk hunting—and head into town. He let Scout back in the house and drove. Tom worked the wheel to keep the tires in the ruts, already hardened into icy grooves.

The sun dazzled across the snowfields, glittering beneath a sky of taut blue purity. The brightness assaulted him, heightening the tangy sense of guilt he felt in his stomach. When his attention turned to this feeling, part of him rose up in protest, arguing: *I don't owe her anything.*

But he did. Their story was an uncomplicated one, consisting almost entirely so far of her unselfish and his unfinished gestures, reaching a strange anticlimax when he tried to kiss her in a rush over a pizza. But even that implied a legitimacy and provoked assumption, the coin of the realm among righteous gossips and moral guardians. And most other folks just felt like something was going on. If they lived in Great Falls, he wouldn't have to do this; but here, he owed her a visit. No, it wasn't that.

It wasn't Dumont. It was him, what he was learning about life and other people in it. When you allowed people to feel things, encouraged, or at least failed to discourage, those feelings, you fell into their debt. The same was true with his team. He owed them something he wasn't going to be able to own up to. They had not betrayed him—they had been kids growing up in a way they had learned was okay.

He had let them down.

He would have to know that again every time he saw them. And while for a brief moment leaving seemed like an answer, Tom had come to understand that he had left before because it was easy. Staying away was hard, but leaving was the easiest thing he knew how to do.

If anything else was going to come together for him, leaving couldn't be the first option anymore. He parked in front of Jenny's house and walked around the front bumper and up the path cleared in the snow to her front door. The snow squealed under his feet, the sound of painless agony. Tom's eye felt smaller than usual and he had a clear sense of the bags under them. He waited for a few moments after knocking before Jenny's oldest daughter, eight-year-old Erin, opened the door.

"My mom's in the kitchen," Erin said shyly. She squirmed a bit, then simply walked away.

"Jenny?" Tom called as he stepped into the house.

"Back here," came the reply, and he moved back through the hall and into the kitchen. He stood for a moment, staring at her back as she made sandwiches on the counter. She glanced over her shoulder and said a simple "Hi," leaving him almost nothing to go on. He wondered if he should sit. He looked at the harvest table, over which he lunged only a couple nights before, trying to kiss her, and decided to stay standing.

"How are you?" she said, and he caught in her tone an annoyance that she should have to start the conversation.

"Good, fine. How are you? Listen, I wanted to apologize about last night," he said.

Jenny turned, used her wrist to wipe a strand of hair from her eye. "No need," she said. She frowned and finished it with a slight head shake.

"I was coming over, and then my tires got slashed . . ." He held his hands palm up.

"Are you going to take your coat off? I just have to get the kids ready for school. I didn't expect you."

"Sure," Tom said, feeling back on his heels.

"How'd you get home?"

"What?" he asked.

"Last night. How'd you get home with no tires?"

This was a test. By now she might know how he got home.

"That lawyer from Great Falls, the schools' lawyer. She gave me a ride."

"Oh" Jenny said, a simple little "oh." He had no idea what the "oh" meant. It occurred to Tom that, after years of "hello" in the

hallways and idle chatter in the teacher's lounge, then months of
an admittedly one-sided courtship, he didn't know much about
this woman. Jenny cleared matters up somewhat by following
with, "So you were out with her?"

"No," he said. "No. I was having a beer with Krock O' at Pep's
while that meeting went on. She came in for some pizza after. We
were talking about what happened."

Jenny's eyebrows shortened her forehead while her gaze turned
downward. She nodded, pushing her lower lip out just enough to
be noticeable as different from the normal set of her mouth.

Nobody said anything. Tom wondered if he was being evalu-
ated for veracity. He wondered if adding some more detail might
make her tend to believe him more. But he wanted this part to
be over, so he didn't say more from fear it would only prolong the
conversation.

Finished assembling the sandwiches, Jenny snatched a knife
and cut them. Then she started chopping carrots. She did not look
up from her work to say, "I'm not sure what you want, Tom."

Neither was he. He said, "I just wanted to apologize for not
coming over last night. And to talk about what we were going to
talk about." Although the truth was he didn't want to talk about
that now. He wanted to leave that frozen for its moment in time
until he could sort some other things out, then maybe come back
to it. That's what he wanted to say, *I'd like to get back to you on this.*

"No, Tom, I'm not sure what you want," she said again. "That's
the thing."

"I'm the one who tried to kiss you, if you'll remember," he
said, hearing the defensiveness he wished he could choke from
his voice. Jenny was looking at him, her face beautiful in its simple openness, its frank lack of complexity, her features smooth,
untensed, her eyes accessible. The weight of her honest expectation triggered again the rise of the defensive reflex he hated in
himself and before he could stop himself, he had said, "You were
the one who held back."

Jenny's eight-year old daughter Erin took two steps into the room at that moment, stopped in stride, one foot just plopped onto the floor, the whimsical flight that had carried her into the kitchen suddenly redirected. The girl looked at Tom, reading him to make sure he had said what she thought he had. Her hair flipped as she looked at her mother, puzzled. "Why is Coach Warner trying to kiss you, Mom?" she asked.

"He was just giving me a good-night kiss, honey," Jenny said, slicing a look at Tom.

"How come you didn't want to give him a good-night kiss back?"

"Can we talk about this later, honey?" Jenny asked her daughter. "What did you come in here for? Is there something I can get for you?"

"Well, no. I just wanted a glass of juice. And, um, Jonathan is hitting me."

"Are you giving Jonathan any reason to hit you?" Jenny asked.

"No," came the quick reply.

"Are you sure?"

"Jonathan always hits me."

"Do you want me to come and ask Jonathan why he is hitting you?"

"He's just doing it, Mom. He's just, like, hitting me." Erin was staring at Tom now, fascinated and repulsed. "Do you kiss Coach Warner good night?"

"A lot of times adults just give kiss each other to say goodbye and hello."

"In Europe, everybody does," Tom said. "That's how you say hello to people, you kiss them on the cheek."

"Like air kisses?" Erin said. She'd heard of this, or seen it on TV.

"Exactly."

"What kind of juice did you want, honey?" Jenny asked, and moved to pour her daughter a glass of anything she named.

"Grape."

"Drink it down here," Jenny said, handing her the glass. "Don't take it upstairs."

"Okay."

"Promise?"

"I promise."

"If you promise not to give Jonathan any more reasons to hit you, I promise to come and talk to him about it. And I'll come and talk to you about other stuff as soon as Coach Warner goes home. Okay? And brush your teeth as soon as you're done with that juice. We're going to be leaving in twenty minutes."

Erin agreed to that bargain, but couldn't tear her deeply puzzled gaze from Tom even as she stalked from the room. Amazing, Tom thought, that at that age, already she knew he wasn't being straight with her.

"Have you ever been to Europe?" he asked Jenny.

"No," Jenny said.

"Where have you been?"

"What do you mean?"

"Outside of Montana. Have you gone places?"

She seemed to know why he was asking. "I have an aunt in Nebraska. We used to go there. Outside Lincoln. I went to Las Vegas on my honeymoon. Have you been to Europe? Do you want some grape juice before I put it away?"

"No, thanks," he said. "I've never been anywhere, except for road games in college. But for those you just fly in, go to practice, go to the hotel, get up, go to the game and get back on the plane. It never felt like being anywhere."

"Are you planning a trip?"

"No."

"All this sudden interest in Europe," she said.

Any real response to that led down seven paths to trouble, so Tom sat back in his chair and said, "I don't know."

Before either of them could imagine a comfortable angle back into the conversation they'd been having, Jonathan, the five-year old, stomped into the kitchen and burst into tears. Tom couldn't help but notice the sequence.

"Erin's being mean to me!" Jonathan wailed.

"We can talk about Erin as soon as you stop crying," Jenny told her son.

Jonathan shrieked and began some tortured declarations, from which Tom was able to make out something about a phone his sister had taken from him.

Jenny squatted down to his eye level and said, "We can talk all about that, just as soon as you stop crying and calm down and tell me exactly what happened."

"But she's . . ." the rest was stretched beyond meaning by a resurgence of wails.

"I don't know what you're saying, Jonathan," Jenny said. She held his gaze with a marvelous determination. "I can't hear you because you're crying too hard. As soon as you stop crying, you can tell me and we can try to fix it."

The boy, who already had his arms raised and flailing, took a slap at his mother and screeched louder, a long, hysterically undulant rendition of "Nooooooo."

Jenny snatched his arms, held them by their thin wrists, thrust her face inches from his and said, "*You do not hit your mother.*" She pointed to another room and said, "Time out for you."

Unbelievably, the boy's shrieks gained in intensity. Jenny picked him up and hauled him to the other room. Tom was not uncomfortable watching her handle her children, and she reacted as unselfconsciously as she would have had he not been there. That was one of the things admired about her. Adored, actually.

She was always herself. Jenny reentered the room, walked to the sink, and poured herself a glass of water. Looking out the window, she pushed her hair from her face with a free hand, then tilted her head back beneath the glass. Tom saw the hard morning light from the snow outside gleaming on her throat as she drank. He waited until she had collected herself and turned to look at him.

"Maybe this isn't the best time for a real heart to heart," he said, trying to sound hopeful that there would be a better one, and that they still had a need for a heart to heart.

"Probably not, although the fact that we started talking about it at all makes me not want to stop. But . . ." she waved her hand toward the hiccupping cries in the other room.

"When can be a good time for you? Maybe you can get a sitter. Maybe you can come to my place and we can be uninterrupted?"

"I'd like that," she said. "Let me ask around. I'll call you."

"I'll be home after school. Time on my hands," he said. He stood, wondering if he should walk all the way across the distance that separated them and kiss her. He decided that of course he should. She saw it coming this time, and waited, and gave him a smooth expanse of pear-smooth cheek to come down softly upon.

* * *

Later that same morning Marlo went to the high school and sat in the teacher's lounge—a room full of wooden chairs and a couple of tables—and interviewed football players. The moment Marlo saw Wyatt Aarstad, she felt an instant adoration for him. He looked more like twelve than fifteen.

His ears stuck out and his hair held to his head in wiry, uncontrollable cowlicks. Wyatt was accompanied by only his father, who Marlo had seen so much of the night before. He wore the same stained jacket and she smelled the mustiness she knew she would in it, the stale bar stench combined with a cocktail of body odor, garage grease, diesel exhaust, and the moldy fug of years of cigarette smoke. Marlo introduced herself and invited them to sit. She felt Jon Aarstad eyeing her.

"What are you going to do to satisfy me?" Jon asked, enjoying the double entendre a tad too much.

"You may be confused," Marlo said. "I'm not here to satisfy you."

"What are you going to offer to make this go away?" Jon said. "I want Wyatt to be set for life. So you tell me, how far you're going to get toward that goal."

"Mr. Aarstad, I think you've been watching too much TV. I'm not going to discuss the settlement of a suit that hasn't even been brought yet, but I'll tell you that, as an experienced attorney, I don't see any big windfall for you here." Marlo didn't believe that for a moment. A civil jury might decide anything. But she doubted any attorney in their right mind would let it get to a jury. And if there were damages, if the report of sexual assault proved out, Wyatt was going to be a wealthy little farm boy. And that's what she would very carefully have to tease out in the next hour or so.

"If you don't mind, Mr. Aarstad, I'd like to ask Wyatt some questions."

Jon Aarstad stuck out his hand like it held a serving platter, offering his son up. Marlo started asking Wyatt about playing football, why he did it, why he liked it.

"It's great. It's fun," Wyatt said, his voice a cheery peep. "All my friends do it."

"Are the guys on the team your friends?" Marlo asked.

"They're my dawgs," Wyatt said. He beamed, begging her to be impressed with his street accent.

"Even after what happened?"

"Aw yeah, they didn't mean nothing by that. It was just goofing."

"Did they manhandle you to get you up on the rack?" Marlo asked.

Wyatt paused for a minute and scrunched his face to the side. He swung a glance at his father, who was too busy glaring at Marlo's breasts to notice. Wyatt's hesitation signaled to Marlo that what came next would be a lie. Still, she didn't care. She couldn't help thinking he was the cutest little guy she'd ever seen.

"Just whatever it took," Wyatt said, and he let it go at that.

"So they, like, grabbed you and wrestled you up there?" Marlo asked. "Did you struggle?"

"You gotta struggle a little bit or everyone will think you're a pu . . . sissy."

"Did you ask them not to do it?"

Now she could see Wyatt calculating, wondering if she'd heard something different from someone else. "No," he said at length, the disappointed admission of someone whose lie has been revealed after so recently being minted. Now his father's attention swerved toward him and Wyatt seemed to flinch. "They just said they were gonna beat my ass if I didn't go along."

Marlo watched the boy, making a mental note to check this detail with the other stories.

"It was a joke. That's just what the guys do," Wyatt was saying. "It's what we do on the team."

She asked him about the team and his role on it. The story Marlo heard from Wyatt was of a boy who craved attention and wanted to hang with the boys who commanded it. He wanted friends. And he thought the way you gained them was through mouthing off and playing pranks and getting pranked. He was the kid that was always poking, so you'd at least notice he was there.

"Wyatt, if the pictures hadn't come out, would you have told anybody about this?" Marlo asked.

"No way," Wyatt said. "I'm no squealer."

"You wouldn't have wanted to get the guys on your team in trouble?"

"No way."

"Did they do anything to you that you didn't like?"

"They stuck their butts in my face, but that isn't anything."

"Wyatt, it's important that you be very, very honest here. Did anybody on the bus touch you in a way you didn't like? With their hands or any objects?"

Wyatt thought that one through, weighing in his father's anticipation. Then he said, "I mean, it wasn't the best time I've ever had. It might have gotten carried away."

"What about that candy bar?" Jon Aarstad burst in.

Wyatt looked at her as if he were about to be reprimanded, but Marlo nodded. "What did the boys do with the candy bar?"

"They just kind of stuck it in my . . . butt cheeks. For a picture."

"Did they penetrate you in any way?"

He flinched with an undertone of *gross*.

"Did they touch your anus with the candy bar or anything else?"

Wyatt blushed. It was clear "anus" and "penetration" were not topics discussed frequently in his interactions with adults.

"Do I have to talk about this?" He seemed disgusted, but also amused the way only teenaged boys can be about bodily orifices.

Marlo felt like she had him on a truth streak and she might as well try the hard one. She kept her voice analytical, and tossed the next question out like it was his to do what he wanted with. "Wyatt, did you feel like they were doing something to you, to your anus, that you didn't want them to?"

"Who wants a candy bar in their ass?" Wyatt said, and he beamed as if expecting some feedback for being so clever.

"Tell her what you told me," Jon said.

"It wasn't the best time I've ever had. I said that," Wyatt said. "I felt like I was up there in front of everyone and they were doing things to me."

Marlo couldn't help but notice that Jon Aarstad nodded on each of Wyatt's points. "Did any of them touch your face with their penis?"

"What? Why you gotta be sick, dude?" Wyatt said, and flinched away from her.

"I saw the pictures, Wyatt. Did they touch you with either their penises or their buttocks?"

"I don't think so," Wyatt said.

"You don't think so?"

"Think you'd remember something like that, son," Jon Aarstad said.

"I don't know," Wyatt said.

Marlo asked, "Were you afraid of them?"

"Not really," Wyatt said.

"Have any of them ever hurt you before?"

"Sometimes they hold me down and give me a redbelly. Stuff like that. It doesn't really hurt for very long."

"So were you scared of them at all?"

"Why would I be scared of them? They're my dawgs."

"Wyatt, why is the TV news saying that you were sexually assaulted?"

"I heard some guys pranked them," Wyatt said, breaking into a grin as if he wished it had been his own idea.

"What do you mean?" Marlo asked, trying not to appear astonished.

"I heard some guys from the team called that reporter's hotel room and told her all kind of nasty stuff happened," Wyatt seemed to think this part was a most excellent coup.

"And she reported that?" Marlo struggled not to add, *Are you fucking kidding me?*

Earlier that morning, when Marlo had left her own hotel room, she had been waylaid by the TV reporter, Penny Meriwether, who had, of course, stayed in the Sportsman overnight. Penny Meriwether had pretended she hadn't been sitting in the news van for over an hour, waiting for Marlo to emerge, though Marlo knew she had been. She'd heard the van's engine start shortly after she rose and peeked out to see the news crew loading up, and Meriwether, twisting the van's side mirror to apply lipstick, a mic dangling over her shoulder like a pelt.

Meriwether had at first asked politely if Marlo would go on camera for an interview, which Marlo declined. Then she had signaled her cameraman, who zoomed in on the scene as Meriwether began firing questions. Marlo struggled to remain polite and cool while saying "No comment. No comment. It would be inappropriate to comment on that at this time. Sorry, I can't comment" until the exercise was over.

"Why does your father think you were sexually assaulted?" Marlo asked Wyatt.

"Those boys jab-assed my kid and everybody's talking about it," Jon howled.

"That doesn't seem to be what he's saying."

"It's all over the school! Everybody thinks the kid got jab-assed. I'm catching six flavors of shit at work over it."

"All due respect, Mr. Aarstad, you were the one on TV last night crying sexual assault," Marlo said. "You're where the innuendo came from."

"I was just saying what everybody else was already thinking," Jon blustered.

"Okay, Wyatt, I think we might be almost done," Marlo said, while Jon fumed and tried to dream up a way back into his defense. "Have any of the guys on the team said anything to you about all this since it happened?"

"They told me to keep quiet, like everybody was gonna."

"Who told you that?"

"Some of the guys. They said just told me to keep it shut."

"Which guys?"

"Couple different guys."

"Who?"

"I don't really remember." He was closing down. Marlo wanted him back. "One more time—you were naked and taped up. Did anybody touch you in an inappropriate way?"

"Well, I was naked and taped up. All those cheerleaders were there. I couldn't cover up. I didn't like that too much."

Marlo felt something giving way. "And the candy bar?"

"Yeah, they put it in my butt in front of those girls. I didn't want that. I was okay with them taping me up, it was a goof, a picture for the yearbook."

"A naked yearbook picture?

"At first they were going to tape me up and hang me from the book rack. They texted those girls to bring the yearbook camera over. I had my clothes *on*. I didn't know they were gonna, like, yank my pants down."

"Were you penetrated in any way? You've got to answer this one, Wyatt."

Wyatt looked at the floor, his eyes scrubbing back and forth.

"It's okay, Wyatt. It doesn't make you less of a man."

Wyatt said, "I . . . I don't know."

"You know, Wyatt. You definitely know. The sheriff's going to want to know, too. I know it's hard . . ."

Wyatt looked at his father, who was staring at him. "Maybe I'll remember better when I talk to the sheriff. Will there be a lot of people there?"

"Is it because I'm a woman, Wyatt? Is that why you don't want to tell me?"

"Maybe."

"Okay, what about the boys who put their buttocks or their penises in your face?"

"That's stuff that just happens," Wyatt said.

"Really?" Marlo asked.

"Sure."

"Who put their buttocks in your face?"

"Matt, Waylon, Alex."

"Who put their penis in your face?"

"Matt and Alex."

"Did you want them to do that?"

"It was just goofing for the girls. Stuff seniors do to freshmen."

The girls, Marlo thought.

* * *

Josie Frehse sat at a table with Ainsley Martin and Britnee Mattoon, and they talked about what they assumed everybody else was talking about.

"Did you see Matt do the candy bar thing?" Josie asked the two girls who had been on the bus when it all happened.

"I didn't," Ainsley said.

"I kind of did," Britnee said.

"Did he do what they said?" Josie asked.

"Don't you talk to Matt about these things?" Ainsley asked.

Josie sat, stumped. She had talked to Matt about it but he hadn't really told her anything. She kept thinking he would. She kept thinking she wanted to know more before she brought it up again, wanted to come to the conversation armed.

"Is Matt, like, into that?" Britnee asked.

"Into what?"

"You know . . . butt stuff."

Ainsley's face wrinkled in disgust, but clearly she wanted to know this, too. Britnee laughed at both of them.

"No," Josie said. Then she really got it. "Oh, they all talk about it, but not with me. God no."

"I've seen it in pornos," Britnee said.

"That would be so gross," Ainsley said.

"So gross," Josie agreed.

Britnee laughed at them more, because it was her job, in the group, to be shocking, and she had just done well.

At that moment, Mikie LaValle shuffled by the table and then paused as if he were going to start talking to Josie. This was not the most unusual thing in the world. Dumont's cafeteria— the high school itself—was not so stratified that certain people feared interacting with others. Well, Mikie probably wouldn't stop by the football player's table, or talk to her if Matt were in the cafeteria.

Kids knew each other from helping out on neighbor's or uncle's farms, from sticking together at sports camps in Havre or Billings, from parents getting together for dinner or at the bar. Everybody knew each other, and had brothers who were friends with some- one's else's sister, or cousins who hung out together. There were factions, just as factions existed in town. Josie wondered if any time you had two people in a room, you had factions, if it was part of being human. But it was hard to stay distinct.

Which was why Mikie LaValle stopping at her table neither surprised nor informed Britnee Mattoon or Ainsley Martin, who were used to seeing her talk to people from all the different groups in school. They knew that Matt was developing some sort of grudge against Mikie, and suspected it was based in possessiveness, but they also knew Josie didn't let Matt's petty jealousies gain traction and refused to let him tell her what to do, which made theirs not the smoothest of relationships, and caused her classmates to form opinions about her—she was either being a strong role model who knew what she wanted, or just asking for trouble. The views divided neither along lines of age nor sex.

Plenty of girls in school thought she was asking for trouble, and might even be trying to steal their boyfriends or crushes. Some girls thought Josie wanted to have a boy on every hook, and they deplored what they saw as greed in a place where even marginally attractive boys were so few and far between. On the other hand, most of the boys loved that she talked to them—even if they thought Matt would prefer she didn't.

So when Mikie LaValle scuffed to a halt beside her, Josie looked up from her fish stick and said, "Oh, hi Mikie. 'Sup?"

Mikie held his tray and looked at the other girls at the table as if they were contagious, his distrust palpable. Josie could see he would much prefer to talk to her alone and, while she had no desire to make him feel uncomfortable, she didn't see why she should have to leave her friends to talk. She had, the way she saw it, no secrets.

Except of course there was the night at the reservoir, which was definitely still a secret, even though nothing that needed to be kept secret had happened. And she had passed a few notes that she had gone out of her way to conceal or disguise. And there had been some phone calls that nobody at the table knew about.

"Hey," Mikie said, and it sounded as if he were wondering if that was the right thing to say.

Oh come on, Mikie, Josie thought, *don't geek out on me now.*

"What are you doing?" Mikie said.

"Just having some lunch," Josie said.

"You got something going on after school?" Mikie asked.

"Yep. Basketball practice starts tonight," Josie said, happy to be able to perk up about something. "Unofficially, of course. Shoot around."

Another boy stopped a few feet behind Mikie, his friend Arlen Alderdice, who was every bit as skinny as Mikie, only four inches shorter. Arlen wore glasses with rims that were too thick and toted his lunch tray like everything on it was trying to get off. He stared at Mikie, watching something he was not sure he believed, and seemed to anticipate some sort of ultimate failure.

"You gonna go out for basketball?" Josie asked, glad to be able to sound so enthusiastic—she was this way whenever she talked to anybody about basketball—and glad she could be nice to Mikie in front of everybody.

"Maybe I will."

"Why not?"

"It's not rez ball," Ainsley Martin said, sounding like he'd been arguing that it was. Josie turned and stared at her, baffled. Mikie's glance carried more heat.

"Yeah, well, hey, I'll see you around," he said, and moved off in a stride that was somehow long and bouncy at once. Arlen Alderdice swirled along, sucked away in his wake.

"What was that?" Josie demanded of Ainsley, once Mikie was gone.

"Rez ball is different. I didn't want him to be disappointed."

"I think you managed to do that anyway," Josie said.

"I would never hook up with an Indian," Ainsley said, "They're all so gross."

Britnee leaned in conspiratorially, and when it became apparent nobody was tilting to meet her, she went ahead and said, "I heard they're never circumcised."

"No way," Ainsley said.

Britnee shrugged, dared them to believe her, "I guess it's spiritual."

"You're just making that up," Josie said. "Anyway, Mikie's only half Indian."

The other two looked at her as if trying to figure out why she was defending herself.

"Well, you can't just make generalizations about people," Josie said.

"God, Jos, Matt's in trouble so now you're going native?" Britnee said.

"That's not even funny."

"Maybe you and ol' what's-his-name can move into a nice trailer at Fort Miles," Ainsley said. "Play Keno on Saturday nights down at the gas station and get hooked on meth."

"That's just . . . don't even talk like that," Josie said. "And for god's sakes don't talk like that around Matt. He already wants to beat the crap out of ol' what's-his-name."

"Mikie," Britnee said. "Mikie LaVagina, so you don't have to pretend you don't know."

"Matt's not the only one who would beat the crap out of him," Ainsley said. "Your brother would scalp him. Probably scalp you, too. Can you imagine?"

Ainsley let them imagine. Josie was confused about what she was supposed to be picturing. A scalping?

"That's, like, the worst thing you could do to your parents," Ainsley said, talking hypothetically now. "Bringing home an Indian. God, my dad would skin me alive."

"I don't think my dad would care," Britnee said.

"Really?" Ainsley asked, sarcastically.

"Seriously," Britnee said. She shrugged her lips. "If he was a nice guy and treated me good, they wouldn't care. My parents aren't like that."

"Josie's are," Ainsley said.

"I don't know if they are," Josie said. "My dad? I doubt it. My mom might worry but only because she knows how some people," and here she made it clear she was referring to some people like Ainsley, "treat mixed-race couples. She'd just worry about whether I was happy."

"All I know," Ainsley said, petulant after suddenly finding herself in a minority of what she clearly felt was superior thinking, "is that Matt has enough troubles right now."

Josie hadn't thought they were talking about Matt, but she wasn't going to let any ember of rumor flitter toward flammable material. "I'm not interested in cheating on Matt with Mikie LaValle," Josie said, her tone slanted toward pointing out how ridiculous the idea was. "Just so we're all clear on that."

Ainsley gave her a *whatever* shrug, implying Josie was the one who'd started the implication.

"Be serious," Josie said. She felt a compelling desire to look over her shoulder at where Mikie LaValle would be sitting, where he always sat, to see if he was watching the exchange. She wondered if he could hear any of it, or pick up from their gestures that they were talking about him. She hoped he wasn't noticing. But mostly, she knew she couldn't look—for his sake as much as for hers.

* * *

Matt Brunner sat at a desk, flanked by his parents, and told Marlo there was no way the school could keep him off the team. "If I don't play," he said, "we lose."

"Matt, I think you may have to consider that the school is looking at punishments that go beyond Saturday. You could be expelled," Marlo said.

"They won't kick me out," Matt said, slouched a little too coolly. "They *need* me for basketball. If I don't play, they don't even have a team."

Her first reaction had been: *asshole*. But the kid's affect was so flat she had an instant understanding of how much Matt simply believed what he was saying. His parents looked on, apparently in complete agreement.

"Matt, several people I've talked to think you're lying about your role in what happened. I'm going to give you a clean slate and the benefit of the doubt. Let's start at the beginning and you tell me what happened."

She let him tell his version of events, which mainly included him sitting in the back of the bus having nothing to do with any of it except helping to tape Wyatt Aarstad to the rack. The whole thing was stupid, he said, immature.

"What's the big deal? We shower together every day. We see each other naked every day." Matt said. "People are always mooning each other. I mean, to us, it's no big deal to stick your butt in someone's face."

"Don't you agree, though, that there's a difference between seeing each other naked in the shower and what happened on the bus?"

"Maybe you just have to be seventeen and a guy," Matt said. "I get mooned all the time. If it bugs me I just push them away. It's just not the big deal everybody's making it out to be. Wyatt didn't care. I mean, you have to know Wyatt. He's the mouthiest runt alive. He wasn't mad at us. I shot some hoop with him two days later. He's always hanging around us. He doesn't get upset."

Sensing a stymieing, Marlo switched tactics and flipped up a photograph of Wyatt's face next to a pair of pants unbuttoned and partially unzipped. The base of a penis was apparent in the photo, amid a curling of pubic hair.

Marlo stared directly at Matt while he took a quick enough glance to see what the picture was, then let his attention bounce out the window.

"Is this you?" Marlo asked, daring him to make eye contact.

"No," Matt said. He was sitting with the backs of his fingers pressed against his mouth, not quite curled into a fist.

"Lying isn't going to help you anymore. The toothpaste is out of the tube."

Matt looked at her finally, and while she wanted to see confusion or fear, a hint of comeuppance, instead the closest redeeming quality she could identify in his expression was frustration and disgust. "What toothpaste?"

Recognizing that it was probably too late to play Good Cop, Marlo tried to jigger the power balance in her voice so Matt could feel on a level. "I want us to work together on this, Matt. I understand how these things go, and I know you all agreed not to tell all the details. But everything has changed now. This is really about your future. I need you to give me a chance to work with you. Now I'm sitting here, looking at the picture, at the belt on the jeans in the picture, and I'm looking at you sitting there, wearing the same belt on your jeans now. That tells me you're not treating me with respect, Matt. You think I'm stupid. You think all of this is stupid." She stopped to let that settle in before adding, "I respect you, Matt. I respected you enough to ask for your side of the story. Work with me a little bit."

Marlo would wonder for a long time afterward if it was the business about respect, or just leveling with the kid. In either case, she witnessed a visible thaw overcome him. It started with him slowly chewing—almost kissing—the fingers at his mouth. His eyes welled, and his mouth gathered and twitched. She saw him slump, the rigidity of even his slouch melting out until he seemed in danger of sliding onto the floor in a puddle.

"Okay, it's me," Matt said. He started to cry, almost simultaneously looking around the room to see if anybody was watching. His father's eyelids dropped halfway. His mother took a sharp breath and held it, her mouth shrunk to the smallest pucker she could press it into. "I just want to play ball," Matt said. "That's all I want. It's all I have. Don't take it away from me."

"Do you feel like you did something wrong?" Marlo asked.

Matt sobbed a long shaky inhalation. The sound he made could not be faked, and it hurt Marlo to hear it.

"I guess," he said, his voice warped and warbling. He looked at his father. "I'm sorry. It was all so stupid." He turned to Marlo. "I'm sorry. I'm so sorry. All I want to do is play ball."

The voice that chilled Marlo was the father. He was not loud, spoke in a whisper with a searing edge, but laced with disgust. "Jesus Christ," was all he said.

* * *

After his junior American history class, Tom was looking at his notes for the next class period and was surprised to notice a student standing in front of his desk, saying nothing. Tom looked up. It was Mikie LaValle.

"Mike," he said. "Can I help you?"

"Um, yeah," Mikie started. "Uh, I was wondering if you know some books I can read about Louis Riel and Gabriel Dumont?"

"Sure," Tom said. He started digging around on his desk. "You bet. First, take this textbook." It was a Canadian history textbook that Tom had special ordered.

"Cool," Mikie said. "I just want to learn more."

"Sure," Tom said. "Makes sense."

"Because I'm, you know, like, Metis. Mixed blood."

"Right," Tom said. "I get it. Yeah, heck, I'm glad to know you're interested. There's another really thorough book called just *Riel*, I think," Tom said. "It's Canadian."

"Oh," Mikie said. "I'm not allowed to go to Canada."

"Why aren't you allowed?" Tom asked, thinking the kid was young to already have a drug bust or DUI on his record, the usual reasons for people not being able to cross the border.

"My mom won't let me," Mikie said.

"You know, I think you can probably order it on Amazon."

"Oh. Okay."

Tom had observed Mikie in class, of course, but there Mikie cloaked himself in silence. Here now, one on one, Tom thought the boy might explode from nervousness. Mikie was digging at his cuticles so fervently Tom feared they might gush blood. The boy failed to meet his eye, looked at his fingers or across the room and

out the window, like his gaze was hauling him toward some soothing respite on the other side of the distant horizon. Tom tried to
think of something to say to help put Mikie at ease. He thought
he remembered knowing the kid's father wasn't in his life. "How
come," he asked, "you don't play any sports?"

But that didn't work at all. He could see Mikie burrowing deeper
into his insecurities.

"I mean, you look pretty athletic," Tom tried. "Just the way you
carry yourself and the way you move. I'm a pretty good judge of these
things. You look like you could play some ball. You play hoops?"

"Yeah," Mikie answered quickly in a thick voice that sounded
dumber than anything he'd said so far.

"I bet you're good at that," Tom said.

"Cause I'm Indian?" The kid seemed suddenly offended.

"No," Tom said. "No. You just look athletic. Do you run?"

Mikie looked around the room. "I don't know."

"I mean do you ever go for a jog, anything like that? To stay in
shape?"

"Yeah," Mikie said, "Not that much."

"Because you might be good at that, too. And, yeah, a lot of
Indian kids are good runners, especially distance," Tom said. He
thought he saw something light up in the boy—irritation, at first,
at the heritage comment, which Tom threw in there to make sure
Mikie knew he wasn't afraid of it, but then a slower satisfaction—
and that made him think he knew how to appeal to Mikie. "You
can imagine the endurance and stamina those Metis people out
on the plains needed. A lot of times, that makes for good distance
runners."

Mikie seemed to be chewing this over. "Indians could run for
days, man. I read about it," he said.

"You want, I can give you some workouts to do," Tom said,
holding his hands up quickly when he saw the flash of fright in
the boy's eyes, "You can do them all by yourself. I'll just give you a
schedule of what you should be trying to build up to. You can start

running on your own, build up on your own. You feel good about it, maybe you can try out for track in the spring. Be good to see you on a track or a court or something."

"Ah, man, I don't know about track," Mikie said. He turned his head and looked at the floor.

Tom had seen this work dozens of times, had seen the flattery of a coach reach a boy that nobody considered anybody's idea of an athlete. Most of the time, they turned out not to be outstanding performers at all, but that wasn't what Tom was after. He believed that no kid suffered from trying to get in better physical condition. It never hurt a kid try to compete, either, to learn about what competition could do for them, what it meant to work for something, as long as their progress and losses were carefully managed. It never hurt loner boys like Mikie to join a team—even if at first they found themselves harassed in the locker room, it never hurt them to persevere and win the respect of their peers.

But most importantly, it never hurt these kids to think that somebody cared enough to watch them. Even though Mikie seemed shy and indecisive, his body language had already puffed up. He stood straighter and seemed able to hold his eyes in Tom's direction.

"You'd have to give up the smokes," Tom said. He half laughed to let Mikie know he wasn't judging him.

"Aw . . . it's not like a habit, or anything."

"Okay," Tom said. "Easy enough then. Give it a shot. I think you'd find out something about yourself that you'd like."

"I don't know about that," Mikie said. "I'm not, like, the strong football type."

"There's lots of different kinds of strong. Listen, let me tell you something about me, with the preamble that I realize going into it this may or may not be how you feel or what you want at all. But I can tell you that when I was a kid, I didn't want to play sports for a long time because I was scared. I was afraid of what it might feel like to be tackled in football. I was afraid of making a fool of myself on the basketball court. I was afraid to come in last on the track. I was afraid a baseball might hit me in the face and break my teeth out. I was afraid of everything you could be afraid of. I was afraid the other kids would laugh at me, most of all.

"Eventually I said to myself, Yeah, I'm scared, but I'm going to try it anyway because I think I'm missing out on something. And you know what happened? Every one of the things I was afraid of happened. I got drilled by kids who were bigger than me on the football field, knocked silly. I got the basketball stolen from me, had shots blocked, made a fool of myself on the court. Got hit in the face by a pop fly I failed to field—didn't break my teeth but I bled like a stuck pig. And the other kids laughed at me. They called me Ten Thumbs Tom and Dork-o and other names I can't repeat. But you know what I found out?

"After the first couple times I got hit in football, I learned to lower my shoulders and lean into the contact. And after that first baseball smacked me, I wasn't scared to get my glove up—what could happen that was worse? And pretty soon I learned when to pick up my dribble, and how to move my shot so it didn't get blocked. And the kids who laughed at me? I figured out pretty quickly that they laughed at everybody. It wasn't just me. That's when the fun started." Tom held his hands out. "I'm not saying that's your life, or even that it might happen the same way for you. But I know that getting on a team, having teammates, playing for each other, that was something I wouldn't have missed for the world, man. That was the greatest fun I ever had."

"I'm not a sports type," Mikie said.

"I know you think you're not," Tom said. "I thought I wasn't either. Then I was. Life's like that. You can be what you decide to be."

This last sentiment seemed to make more impact on the boy than everything Tom had said up to that point. Mikie looked at him quickly, off guard, as if to assess whether Tom was being flippant. Tom shrugged, said, "Think about it."

Then the moment of unguarded enthusiasm was gone and Mikie's eyes hooded. He snorted. "Maybe I'll just be a Metis."

"Sure, that too," Tom said.

* * *

Brad Martin preceded his son into the room and showed the boy where to sit. Alex was a handsome kid with fluorescent blue eyes made more vivid by a frame of hanging dark hair. He was tall and rangy with the foot-flopping, slightly pigeon-toed walk of a kid physically coping with a growth spurt. He was nearly a foot taller than his father, and Marlo noticed that his mother, Sharon Martin, was also taller than Brad. Sharon started silently weeping almost as soon as they sat down and, without saying a word or sniffling or in any other way being present, continued to do so for the entire interview.

Alex fessed up at once, admitting to owning a pair of buttocks in question when Marlo slipped the copy of the photo under his nose. "I shouldn't have done it," Alex said. "I know it was wrong. We just got carried away and . . . I made a mistake."

His words struck Marlo the moment she heard them as honest, the way only unscripted sincerity can.

"Look," Brad interjected, "you're talking about a kid who has a 4.0 grade point. He has a great talent for basketball. He's a good kid, a good citizen. He's never been in trouble before. He got himself into a bad situation and made a stupid mistake—kids do that, Ms. Stark, they make mistakes."

"I appreciate all that," Marlo said, and she had been perfectly willing to listen empathetically until he kept going.

"Between you me and the fencepost," Brad said, "that kid they taped up, that Aarstad kid? He's not going anywhere. He's got no future. My boy has a future. He's a good student. He's an outstanding athlete. He's got the tools to take himself away from this town and make something of himself. So do some of these other boys. They're going to get scholarships. Jon Aarstad is looking for a payday to balance out the fact that he never amounted to any-thing, and his kid will never amount to anything. We can't let that come at the expense of our kids who worked hard to do well in school and excel in athletics."

Marlo pumped her brows to let Brad know she heard him and that he'd said a mouthful. She had a job to do, and she told him so. She wasn't there to straighten out generations of relative suc-cess and failure. She was only there to find out what happened on the bus.

"For years and years, you can talk to anybody, they'll tell you that this kind of stuff has always gone on," Brad said. He seemed wounded by the very implication that it could be anything else. "When I was in school there was something called a brown eye. Do you know what a brown eye is?"

"No," Marlo said, "do I need to?"

"That's when the senior guys, they'd hold you down and one of them would squat over you and start to . . . start a bowel move-ment. Only at the last second he'd try to pinch it back."

"Jesus, Brad," Marlo said.

"We . . . they still do it," Alex chimed in.

"The only reason I'm telling you this," Brad said, "is because *I know* it's been going on forever. *I know* what kids do and have done for decades. The only difference now—the *only* difference— is that there weren't digital cameras back then. Now you can't pick these kids and make an example out of them when *I know* this kind of crap has been happening since all of us were in school." Brad sat back as if he'd just presented his case in a deal negotiation. Then, as if he couldn't resist making one more point, he leaned quickly forward. "I can't, in good conscience, let you ruin my son's opportunities, his future, over something that every single male who ever played sports in this town has been guilty of."

"First of all, I'm not in charge of ruining anything," Marlo said, "I'm the school board's counsel. All I'm trying to do is sort out the legal implications."

Marlo left second of all alone. Second of all, Marlo thought there had always been a divide between who was squatting and who was being held down underneath them.

Waylon Edwards was next and last on her list, scheduled so a parent could be present during the interview. But Waylon's parents didn't show up. Waylon claimed to have no idea where they might be—or, at least, where his father might be. His mother had left the family years before, bound for South Dakota with a railroad engineer. She had left Waylon and a sister with their father and his new girlfriend, who worked in a bar in Fort Miles. Waylon told Marlo he had informed his father of the interview, and had every expectation that his dad would show up. But it didn't happen.

Marlo wouldn't interview him without an adult present. A parent was ideal. She had thought for a bit about calling in Dave Cates, but given his pending suspension, she thought it best not to involve him. So she'd been faced with a dilemma. The school board had promised the community a full report the next day, Friday. There was, after all, a playoff game on Saturday that the assistant coach was preparing the team to play. Everybody wanted to know who was going to take the field.

Marlo left the school building, walked out into the cold, heading across the parking lot to her vehicle. Though there were a few hours of light left, she could already feel the day tipping toward darkness, calling it quits early. She tugged her cell phone from her purse to call Chet.

Next she drove to the Farm and Fleet store on the edge of town. She purchased a Carhartt overall suit, quilt-lined, one-piece, and as warm as she could hope to stay. Oddly she found herself liking the way she looked in the brown jumpsuit, though it did nothing to flatter her.

It felt like the right thing to be wearing in Dumont—too new, too clean, but at least she was in the right label. She bought a pair of insulated gloves and a brown Carhartt stocking cap, too, and wore them all, along with her Sorel boots, out of the store. If she was going to be here for a couple days, she might as well look like it.

* * *

That late afternoon, the sun shouted off the aluminum paint of the three tall grain elevators like a campaign promise. The snow was starting to melt, only to ice up overnight. Tom would have loved to watch Slab Rideg run the boys through practice, but walked into town instead. The sheriff's cruiser's taillights flashed as Sheriff Rue dropped it into reverse on the way to pulling off the curb. Across the street Tom saw two men smoking cigarettes outside the Mint bar, pinching the butts like convicts. He ducked into the IGA. Hannah Alderdice peered out from behind her cash register and beamed and said, "Hello Tom!" like she'd been waiting to see him for a long time.

He said hello and she said, "Well, just what kind of shame is going on over at the school, Mr. Football Coach?"

"Well," Tom said.

"Well," she said, "I swear I just don't know any more." Tom moved on into the store, five low rows of grocery items, but her voice stopped him again. "How are you treating our Miss Calhoun?"

Tom looked at Hannah, who gave him every bit of knowing in her return stare. So he winked at her and she pointed a finger at him and he started shopping, such as it was. Here they were, surrounded by fields in which grew millions of dollars' worth of commodities, but just try to find a fresh tomato. A thought probably sparked by his craving for a bottle of Clamato juice and the thought that a summer sausage might be nice to gnaw on.

Then he realized how much that sounded like just craving salt in different textures. So instead he let himself follow some mixed ideas and half-finished impulses and picked up a liter bottle of Diet Pepsi and a wedge of cheddar jack cheese and some tortilla chips, a pound of hamburger, a head of lettuce, a red pepper, and some spaghetti noodles.

He was wandering in and out among the five low aisles with all of these things gathered in his arms or hanging from hooked fingers when he spotted over a shelf a hank of hair color that could only be Dotty Lantner's. He switched direction so they met at the end of the aisle. Dotty might have wanted people to notice the rhinestones surrounding the smooth rounded seat of her jeans, but Tom noticed the way her belt puckered the waistline.

"Hey there, Dotty."

"Mr. Warner," she said, laying it on thick for the Mr. part.

"Mr. Warner," Tom repeated, as if he deserved that.

She narrowed her eyes and started to step away.

"Dotty," he said.

"What do you want, Tom?" she asked.

It was a fair question. There wasn't really a thing she could help him with. "I just . . . I know you have some ideas about me." He nodded to add some punctuation. She nodded as an answer with its own emphasis.

He jerked his head to the north, the direction of Pep's bar. "Can I buy you a drink?"

He watched her cheeks pull the "no" back from her lips. A calculus unfold in her eyes. And it wasn't very nice to turn down a drink from someone who asked so directly about it.

"You gonna pay for all that . . . stuff?" she asked, nodding at his armload of groceries.

"Can I meet you right over there?"

"I'll come," she said. Then louder, including Hannah Alderdice. "I gotta feed my family. God knows they'd starve if they had to feed themselves."

"Won't hurt them none to wonder where you are for a bit," Hannah said.

"Might remind them I exist," Dotty said.

Tom paid for his groceries, set the bags in his truck cab, and stepped up the street to Pep's. He opened the door into its darkness, took a half step through, scanning the premises before committing. Only a couple of drinkers at the bar. Sam Hendricks and Randy Bury caught reminiscing about something they both found pretty funny but probably shouldn't have. One of the older Aarstad brothers. Nobody under seventy except Hal Hartack behind the bar. Tom went to him, ordered a beer.

Hal just shook his head so his chin waggled counter to his forehead. He set the beer down in front of Tom, took the five-dollar bill, and rapped his knuckles on the bar as he walked off with it. There would be change, but Tom was going to leave it and sit at one of the tables in the back of the room by the Keno and poker machines. Dotty spent a full twenty minutes in the grocery or somewhere before she walked through the ingot of light into the bar.

"Vodka and soda with a lemon," she said to Hal as she walked past him and sat down opposite Tom.

The first drink helped, but not nearly as much as the second and third. The early ones went quick and Tom and Dotty worked through the weather and wheat prices and whether cattle was ever a good idea. "You gonna ever do the right thing with Jenny Calhoun?" Dotty asked.

"I need this twice today?" he said.

"You need it until you do the right thing," Dotty said. Then they got into the school and rules and by the third time Hal Hartack clanked glasses on the table, they were ready for the brass tacks. They both leaned into the table.

"Dotty, why I wanted to talk to you . . ."

"I was wondering when we'd get to that. Didn't think you were trying to get me drunk and take me back to that lovely little farmhouse you rent with that dog."

"These boys, Dotty. That's what it's about."

"You're quittin' on them but you want me not to?"

"You know why I had to do what I did," Tom said.

"I'm not sure I do."

"You would have if I didn't, for starters."

"True."

"And I think those boys need to see some consequences. I'm not against consequences. I mean, they screwed up royally. I'm not bucking against that. But if you could find it in your heart to see them as boys and not as some kind of full-grown TV villains . . ."

Dotty sat back now, let her ass slide to the edge of the chair. She looked around the bar, keeping her eyes high, toward the seams of the ceiling, corralling thoughts. When she had a few together, she slid her seat again to tilt forward at him and they lowered their voices and started whispering ferociously over each other. "Here's the thing, coach. I don't like you—"

"So punish me—"

"It isn't even that I don't like you—"

"But don't punish them because you don't like me. That's unchristian."

"Might even turn out that I do like you, and when did you get so fucking concerned about my Christianity?"

"It's the rest of their lives—"

Dotty checked back over her shoulder to see what Hal was doing before getting both her elbows on the table and finding a tone that shut Tom down. "I probably do like you, Tom Warner. I probably like you a lot more after this conversation than I did before. But I don't like the idea of you. And I don't like the idea of him"—she hooked a thumb in the direction of Hal Hartack— "and I don't like this town's idea of what it means to be a Dumont football player. I'm sick and goddamned tired of everybody thinking these boys walk on water and do no wrong, and everybody bending over to excuse them for everything they've done. You want to talk about the rest of someone's life? You try being a young girl out in a pickup with three football players some night when you've all had too much to drink and I guarandamntee you the things that happen will change the way you are for the rest of your life."

The sudden silence seemed to be a direct effect of the finger she stabbed into the table. Dotty's eyes glistened with intensity, seemed to shimmer as they shifted back and forth between his. Her upper lip pressed so hard against her lower he could see it quiver.

"Dotty," he said, softening, inviting her to soften. "Dotty, I'm so sorry for anything that might have happened to you."

Her finger levered up as a warning and she met his eyes as hers glistened. Only the ringing hammers of time could temper a gaze to such a hardness.

"I don't know what to say," Tom said. "I know that the boys on my team didn't do anything to harm you and they didn't do anything as harmful as what you just talked about. Somebody might have, but it wasn't the boys on my team. And I know that what you do next could seriously harm the rest of their lives. Do you think that's just?"

"I think it's just crap."

Dotty wasn't able to find his face with her eyes anymore. She'd returned to the ceiling, to the memories and ideas that lingered there with the years of muzzy cigarette smoke and dust against the stamped tin.

"I've been learning through all this that right can be a temporary point of view," Tom said.

"But we don't live in a temporary world, do we, Coach? Things just keep going on."

"Well, I guess that's right."

"And you want to be on the right side of history. Isn't that what people talk about now?"

"I think we're getting on the right side of it," Tom said. "I don't think what we're doing with these boys is ignoring that. I resigned over it, Dotty. But I think there's a difference between being hard and being strong. Isn't there a way to punish them without ruining them?"

"They ruined themselves," Dotty said.

"But isn't there a way to punish them without ruining them more?" Tom repeated.

"That's just a sort of pissed-off optimism I see too much of around here. I just get fed up."

"What if you could help them get on a better track, be better people?" Coming back to the Christian angle for a good church-goer like Dotty.

"I gotta go home," Dotty said.

"Let me walk you out," Tom said. But she was up and moving, and he had to pay. He was throwing bills on the bar as she opened the door into a considerably less-bright day.

Hal Hartack said, "I give her credit. She didn't play the sympathy card after that house landed on her sister."

Tom ignored him, hurried out, managed to reach Dotty's elbow just before she got to her Suburban. She didn't yank her arm from his hand.

"Dotty, what you told me . . . I'm sorry. For whatever might have happened along the way. If you ever need to talk . . ."

"I don't ever talk about that," she said. "Not with football coaches. Not with men."

"Understood. Understood. If you ever decide you need to," he said. "I'm a person, not just a football guy. I can feel for people. I feel for you. I want you to know that." He slipped around her and opened the vehicle door for her.

"That's real nice," she said, but he could practically see her slipping back into her coating of condescension and the moment when he thought he could say things like that to her passed right there on the sidewalk, as the late fall afternoon sunlight turned brassy and cold.

She said, "Thanks for the drinks" and "We'll see you at the meeting tomorrow" while she fished around for her keys and stuck them in the ignition and fired up the big Suburban and blasted backward into the street before lurching and wheeling forward and over the slight dip in the row, obvious now in more shadow, and then past the buildings and off into the empty distance surrounding town.

* * *

If the previous meeting had been a dog and pony show, the Friday night school board special session, held again in the gym, was an angry circus. People had come from neighboring communities, starving for entertainment. By now Dumont had had time to settle into camps. Rumors had multiplied and whether anybody knew what really happened on the bus, everybody thought they did.

The meeting was called for 7:00 p.m. An hour earlier, Marlo met with the school board *in camera*, in the teacher's lounge again. She presented the findings of her interviews with the kids and made her recommendations.

"I want to know," the second woman on the board, Amy Sibra, said, "if there was sexual abuse involved or not. And if there was, I want to know exactly who did what."

Marlo's report had not been crystal clear on that point, she knew, but her vagueness had been deliberate. "I can't say for sure, Mrs. Sibra, if a sexual assault occurred. The testimony was inconsistent. But that's not my purview. That's a question to be answered by trained investigators and maybe jury. Our job is to determine if something inappropriate happened, if it threatened—and that's a key word, 'threatened'—the safety and well-being of the kids on that bus, who we're in charge of when they're in school activities. And, if there was a threat, we're charged with defining what an appropriate punishment might be."

"I'm the mother of four children in this school system," Amy Sibra said, "and I don't know how any of you can look me in the eye and tell me my children are going to be safe from something like this happening again on a school bus."

"That's an issue," Marlo said. She took another long look at Amy, noticing her crossed legs and the foot rapidly tapping the air like a metronome for some long-buried neuroses. She couldn't remember Amy being so animated in the first meeting. Marlo turned to Brad Martin. "Anybody want to address it?"

"You've got four kids in school, Amy," Brad, who seemed put out by having to argue his points, said, "Has anything ever happened to any of them?"

"Not yet," Amy shot back. "But I wouldn't let my eighth-grader get on a bus with your son."

"That's bullshit," Brad said, sudden anger whipping his words. "That's unfuckingcalled for. My boy's as good and decent a kid as there is in this whole goddamned town. What has happened to you people? All of a sudden I'm surrounded by a bunch of snowflakes. "

"Snowflake!" Dotty Lantner said. Marlo thought she might come out of her chair. "I've never been a goddamned liberal in my life."

"Well, you're sure acting like one."

Dotty pinched her cigarette between two fingers and jabbed at Brad. "Don't you ever make a personal attack at me like that, Brad Martin. Don't you ever!"

A fraught silence held the room still. Marlo was afraid to break it. Here, she thought, was a bloc coalescing. There was Brad Martin and the truck driver, Josh Danreuther, on the other side. Nathan Merrill was going to be the swing vote, and he was keeping his mouth shut, watching with interest how Brad answered the questions.

Dotty muttered, "Goddamned snowflake. Jesus. I don't want kids to get raped on the school bus, and now I'm a liberal."

"Nobody got raped on the school bus," Brad said. "That's not what we're talking about."

"It is what we're talking about," Amy said. "You just aren't listening."

"Oh you fu . . . you women, I see what's happening," Brad said. "You got together and clucked like a bunch of hens and now you're going to take it out on those boys. Because you"—he pointed at Dotty—"are still pissed about your nephew who couldn't get his fat lard ass off the bench and onto the field, and you"—the finger swinging to Amy—"are stupid enough to let her talk you into it. That's fucking great."

"Brad, uh, you're letting this get a little personal," Marlo said. "It's inappropriate."

"And you're siding with them. Woman power. Beautiful. You all are just beautiful."

"Well, aren't you a whole mouthful of nothin'?" Dotty said, looking right at Brad.

Marlo saw Brad make the slightest lurch, but he said nothing more. "Okay, maybe we all take a deep breath. Relax. Step back," she said. "There are some things we don't know . . ."

Brad interrupted her. "If I cared about all the things you don't know in the world, I'd die of a broken heart."

"Brad!" Marlo said harshly. "We hear you. We have business and we have decisions and you don't have to like any of us, but you have to help us reach these decisions. Got it? Business now."

For the next forty minutes, Marlo managed to guide the conversation through a series of questions designed to point the group toward decisions. But by seven o'clock, the voting blocs had settled into hunched silences, Nathan Merrill had said nothing to tip his hand, and when they filed out of the room, Marlo had no idea how the public meeting would turn out. It was exciting, she thought, but, like all exciting things, a little bit terrifying.

* * *

By the time Josie arrived at the gym with her parents, two camera crews lit small circles where reporters did stand-ups and tried to snag interviews. But the citizenry of Dumont was more reluctant to talk on camera now. Even the school kids, some of whom could not contain their desire to be on TV, spoke with a measured sense of what people should know about their town. Again, Josie sat with Matt and Jared.

Her parents sat in the same row, on the other side of Jared. The Brunners sat on the bench right behind Matt. On the floor, Brad Martin opened the meeting by saying they were here to discuss what had happened on the school bus last Saturday and to determine if any punishment should be handed out. The way he said punishment pumped up Brad's faction in the stands. Josie could feel the energy roll through. She heard Gary Brunner say, loudly enough for anybody to hear, "That's bullshit." Her own father looked at her, his eyes beseeching, as if to ask, do you see what's right here?

But she didn't. Josie felt more confused than ever. She wanted it to be okay for her brother and for Matt. But if the school board all turned to her and said, "Josie Frehse, you cast the final vote—what do you say?" she could not say. Beyond certain leanings she could have already guessed, nothing seemed apparent. Is this, she wondered, how important decisions always get made? What happened to decisive leaders? Where were Louis Riel and Gabriel Dumont when you needed them?

Dotty Lantner said, "Let's go, Brad."

Brad looked at her. It was clear he didn't want to go. He wanted to work the crowd some more.

"Right now we're going to open the meeting to public comment before voting, so if any of you have any comments on the information that you know nothing about," Brad said, "please come forward and express your valid opinions."

Josie could see what he was doing, but also saw how it failed. She wondered if Matt or Jared would go down and take the microphone. A few football boosters stepped up and talked about the players and what good kids they were. Carson Hovland's father stood up and said, "These kids have a chance to make history, to win a state championship. Don't take that away from them. You know me. I've never been big into athletics or anything like that until my son got involved. But I've seen what it's done for him. It's done a lot of good. It's built his character. He didn't have nothing to do with what happened. Why would you take something so great away from him?"

The next speaker, a football mother, said, "These are our boys. Our boys from our town. You know these boys. Sure, they got up to some shenanigans, like boys do. But they're good boys. I'd let any of them take my daughter out on a date. Why are we going to punish these kids? Why aren't we punishing the kids coming off that reservation who are selling dope and stealing and causing real trouble?" This brought whoops and a round of applause.

The last speaker surprised Josie. It was Jenny Calhoun, whom Josie had never known to involve herself in anything that required taking sides. She had small children, still in grade school, a boy and a girl, Josie remembered. She noticed how the room fell silent for Jenny. "One last thing I want you to think about," Jenny said talking directly to the board members. "What if that had been a girl on the bus last Saturday night? What if those boys had taken one of your daughters or granddaughters or nieces and taped her up so she couldn't struggle, and then did these things to her? How many of you would be defending what happened then? That's all I want to ask you to think about."

Jenny walked away from the mic and out one of the side doors as if she was leaving the building. Maybe she did. She left a sudden chill behind her. All along Josie had been able to frame the question in terms of boys and what boys expected. She knew boys did things she would never understand. But what if it had been Britnee Mattoon taped to the rack, with her pants down . . . what if it had been herself?

Was it so different, the way boys could horse around with each other—always a big joke, according to them—and the way they could approach girls with the same stuff? Josie had to recall the first time she had had sex with Matt—her first time—and was reminded that only the loosest definition of approval would apply to what had happened. Matt was so much stronger than her, and he took what he wanted. She had known it would be coming, had even thought of him as the boy who it would happen with, but it was not at all the way she wanted it to happen. She had said no—though she had said no to a number of things along the way and never complained after—and had told him very clearly the way she wanted it to happen. But he had done what he wanted in the end.

Which made it hard to hold Matt's hand anymore. She wanted to. Yes, Matt had not been perfect, but he was what she had so far. He was not what she would have forever. She knew that now. She would leave, go off to college, become someone different, a woman who wore professional clothes. A woman who could wade into a gym full of hostility and ask people if they would talk for the camera.

She believed that more than she had believed anything in her life. Josie counted on her life to change, prayed for her life to change, for the world to be different than everything she had known so far, different from the wind-driven dust in her teeth, different from driving trucks during harvest, different than watching boys shoot rattlesnakes and gophers and whoop when one of them dissolved in a pink mist.

But Matt seemed pretty determined to stay who he was. On the floor in front of her, things started happening quickly. Brad Martin said her boyfriend's name. The school board voted. By a count of 3–2, Matt Brunner was suspended from extracurricular activities for the remainder of the school year. Waylon Edwards was suspended from school activities for the year.

Then Brad said, "Somebody else is going to have to do the next part. I'm a parent," and he left the mic and walked into the audience and sat down beside his wife and son and daughter.

Nobody seemed to know what to do. The board members looked at each other. Nathan Merrill leaned forward and looked down the row at Dotty Lantner. Dotty twirled her hand as if to say, "I guess . . ." and went to the mic.

"Our last order of business tonight concerns Alex Martin."

In the audience, Brad Martin stood and said, "Just so you know, I've talked to some parents." He looked up toward the Brunners and Frehses. "We're prepared to file a suit for damages over this."

"That's interesting, Brad," Dotty said. "Thank you for sharing."

Some laughs tittered through the audience, many met by scowls. Dotty Lantner tallied the votes. "With board chair Brad Martin abstaining, the vote is 3–1 to suspend Alex Martin from school-sanctioned extracurricular activities for the rest of the school year."

Matt had pulled himself away from Josie without really making a move. She knew what was next, how quickly he would grow isolate and inviolate, and then how he would come back to her—hurt that she hadn't cared enough to puncture his insular bubble. It was her job to stand aside for a while, until he was ready.

So she let him pull away from her and stand up with his parents and leave. She couldn't believe how quietly the full gymnasium emptied. The reporters chattered animatedly at their cameras, but everybody else just shuffled out the door.

So that was that.

* * *

Tom had stood in one of the doorways and watched the proceedings. Jenny had talked about getting a sitter and coming to his house tonight, but he had put her off, telling her he wanted to come to this meeting. He hadn't wanted to call attention to his presence, so lurked a bit in the shadows. He wasn't sure why he had come—to find out what happened to his players, or because he wondered what Marlo Stark would do afterward, or to avoid the talk with Jenny.

He'd been surprised when Jenny arrived at the meeting, stood up, and spoke. He'd liked what she said, and wanted to tell her so, but she walked right out and left afterward. He didn't even know if she'd seen him. Tom was less surprised that the boys were suspended.

Or he thought that was the right thing, but was mildly surprised that a board made up of Dumont residents had actually done it. All along Tom had felt like, with this one, a line had been crossed. He suddenly felt aware of lines all around him, crossed or waiting to be.

Now the crowd flowed out of the gym and Tom couldn't stay where he had been, in the doorway, without attracting notice, so he dropped back into the parking lot. He saw Marlo's vehicle and lingered near it, trying not to meet anybody coming from the meeting, though plenty of people moved past him and nodded. One man even grasped Tom's shoulder and upper arm as he walked by and said, "Sorry it turned out this way."

He stood in the night seeing far in the distance the low line of mountains, polished a cold white under the moon. He watched his breath float away in frosty patches, lifting toward the stars, and then Marlo walked out of the building, by herself. She carried her briefcase and walked straight to her rig, not slowing when she saw him standing there. She opened the door and swung her briefcase onto the passenger seat, then backed out and turned to face Tom.

"Tough night," she said.

Tom looked at her, trying to see what was there for him.

"I'm heading back to Great Falls," she said.

"Tonight? That sounds like an unsafe idea."

"It's just time." She stepped forward, put a hand on his shoulder, touching him but at the same time creating a barrier against his coming any closer. "It was really great getting to know you. I wish the circumstances were different . . ." She waved a hand vaguely at the school building she had just walked out of. "I wish you a lot of luck, sorting everything out."

"Thanks," he said. "I liked getting to know you, too."

"I'm sure I'll be back," she said. "I need to go now."

Marlo ducked into the vehicle and closed the door. She looked at him through the window as she backed out, smiling, but offered no finger wave this time. She seemed, he thought, very happy to be getting on the road.

* * *

Tom went to the field on Saturday because he wanted his players to know that he cared about them. He wanted to support Slab Rideg. He did not want to pout. He didn't need to be noble, but he didn't think he could deal with his own petulance. *Just a week ago*, he thought while he walked among the people already gathering at the field, the boys' red helmets shining in the sunlight.

The day was bright, a problem in that the snow from the blizzard had begun to melt in earnest. The front had been a fast moving storm, and behind it came chinook winds. Jimmy Krock had driven an ATV-mounted snow blower to clear the field early in the morning, while the snow was still light enough to move, but what he missed melted to mud. That late in the fall, hardly any grass remained in the middle of the field.

By game time, the sidelines were slop pits. The girls taking money at the gate were confused about whether to charge Tom or not, but he handed them a five and didn't wait for his dollar change. He had arrived a little early, watched the team warming up. Tom strode to the border of yellow twine staked around the sidelines and waited until he caught Slab Rideg's eye. Slab said something to his last remaining team captain, Jared Frehse—telling him, probably, to run the calisthenics—and then walked on a beeline to where Tom stood. Tom thrust out his hand. When Slab grabbed it, Tom could feel the new dynamic in his grip.

"Coach," Tom said. He meant to smile broadly.

"Coach," Slab said.

Standing there, Tom realized he hadn't talked to Slab much while everything unwound. Now he felt badly about that.

"I'm sorry this got to where it is the way it did," Tom said.

"We gotta play out the string," Slab said.

"I wish I could be with you."

"I do, too, Coach. I really do." Tom felt Slab's hand grip his more tightly. "Means a lot, you coming."

"Paste their asses," Tom said.

He swatted Slab on the shoulder, let go of his hand, turned and walked down the sidelines. Behind him he heard Slab say, "Glad you came, Coach. Hope you enjoy the show."

The Absarokee team had driven eight hours to make the game, starting some time the night before and spending the night in Lewistown on the way. They played like it at first. On Dumont's opening play from scrimmage, a toss sweep, Jared Frehse outran everyone to the corner, then to the goal line. Cheerleaders chanted and leapt. The crowd, larger and more vociferous than Tom had ever seen in this town, erupted in a sustained and somewhat savage bout of satisfaction.

But Dumont's problem was the missing players. No Matt Brunner and Alex Martin in the defensive backfield, no Waylon Edwards to blow up the line and bring pressure up front. Jared was able to cover Absarokee's best receiver. Carson Hovland was athletic enough to range around, but he was nervous in his first start as a defensive back. Absarokee had not made the playoffs by being shabby. They were well-coached, had a smart quarterback, and knew how to pick on the youngsters. They marched down the field and scored on their first possession.

Tom stood along the field, behind the yellow rope, and watched as the teams traded punches. Dumont's second possession lasted six plays before Jared Frehse scampered through a hole, cut against the grain, and sprinted down the left sideline for a score.

On the third series it became clear that Absarokee didn't believe Dumont's new quarterback, a sophomore named Johnny Baken, could throw the ball. They crowded the line and blitzed and blitzed. They followed Jared Frehse wherever he went on offense. Jared found angles and corners, made cuts, broke tackles. He scored on their third and fourth possessions, but it was wearing on him.

He was doing hard work. And Absarokee answered, throwing and running, matching Dumont touchdown for touchdown. Tom had never watched a game he cared so much about without being involved in the outcome. Knowing so much about the players, watching the linemen, the Hansen kid, knowing their flaws and vulnerabilities—he thought this must be what punishment that fit the crime felt like.

And then Tom saw something that made a broad, genuine smile spread across his lips, a subtle thing he understood before the rest of the crowd did. Slab had been thinking. Slab knew that Absarokee was going to load up on Jared and Slab had schemed for it. On Dumont's fifth possession, Slab had his new young quarterback, Johnny Baken, fake an off-tackle handoff to Frehse, keep the ball and sprint around the end. The defense collapsed on Jared. Tom and Slab knew Baken could run. He wasn't Jared Frehse.

But he could hoof it, and with so much green in front of him, he rolled easily for the score. That was the half, and Dumont went into the locker room leading 35–28. Tom watched the crowd after the kids left the field. He'd never been around for this part of it, the cheerleaders, the eight-person marching band. The trumpet player wore gloves. All of their breaths steamed around their instruments. Tom couldn't imagine putting his lips to a cold brass mouthpiece today. He strolled along the sideline, not sure where he was headed.

He spotted Brad Martin standing in a tight group with three other men. Brad stood with both hands shoved deep in his pockets. The other two seemed to take turns staring at everyone and kicking the ground. The cheerleaders wore jeans under their skirts against the cold. People moved about, momentary groups forming as neighbors said hellos and discussed what they were seeing and which of them understood the weather forecast better. Tom nearly walked up on Dotty Lantner, wearing a Dumont cap under a Carhartt hoodie, before he recognized her.

"Tom," she said.

"Dotty," he said.

"I'm supporting these boys," she said, like he'd accused her of not doing it.

"See that."

"Slab's making chicken shit into chicken salad."

"He's doing good."

"I hope we win," she said. "I hope you know that."

"I do," he said. "I hope we win, too."

He kept strolling. A skein of five young boys threw a football around, chasing whichever of them caught it and tackling him in the muddy snow. One rose from the ground, his front smeared with mud, clenched his fists, and raised them to the sky. They'd apparently not got the memo about football, Tom thought. He had turned and started back to his post at the far end zone when he saw Krock O' step out toward him.

"Slab's got 'em going," Krock O' said.

"Helluva job," Tom said.

"Killing ya?"

"Honestly? Yeah."

"Helluva thing." Krock O' looked up at the sky, then around the field. Tom did too, the field and empty hole in the circle of people, now that the cheerleaders and band were gone. He looked beyond, to the fields racing away to the horizon. This place was so full of noise—the asynchronous and off-key band with its tuba farting loudly every time the player caught his breath, the hum and brabble of jazzed-up folks. Out there, beyond their thin ring, the land circled for miles, soundless in the horrible silence of beautiful places. Then Cal Frehse moseyed over to where they stood.

"Tom," he said, like it was nothing.

"Jared's doing great," Tom said.

"He's trying."

"How's you?" Krock O' asked.

"Oh shit, I'm fine. I don't think Gary Brunner is, though."

"Why's that?" Tom asked.

"He missed the spike pretty good on spring wheat, and he needed to hit it."

"Did it peak?" Krock O' asked.

"Christ, it's falling off a cliff now. I sold lower than I would have liked, but higher than it is now. Some people are gonna lose their ass, and I don't think he's got much ass left to lose."

"That's a goddamned shame," Krock O' said.

Then Greg Hovland appeared and Cal said, "You get that buck?"

"I'm leaving him for Carson."

"Jared said he's huge."

"It's like he's carrying a pipe rack on his head. Just enormous god-damned horns. Biggest mulie buck I've ever seen around our place."

Was this, Tom wondered, what people talked about at football games? But why wouldn't it be? Some of these people, Tom realized, lived on adjacent farms but probably didn't see each other more than once or twice a week. The ones who lived north of town might not see the ones who lived south of town for a month at a time. The Absarokee fans stood along their sideline, an impressive contingent of sixty to a hundred folks who had made the long drive. Likely they were discussing similar subjects, and maybe comparing this landscape to their mountainous one.

Tom felt surprised by how friendly this all looked. Like a county fairgrounds, or a small outdoor concert. Coaching, during the game, he was always so focused forward, always thinking about hitting and tackling and outrunning, angles and plays and players and ways to make them all work better. He never saw these handshakes and elbow pokes and shoulder claps and small conversations that had nothing to do with football.

But would it kill them to pay a little tribute to the effort their boys were pouring out all over the field? Shortly after the boys came back, it was apparent that halftime hadn't been enough. Jared Frehse started getting caught from behind. Slab introduced a new wrinkle: he let the new quarterback throw. And there, Tom

thought, Slab out-kicked his coverage. Johnny Baken was a sophomore and played like one.

He threw a pick-six on Dumont's second possession in the
third quarter. The next time Dumont had the ball, Baken got
sacked on second down and on third tried a long out that he
didn't have the arm for. It bounced. Dumont managed to capi-
talize on Absarokee mistakes in the next series. The Hansen kid
stuffed a fourth-and-short attempt. Tom knew Slab would have
to go back to Jared, but he knew the Absarokee coach knew
that, too.

But Slab adjusted. He had Baken fake to Jared up the middle,
then ran off tackle for thirty yards. Then Baken dropped back to
throw and instead ran a draw—twenty more yards and a first and
goal. Three plays later Frehse found enough wiggle room to score.
Dumont missed the extra point. They entered the fourth quarter
trailing Absarokee 49–48.

During the break between quarters Tom observed the boys he'd
taught to play football. He saw the twenty-six-year-old coach he
had mentored, his face a knotted red scowl, his chin bouncing as
he exhorted his players. Tom saw the Hansen kid, the boy people
had given him shit about all year long, saw his uniform mudstained
and torn, the blood trickling on his forearms, steam pouring off his
unhelmeted head. Carson Hovland had been beaten and beaten
and beaten on long passes, but kept at it, kept going, kept trying
to finish the job, and had made a couple big defensive plays that
affected the game. Jared Frehse—Tom didn't think he'd ever seen
such heart. By the fourth quarter the field was a black mud pit.

There was nothing to do about it. Jared's speed was dulled by
slipping. Absarokee's passing game suffered from receivers sliding through cuts, and the wet, sloppy ball. Absarokee threw two
incomplete passes to open the quarter and then a long touchdown
that left Carson Hovland reeling to catch up and Dumont trailed
by eight. That's when Slab surrendered.

He quit trying to outthink anybody and started running the play the boys called "Six." He ran it three straight times, Jared sprinting around the corner and picking up yards on each play. Then he let Johnny Baken throw it again, but the young quarterback threw it behind a wide-open Carson Hovland. Slab called the Six play again. Jared took the pitch and bolted for the corner. Tom caught the way he high-stepped a bit, the overwrought head bobbing. Jared was selling something.

The Absarokee defensive end was buying, hustling like mad to beat Jared to the corner. Then Jared cut upfield inside him. He had the kid beat. But Jared's plant foot slipped in the mud and he found himself straddled over cleats that were splitting far apart from each other. He put his hand down to stop himself, and while he hovered there, defenseless, the defensive lineman found his bearings and blasted him. Jared hung onto the ball, but came out of the game.

The kids always said when someone got hit that hard they'd have cartoon X's for eyeballs. On the next play there was no decoy. Johnny Baken dropped back to throw the ball, and it was exactly what Absarokee anticipated. Absarokee defenders dropped back into coverage. But Slab was faking again. Baken took off on a planned run. The receivers blocked.

Baken ran into open field, but this, Tom knew, would eventually happen: Johnny Baken was a sophomore and he would play like one. He ran down the field with the football gripped in one hand like a cheeseburger. The Absarokee safety lunged, swiped, and swatted the ball loose. An Absarokee player trailing the play landed on it. Absarokee scored three plays later to take a 63–48 lead.

Jared Frehse returned to the game to field the ensuing kickoff. He caught the ball, ran five yards, got hit, seemed to be going down, but the contact spun him completely around. Unspiraling, taking several steps forward with a hand jabbing down to keeping him from torpedoing into the ground, Jared managed to get over his feet and ran straight up the wide-open field to score. Dumont converted for two points.

Now they trailed by seven. Tom found himself wishing for the things that he knew would not happen—a late-game fumble, an interception. He watched the Absarokee coach, and old adversary and friend, take time off the clock, running up the middle, picking up first downs with quick outs when he needed to. The afternoon waned.

It seemed to happen quickly. Light slipped like hope from the sky. The pickup trucks surrounding the field switched their headlights on. The home crowd voice seemed to grow hoarse, or just lost. Absarokee had a first down on Dumont's fifteen-yard line. Tom watched Jared Frehse standing with his hands on his hips, chin on his chest, staring at the ground, breathing with his mouth open. He saw Carson Hovland line up over his receiver, fingers curling into fists and springing open again. Johnny Baken was too close to the line of scrimmage. Tom could see that if Absarokee called the right play, Dumont was burned.

He nearly ran onto the field, screaming, *Time out!*—before he remembered he couldn't anymore. He nearly yelled at Slab to call time out. But he'd given up that right. Then Absarokee snapped the ball. The entire Dumont defense blitzed.

Everybody. Tom couldn't believe it. It was either the boldest or the craziest call he'd ever seen a coach make. The linebackers did beautiful, ballet-like stunts where they each took a step back and then looped into each other's places, causing confused offensive linemen to lunge and miss. The whole Dumont defensive backfield charged. All the Absarokee quarterback had to do was stay cool. All he had to do was keep his feet settled and light.

All he had to do was float one pass into the darkening blue of sky. Toward anybody. There were no defenders in coverage. His receivers were wide open with clear shots to the end zone. The Absarokee quarterback was an athletic small-town high school kid with a decent enough arm. But he was no football genius.

And when he saw crimson and blue jerseys pouring through the line, sprinting from the corners, he panicked and tried to scramble from the pocket. He sprinted directly into the path of a hard-charging Carson Hovland. He tried to throw it at the last second.

Hovland hit him and Jared Frehse hit him at almost the exact same moment. The quarterback's throwing motion continued, fractured, even as he fell backward, and the ball sailed up almost straight into the air. Johnny Baken caught it and was smart enough to fall on it. Or he was falling already.

Either way, the crowd erupted again and Dumont had the ball. They had sixty-five yards to cover and less than two minutes to cover it, but they had done something every coach everywhere wanted their kids to do. They'd not given up.

They'd believed in the chances their efforts could bring them. Dumont ran the Six on their first play. Jared Frehse made his cut and somehow managed to run twenty yards before being dragged down from behind. Tom was ecstatic. He'd never seen Jared caught from behind, but he'd never seen one player exert so much will during one game. Slab pulled Jared for a play, called a quick out that Johnny Baken overthrew. Jared returned as a decoy, which let Johnny Baken run for nine more yards.

On the next play, Slab called the Six again, Jared taking the ball on the pitch, sprinting to the corner. He faked an inside cut and froze the defensive end, then ran around him to the outside.

The far-side safety closed on an angle. Jared held a stiff arm out, caught the safety's helmet with his hand, and shoved. The safety's head bent back and he skidded onto the mud. But this was the kind of thing that happened on muddy days with high school kids, the kind of thing that defined coaching careers: the Absarokee safety slapped one of Jared's feet.

On a dry field, if he hadn't run for over two hundred yards already, if he weren't playing on sheer will, Jared might have recovered—Tom had seen him do it probably a hundred times.

But on this field, on this day, when he staggered to try to stay upright, Jared's right foot clipped his left and slipped when it found the ground. Then his left foot slid out from under him, and he was going down. He held the ball out, lunging for the goal line. The ground gave him nothing. He fell flat.

And this, Tom saw, was how you lose. Jared had gained enough yardage for a first down, which stopped the clock. They had one more shot from sixteen yards out. Tom looked at Jared, his fingers interlaced on top of his helmet, mouth agape, a sort of shock on his face that it wasn't over yet. Tom thought: *What a beautiful football player*. He had no idea what kind of life Jared would one day have.

He didn't know if Jared would even play for a college team. But here, in this season and in this game, Jared Frehse had played harder and better and more beautifully than anything Tom had ever seen.

Exhausted, probably injured, Jared had formed on this field a piece of the man he would someday be. Before the game ended, Tom understood it. He hoped Jared would one day, and that it wouldn't take him too long, wouldn't ruin too many other things before he figured out how he had done it. Johnny Baken walked from the huddle to his spot under center, his feet crossing over each other like a drunk's.

On the sideline, Slab Rideg's hands extended in front of his chest like he was trying to grasp an unreasonably heavy invisible object. Tom could see him trying to say something—the right thing—and confounding himself to silence. Down the sideline from Tom, Brad Martin stood with his arms folded across his chest, silently furious about everything in front of him. Tom's eyes slid to the field, patches of yellow mostly submerged by dark mud, the center of the field churned. He wished he could feel it on his feet.

So much of his life had happened with field grass under his feet, green grass, white lines. But he could clearly see his distance from this field, the dozen or so steps he would have to take just to reach the Dumont sideline. Open space he was no longer able to cover.

He heard Baken bark under center. Heard that clatter of pads and the grunts of effort. Baken pitched the ball to Jared, the play everybody knew was coming. The whole Absarokee defense knew it was coming and sold out to attack Jared. Jared made a ridiculous jump-cut toward the edge. Tom couldn't believe the kid still had enough leg strength, but that's what Jared always did—headed in one direction and then suddenly bounced out, landing in a different spot, on a different vector than anybody could have anticipated, usually with nobody near him.

This time four Absarokee players drove toward him. Jared fought like a wild animal, throwing them off with his arms, gnashing the ground with his legs. Then a fifth and sixth Absarokee defender crashed into the pile. Jared would not go down, his legs driving. He bucked and twisted and thrashed, but the pile of Absarokee defenders shoved him backward into his own backfield and then the whistles started blowing, Jared still on his feet, still trying to charge even as he was thrust backward, and the whistle blew enough that the Absarokee players let go of him and ran across the field with their arms upraised and Jared, finally unencumbered, quit trying to run and tossed the ball aside and turned and ripped his chin strap loose and started walking the other way down the field , and it was over.

The game was over and Jared's career with the Wolfpack was over and Tom watched him walking away from something he'd known a long, long time. For a stretched moment, Tom heard the sudden quiet of the afternoon, even though it was quickly broken by a scattering of cheers that seemed far away. Across what seemed like an ocean of field, a group of Absarokee fans jumped and screamed and held onto each other and shouted. The Absarokee players, looking so small, like miniatures of football players, raced onto the field and fell all over themselves. But then Tom heard something different, a deeper, stronger note.

The Dumont fans were all staying put, all on their feet, clapping hard and shouting. Some men stuck their fingers between their teeth and loosed long, shrieking whistles. On the small section of wooden bleachers, people stomped their feet. Very quickly, the sound of the Dumont fans drowned out that of Absarokee's victory shrieks. Tom turned and saw ranchers and farmers staring at the field and risking their stoic faces, risking wet eyes. Mothers pressed their lips together and let tears stream down their cheeks. Tom watched Slab Rideg walk across the field, hand outstretched.

The Absarokee coach ignored the hand and wrapped Slab in a two-armed hug. The two men stood like that together for a moment, and Tom could see the Absarokee coach talking with animation into Slab's ears, saw the Absarokee coach swat Slab on the ass with his laminated play sheet, and heard, as Slab turned and came back to his team, the crowd thundering louder, a step-change that made even Jared Frehse pull his head from his hands and regard the scene in front of him. Dumont was celebrating its children.

Tom felt himself slip even deeper into the world he'd chosen to inhabit, the world of guts and effort and choices. He realized he was pounding his hands together so hard they hurt, stinging right down to the bones. He had not, he knew from the pangs he felt swelling into his chest, completely lost them. They were still his boys, too.

* * *

The party Saturday night took place at the Martins', a split-level ranch on three acres of knoll just far enough from town to look down on it. What mattered most to the boys were the Xbox and HDTV sets in the finished basement rec room. Alex Martin, Matt Brunner, and Waylon Edwards had been rotating turns on the Xbox and drinking beer, swapping barbs about each other's relative lack of abilities in video gaming. They had stolen the beer several months earlier from a train car that had stopped to load grain at the elevator.

The train had idled overnight at the elevator siding and Waylon Edwards had spent some time after dark crawling around among the boxcars. When he was able to slip into a gap left by a loose locking mechanism and noticed the bounty of craft from the micro-brewery in Great Falls, Waylon had quickly called Matt and Alex and Jared, and the four of them had spent several hours in the middle of the night offloading cases and shuttling them in pickups to an abandoned homesteader shack twenty miles north of town where, in better weather, they hung out and shot gophers.

They had stolen almost sixty cases of beer, lifting them from the middle of the car so that, at a casual glance from the outside, there had been no apparent molestation of the cargo. They'd stacked hay bales around the beer and covered it in blankets against the cold. The great train robbery had occurred in early August and they had been enjoying the beer in select moments, rationing it, ever since. Though it was an open secret at the high school that the booty existed—even its whereabouts were broadly known—nobody seemed interested in stealing from the thieves, who were anyway fairly liberal about distribution of their product.

The boys had thirty cases left, and this Saturday afternoon seemed like the kind of day that hijacked beer was made for. Though many bottles had exploded during the cold snap, the bales and blankets protected enough for one last party. The boys spent a great deal of time drinking it and playing Madden and comparing themselves to the artificial players on the screen.

"Can't stop talent," Alex Martin said, as his avatar juked around Matt's and scored.

"But you can outwork it," Waylon said, a crude imitation mocking the source of the sentiment, Coach Warner.

"Warner is rearview mirror, dude," Matt said. "I just want to forget I ever saw that bastard's sad face. It's hoops season now."

Matt had called Josie to come over, and she had said she would later. Ainsley Martin and Britnee Mattoon were also coming, and anybody else they told who wanted to. Cell phones were deployed. Even as they sat, word was sizzling around town. Alex and Ainsley's parents had planned to watch the playoff game and then were off to Missoula for several days to visit relatives.

"You pissed at Coach?" Waylon asked.

"Fuck Coach," Matt spit back. "Guy ruined my fucking career."

"That was a hell of a lot of work," Alex Martin said, "just to be over."

"We were gonna win, too," Matt said. "We were gonna crush Wibaux . . ."

"They almost beat Absarokee without any of us," Alex said.

". . . and then we were gonna beat Drummond. We could have gone anywhere we wanted, after that."

"And we don't even get to try," Alex said. "Because of such a stupid reason."

"I don't hold nothing against Wyatt," Matt said. "What's fun is fun, you know. It's not his fault. But Coach Warner, man, he sold us out."

"And he *played*," Alex said, as if this were the crowning stupidity. "He did the same shit. I *know* he did. Things aren't that different in Winnett or Jordan, or whatever butt town he's from. He did everything we did."

"Warner sucks," Matt agreed.

"The whole school sucks," Alex said. "That shitbag Dotty Lantner—like she doesn't have something to prove because somebody gave her nephew a browneye last year."

"That was Pete Dodd that gave him the browneye," Waylon said. "I remember that. I was laying low, afraid they were coming for me next."

"Pud?" Alex said.

Matt barked out a laugh. "Ol' Pud couldn't put the brakes on in time."

They all laughed.

"That was one of the nastiest things I've ever seen," Waylon said.

"He browneyed me the year before," Alex said. "Kept it tucked, though."

"Cost us our season, boys," Matt said. "Right there—Pete Dodd and his untucked sphincter."

They all looked at each other, unable to decide what to make of it. "That'd be really funny if it wasn't true," Alex said.

"True doesn't make it not funny," Matt said, "No use warming beer about it." He scooted his bottle over his head, upended it, and drained the contents into his open mouth, swallowing hard to keep up. Some of the beer spilled over his cheeks, but most of it went down his throat. He belched explosively, wiped the back of his forearm across his mouth, and left in its wake a broad, beaming grin. Matt looked ready to will himself to say to hell with it all, an old trick.

* * *

Mikie LaValle was sitting in his room, staring at his computer screen. His avatar had just reached a new level, and while in the past this sort of feat of virtual derring-do had made playing the game what it was, now it felt less than thrilling. The truth was Mikie had once spent most of his time playing World of Warcraft and he still did, but not with quite the verve. The funny thing that had happened to Mikie LaValle was an awareness that what went on around him wouldn't go away when he escaped into the cyber void any longer.

Like many confused teenagers before him, Mikie had taken refuge in books, usually fantastic novels involving outrageous fortune and vengeance, not unlike the video games he played. But as of quite recently his fascination turned to history—specifically the history of the Metis people, the Riel Rebellion and Gabriel Dumont. The county library was predictably short on books about the Metis, but Mikie had borrowed books from Coach Warner and immersed himself. And yet even the fascination with a lost people—a culture of relatively recent invention, created by the clash of Indian and white blood he felt coursing through his veins—could not distract him from something that was becoming painfully, painfully obvious.

He could not stop thinking about Josie Frehse. So on a cold Saturday afternoon in November, Mikie's attention drifted from Warcraft. He thought for a little while about why she was so nice to him, nicer than anybody else in school was. He wondered what that could possibly mean for him. Did she like him? There was no way she was going to dump Matt Brunner because she liked him. But Brunner had done some dumb things now—not any dumber than a whole litany of experiences Mikie had with Matt, he thought, but dumb in the eyes of public opinion, even the eyes of jock-crazed Dumont—and maybe that made Josie reconsider.

And maybe in the reconsidering, she would consider him, and maybe . . . and soon he found himself drifting off to imaginings about how Josie would come to him and tell him that she'd been thinking a lot about him and how she wanted to try it with him, and see what it would be like. And in a not too sluggardly pace, those imaginings became infiltrated by adolescent hormones and flourished with lust. The fact that he had never actually done the things he began to envision doing with Josie made playing out the fantasy difficult, so he concentrated on a few words from her, a few reactions he ascribed to her.

Soon this was not enough, and he wanted to hear her voice, although that could be a delicate risk. If she did not talk to him in the sweet, approving and somewhat longing voice he imagined for her, his day would begin to pool. He knew this from other experiences of having fantasized about how she was starting to like him, how she was wanting to be with him, and then actually talking to her only to find out that Josie was not spending a lot of her time imagining their life together.

Or any. That reality was dousing, although it turned out that if she was only nice to him, only sweet and seemingly interested in what he was talking about, he could find enough lift to refuel his ravenous needs. Mikie tried DMing her to see if she was online, but then remembered the game and that afterward Josie cleaned the church on Saturdays. She would be around, somewhere. He tried texting her, a simple 'Sup?

Cleaning 4 god, she texted back, within a few seconds.

L8ter?

Party @ Martin's. U going?

Doubt, he texted back. The truth was he hadn't known about it. Mikie went to keggers in the boonies, parties where anybody was welcome, but Martins' was the territory of a specific clique.

Next, Mikie texted Arlen Alderdice, who had already known about the party and was planning to head over with his cousin Wyatt Aarstad. Mikie begged a ride and was told to be ready in forty-five minutes. He headed for the shower.

* * *

Caroline Jensen was not accustomed to her son showering on Saturday afternoons. It was piker's work to get him interested in showering most mornings before school. So many things were happening with this boy, new and unusual behaviors that only served to clog up her sense of how their little family operated in the open, and that made her inexplicably sad. He should be growing into new social situations, and, as his mother, she should love that, feel excited for him, thrill in his expansion of the boundaries of himself. But she didn't. Because now she was pretty sure she knew who the girl was.

Because she was not Mikie's girl and would not be. Caroline knew how these things worked. Josie Frehse was a darling, a flower of the community. She belonged to Dumont, not to the characters on its fringes, not to half-breed boys that nobody knew. She was athletic and smart, not just polite but genuinely sweet. She would, in all likelihood, not stay here, because the pressure of belonging to the town would grow overbearing, and the bigger world was meant to draw girls like Josie from them, take her to huge anonymous cities, where excitement and opportunities were stacked and waiting for girls with a pretty smile and sharp mind and men who knew how to get what they wanted out of that.

If she did stay, Josie's life was so bound and wound in the lives of Brunners and Martins—and Danreuthers and Woleslagels and Alderdices and Aarstads—that she could not, Caroline knew, break from the perfectly normal expectations created by the lives of those families to form an existence with someone like Mikie. Even if she wanted to, even if she was aware enough of the way life worked, the way love lurked and lurched and the way everybody's high school romance eventually became dinner in front of the TV, even if Josie could step outside the inward-peering view of her teenaged world, and that of her friends, to lay eyes on an outsider like Mikie, Josie would never let them be happy, not in any enduring sense, not if they stayed here.

Caroline believed, too, that Mikie was in no way prepared to have a girl like Josie in his life. He fixated too sharply on things, extended too quickly and broadly his sense of ownership over those elements of his life over which he exerted some control. He would never be able to withstand the constant attention from outsiders that a girl like Josie generated wherever she went. He was, simply, too petty and jealous.

And lazy. Had she made him that way? She had to admit that sometimes when she thought about mopping the bathroom floor she thought, *Why bother, I own socks.* A defining characteristic of human behavior is imitating other humans. That's how life got done. Her role modeling must have had something to do with it—another in the thousand cuts on her heart. Mikie would always feel that he didn't measure up to a girl like Josie.

Well, he wasn't mature enough, was what Caroline came to. He was petty and jealous and controlling because he hadn't experienced enough of the world to know that those tactics would always fail him, and that, of course, was Caroline's fault, too. She hadn't exposed him to situations in which he could learn about the shortcomings of possessiveness and the undesirability of even minor rage.

He was still confusing intensity for intimacy. The night they had seen Tom Warner in Pep's, starting on the drive home, Mikie had gone into a sulk from which he'd still not emerged, not for Caroline's benefit at least. Caroline had been feeling good from the two cocktails she'd had, her eyes stimulated by the blinking of the Keno machines, her mind awhirl from talking to people who almost never talked to her. The smell of the pizza like a hot, sloppy promise had billowed from the back seat. Mikie, slunk behind the wheel while she sat intoxicated in the passenger seat, had said, "You're so stupid."

This alone would not have bothered her. But this time his tone was rinsed in acid, and he seemed to feel that her stupidity had somehow insulted him.

She remembered even now how the ominous sound of him had pinched a deep tug in her belly, the bruise from which she still felt. She had gone ahead and asked, "Why this time?"

"You think he likes you?" her son practically spat. "You're old and ugly and fat."

"What are you talking about?" Caroline had asked, feeling sharp fingers grasping a vital organ and digging in. "And watch your language."

"He doesn't like you. You go in there and throw yourself all over him like some slut . . ."

"What?"

"You're a mother, for christ's sakes," he said. "My mother, although I wish as much as you do that you weren't."

"Mike LaValle, you shut your mouth right now and think before you say any next thing."

"Then you could go out and slut it up all you want," Mikie said.

"Just shut up," she said. "Shut. The fuck. Up."

He turned his face to her as if he were going to say something even more vicious, and the expression she saw on him, the bared teeth of a beaten and terrified dog lashing out at its tormentors, chilled her. But it also rallied her self-defense mechanisms, and she reached across the seat and dug her fingers into her son's cheeks, clutching with all her strength. Then she threw his face away from her. "Not another word," she said. "You've said enough."

The violence of her reaction had seemed to impress a silence on him, letting him know both that he'd stabbed deep into her, and that he wasn't going to be allowed to get farther. Mikie sneered and stared through the windshield for the rest of the ride home. Caroline's own anger had risen, pitched and blown away quickly, leaving her again—this seemed to happen so often—sick with the knowledge that she had deeply embarrassed her son, a boy who seemed so deeply and easily embarrassed, and she wanted to know how she could avoid doing it over and over. A man like Tom Warner, she thought, would actually do wonders in the life of a boy like Mikie.

A stalwart man who could make ethical decisions and stand by them even when those decisions proved unpopular? She had wanted Mikie to understand that Tom Warner was an example— and it wouldn't hurt one bit if they had some personal interaction, to boot. Instead Mikie had chosen to cast the coach as the worst kind of threat. And, sitting in her kitchen, listening to the sound of the water pump filling the pipes to rinse her son's greasy hair, she felt another sadness that she realized she could no longer deny. Part of her had hoped that Tom Warner might notice her.

Part of her had let herself listen to Pearl Aarstad. What was she going to do about that? She was going to light another cigarette. And listen to the wind cuff the side of the trailer house.

* * *

By the time Josie Frehse arrived at the party, a half moon had risen, pale and rocked back, just above the horizon. A cadre of four kids, mostly wearing black Carhartt hoodies, huddled outside the Martins' back door, huffing cigarettes. The cold built steam onto their smoky exhalations, clouding their faces. Inside, the party had moved out of the rec room and spilled upstairs into the kitchen, where Ainsley and Britnee were watching Waylon Edwards rifle through the refrigerator.

Britnee had had at least one beer, which meant her smile became permanent, her shirt rode up to reveal more belly, and her butt was a little loose on its rack. Her voice accelerated in both velocity and amplitude. Josie said hello and exchanged chitchat. Downstairs she found a girl named Kelsey Aarstad sitting on Alex Martin's lap like she intended to keep him in his chair by sprawl. Steve Dodd and Carson Hovland had taken over the Xbox and shouted insults at each other. Two rodeo boys, who eschewed football for tests of masculinity versus large farm animals, shot a game of pool and sipped from brown bottles.

Several girls from the junior class stood together on one side of the room and watched the pool game, occasionally adding commentary. Josie saw that Matt was busy talking to a group of sophomore girls who were standing with their heads hung stupidly from the ends of their necks like cows in a tight-shirted knot.

That was her fella. All hulked up and driving under the influence of his own body language. Josie didn't love the fact that her boyfriend seemed to be volunteering as a focus for these girls, but she knew Matt's need to be at the center for what it was, and was working on her reactions to it. She liked the sophomore girls. The Merrill girl could be sloppy, and the Danreuther girl rarely said a word out loud, but they were nice. Josie remembered how she felt when she had been a sophomore and the senior boys had flirted with her, the possibilities she let herself believe then—still did sometimes when she met boys from other towns, or thought about the boys she would meet in college.

She knew those girls were looking at her fella and thinking he was all kinds of right. And everybody knew sophomore girls couldn't handle beer, which could become dramatic later. When Matt saw her, he did not step away from his adoring satellites, but rather threw his head back in greeting, said, "JF. You are far behind, girlfriend."

Josie said hello to the girls, saying each of their names. She forced a laugh and said, "Better start catching up," and walked away, over toward the cooler where the beer was iced. Josie twisted open a top and took a swig, cringing at the half-cooled hoppy flavor that flooded her mouth. She didn't like beer to start with, and these fancy beers only accentuated its drawbacks—the yeasty smell, the bitter tang.

But she knew she was going to have to drink a couple if she was going to enjoy herself with this crowd. She knew, too, from Matt's cool greeting that they were going to play a little game tonight. Matt was going to be hurt by some imperceptible slight that she had either already committed or would commit at some point during the early part of the party, and she would have to guess what it was, then make it up to him. She was sick of that game, but found herself already trying to figure out what had upset him—that she was late?

That could be it. Or maybe she was failing to understand how hard the public humiliation or the loss of football was on him, failing to be consolatory enough. And, she thought, truth be told, there might be something to that. It was a huge part of his life, and she could display a bit more sympathy than she had so far.

She could cut him some slack on that score. This was a hard day, for Matt and for her brother. For all the guys. They all seemed to be taking it well enough, but it scared her, the momentum that had built so early in the outing—it wasn't seven-thirty yet and everybody was drunk. The boys seemed to be burning energy they'd stored up for a different end to the season.

They were staying on the safe side of shits and giggles for the moment, but Josie had a sense that somebody would be crying before this night was over. Then Josie's brother arrived and an uproar commenced. Somebody yelled, "Mr. Freeze in da house!" and everybody cheered, whether they knew what they were cheering about or not. The seniors and Waylon surrounded Jared in a swarm of ritual bro-hugs and drunken assertions about how awesome Jared had been.

He had been awesome, Josie thought. She was proud to be his sister at this moment. She watched him, appreciative but humble, his natural smile making people want to tell him more about how much they appreciated what he'd just done. Josie slid away from Jared's big moment, swallowed a beer, and spent time talking to several schoolmates before she tried approaching Matt again. He'd grown bored of the sophomore girls and seemed to want to focus his attention on attracting more of hers. She sidled up to him and slid an arm around his waist, earning one of his looped over her shoulder.

"JF," he said. "Your brother was so fucking hero today."

"Frehse genes," she said, and shrugged. Then she whispered into his ear, "I'm really sorry about the season."

"Sucks," he said, in a chipper sort of manner.

"Well," she said, and kissed his cheek. "I'm really sorry about it. We can talk about it later if you want."

"Nothing to talk about," Matt said, then flipped to cocky. "And later I don't want to be doing much talking, if you know what I mean."

She knew what he meant, but didn't put much stock in it. She had a feeling that later she'd be lucky to get him home without assistance.

"People just take shit from you," Matt said, another sudden switch in tone. He seemed bitter now, but equally puzzled. "Like it's theirs to take. Just take away everything. Just like that. They can just take it."

"You still have a lot," she said, trying to be cheerful.

"That's a big old fat load of crap," he said. "I just got you."

"You still have a lot," she reemphasized.

He drew her to him in a jerking squeeze, and said. "Don't ever let them take you from me."

"No, sweetie. They won't," she said, being held tight, too close to his face.

"Don't let them," he said, and he seemed to be scolding her, or maybe warning her.

"Nobody's taking me from you."

"Promise?"

She had to answer quickly here. "Of course I promise," she said. That was true. Nobody would take her from him. She'd do that all by herself.

"What do you promise?"

"That nobody's going to take me away from you."

"That you're never going to leave me?"

"Matty, I'm going to leave you right now," she said and threw a big grin at him while peeling his arm from her, "and fetch me—and you—another beer. That's all the leaving I'm doing."

Matt's face pressed into a smile that showed no teeth. He looked at her as if he found her surprisingly more beautiful than he had remembered. "Goddamit, that's my girl," he said, and swatted her on the behind as she slipped away toward the cooler.

Close one, Josie thought. She didn't like to make promises unless she could make them true. Josie liked to say true things, but promises meant even more to her. She still believed you could keep them all. By the time Josie returned with Matt's beer, he was done with melancholy and love.

He had heard that Waylon was upstairs in the kitchen challenging Alex to chug-offs involving various condiments. When Josie and Matt got up there, Alex was guzzling the juice from a jar of pickles. Waylon chugged several gulps of ketchup. Alex tried salsa, but that tripped his trigger and sent him staggering to the sink, vomit spewing in sprung streams from between the fingers he had clapped over his mouth. Whooping applause followed him.

And then a quiet spot opened up, just a slight hitch in the flow of the party. Most people probably didn't notice, Josie thought, but she did because at that moment Mikie LaValle and Arlen Alderdice and Wyatt Aarstad walked through the back door and into the kitchen. They stood with their heads stuck forward a little bit, eyes hooded, gazing around, unsure of what to do. Wyatt was able to nod a few hellos, but was clearly unsure about how he'd be received. Mikie stood staring only at her. Josie lifted her hand and wiggled fingers at him. From the moment he arrived, Josie felt Mikie watching her with hungry, wary slices of glance. It was a bad night for that, she thought.

She stayed close to Matt, even slinging her thumb through his back belt loop for a while because she felt it was important to make sure everybody knew where everybody stood.

Matt yelled, "Wyatt Aarstad, you little punk. I'm going to tape you to the kitchen cabinets."

Wyatt grinned. "If you don't get your ass beat trying," he said.

This inspired a genuine hoot from Matt, and by the time he was finished laughing, the party was rolling again, people falling back into their enthusiasms and agendas, most of which tilted toward annihilation. Mikie seemed to disappear, which Josie attributed to his propensity for smoking outside. She let her ease slip back in. These were her people, after all, classmates and friends, her boyfriend and her brother. Four girls were dancing in the living room. A couple of boys made hip hops moves close to them, like apes mating. Josie went downstairs, where Matt, Jared, and Alex all had donned irrigating boots and divvied up the darts from the dartboard.

They were running around the pool table, throwing the darts at each other's feet. The game should have ended when Matt flicked a dart that dangled for a moment in Jared's hip, but the boys played on until Matt skewered Alex's thigh. A crimson rivulet ran down the outside of his jeans. Alex plucked the dart out and stood squeezing his thigh, trying to get more blood to flow, but pulling the dart caused all the blood to flow inside his jeans, so he took them down to his ankles.

Neither boot-darting nor condiment chugging nor partial nudity were unusual when the boys got wound up, but these things rarely happened within the same hour.

* * *

Tom drove home after the game. He toyed with the notion of hitting Pep's, but couldn't imagine the mood there. Instead he bought a six-pack of Bud Light at the IGA and drove to his house. It was over, he kept thinking. His mind played the refrain like the hook of a favorite song: *it's all over.* He wondered what was next, as if it were the next turn in the highway, not something he planned or had anything to do with, but a feature of the geography he was traversing.

Wasn't there always next? He was going to teach out the year, but everything else seemed in flux. Tom had until quite recently imagined himself a Dumont resident for good. Would he stay now? The town would never let him forget the bumbling of its greatest football team ever.

He knew that, if he let things calm down, he would have opportunities in bigger towns, maybe even a spot on a college staff. But he liked it here, loved the prairie and the sky, found comfort in knowing the town, admired and respected the people. Maybe teaching would be enough. He wished he could find the part of himself that had so recently cared so much about football. Hadn't it been everything?

Hadn't it been what carried him through the split with Sophie and the mundanities of the divorce? Hadn't throwing himself into the lives of kids been the only way to compensate—even if that compensation was woefully incomplete—for the loss of his son? Football had been everything he thought about—only he realized that it hadn't.

He'd wanted it to be, but everything else kept spilling in. He'd tried to seal Jenny Calhoun out, but she seemed to be something worth grasping for. Marlo Stark made him see that. The sun was gone beyond the empty land to the west, a strange, humid twilight gathering close to the snowpatched ground.

The shelterbelts huddled dark and bristly. When he made the turn into his yard, Tom found a surprise. Strung across the front of his house Tom saw a broad white banner that read, in alternating crimson and blue letters: "Great Coach, Great Season." Along the steps to his back door he saw planters of flowers, and three or four gift baskets filled with homemade jams, sauces, and soaps. Taped to the storm door was a sign that read, "Thanks, Coach Warner, for getting us where we needed to go." It was signed by all the players on the team—except the boys who'd been kicked off—and the cheerleaders.

Some of the players had written personal notes. The Hanson boy's said, "Thanks, Coach, for making me a better lineman and a better player and a better person. I won't ever forget this year." Tom set the plastic bag with the beer cans down on the ground. Inside, he could hear Scout whining. She knew he was out there. He stared at the banner, the flowers, the sign, symbolic logic from forsaken friends. He knew what he wanted to do in that moment— he wanted to cry. But he couldn't. He felt a hollowness well up in his chest.

Why couldn't he cry? What the hell was wrong with him? He started thinking about how he would clean this all up. He moved toward the door, to let Scout out. He could hear her clawing on the wood now. And then he saw, right in front of his door on the worn foot mat, a pie wrapped in foil. He suddenly remembered a line from a song Sophie had liked: "When you live in a world, it gets into who you thought you'd be."

He couldn't remember who sang the song, or even the tune, but those words chased each other around the inside of his skull, and he turned and sat on the step and buried his face in his hands and wept while the dog clawed the other side of the door. He cried for his past, for his lost love and his lost son, for the future he had once believed so fully in, but would never have. Most of all he cried for himself, for feeling so frozen and empty inside and not having any idea what to do about it for so long now.

* * *

Josie slipped through a doorway, down a narrow hallway to a bathroom at its end, passing a darkened utility room. Just as she was about to close the door behind her, Mikie slid in.

"Close it, close it, close it," he said in a fast whisper.

She held the door mostly closed but open a crack. "What are you doing?"

"I need to talk to you."

Josie let her assessment of Mikie build for a long moment, tried to take as much in of him as she could. *Was this the kind of guy he was going to be?* She felt a long blade of sadness reach into her, like she was losing someone she hadn't met yet.

"This isn't such a good idea," she said.

"Just close the door," he said. "I just want to talk to you. You're not going to talk to me with all your friends out there, are you?"

"Why can't you be normal?"

"Oh, you mean like the guys throwing darts into each other's legs?"

"Why can't you just enjoy yourself? You don't have to hold yourself aside and, like, *lurk*. Just sit down, and talk to some people."

"Yeah," Mikie said, his eyes wide. "Everybody here is dying to talk to me."

"Well they might be if you let them know you at all. You always hold yourself aside, like you want to be so different from everybody."

"I am different from everybody."

"Not really," she said. "Not any more than anybody else."

"I thought if I came here you might be nice to me," he said.

"I am being nice," she said through exasperated clenched teeth. Then she relaxed and repeated, "I'm being nice. What more do you want me to do?"

"You could act like I exist."

"I do."

"Not when he's around, Captain Football Man."

"It's a hard day for him, Mikie. He's blowing off steam. It's not evil."

"So that's going to be the party line, eh? Stand by your man?"

She held her hands out and gave him a seriously dubious look. "Did I ever indicate to you that I wasn't going to stand by my man?"

"Yeah, right," he said, falling into a mumble. "Whatever. I just wanted to talk to you."

"You can talk to me. Get out of here and let me pee, and we'll go right out there and I'll talk to you like you're anybody else. Now get out. Before someone else comes down here." She pushed him out of the bathroom, feeling him at first stand firm, then seem to let her wrap into him, halting a moment before he let her push him out the door. She shut it behind her and, after a second thought, turned the lock.

When Josie came out of the bathroom door, Mikie was still waiting in the doorway, and there were people coming down the hall. Matt's voice said, "What's this all about?"

"What's what all about?" Josie asked. She had stopped in the act of scooting past Mikie in the hall.

"Some secret meeting?" Matt asked. "Some powwow?"

"Matt, cool it," Josie said. She stepped forward now, to intercept him before he came too close to Mikie.

"I'm talking to him," Matt said. "Mike LaVagina." Josie could see Mikie's face fall a deeper shade of red. "You having a powwow with my girl back here, LaVagina?"

Josie's brother and Alex Martin had filled the other end of the short space, forming a blockade.

"I'm just trying to take a piss," Mikie said, his voice a shuffling whisper. He flicked a glance at Josie, and she saw the betrayal he felt.

"What's that?" Matt asked.

"Just trying to take a piss," Mikie said, louder, but he couldn't look at Matt. His eyes shied to the side, the curve of the white showing.

"You can't piss outside like the rest of the boys?"

"Jesus, Matt, don't give the kid the third degree over his bathroom habits," Josie said.

"You think you can just show up here and start putting some moves on my woman?" Matt yelled at Mikie.

"Jared," Josie implored, "could you help me drag my idiot boyfriend out of here?"

Josie wrapped her arms up under Matt's armpits and tried plowing into him, which was as futile as trying to tackle a pickup truck. They stood, tilted against one another. "Jared," she said, this time as much warning as plea. Jared came forward then, wrapped an arm around Matt's shoulders, but also close to his neck. He tightened his grip and gave a few good ol' boy hooks, pulling Matt toward him.

"Come on, Mattie," Jared said. "It ain't worth it. Let's go drink all that beer."

"That motherfucker is going to make me do a little paleface stomp on his ass," Matt said.

Josie let go of him, backed up a step and stomped forward again, jamming the heels of both palms into his chest. "Don't talk like that."

"I ain't just talking," Matt said.

She whacked both palms into his chest again. "I'm going home."

Josie brushed by him, desperately hoping he might take the bait and follow. Jared pivoted to turn Matt in the direction she was walking and shoved him. "Go talk to her," Jared said.

Matt stumbled a few steps after Josie, then seemed to change his mind, righting himself in the direction of Mikie. But Mikie had slipped into the bathroom and closed the door behind him.

"I oughta rip that door off its hinges," Matt said.

Alex, who had been watching quietly, said, "I wish you wouldn't."

Josie crossed the rec room and paused at the bottom of the steps, hoping he'd see the hesitation and follow. But Matt rushed the bathroom door, wound up his arm and threw his fist into it. His body followed. The door didn't budge. Matt screamed into the wood, "I'm going to beat seven colors of shit out of you, LaValle. I might just kill your stupid Indian ass. Don't let me catch you!"

Jared and Alex both latched onto Matt and dragged him from the door. Josie started moving away again, and Matt followed. Jared and Alex stayed with him, though they had to dodge Waylon and Wyatt Aarstad, who were wrapped up in a new round of boot darts.

Upstairs, they went right outside. In the cold dark, Matt stopped and seemed to shrug the other two boys off him. Josie had pulled her coat on before getting out the door, but Matt stood in a T-shirt, his hair spiky from running around and then the short wrestling match in the hallway. Prompted by nothing, he began to speak as if he had an audience that had asked him his opinion.

"That Wyatt, he's spunky, man. He keeps coming at you. Mikie LaValle is just a punk. What's with that black wardrobe?" he asked his arms reaching into the darkness for some sort of answer.

"I heard him the other day saying he's a Metis now," Alex said.

"He's a half-breed from Fort Miles, and I'm gonna kill that little fuck if I catch him near my woman again."

"He's from Browning," Josie said. She leaned against the fender of an F250, her arms wrapping herself for warmth.

"How do you know that?" Matt asked. He took a step like he was coming toward her, but made it a feint, as if they were playing a game.

"I don't know." Josie shrugged. "Everybody knows that."

"I didn't know it. How do you know?"

"I just know. I'm in class with him. We talk. I talk to people, Matt."

"I'm going in," Jared said.

"Go," Matt said. "You don't give a shit anyway. You got to play."

"Give a shit about what?" Jared asked.

"Just go."

"Whaddya think, Joser?" Jared asked.

"I'm fine," she said.

"What, are you protecting her from me now?" Matt said. He'd just caught on. "Like you could."

Jared stood long enough to let Matt see he wasn't turning tail. Then he looked at Josie, and she nodded. "We're fine."

"Fuck you, Frehse," Matt said.

Jared rolled his eyes Matt's way. "Just . . ." He made a gesture with his finger like turning a knob. "Dial it down a touch, bro."

Then Jared went back inside. Matt didn't move. He was going to make her come to him, and she did. He stared down at her and said, "You don't support me. My whole life is coming apart, they just took away the only thing that matters to me, and you don't even support me."

"I thought I was part of what mattered to you," she said.

"You were, until you decided not to support me. Now I don't even have you on my side. Everybody's against me. What did I do to deserve this?"

"I support you, Matt," Josie said, "but not when you start acting like a big puckered ass."

Matt looked at her then with an obtuse sadness in his eyes. He seemed unable to understand why she had said what she just had. He threw her hands down and wailed, "Nobody gives a goddamn what happens to me." And he took off running.

Josie shouted and followed, but she couldn't keep up with him as he headed into the snow drifted across the field. She turned and ran back into the house and found first Waylon, then Jared and Alex.

"He's running again," she said.

Matt's teammates took off across the field after him. She watched their backs, rectangular patches of brown and black jackets hovering over legs that flickered as they disappeared into the dark.

* * *

When he decided to call, Tom was actually thinking about Italy, about the places Marlo Stark had talked about.

He wondered if people there looked different, if they spoke in different voices—languages, sure, but were the tones different? Did they wear different clothes? He had always imagined foreign countries like that, folks walking around in traditional costume, the way movies set in the Middle Ages looked. It was, he assumed without dwelling on it to much, another of those holes in his imagination. Tom did not consider himself naïve, or inexperienced.

He felt that he had loved and been loved. And he didn't blame any of the women who loved him for no longer being in is life. Even Sophie, whom he had believed in so completely . . . he knew that statistically a couple who loses a child is far less likely to find a way through. He had thought they would be different, believed, and been wrong. That the mistake held such high stakes did not mean it was any less honest than other well-intentioned mistakes.

Nor did he blame her. Tom remembered how impossible he had found it, sometimes, just to be in her presence, just to stand under her gaze. He had been driving. He had done nothing wrong, but he had been driving. And whether she actually could or not,

Tom's experience led him to believe she would never forgive him for being the driver when her son died. He could never touch her in her grief. For the entirety of their relationship, Tom had found such confidence in the notion that, no matter the problem, Sophie thought of him as the first choice for a solution. And then a thing happened that wrecked each of them inviolately, and he could no longer access her searching.

It wasn't her fault, just the foolish belief that lives will always mean what you think they can. He had never answered her email. *I feel bad about so many things*, she had written. So did he, but that didn't mean he knew how to make them different. Nor, until this moment, did he know anything to do about Jenny Calhoun.

He had disrespected her by bringing the young lawyer from Great Falls into his house, making her a drink, talking into the night with her. If Jenny knew about that—and people in Dumont seemed to know about every coming and going—she would probably feel disrespected.

Jenny was an honest woman. He suspected she would forgive him, thought that's what the last pie meant, but he was not sure he was ready to forgive himself. He found her beautiful in so many ways, even more so in her grace, but that was the heart of it. He knew now that he had been so attracted to Marlo Stark because he felt Jenny getting close. The problem with Tom's coping mechanisms, developed through a life lived mainly in small towns on wide-open plains, was that they relied so heavily on nothing much ever happening.

But then things did. He had made a fool of himself, and of Jenny. Maybe it was knowing that. Maybe it was knowing the outcome of the season finally, feeling released from the burden of how everything was going to turn out. In any case, he called.

"Hi, Tom," she said. "How are you?"

He tried to picture her, sitting in a chair at the table in the kitchen, where her voice would be least likely to carry up the stairs to the children in their beds. Or maybe she was on the sofa, reclining in the dark, bare ankles crossed. She was speaking softly, which made her sound either exhausted or urgent, Tom couldn't figure out which. He said, "I've been here thinking."

"What about?" she asked. Her voice sounded so welcoming, like a soft place to land.

"Well, I know I said I was going to call before, but then things just sort of got away from me," he said.

"Okay," she said, and he heard not a forgiveness or acceptance, just an acknowledgment that maybe things do sometimes get away.

"So I'm sorry for that," he said.

"It's okay," she said.

"And then I've been thinking a lot about how I really wish I could have talked to you more about what's been happening."

"Well, you can," Jenny said. "You know, I really admired how you did what you did. Even though I know it must have been so hard for you."

"Do you think it's possible to see each other to talk about this stuff?" Tom said.

"Sure," she said. "I'd like that." And there was a long pause. But he didn't want there to be a long pause, so he said, "Well . . . how're the kids?"

"They're great," she said. "How's that dog of yours? How's Scouter?"

"She's good."

Tom let the silence hang. He felt it palpably unbalanced, wavering around some tipping point, as if the wrong words from him would topple it crashing over. He started to notice his breathing and tried to keep it deep and even, a way he liked to cope when things seemed out of his control. It wasn't impossible to miss Sophie and his boy Derek and also want this. It wasn't any violation to miss things he loved about his old life and to still want a new one. It didn't make him a greedy person, or unreliable.

"Is there a time you had in mind?" she asked.

"Tonight is good," Tom said.

"Oh," she said, and he could hear the smile. "The kids."

"Right. Of course."

"I could get a sitter for, say, Thursday?"

"Thursday would be great."

"Let's do something Thursday. We can think and figure out the details later."

"Okay, good. That's good."

"Listen, there is one thing, Tom," she said. "I don't want to feel like I'm just because there aren't any other choices."

"No. I don't want you to feel like that," Tom said. "Not at all."

When they hung up, Tom sat in his sparsely furnished living room, alone with the TV sports newscasters, the cuts to highlights altering the dim flicker of light in the room. His fingers felt short furrows in the wooden arm of his chair, scratches from when Scout was a pup. The springs in the cushion remarked on his nervous weight shifting. He heard the wind moan outside and felt a strange comfort in it, as if the slipstream around the house's outer walls had formed an eddy where he might find shelter.

* * *

On Sunday, the day after Dumont lost their last football game of the season, Josie lay in the half-sleep before sunrise, knowing she could sleep more if she wanted because it was Sunday, but so used to waking this early. And then she heard the shots. They weren't loud, just pops—one followed by a loud squeal, and then a moment of quiet and then another pop, but Josie knew gunshots when she heard them. By the time she had pulled a coat over her shoulders, slipped into her muck boots, and headed outside still in her plaid flannel pajama bottoms, Jared had started up his pickup and was backing it toward the barn.

Josie raised her hands in the air, a gesture of question. But as soon as she saw Jared ram the pickup into park, then sit with his hands on the wheel staring out the glass in front of him, she knew what had happened. Hot exhaust streamed from the tail-pipe into the cold morning. The frost hadn't completely cleared from his windshield yet. Josie walked to the passenger door and opened it.

"You did it?" she asked.

He didn't speak. He pressed his lips together hard.

"Do you want some help?"

Jared shrugged. His eyes brimmed with tears that hadn't fallen yet. Josie legged up into the truck. The shotgun lay across the crew seat. Jared dropped the transmission into reverse and Josie felt the truck settle under her. Looking out through the windshield, she could see her father standing in the window of the house, a cup of coffee in his hand, watching them.

"Sorry," Josie said softly.

"Dad was right," Jared said. "I couldn't breed them. I'll be gone next year. It wouldn't be fair."

He backed the pickup around behind the barn and then up against the pig pen. They both got out and Jared dropped the tail-gate with a clang. He shoved open the gate in the pen. The two bodies lay in motionless humps. First they grabbed Chops by his legs and heaved him up onto the bed of the truck with a whump. He was heavy and awkward, like a sack of grain with a spine in it. They did the same with pretty pink Carnitas, her head a bou-quet of gore, swinging and smacking against Jared's leg when they heaved. Jared climbed into the bed of the pickup and hauled on the corpses so they weren't on top of each other.

"Where are you taking them?" Josie asked. Jared dropped down out of the bed, turned and slammed the tailgate shut.

"That guy in Havre," he said.

"Is he there? Does he know you're coming?"

"I don't know. I'll hang around until he is."

"Want company?"

"Sure." They didn't say anything else. Jared drove and the pickup rolled over miles of highway, rolling past wheat fields and coulees, past farm houses and herds of cattle. Josie stared out the window, knowing Jared would talk when it was okay to. Until then she noted for the ten thousandth time how, when the wheat rows were perpendicular to the highway, the lines of stubble seemed to converge far away on the distant horizon, and thought about how, if she ever went to that point, they wouldn't be any closer there than they were on this end.

* * *

On Monday, Josie stood in the lunch line, waiting to grab a tray full of whatever was being served. Some sort of beef, it smelled like, and she was seeing buns on people's plates. Must be hamburger day, not her favorite. Matt would be happy. He loved hamburgers, even school hamburgers. He would pile several meat patties onto a bun and slather them with ketchup and mayonnaise and probably go for seconds. She was just glad lunch wasn't pork. The cafeteria seemed dark and cold—Josie was wearing a hoodie to stay warm, and some girls wore their jackets. November.

Almost Thanksgiving. The end of autumn had seemed dark and cold, more so than usual. The snow had melted to mud in most places, then the ground froze solid and it was snowing again outside. Even though it was basketball season now, her time to shine, Josie's personal situation made it hard to relax and let Thanksgiving be Thanksgiving.

Matt moved through the cafeteria lunch line several people ahead of her, Jared and his friends knotted around him in some dumb-looking entourage. They were afraid—afraid not to stand near him, afraid to be cast out. Sort of the same way she was afraid to walk away from their relationship. For so long, Josie had breathed in the mixture of wheat chaff, dusty soil, workout sweat, sweet beer breath, and the stale cafeteria food smells. What if, when she breathed it all out, there was nothing to breathe in again? Her mother was no help.

Sunday morning over breakfast, when Josie and Jared had talked about Matt's long attention-getting gallop through the darkness Saturday night, Judy Frehse had said, "I didn't raise the kind of girl who abandons her friends because it's easier than sticking by him." Now Matt was smiling to Pearl Aarstad, telling her how much he loved her cooking.

And then he slid his tray down farther, in front of Caroline Jensen, Mikie's mom, and his eyes deadened, his face falling slack. The sudden coldness shivered through Josie as she watched. It was over in a second, Matt making some wisecrack to Jerry Brown, the dishwasher, and then ambling over to the senior table, surveying the lunchroom as he walked with his bouncy, bundle-of-muscle pop.

Josie thought she saw him lock for a moment on Mikie LaValle, who was already seated with Wyatt Aarstad and Arlen Alderdice at their usual table, checking his phone—probably checking for a text from her. She caught herself realizing her observation could have been more about anxiety than reality.

Except it wasn't. Matt veered right toward Mikie's table and, so fast that it hardly looked aggressive, snatched the phone from Mikie's hand. Mikie thought about trying to get his phone back, lifted from his seat a bit, then sat back in it, and opted for a smug expression that wanted Matt to know he was making a fool of himself. Even from the distance she stood from them, Josie could hear Matt say the words "Metis warrior" but nothing around it.

Mikie looked up, pretending he had the wherewithal to be properly disdainful of Matt. It didn't help that Mikie was wearing a black T-shirt, across the front of which he had scrawled "Represent" in permanent silver marker and "Batoche" on the back. Matt stood, glowering at Mikie, fiddled with the phone until he saw something he either did or didn't like and stood for a moment straighter. Then he bent at the waist, still holding his tray full of lunch, and lowered his face close to Mikie's. Josie couldn't hear what he said next, but she saw Mikie's lip shortening into a snivel, fear laced with resentment, but also a resignation, the dog that knows it's about to be kicked.

He looked so weak that sympathy and revulsion fizzled against each other within her. Matt pitched the phone from close range into Mikie's chest, and it clattered to the floor. Mikie was too paralyzed with anxiety to try to stop it. Josie caught a bit of movement coming into her vision, Mr. Potter, the math teacher, walking from the teachers' table.

"Matt, is there a problem?" Mr. Potter called.

Matt turned to Wyatt Aarstad and hissed a whisper at him. Wyatt said nothing back, and as if he hadn't heard, perhaps, stared across the lunchroom at a wall. And then Matt walked away, and it was over, whatever it was.

Mr. Potter stopped halfway across the open floor. Matt stalked over to the senior table and sat down with Jared. Josie watched Wyatt, Arlen, and Mikie suddenly huddle.

Matt was . . . he had never been easy. That's what he wasn't. He was not easy to figure out and there were things about him you just had to accept. She slid her tray in front of the window where Pearl Aarstad and Caroline Jensen were serving. She made a specific point of saying good morning to Mrs. Jensen.

"Could I have a little extra corn, please?" she asked Caroline. "I love the corn."

"Everybody does," Caroline said, shooting for cheerful, but Josie always felt Mrs. Jensen's wariness around her. Josie understood why, too, and it was another step in understanding how complicated things could be.

* * *

On Tuesday afternoon after school Tom walked through a coulee, following Scout, when his cell phone rang. Another cold front had come through during the night and early morning and left a couple inches of new snow. Cold sharpened the brightness of the colors, made them ring against each other. The shadows of the deep coulee still held some hardened snowdrifts from last week's storm. Tom was happily thinking about Jenny and a conversation they'd had during lunch in the teacher's lounge. She was making a cup of coffee and asked if he wanted one. He said he did and could she add two sugars and two creams. She'd looked at him over her shoulder and said, "That's not really a coffee, is it?"

The way she'd said it, the familiarity of the tease. He liked it. He was as anxious for their date on Thursday as he had been for any playoff game. He did not recognize the number on his phone, and answered. The voice announced itself with a confident vigor.

"Tom? It's Marlo Stark."

Tom stopped walking then, his feet just coming to rest beside each other as if they had decided it. He stared at the shards of slopes cutting down to the coulee in front of him, brilliant in the hard glancing light, then at the furrow sunken through the landscape, clotted with thick russet and brown brush. The wheat and grass poking above the snow gave the land a gold and tan nap against a bright blue sky. He saw a harrier hovering over the hillsides, not ten feet off the ground, climbing steeply and pouring downwind before turning, and, with invisible flexes of its feathers, hanging almost completely still in the cold air a few feet above the brush.

He found himself fascinated by how still the hawk could hover, by the power feeding that lack of motion. Then the bird tilted its wings and climbed steeply, flowed downwind, and looped back before dropping again, floating on some invisible welt of current.

"Tom? Are you there?"

"Yeah," he said. "Sorry. I'm in the field. Bad reception."

"Are you hunting?" Marlo asked.

"Just walking," he said.

"I wish I could have gone hunting with you. I would have liked that, I think," she said. "I would have liked to have seen your dog working in the field."

"That," he said, "would . . . have been nice."

"I saw you guys lost on Saturday," she said. He wondered if that was just to let him know she was keeping up on things. "Sorry about that."

"Yeah," he said.

"Did you go to the game?"

"Yeah. Listen, you're breaking up here, and I've got Scout running around out in front of me. I better hustle along."

"Okay," Marlo said, and Tom could hear her disappointment, wondered if it was in him or in herself for having called him. She rallied some brightness into her voice to say, "I'll probably be over there this winter for some school business. If you want to get a beer?"

"You bet," Tom said and clicked off the call, then shut down the phone. He had no idea where Scout was. The harrier still levitated along the edges of the coulee. Hunting by holding still.

* * *

The following evening after basketball practice, Josie told Matt she was going to do some extra work cleaning the church kitchen and drove instead to the reservoir. The road was slick with wind-scoured ice, and she wondered how she would explain what she was doing out here if she got stuck and had to call for help. She was there because when she had opened her history book she had found stuck in it a note, folded in a small, thick triangle.

She had opened the note after examining it for a few moments, enjoying its presence. It had not occurred to her to be furtive, until she saw the scrawl inside. It was not every day someone received a note in school; it would be something worth speculating about for certain people—or an excuse to speculate, at any rate. The note said:

He saw ur number in my sent calls. He said if I call u again he'll kill me. Your man sucks Jo. He owns u. U told me we could be friends. What kind of friends is that? I thought u were honest & good, but ur just like him if u let this keep happening. Meet me at our place after practice to talk.

"Our place" meant the reservoir, and Josie resented him appropriating it, as if by reserving a place, he could create some alternate reality in which there was a "them." Josie had promised Mikie over and over she would be his friend, that they could talk about things, that he could call her.

And Matt preemptively deciding they couldn't angered her. She'd received several texts over the course of the afternoon from Matt saying, "We have to talk" and other equally strident suggestions that something very big was very wrong. But she'd managed to avoid him and told him she couldn't tonight—first citing homework and then her responsibilities to clean the church kitchen.

Matt would have to wait until tomorrow after practice. When he'd called, she hadn't answered, just by way of letting him know she was royally pissed. She knew he imagined himself even more angry. He would have ginned up all manner of outrage and hurt and self-pity, would convince himself he stood firmly on higher moral ground and could unload on her with relative impunity.

He wouldn't see anything wrong with the way he had acted. But she was tired of people telling her things about herself. She had spent the afternoon thinking, at first urgently but then with a dreamy, finely detailed imagining, of how nice it would be to be Jared, or at least Jared's age, and to be going off to college in the fall—not too soon, because there were friends here to miss, but soon enough that she could imagine being her own person, a person she started with and built from scratch, who reacted to things the way she wanted to, not the way she was expected to.

She could start all over with relationships, not be in any for a while, just have her head to think what she wanted in it. There would be no Matt being Matt, and no Mikie guilting her into meeting secretly. She'd start all over and be a much better judge of character and motivation next time. Josie's headlights swung over the barren grasslands, over hummocks of snow. She could feel her tires slide as they rotated over ice in some low spots. *Please don't let me get stuck*, she kept thinking. *Please, please, please.* At the access pull-off, she saw no other car so she pulled in, searching for highest ground. Josie switched off the ignition and sat for a moment.

She felt the wind shoving across the plain, rocking her car on its springs. In the moonlight, in the water not yet covered in ice, curved silver slivers pushed over the surface of the reservoir. A lot of days, when she gazed out over the miles of empty space around her, she thought about how she would miss this landscape when she was living at college somewhere on the East Coast, or in Seattle or Portland, the openness of it, the sense that you could see all of it. Tonight she found it all oppressive, all that space and nothing to do in any of it, the snow that never could remain unbroken, drifts that the wind bored scoops out of, underneath it the vale of mud and dirt.

The door to her truck flew open then, the bright dome light shocking her as much as the sudden motion: first the sucking of the door opening her quiet cocoon to the night outside, then the thrust of Mikie stuffing himself into the passenger seat. The reek of pot followed him in.

"What are you doing?" Josie asked without thinking.

"Having a seat," Mikie said. She could tell he was proud of himself about something, thinking he was clever. "I assume you're here to see me."

"How did you get here?" For a moment she was struck by the horrifying notion that he had somehow stowed away in her vehicle, that things had possibly turned that weird.

"I followed you," he said.

She whipped around to look for his car and spotted a glimmer of moonlight on a old sedan, parked several yards away from her rig. He apparently read the confusion on her face when she turned back and said, "I drove with my lights off. I'm getting good at it."

"Why?" she asked.

"You never know."

"You never know what?"

"When you're going to need to drive with your lights off," Mikie said. His wore his pride at this skill with an unconsidered brio.

"Mikie, what? Are you running drugs now? Or is this some ancient Metis lore about driving with your lights off? Why do you have to be so goddamned weird all the time?" Josie regretted making the slur as soon as she had done it, wished she had settled herself before speaking.

"I'm not being weird," he said. "I'm being cautious. A few nights ago your boyfriend threatened to kill me if I even talk to you, if you want to remember."

Great, Josie thought, now Mikie had found an excuse to go all 007, a wrinkle in his persecution complex he'd probably been waiting to have triggered.

"Matt's not going to touch you," Josie said, though she hoped she sounded more sure of that than she felt.

"He'll be sorry if he does," Mikie said.

A perverse part of Josie wanted ask, *Oh yeah?* She couldn't imagine what Mikie thought he could do to Matt, how in any kind of physical confrontation Mikie could make Matt sorry about anything. Mikie must have read something in her expression.

"I got a pair of brass knuckles," he said, smug again. "Wyatt and me figured it out. If I know Matt's coming for me, I'm going to coat my arms with Vaseline, so he can't hold onto me. And then I'll just keep hitting him with the brass knuckles. Bust his fucking face for him."

"Don't even talk like that," Josie said.

"I'm not shitting," Mikie said. He lifted his hand above the dashboard in a fist and Josie could see metallic bands looping above each of his knuckles. She'd never seen anything like this and, oddly, the brassy shimmer made her think of a wedding ring on each of his fingers. The weapon was obviously too big for his hand, but she imagined it could hurt somebody even in his fist.

"Where'd you get that?" Josie asked.

"Over on the rez. My cousin."

"Give it back to him."

"No way. And don't you tell your hunky honky, either. If he comes after me, he deserves a surprise," Mikie said.

"He's not coming after you."

"Did you tell him?"

"Tell him what?"

"What you told me before—that he couldn't tell you what to do. That you'll talk to me if you want to." He might have remembered her telling him these things, though Josie couldn't pinpoint the exact conversation in which they'd occurred. She'd certainly told anybody who wanted to listen that she decided who her friends were.

"I haven't talked to him," Josie said. "I guess I've been avoiding him."

"He owns you, that's why," Mikie said.

"Why do you keep saying that?" Josie said. And now here was a time that, if they were really friends, they could talk about her. "What do you hope to accomplish by saying that? It hurts my feelings every time."

"Maybe because it's true."

Josie abruptly resettled herself in her seat, turning more toward him and pressing her back against the door. "It's not true. He doesn't own me. But, Mikie, I *am* his girlfriend."

"So? Does that mean he can tell you who to talk to?"

"It means I should have his best interests at heart," Josie said. She hoped the way she was looking at him would tell him something more obvious. She hoped he wouldn't make her say it out loud.

"What about your best interests?" Mikie asked.

Which made her realize she was going to have to say it out loud. "Mikie, I'm not exactly sure you're my best interests." She saw right away that she'd hurt him, and was sorry and started scrambling to undo the damage. "I want to be friends. I want to talk. I'm just saying I'm not sure what my best interests are. I've been with Matt for two years now, and he'll probably go away to school next year—well, who knows now, but maybe. I'm going away the year after that. I'm only sixteen."

"Man," Mikie said. "Man . . ."

Josie felt suddenly weak under the burden of his sensitivities. She was so tired of trying to keep everybody's feelings unscathed all the time. "I also know," she said, "that I don't much appreciate sitting in a dark car with a guy wearing brass knuckles who followed me out here with his lights off. That's just kind of creepy, Mikie. I feel like you're needing to push me into a corner and make me make choices that I shouldn't have to make."

Mikie glared at her, and what she thought she saw was a pure form of loathing, one that spends most of its time aimed at the self. "I can't believe," he said, "you would sell me out like that. You of all people, Josie Frehse."

He had the car door open and was out in the night before she could think what to say. Mikie bent, his head and shoulders leaned in to fill the open door, and added, "Tell your boyfriend to leave me the fuck alone." That was punctuated by the car door slamming. Josie was still staring into the empty space where he had sat when she heard his engine huffing behind her, then the spinning tires, muddy snow splatting against her vehicle, as his red taillights fishtailed away. *I'm just a girl*, Josie thought. *A plain, ordinary, normal girl. Why won't anybody in this town let me be that?*

Josie lingered at the reservoir for a while, looking out at the blue light on the snow, following the ribs of drifts and the stridulations of broader wind shapes. She saw a coyote trotting across the frozen part of the reservoir, a mercury mix of reflection and shadow traversing the moonlit ice. There was so much to love about this place—this moment, when she was all alone with the ice and the coyote and wind, feeling as safe as she ever had, wrapped in her own sense of wanting that had nothing to do with anybody else.

She could sit and stare up at the scattered stars for as long as she wanted, watch the moon track across the dome of night, roll down her windows and feel the shock of wind on her cheeks. She could think about songs she liked, what she'd wear to her first college party, an imaginary three-pointer to win a playoff game, her dream man—whomever he turned out to be.

So she stayed for a long time, silent in a night orchestrated by wind, ever-altering gusts stretching long notes through the distance. It seemed sad that indulging her own sense of longing required her to be separate from everybody she knew. Then she thought she should make an appearance at the church, just to let people see her vehicle there in case she needed that cover.

When she pulled into the lot, her headlights swept across a black Silverado, gleaming as the splinters of light traced the shapes of its quarterpanels. Her stomach dropped. Matt stared out the closed window at her, his face a fist.

His mouth pressed shut. *Shit*, Josie thought. Matt's door swung open and a booted leg reached the ground. Josie jammed her truck in park and dug around on the seat beside her, moving her phone and handbag, trying to imagine what she might be pretending to be looking for. The key to the church, maybe. She pretended to put it on her keychain, where it already was. She tried to think of what she needed to say to get out of this. Matt tried to whip her door open, but it was locked.

"Where were you?" he growled.

Josie stared at him through the window, leveling a gaze meant to tell him not to overdo this. She clicked the lock.

Matt grabbed the handle and practically ripped the door from its hinges when he flung it open. His face wrinkled into a scowl and he thrust his head further into the car, sniffing.

"You smoking dope?"

"No," Josie said.

"Why's it smell like a pot farm in here?" he asked.

Josie shook her head.

Matt stood back. He gnashed his teeth so hard she feared he might pop them off. "He was in here? You had that fucking punk in this car?"

Josie swung and sat sideways in her seat, her feet in the open door space. She put her elbows on her knees and rested her chin on her fists. She felt a tremendous sadness, knowing that whatever was going to happen now would probably change everything that followed.

"Cleaning the church?"

"That's what I came here to do. I got hung up earlier."

"Hung up?"

"Matt."

"Where the fuck were you, Josie? You owe me that."

"We don't owe each other things," Josie said. "We give each other things because we want to. At least that's how it should be."

"When I spend two years of my life on you, you owe me things," Matt said. He wasn't quite yelling now, but she could see that he was looking for his excuse to let himself go.

"Maybe that's our problem," Josie said and shrugged.

"Or maybe our problem is that you're sneaking around with that half-breed fucking mutt." There it was.

"Matt . . ."

"Don't even try it, Josie. I know where you were. I can smell it on you."

"Matt, I'm going home now. You're starting to scare me."

"Why are you doing this to me? You want to do him? Is that it? You want to fuck that scrawny little piece of shit? You want to suck his skinny Indian dick?"

Josie closed her eyes and let her head shake slowly. She remembered how hard it was to think like a boy, to try to understand those gashes of insecurity that opened so suddenly and gouted the precious emotions boys usually cradle and grasp so close to themselves.

"Were you with him?"

"Matt." Josie dropped her hand to the door armrest, as if to start pulling it closed. But Matt stepped in quickly, blocking the door with his body.

"No," he said. "Did you hook up with him? I want that one answer."

"Matt, don't be an idiot. It's late."

"Too late to clean the church, I guess."

"Matt, stop."

Matt stepped into Josie, slashing a finger in front of her face so closely that she jerked back. He kept bearing in with the finger. "Did you hook up with him?"

Josie said nothing. She tried to glare at Matt. For the first time in her life she actually let herself hate him a little.

"Tell me!"

It would have been easy to say no, but that would be a sort of gift. Josie didn't want to give him anything anymore.

"Matt, fuck off."

"Fuck off?" That seemed to surprise him. Matt responded by snatching her hair and pulling her head forward, yanking her from the truck and piling her on the ground. Josie started to shout but wound up shrieking. She felt his boot tip spear her buttock, another one lance her lower back, a few more in her ribs. Then a single heel stepping on her back, crunching her to the ground. She lay on her stomach, throbbing aches mapping the places he'd kicked her. Still holding her down with one heel,

Matt squatted beside her, wrapped his fist in her hair, lifted her face off the gravel.

"Fine, don't tell me. I'll beat it out of that little fuck. It's up to you."

"Don't," Josie said. "Leave him alone."

"I am not going to leave him alone. Oh, no. He's going to be anything but left alone for the next little while."

"He's a poor kid who just wants friends. That's all."

Matt raised an open hand, poised to strike. "Has he felt you up yet?"

"No!" she said, fear and anger scored the counterpoint to her breathing. "God, no. Can't people be friends without getting felt up?"

He moved the hand to make sure she could see it was ready to hit her. "Has he touched your pussy?"

This time Josie's voice fell to a low grunt, devoid of energy. "No."

"So that's the Josie Frehse version," Matt said, opening his fingers and letting her hair drop in strands from them. He rose, stepped off her back. "Next we're going to hear the Metis Mike version. Can't wait to see how they stack up."

"Leave him alone, Matt. What are you going to prove?"

"You fixed it so I can't leave him alone. I could have when it was just mooning at you in school. But now you're sneaking out for meetings with him—whose idea is it, anyway? His? Yours? Don't want to tell? It's okay. He'll tell me." Josie hated the smile she saw on Matt's face, hated its smugness, but also the edge, the tilt toward oblivion, that Matt didn't seem to have a handle on.

"What are you crying about?" Matt said.

Josie was crying because she'd been violated, jerked by her hair to the ground and kicked. Crying because she felt scared for Mikie, upon whom Matt, she knew, was pointed his furor at next. Crying because, as she sat looking up at Matt, she saw no glimpse of the boy she'd spent her first real love on.

Then she saw him duck his head and flash a thumb toward his eye, sweep away a tear from his own face, before stuffing his hands in his front pockets and turning to face the wind. He started walking to his truck, took one sidelong look at Josie, but didn't break stride. Matt started his truck and just before he closed his rig door, he turned down his car stereo so she could hear him say, "I'll see you real soon."

* * *

Later that night, Tom waited in his kitchen for Jenny to show up. He didn't know what to do with her, felt wretched and shabby offering her a place as spare, dim, and dog-hair-drenched as his house. He had offered to make dinner and felt deeply relieved when she said she would eat with the kids before coming. He'd driven all the way to Malta after school to find a bottle of wine you couldn't buy in a gas station. He'd bought three bottles, knowing she didn't drink much, but feeling he might have to. He wondered if his house smelled.

He'd noticed some houses smell musty or moldy or like smoke and dirty overalls or wet dogs. They were often the houses of old people or single people. Probably the people living there didn't notice it anymore, was all he could think, because how else could they stand it? For a brief moment he fought the impulse to break out the housecleaning supplies and wipe down the kitchen, just to telegraph the impression that he tried. But it was too late. She arrived, her hair hanging in lush, shiny arcs on either side of her face. Down, he noticed.

She rarely wore it down. She looked gorgeous, and he could suddenly see her as a young girl, years ago, a teenager. For some reason he saw her leading a horse or at a corral, wearing a low-slung rodeo belt buckle, a ponytail pulled through a cap. Deep-set eyes that looked at you from a long way away. Her long slim nose, lanky hips, narrow lips, red weathered cheeks, and a sloping jawline to a rounded chin. The back of her jeans higher than the front.

Cowboy boots making her hips lead her walk. All of it in a sudden flash. And then she was herself, walking through his door in a barn coat and a pair of wool twill pants he'd never seen her in, black pants that framed her hips and hung loosely down her legs. She must have been cold, he thought. But she wore them anyway.

Christ, the dog hairs she'd collect on those by the end of the night. She wore a red sweater with white sprinkled throughout. Maybe it was a snowflake design. Her breasts rounded it on the sides. He made sure he didn't look too long, tried to meet her eyes, a gray-blue gleam that regarded him too earnestly.

"So this is where you live," she said, stepping in. "I've been out here, but I've never been in here."

"Yeah . . . yes." What to say to that? He hurled his gaze at the floor, pushed it around like a broom, wishing away food scraps or dust bunnies that might be lying there. "Let me take your coat."

She handed him a bottle of wine, not the kind you buy in the gas station. He wondered if she had gone to get it, or had been saving it for something. *Better get into that pretty quick*, was what he was thinking.

"Should we open this?"

"Oh, Tom, can we just open that bottle and drink it and not talk about serious things. I feel really nervous, and I don't want to. Can we agree to that?"

"I think that would be fantastic," Tom said. He didn't sigh, but not because he didn't want to.

Tom made a hash of the cork, which was too dry and fell to bits beneath his overpowered augering. *Well, shit*, he wanted to say, but didn't.

Jenny busied herself talking to Scout, then stepped to the threshold of the living room and stood there, peering about.

"How are the kids?" Tom asked. "There's something wrong with this cork, is why it's taking so long."

"Oh, no worries," Jenny said, but he was pretty sure he could see her wanting a drink.

Worse than high school, he thought.

"The kids? The kids are great. They're . . . constant. Erin is so cute. Yesterday, I saw her plinking on this little toy keyboard she has, like a toy musical keyboard kind of thing my dad bought her, and she was plinking away and then she'd stop and write something down and I said, 'What are you doing, honey?' and she said, 'I've been wanting to write this song for years, but I've been so busy.'"

Tom laughed too hard.

"It's funny the things they come up with," she said. It sounded like she might go on but she stopped. Tom finally managed to drill out the last bit of cork, though crumbs had fallen into the wine. He poured her a kitchen glass full and handed it to her. He didn't know what to say, and noticed that she was still not talking. He looked at her, and wondered if she could see how baffled he was.

"I'm sorry," Jenny said. "I sometimes forget that you didn't get to have that. Or that you had it and then . . . you didn't anymore. Which I'm sure is even worse."

Tom felt the enormity of that wallop him, and felt socked into silence. He drank about half his glass of wine in one gulp, nodded his head up and down while looking back to the floor.

"I'm sorry," she said, letting out a confused breath. She took a healthy swallow of her wine. "I didn't mean to . . ."

A little silence ensued before Tom said, "Can I ask you something? Does my house smell?"

Jenny stared for a moment, then burst out laughing.

"What?" he asked.

"Does—" But she was laughing too hard to finish.

Then Tom laughed. They both bent in a heightened, nervous laughter.

"Does my house smell?" she managed to squeeze out before needing to inhale.

Tom realized he was laughing at himself, which made him roll into a new round.

"Does my house smell?" she said again, though it took two breaths to say it.

Jenny let out a long cooing sigh, then said, "Oh Tom, do you take anything for your anxiety?" He looked at her, ready to start laughing again. She said, "Is there anything I can take for your anxiety?"

And he broke up again. He tried to slug back more wine but he choked on a drop and sprayed some of that in the sink.

"Listen," Jenny said, "I think we're going to need all of that."

"Ah, shoot," he said. "You wanna sit down?"

"Are there . . ." she giggled a bit. "Are there enough places for both of us?"

"I got two," he said. But when she sat on the couch, he plopped down beside her, making her self-consciously bump over a bit to put a bit of space between them. It wasn't anything he planned, but he liked the way that unfolded.

"When you walked in here tonight," he said, "you looked so pretty for a minute I was imagining what you must have looked like when you were a young girl. Not saying you're old, but, you know, young. High school. When you're first learning about the effects you have on boys."

"Oh, I don't know that I ever learned much about that."

"Then I realized I don't know anything about then. You when you were young."

"Not much to know," she said. "I doubt I was different than anybody else."

"Oh, I don't know. Not a lot of farm girls were reading Jack Kerouac and crushing on Neal Cassady."

"Yeah, but I also crushed on Boyz2Men. And whoever was winning the bull riding. I was just a girl."

"You had horses." It wasn't a question.

"I could ride the hair off a horse. I grew up on the farm, west of town, out closer to the mountains. We always had a couple horses around. We had them until one of them rolled down a coulee bank and pinned my father under it. Broke his hip. He got rid of the horses after that. First time a man ever broke my heart. But farmers can't afford to break their hips."

"Something tells me you broke a lot more hearts than the other way around."

Jenny looked out the window behind them at the night, away for a moment, then back at him. "It's funny how people have ideas about you. It's mostly their own story they put on you. I didn't break a lot of hearts. I tell you what I did. When there was a boy I was interested in, I moved deep into like really quickly so that, should love come along, I'd be right there ready for it."

"A strategy. See, most people don't have one of those for love."

"Didn't matter that much. Love didn't really come along so often."

"It came along some. You got married."

"Well, that was more I let him chase me until I caught him."

Tom let that sink in, liked the way she could admit it so clearly. He had an idea of who he thought she was and she was going to complicate it. The first wine bottle was gone so he opened a second.

"I was dumb, like all of us," Jenny said. "Young girls spend their time picking at the bones of why they aren't getting what they need. When you spend so much time thinking about how things should be, it's hard to see how they really are. I wanted the quarterback, even if he wasn't worth having. I wanted him because everybody else wanted him, and if I could get him then I'd know that was about as good as I could do. I was a lot like Josie Frehse, chasing after Matt Brunner."

"I'm not sure how much chasing she does," Tom said.

"It's all over them, clear as Romeo and Juliet. She's such a lovely girl. So much potential. She's smart, pretty, athletic, great people skills. But she's locked into that boy, and he's going to drag her down."

"I don't know," Tom said. Here Jenny was putting her own story on someone else, maybe. "Matt could get out of his own way, he'd be all right. If he survives high school, goes somewhere where he hasn't been king banana his whole life, gets kicked around a bit. He's a competitor. He knows how to work. He's not dumb. He's just . . ."

"Dumont," she said.

"Yes," he said. "But that Josie, I think she's going on. She'll get a basketball ride somewhere—she's one of the best point guards I've ever seen."

"If she can get away from Matt."

"I think . . . I don't want to say break free, because that implies there's something bad here that holds her back. But I think she'll go on. I think she'll outgrow him, and here, and make a go somewhere else in the world."

"I hope so," Jenny said.

Tom thought he knew why she seemed so invested in Josie Frehse. The same reason he was. The same reason he wanted her brother Jared to leave Dumont, the same reason he wanted Alex Martin and eventually Waylon Edwards and even Matt Brunner, even Mikie LaValle to leave, to see a bigger sense of their place in the world.

Tom had left his little Montana town and, while it was true he had come back to life on the plains, he had done it deliberately. He had gone out and seen what the rest of it had to offer. He had gone to college. He had smoked pot with his hippie wide receiver and become friends with the black linebacker from Texas who beat him out for the starting job. He had rented his own apartment, fallen in love, had his heart broken, stayed up all night just talking to a woman he never kissed, drove twelve hours round-trip to go fishing because he could, paid bills, created choices about jobs.

He'd lived for eighteen months in Boise, gone to work every day in a radon testing business. He'd led a bunch of life on purpose. And he'd come back to the prairies. On purpose. You return to places to learn why you left them. He poured some more wine.

"How'd that all end up? You and that quarterback."

Jenny's face took a different cast, now that they were talking about her again. Her eyes went hard, looking inward. "I have the gift of pouring trust into people who don't deserve it. And then after a while I just started to feel like a tiny approximation of myself."

"I'm sorry," he said.

She brushed that off with a flip of her hand. "What about you? Weren't you basically Matt Brunner?"

"Oh, well . . . no. I can see how you'd think that, but no."

Now Tom took a moment to see around him. Scout lay on the floor, chin on the floorboards, resigned to not being the center of attention. Jenny was on the couch beside him, her long legs up on his coffee table, feet in socks. Her black slacks looked like someone had grated a dog on them. She leaned back in the couch but angled toward him. Her face tilted his way.

Her arm, the one not holding her wine glass, lay beside his thigh. Because he had slouched a bit, he tilted toward her. It hadn't happened at any one time, just a function of leaning to pour wine—they were deep into the second bottle by now.

"What were you like?" she asked.

Tom moved again, sinking into the couch, but rolling a shoulder closer to her.

"It's funny. So much happened since then. I sometimes get my own experience mixed up with movies I like."

"I don't buy that."

"It's true," Tom said. "I think maybe it's shock. Trauma. I just spent so much time trying not to think about certain things so that I could live a daily life that eventually my memory of those things is completely unreliable. I don't remember much about being a kid. I wasn't happy, I know that. I was good at football and that brought certain notice, but it also brought a lot of attention and expectation and, to be honest, I liked to read books. I liked to go off in the hills by myself and hunt and fish. I was a loner. I didn't really have a high school girlfriend. I didn't understand how you could, I think."

"It came along some," she said, smiling. "You got married."

"It came along for me in college. That's where I learned to be who I was. I had a college girlfriend. I really liked her. I still really admire her. She taught me a lot."

"The ways of the world?" Jenny said. She was teasing, but prying, too.

"I guess, but not just that. She was a real free spirit. She wanted to know a lot of things about life and she went about finding out. She taught me a lot about how to let myself be me."

"Ah, back when lovin' was easy," she said, and he knew she was poking him. "By the time I got to college, free spirits were when someone else was buying at the bar. I was already pretty much roped to what I ended up with."

"Funny how it works."

"What happened to your marriage?" He'd known it would come. Almost as soon as they'd quit laughing about the house smell, he'd wanted her to ask, felt like he'd be able to tell her. And to make it even bigger, Jenny let her hand drop on top of one of his and squeezed.

"I don't think," Tom said, because he'd been wanting to say this to someone for a long, long time, "that I ever dealt with my divorce. Processed it. And I think we got divorced because I've never dealt with, processed, my . . . the loss of our son."

She winced to encourage him to go on.

"After we'd had some time to mourn, my wife and I never addressed the 'us' part, the part that fell apart after our boy died."

Sophie said she didn't blame him for Derek's death. It had been an accident. He had been driving. He accepted the fault. That was the thing about blame and fault, though. One you take and the other you give to someone else. That give and take was what had silently ripped Sophie from him.

Sophie had been so unreachable, impenetrable, and his aimlessness had not allowed him any purchase against her seamlessness. On the odd occasions he did seem to find a grip, he couldn't remain focused long enough to find other handholds nearby, to create a locus of attachment to which he might have clung long enough for her to take notice.

He became dreamy, instead, believing his dreaming world had taken on a greater significance than his waking one. He imagined scenarios that were much more interesting than real. And when both of them finally looked up from their preoccupations, they had swirled so far apart from each other, could barely make out each other's features against the sky. He was mad at her for letting herself get so far away from him, for not calling for help earlier.

But he had done the same. The energy it would take to move back to closeness seemed too wearying when their sense of familiarity with the world had been so stunningly and irrevocably altered. It was easier for each just to let the other go than to deal with their disappointing selves and all it would take to get over coming back. Tom had believed Sophie was the great love of his life, that once-in-a-lifetime person that always has a piece of you, no matter how things turn out on the ground. He had believed he would never love anybody as both profanely and profoundly as he had once loved her.

She had said the same about him. What was between them would always stay between them, and that was the glory and the tragedy. She was gone—and that was the reality. She was not someone he could be with. Jenny Calhoun was right here, in his house on this night. She was so plainly beautiful and not going anywhere.

"I used to spend a lot of time being sad," Tom said. He turned the hand that Jenny had been holding, turned it over so it was holding hers, and he put his wine glass down to hold her other hand. He didn't look at her while he talked. He looked to where Scout was stretched on the floor, or to the silent, empty TV screen. "And then that changed, and I spent so much time being anxious. It was like I feared that the sadness could hurt me, like sadness was a reason for fear.

"My wife used to spend a lot of time reading about Buddhism after we lost Derek. My ex-wife. Those Buddhists she started to believe in emphasized present moments. She was always trying to get me to be more involved, be more present. But I was never really being present because I was so busy pretending to be. Back then, for me? There was no such thing as the present. There was only memory and anticipation. Sophie grew so hard around that. It made me feel weak."

"There's a difference between being hard and being strong," Jenny said.

Sure there was, Tom thought, but who had been telling anyone that back then?

There was no pretending that somewhere along the way their thighs hadn't pressed closer to each other. He felt happy that it was happening this way, that there weren't fits and starts. That they had been so open and were both being so forward. He looked at her now, and saw what he hoped to see, the yes in her eyes.

"Do you have to be home at any certain time?" he asked.

"The kids are at my sister's for the night."

He nodded. No smile. He wasn't trying to be charming. Didn't feel like he needed to be. All the want had already been there, for a long time. They just needed to get some honesty out of the way. He felt the way clear.

Jenny said, "We're going to do this?"

"I sure hope so."

"One question," she said. "Just one."

"Fire."

"Did you sleep with that lawyer from Great Falls?"

"I did not."

She nodded, securely. She sat up then and brought her face to his and looked into his eyes and kissed him. One long kiss that started timidly and quickly opened and deepened until they were both breathing deeply through their noses, still kissing. And then she broke it off. Stared into his eyes.

"You think I'm some fragile thing. I'm not."

She stood up and started walking toward the bedroom as if she'd been there a hundred times before.

* * *

Thursday at practice, Josie had the dropsies and everything she put up clanged off the rim. A pass she wasn't looking for hit her in the side of the face, stinging and ringing her ears. Her own passes skidded behind her teammates, or sailed beyond their reach. And it hurt. It hurt because the court was where Josie felt so free.

Nobody could touch her here. When another team had a great player who would front her, Josie had always been able to dig in and lose herself to being better than every one on the court. She could so focus on moving her feet, being where she knew the ball was going, seeing open lanes that she rarely had any idea how many points she had scored until someone told her later. The focus took everything away.

It made her know she was good. Tonight was only practice, and there was nobody on the Dumont team who could slow her down—except, apparently, her. Midway through a three-on-three drill, Coach Bury sat her. He didn't criticize, just whistled, shouted, "Frehse, have a seat. Engstrom, get in there," and the drill rolled on. Josie sat on the bench and acted like she was watching and fretted over what she would say when Coach asked her what was wrong. *My boyfriend kicked the shit out of me.*

Was that an answer she could give to an adult? There really wasn't much practice for her after that. A few shooting drills, through most of which she was preoccupied with hoping Coach Bury wouldn't question her. In the end, he let her walk into the locker room with just a long look. She had shaken her head. He trusted her. That much she knew.

But she had no answers for him. Nothing he would understand. Nothing she could understand. She could not imagine being one of those women she read about in books and saw in movies, women who let men beat them up, let men dominate their lives. Matt was a loose cannon, sure, but never to her.

Never. When she had gone home the night before, after the church, her mother had still been up, sitting at the kitchen table, searching for pieces to a huge jigsaw puzzle.

"Where have you been?" Judy asked without looking up. "I was going to start looking for you on milk cartons."

Josie didn't want to say where she'd been. She had no clever retort. Her mom had looked up slowly.

"I think Matt's, I don't know . . ." Josie had said.

"What's going on with Matt?" Judy Frehse had asked.

"He got . . . really angry," Josie said.

"Angry how?" her mother asked.

"Like, furious. Like, physical."

Her mother stood up, walked to fridge and half-filled her glass from the filtered pitcher. She turned and leaned against the sink. Josie looked at her, try to read her, to know how much to tell her. But her mother was so . . . certain. She wore the same clothes always—jeans and button-down shirts, no variation in theme, never a dress unless there was a wedding or a funeral. Her hair, the gray-blonde wings hanging beside her face, was always the same, and had been for all of Josie's life.

"What happened, Jos?" her mother asked.

"Matt got really mad and . . . he lost it."

"Lost it how?"

Josie sobbed, once. Then again and then she was crying. Her mother put the glass down and opened her arms and came forward, "Come here, Jos," Judy said, and she held Josie close, squeezed her in. "What is going on with you?"

They stayed wrapped together that way for a while, neither of them speaking until Josie stopped crying and could feel how fast her mother breathed, how firmly her mother's wiry arms wrapped around her. Judy said, "Are you okay, baby?"

"I was really scared," Josie said. "He hurt me. He threw me on the ground and kicked me."

Still wrapping her, Judy Frehse said, "Oh good Jesus, baby. Why would he do that?"

"He thinks I'm cheating on him," Josie said.

Silence from her mother, whose face Josie couldn't see.

"I'm not, Mom."

Her mother said nothing, just held her and stroked her hair.

"I'm not cheating on him."

"He can't do that to you, baby. He can't hurt you."

"I'm not cheating on him, Mom." Josie was crying slowly now, just tears.

"Such a mess," her mother said.

"Don't tell Daddy, okay?"

Josie was crying hard now. Her mom was silent.

"Okay, Mom? Please?"

"Let me tell him what he needs to know, but not right now. I won't tonight. Okay?"

"Why did he do that, Mom? He's supposed to love me."

Her mother was rocking her a little now.

"That boy's going through so much."

Josie jerked away, bounded up, leaving her mother holding the shape of where she'd been. "God, Mom. Whose side are you on?"

"I'm on your side, Jos. I am always on your side. I'm just trying to figure out what's going on. You kids are so secretive about your lives. Until something bad happens."

"This isn't something I did, Mother. This is something someone did to me. Someone who I thought I trusted."

Judy Frehse quit the pose of a mother whose child has left her embrace, dropped her arms, let her hand rest on the frame of the ladderback chair.

"I just wish I knew more about what was happening before the bad things happen," she said. "That's all."

"God, Mom, this isn't about you," Josie snapped. She whirled and ran to her room, her back and ribs flashing with pain.

Later, her mother came into her room and stood in the doorway and said, "I think you'd better not be around Matt until he's had some time to cool down. You can tell him we said you're not allowed to see him. And maybe you could think about whatever it is that made him so mad. If there's anything you can do about that."

Josie spoke evenly and quietly. "I did not ask to get dragged out of my truck by my hair and kicked in the church parking lot, Mom."

"The church parking lot?" her mother said, and then clipped her tone. "I . . . we hear things. Around town. You know? People say things. I don't believe everything I hear. But I want to hear them from you."

So you can blame me? Josie thought. But she lay silently until her mother leaned over, brushed her hair from her forehead and kissed it, then left.

And now practice, the place where she could always disappear, was over without offering her any solace and she didn't want to go home and listen to her mother—didn't even want to have to look at her mother—and who knows what her mother might have told her father by now. And she was hungry. So she went to Pep's.

She ordered cheese fries and sat at one of the high tables back from the bar, sipped a 7-Up through a straw and scrolled through her phone while she waited for the food. Everything on Snapchat seemed thoroughly childish at the moment. She'd answered few of the texts she had received throughout the day—dozens from her girlfriends, who knew nothing of what had happened and were caught up in tiny invented dramas. Matt had texted once: I want to see you.

Well, dead people want out of hell. Mikie had sent a DM through Instagram, his new secret way of contacting her. "Sorry about last night," he'd written, "but your boyfriend makes me feel bad about you." *He makes me feel bad about me, too.*

That Mikie, what a weirdo. And then her food came and while she ate the door to the bar opened, and Mikie's mother walked through it. Josie immediately dropped her eyes back to her phone, but Caroline Jensen had seen her. She knew that. She was going to have to look up again and pretend to just notice her and then say hi and be friendly.

What she really hoped was that Mikie wasn't walking through that door next. Josie chewed some fries, scrolled through some more Snapchat videos. But she was sick of the food now and just wanted to leave, to go home and go to bed. She pushed her stool back, dug some bills from her wallet to leave on the table—she knew how much cheese fries cost—and wandered over to where Mrs. Jensen sat at a Keno machine, a short glass full of ice and clear liquid in her hand.

"Hi, Mrs. Jensen," she said.

Mikie's mother looked her over, taking her time. "Well, hello there."

"Having any luck?"

"Luck?" she seemed to be scoffing. "Luck is for young people." Caroline's tongue sat forward in her mouth, filled up space behind her teeth.

"Well," Josie said, "I just wanted to say hi."

"Hi, then," Caroline Jensen said. She kept looking at Josie, looking her up and down like she was trying to figure something out about her.

But Caroline Jensen already knew everything she needed to know about the Josie Frehses of the world. Caroline had known plenty of those girls when she was younger—knew several still. Pretty girls. The world an oyster.

Boys to be toyed with. They had the singing sword, the beauty and untarnished sexuality. This girl, Caroline could already tell, was going to wreck her boy. She wasn't a terrible girl, and it probably wasn't all her fault that she inspired the kinds of hard-ons that drained the thinking juice from men's brains. She was actually sort of nice. But it didn't matter.

She had the singing sword. And she swung it around, oblivious to whom it gashed. Caroline could see that Josie was about to turn away, leave. "Hey," she said. "How are things in school?"

"They're fine," Josie said.

"Can I ask you something serious?"

"Sure."

"Why is your boyfriend always on my boy?"

She watched Josie take a step toward the door, an unchecked instinct, before she gathered herself and said, "That's really complicated. I don't even know. I gotta go, Mrs. Jensen. I haven't even been home from basketball practice yet."

Caroline caught the shift in Josie's demeanor when she mentioned Matt Brunner, saw there was something she hadn't known before. She might not have cottoned to the scope, but she had been a beaten woman, and she recognized a girl in that trap. Maybe he hadn't started yet, but he would. Caroline saw that Josie knew it, too.

"Hey, kid," she said. Josie looked at her. "Misery is optional."

Caroline liked the way that hit the girl. Josie had been leaving, but now stood there.

"You ever need to talk," Caroline said, "I know I don't look like it, but I know some things. I've been through some things. You know what I'm saying?"

Josie wouldn't want to admit to herself that she did know what Caroline was saying. And that was fine. Caroline felt better just having offered. She felt better knowing that Josie had a problem.

Life just got a new layer for that girl. And that Matt Brunner . . . Caroline only hoped her son would stay out of that disaster, though it was clear as day that he was trying hard to walk straight into it.

* * *

Friday Josie went home after school, before the Whitewater scrimmage. She was far less nervous about the game than she was about walking in the door of her family's house. She was stunned to find Matt Brunner's pickup parked behind the house. She almost turned her truck around and left. But she couldn't think of where she might go. It's my house, she thought. Nothing bad could happen here. She heard their voices first.

Then a laughter, the laughter, the way they were allowed to laugh, boys like Matt and Jared. The way those boys laughed when they scored a touchdown on Madden or shot a coyote or made some stupid sex-with-a-cow joke. Not excited. Just steady and assured and in-the-know. Matt and her father and Jared sat around the kitchen table. Josie walked in, didn't say anything. She swung her backpack off her shoulder and let it hang from her hand and looked at them all. She was pausing only for a moment, then heading for her room.

"Jos." Her father. Now everybody went solemn. In preparation, she thought, to become devout hypocrites. Jared pushed himself away from the table and said, "I've got homework."

"Jos," her father said, "I think Matt came over to say some things to you."

"To be really honest, Dad, I'm not interested in hearing what Matt has to say right now."

Her father looked at Matt as if challenging him to clear that bar. Matt had gone from his swaggering self-assuredness to some sort of choirboy imitation. He sat with his hands clasped in front of him on the table. Josie wondered if that was what he had done as a young boy when he'd been in trouble. Nothing about it was cute. Matt said, "Josie, I'm sorry I got a little excited the other night. I overreacted. I shouldn't have. I'm sorry. But there was a lot going on, and you had something to do with it."

Josie had no desire to argue with Matt Brunner. She wanted to figure out what her mother had told her dad. Her father seemed comfortable with the apology that was being offered.

"Dad," Josie said, "do you know what Matt's apologizing about?"

Cal Frehse checked with Matt, then said, "I think Matt feels a little embarrassed about the way he acted, and he's trying to apologize for that."

"Do you know what 'the way he acted' was, Dad? Do you know what he did when he got 'a little excited'?"

"Josie," Matt said.

"I don't need to be drawn into the nitty-gritty of your relationship to know that you kids have been dating for a long time and it would be a shame to throw that all away over one misunderstanding."

"So, you think I should just calm down and be a good girl?" Josie whirled so her backpack wound up on her shoulder. She pointed at Matt. "Ask him. I dare you." She slowly walked out of the room. Just before she turned to go down the stairs to her room, she lifted her shirt, feeling the cool air on the bruised streaks scuffing her ribs. "Ask him what he did."

* * *

The open prairie never failed to fill Tom up, to take him away from what he was and put him where he belonged on the earth. When he swung the truck north, a sudden distance opened and he could see ranks of clouds that were over Canada, growing smaller as they receded, unabated and limitless, toward the far north. The land close at hand spun by, but the distance sat motionless on a neverland horizon.

All day long it was the workings of the sky that drew the eye, but in evening you looked down, too. Shadow pointed up the high contrast, drew the curves of the land, bringing the ground alive. Tom thought it was amazing what a little darkness can do for light. He pulled onto lane of the farm he was going to hunt, drove past the round bales protected by a high fence and then the huge pile of tires, decades of driving discarded in a heap.

In the coulee bottom the melting surface held a billion dirty little dimples, the reflections of wind currents. Scout was crazed, charging toward the stiff, magenta brushstrokes of old willow. He had wanted to watch the boys' and girls' basketball scrimmages, but too many days of inactivity could blow Scout's circuits.

Plus he was still trying not to be idle, trying not to think about why Jenny could change where his life went. Because that would be a good thing, right? Any change Jenny represented would be one toward an overcoming of aloneness. An unfreezing.

Movement. The so-much-all-at-once of her surprised him and made him think differently about what he should be doing. He thought he should be spending more time getting to know her children. He wanted to spend whole nights with her. He wanted to learn her house, and how to base routines from it. He wanted to see how his dog would get along with her cats. And football?

What of that? Because if he stayed here with Jenny, he would not coach football again. He knew that. Maybe they would let him. Maybe David Cates would ask him to. But he was done. The way everything ended had pulled his string. Slab Rideg had coached so perfectly, he deserved the chance to move the program forward. Dumont would be in good hands. But hadn't football been Tom's whole life?

And what if it was? Was there something better than that, something more? Since football had gone away, Tom was pouring his energy into teaching. He wasn't surprised that discussing extracurricular reading with kids like Mikie LaValle brought him pleasure, but he was surprised by how much it did. Maybe he could become a good teacher, the kind the kids talked about, instead of the cruise teacher teaching the snooze class. He could work at it, get better.

Stay in Dumont and teach and see what sort of life might emerge. Tom tromped through the snow, watching the waggling butt of his small dog out in front of him. Scout ran across a swale of winter-dead buckbrush in front of a tall clay-fronted cutbank. At this age, you don't wait and wait and judge and think. You choose and act and move. Or you should.

He hadn't for a long while. The dog's body folded around itself in midleap at almost the exact same time that a flock of Huns showered skyward. Two dozen buzz-beating sets of wings, two dozen courses leaping away with delicate haste in precisely parallel arcs. It looked too easy, so many targets all tightly grouped. They were even swinging from his left to right.

Tom knew by now you had to pick a bird. You had to single one out. Best to pick a lead bird, so if you miss you get a second shot at a trailer. Pick a bird, shoot it, pick another, shoot it, try for the third. Stay calm. Locate and swing. Locate and swing. Locate and swing. Boom. Boom.

Boom. Three birds dropped. He'd done everything right, all by instinct. If he'd had time to think about it . . . who knew? Tom felt elated. A triple. A rare occurrence. But he needed to know what Scout had seen. She was already circling near the first bird. She'd find that one. He didn't know if she'd watched the second and third. He paused to scoop up the small dead feathered pile Scout was nosing, then started running to where he thought the second bird fell. "Dead bird," he said. "Dead bird!" He swept his hand back and forth, palm down, and Scout knew what that meant. Within five minutes she'd found the Hun, and he collected it.

Now he lined up where they'd found the first bird with the second and tried to extrapolate where the third might be. He jogged and called to Scout, trying to jazz her up again. She ran and looked up at him, ran and looked up, not certain she believed him. When he slowed to a walk and swept his hand around and yelled, "Dead bird!" she hunted and sniffed, arced and circled, scrubbing the snow with her nose. But the brush was much thicker here, and the truth was, while Tom was pretty sure he'd killed all three birds, the third would have been on the outer edge of his shotgun's range.

Maybe he'd stunned it and it hit the ground running. They searched for a long time, Tom walking in spirals, Scout working in sweeps. The snow was too crystalline to hold tracks from such a light creature. There should have been a feather, a drop of blood, but they found nothing. The longer they looked, the further Tom's mood fell. The thought of a Hun or a pheasant on the ground in the night, carrying a shot-fractured leg or dragging a broken wing, always made him sick to his stomach.

They hunted for forty-five minutes for the third Hun. He had lost Scout's faith by then. She quit trying so hard and as the sun slipped against the sky and purpled up the clouds, Tom realized he was going to have to quit, too. He hated thinking of that wounded bird, full of adrenaline and huddled under a buckbrush, hoping . . . what?

That it froze to death before a coyote got it? He'd put that bird in a bad place. And so they'd walked back in the gathering dark in a sullen silence. Scout trotted along beside him, checking in every few seconds, but finding no response she could do anything with. Which made going to the bar seem even more inevitable.

* * *

Josie came out on fire, and for a long while felt great. Felt awesome. Felt unstoppable. She was furious at her father and furious at her mother and wanted to show Matt Brunner who he'd kicked. She wanted to punish someone, and the one person the world let her have her way with was whoever tried to guard her. The gym was more crowded than she'd have guessed for a scrimmage. Farmers were not terrifically busy once the winter wheat was in, and the girls' games started late enough for ranchers to mostly get their chores done. The gym was a warm place away from a scouring cold wind.

Before the suspensions of Matt and Alex Martin and Waylon Edwards, the boys' basketball team had been favored for a deep run in the state tournament. The girls' team still was. Ainsley Martin was a cheerleader in the fall, but played basketball in the winter. She was fast and she could shoot. Jocelyn Aarstad, runty Wyatt's cousin, was five feet ten with soft hands and a big body, and she could pivot. And then there was Josie.

Against Whitewater, when Josie brought the ball up the court the first time, she paid no attention to the play swirling around her. She didn't care about running the offense. She just wanted to see how badly she could beat the girl in front of her. Josie didn't know the girl's name—some new kid that she hadn't faced last year. She just saw the girl's high, tight black ponytail and her fervid slashing of hands and hyper little footsteps. Josie brought the ball up at a loose trot, no hurry, a little head fake here, a shimmy there, seeing what the girl was biting on.

She must be some kind of prospect, if she's a sophomore and they're sticking her on me. Either that or Whitewater had nobody, which was a possibility given the size of the school. Their bench held only three players. Josie brought the ball to the right wing, paused, and twirled her hand signal to start her teammate's motion. She had no intention of passing the ball. She dribbled almost lazily, pretending to watch for a pass she could make. Instead she observed the girl in front of her and listened to the short squeals of shoes on the court as players pivoted around her. She loved that sound.

It placed her where she wanted to be. Where she was good, felt good. The Whitewater guard looked so serious. Josie swung a shoulder fake like she was about to dribble-pass to her left, cross court, but kept her dribble alive, jab-stepped left, crossed over right, and drove three steps.

The girl guarding her fell down. Josie launched a fifteen-footer that splashed in. Next time she'd let her teammates play. Because right now she knew everything she needed to know about the girl guarding her. By the end of the first quarter, Whitewater rotated their shooting guard over to double-team Josie, which was fine with her. The first three times they did it, Josie blasted through the double team, just to let them know she could.

But rotating the guard over left Ainsley Martin open almost every time down the court and Josie assisted Ainsley on her way to a career-high scoring night. But mostly Josie kept beating whoever guarded her and pouring in points. Her overly enthusiastic defense fouled her out early in the fourth quarter. By then Dumont was up by twenty-six, so it wasn't a tragedy. Still, instead of congratulating her effort, Coach Bury stared her down as she came off the floor, and then kept openly gazing at her while she sat on the bench. He wasn't shooting daggers.

He was serving up question marks. Josie shrugged, draped a towel over her head, and stared at her shoes for most of the rest of the game. She went through some feeling sorry for the new Whitewater guard, who was probably a nice ranch girl—not much wheat that far north—and probably worked hard and had cows and ballbuster parents and she had walked into something she didn't know anything about. Josie thought a little about not being the best teammate, too, because she had been so wrapped up in trying to prove . . . what?

Something to herself, maybe, something about her value, about her ability and what it could mean. Although that fell flat even in her mind's ear. Because here she was, after lighting everybody up all night, and nothing had changed. There was still outside in the cold a Matt she could not abide, and right here in the gym a pair of parents who could not understand, and all around her a town she could not please. No matter what happened next, the way people thought of her was going to change. She would be the girl who walked away from Matt Brunner. *Thinks she's too good for him.*

Or she'd be another girl who stayed with a guy who owned her. *They're a cute couple but he sure knows how to keep her in her place, don't he?* And so even the sheer release of performing on the court fluttered out to nothing she could hold onto, a plume of wheat chaff swirled away by the wind. Afterward in the locker room, after all the talk about playing better together as a team, Coach Bury caught her by the elbow and asked her to come into his office across the hall and then dragged her there so she didn't have to answer.

He leaned against the small desk in the office, crossed his arms across his chest, and said, "Josie, if there's something you need to talk about, I want you to know you can talk to me."

"I don't know what you mean," Josie said.

"How long have I been coaching you?" He'd been coaching her since she was a kid, got the bump up to varsity coach the year before she was a freshman. "I just want you to feel like if you need to talk to someone, I can be someone safe that you can trust. You trust me, don't you?" he said.

"Sure," Josie said, *but if you think I'm talking to you about anything personal you're out of your skinny little mind.* "I'm fine, Coach."

"You're clearly not fine," Coach Bury said. "What I'm wondering, after watching that display tonight, is how much your being not fine is going to affect our team."

He let her sit in silence for a moment, so she returned the favor.

"Listen, Josie, sure—yeah, you can embarrass a sophomore from Whitewater. But what's gonna happen when we play Belt? What happens when we play Chester? What happens when there's a legitimate threat lined up across from you and you're out there playing like you hate everybody?"

Josie had been staring back at him hard, but couldn't anymore. Nothing he said was untrue. She'd been selfish and stupid and she didn't see how she could change that, given how she felt.

Coach Bury reached out and put a hand on her upper arm. "Basketball," he said, "is sometimes not the most important thing in the world." He saw her look up and said, "I know I try to make it sound like it is, but it's not."

By now Josie was struggling to not cry openly. Her vision split from the welling of tears in her lower eyelids.

"Josie, if there's anything I can do to help you . . . If there's anything you need to talk about . . . maybe there's something you need an adult perspective on, but you can't ask your parents . . . I'm here. And it stays between me and you."

He knew her too well, was the problem. Nothing reveals the ragged depths of a personality like sports, and she'd pretty much stripped herself naked in front of this coach over the years, competitively speaking. It was, she thought, very sweet of him to offer.

But she could never talk to Coach Bury about anything that was happening. There was nobody she could talk to. She'd done this to herself. Or she'd let it happen to her, hadn't been smart enough to see the way she'd become entangled. The way she'd built her world, the bonds and allegiances she'd chosen to prioritize, they all interwove. And in the center of all of them, criss-crossed and double-braced, stood Matt Brunner.

* * *

Jimmy Krock sat at the corner of the L, like he liked to. Brad Martin sat near him, looking oddly tanned for the week before Thanksgiving, and wearing a golf shirt. Greg Hovland huddled over a drink. A dozen farmers and ranch hands and road workers finished out the crowd. An old-timer with a two-foot spill of wiry white beard, Sam Hendricks, sat upright on his stool, sound asleep, arms crossed over his chest. He had the body of a soup chicken. Around it he wore a Carhartt jacket muzzy with a fourth-century kind of funk.

Tom took a seat between Krock O' and Greg Hovland. Hovland looked like he'd just come in from feeding cattle.

"Well," Krock O' said.

"Greg," Tom said.

Hovland said, "Coach." Brad Martin was going to pretend that they were living in different worlds, although he sat fifteen feet away.

Hal Hartack ignored Tom for long enough to make a thirsty point, then strode down and stood in front of him, across the bar, and said, "You been busy?"

"Can I get a Jefe?"

"Sure you can, Coach." Hal started making the drink.

"Well, shit," Krock O' said. "How's that dog of yours?"

"That dog is okay," Tom said. He wasn't feeling like bragging up a dog that just failed to find a bird.

Down the bar, Sam Hendricks woke long enough to reach out and lift the shot glass from the bar in front of him to his lips, drink half of it, then clink it back down on the bar. He re-clasped his arms and went back to sleep. Hal Hartack slid the tequila, soda, and lime juice on the bar in front of Tom.

"How you feeling?" he asked.

"How am I feeling?" Tom said.

"You know, with the long view of time on your side. Are you feeling righteous? Has it all been a terrible mistake? I get curious about the inner workings."

Tom felt red hot, but fought to keep it in check. Hal laughed at him or the world, tapped the bar twice with an empty shot glass, then moved away. Down the bar, a cowboy Tom didn't know was saying to his friend, "She's like a big bucket of chicken. You didn't raise the chicken. You didn't slaughter the chicken. You didn't cook the chicken. It's just . . . there." Hendricks choked himself with his snoring, jerked awake, looked around as if he was surprised to find himself where he was, then nodded back to sleep.

"How you doing?" Tom asked Krock O'.

"I'm so fired up I can't sit still," Krock O' said and sipped his beer.

Tom smiled at that. "Staying out of trouble?"

"If you haven't heard, you don't need to know," Krock O' said.

The bar door creaked open and an old-timer walked in and Tom saw it was Randy Bury. His grandson, Karl, coached the girls' basketball team. Randy went to the bar and sat near the sleeping Sam

Hendricks, looked him over, and said, "That dumbfuck couldn't drive a round stake up a pig's ass."

The glass of whiskey Hal set in front of him clicked when it hit the bar. Randy had it down his throat in seconds. Hal had brought the bottle over to refill it. The second glass Randy sipped at. Snatches of conversation from the cowboys at the bar rose and fell.

"Let me put it this way. You ever wonder what it feels like to kills someone?"

"Not really, no."

"Well you met my ex, you'd at least learn what it's like to want to."

Karl Bury, the girls' basketball coach, walked into the bar, took a look around, saw his grandfather, and said, "Goddamnit, I got family in here. Ain't that just about all of it."

He pivoted and started walking out.

"Did you win tonight?" Hal asked.

"Yeah," Karl said, and he was back out the door. His leaving proved unfortunate, because no more than fifteen minutes later his grandfather, Randy, tilted his empty glass at his face, stuck it down on the bar and scanned the room. His attention fell on Sam Hendricks, who had woken up for a moment. Without a word, Randy Bury lunged at him, swinging a skinny-armed punch that didn't land, but hooked Sam and pulled him off his chair. Both men plunged to the floor. Bury got both hands around Hendricks's neck and squeezed, but he was an old man and his hands could not deliver the intended effect. Everybody in the bar watched what was going to happen.

Tom slid off his stool and reached down and came up holding Randy Bury's arms above the elbows. "Are we done?" Tom asked.

"You better ask him," Bury said. Appropriate enough, because Sam Hendricks lay back on the floor, lifted a bony leg, and kicked Bury in the knee with his boot heel. Tom dragged Bury toward the door. Hal Hartack came around the bar and picked up Hendricks.

He selected one of the cowboys, a Hendricks nephew apparently, and told him he was driving his uncle home.

Once Hendricks had left, it seemed okay to let Bury back in. Tom went back to his seat, said to Krock O', "What was that about?"

Krock O' laughed. "Oh, hell, that goes back forty years. Bury's daughter was getting married and he hired Hendricks to slaughter a pig he could cook for the wedding. Only Hendricks didn't do it. So there was the wedding and no pork."

"He just didn't do it?"

"I've heard different stories. Heard Hendricks couldn't bring himself to kill his pig. Heard he forgot. They served sides at the meal. Bride was horrified."

"They're fighting over this forty years later?"

"Sometimes they get on fine. Then they want to kill each other. No way to explain it."

The scuffle made less than a ripple in the evening. Cal Frehse came in a half hour later and sat down by Greg Hovland. Krock O' leaned forward and directed a comment to Cal Frehse. "Heard your daughter went off on Whitewater tonight."

Cal grunted.

"Played like she was mad enough to eat bees, I heard," Krock O' said.

Cal didn't respond, said something to Greg Hovland. Tom tried to eavesdrop on them, two football dads whose kids played their hearts out that last game. He used to spend a good deal of time talking to Cal Frehse about Jared, and Hovland used to like to hear about the team, the boys. Now it was just a courteous howdy. The two of them were heads-down in conversation.

Tom heard Greg say, "Well, drinking probably isn't the answer."

And Cal say, "No, but it sure helps you not give a shit about the question."

Then one of the ranch hands Tom didn't recognize said to his friend, loud enough for everyone to hear, "Is it just me, or do battered women sound delicious?"

What Tom noticed was how quickly Cal Frehse's head came up. "That isn't funny," Cal said.

"It was a joke," the cowboy said. "Battered, like, beer-battered? Like fried chicken?"

"I know what it was," Cal said. "What it wasn't was funny. You think I'm wrong, you're welcome to come down here and stand in front of me and tell me all about it."

"Easy, killer. I didn't know you had such sensitive feelings."

The ranch hand's friend said quietly to him, "You're a real asshole sometimes."

"Sometimes?" Hal Hartack asked.

The barroom settled down again, but insensitivity was gaining ground as a mode of conversation. A few minutes later, Brad Martin had had enough to drink that he felt fine striding over and standing next to Tom to say, "Saw you at the Absarokee game. Ol' Slab did a helluva a job. I think we might've found our next coach."

It sounded chatty, but Tom felt the entire bar grow eyes and swing them at him. Cal and Greg stopped talking and peered.

"He'd be a damned good one," Tom said. Tom realized without looking that this was the only interaction happening in the bar now. Brad kept plowing ahead.

"You're not gonna apply again," Brad said, like he knew that.

Tom said, "Lot of deciding to do before next fall. For a lot of people."

"Well, shit, after your fiasco, I don't think the board would look real favorably on hiring you back," Brad said.

Hal Hartack stepped between them on the other side of the bar and said, very quietly, "I wonder if you have as much insight as to what the board will or won't do as you think, Brad."

"What's that mean?"

"You didn't exactly manipulate that process to your preferred outcome the last time."

"Well, we let a bunch of Dotty Lantners get on the board, what do you expect? I mean, sweet bleeding Jesus."

Brad drank from his drink and didn't seem able to stop talking. "This coach here would've let Dotty Lantner's little nephew off the bench last year, none of this would've happened." He scanned the room to see how that played.

"Dotty's nephew was a can of lard," Hal Hartack said.

"And that's how stupid the whole thing was," Brad said. "Just that vendetta."

Now one of the cowboys down the bar piped up. "Those boys didn't do nothin' the rest of us all didn't do."

"Just ritual," another said. "A way of belonging. Like in the military. A whole bunch of kids be better off if they went through something."

"It's all stuff we all did," Brad said. "That's what kills me. It was good enough to happen to us, but not anymore."

"Harmless little rituals. Teach a boy to man up."

"Didn't have to be a goddamned crisis," Brad said. "Look at what they did to Matt Brunner. They took his career away. No football, no basketball. No school is going to look at him with a scholarship. I wouldn't give a bucket of shit for that boy's future. They ruined my boy's career, too."

Cal Frehse sat up a little straighter. He hadn't turned to the room, still faced the bar, but spoke loud enough for everyone to hear. "I don't know about your boy, but Matt Brunner's gone a long way to ruin his own future."

"What's that mean?" Brad said.

The lack of response stretched the tension in the room.

"You know something I don't?" Brad asked.

"I sure as hell hope so," Cal said.

That caused a long pause, during which people were unsure if they should laugh. Tom was one of them. He let a little mirth slip out his nose but didn't open his mouth.

"I don't know what crawled up your ass today, Cal, but that boy had his chance to go to college taken away from him," Brad said. "I mean, he was a sure thing for something. And not to tell tales out of school, but the way his operation is going, I don't know see Gary Brunner pulling tuition, room and board out of his ass."

Now Cal swung on his stool and leaned his elbows back on the bar behind him. "That boy better start unfuckheading his life real quick, or going to college will be the last thing he'll need to worry about."

Brad seemed genuinely puzzled and used that as an excuse to work himself up. "Matt's a good boy, Cal. You know that. He's spirited and he does some silly things like we all did at that age, but that boy's been like a son to you the last few years."

Cal stood up, pulled some folded bills out of his pocket, and threw them on the bar. "He ain't like no son of mine. I got a son that age. He knows how to act." Cal nodded at Greg Hovland and at Tom and walked out of the bar.

After a few beats of silence, Hal Hartack said, "There's a story we haven't heard all about yet."

"No wonder his little girl played so mad tonight," Krock O' said.

"You dumbfucks just can't help minding everybody's business, can you?" Greg Hovland said. He went back to drinking like he was all alone in the room.

Tom already knew something more than a high school breakup had happened, though plenty of those had kept this crowd spellbound through the years. He already knew, without knowing how he knew, that whatever made Cal Frehse so mad had something to do with letting kids like Matt bully their way through life.

* * *

After the game, Josie drove home. She tried to find a sad song to listen to, something blued and bottomed-out enough to fit her mood, but she was almost home before she realized her iTunes didn't have anything nearly bruising enough. She drove down the lane to her house, the shelterbelt rows on either side of her funneling her through the dark.

The she reached the end of the shelter belt, turned left, and dipped down into the yard—only to see Matt's pickup parked beside her father's. She didn't care that everybody sitting in the family room saw her headlights, knew she was coming. She threw her rig in reverse and sprayed gravel backing out to where she could whip the truck around. She saw the back door open and Matt run out and she paused for a minute, wondering if he could see her staring at him this far away in the dark. She stomped on the gas, heard gravel pinging off the undercarriage of her pickup, felt the truck dip with the torque before it gained speed. The last thing she saw was her father coming outside and putting a hand on Matt's upper arm as Matt turned for his own rig, and Matt ripping it away and her father grabbing again, harder, pinning Matt against the truck. Let him follow me, she thought.

I'll drive all the way to fucking Canada. The bed of the pickup tried to come around as she reached speed on the long gravel drive, and she counter-clocked the wheel and then had to go the other way to keep it under control. But she didn't lay off the gas. She hit the highway pavement, turned away from town, and roared off. Quickly she realized she had no idea where to go. Beside her in the center console her phone lit up like a Christmas tree.

But she ignored all that. Then she realized she was driving to the reservoir. She pulled onto the gravel, fought the truck as it slewed and yawed over the snow-slicked ruts. And then she stopped. The silence hit her first. She laid her forehead on the steering and cried. Or thought she would cry.

Wanted to cry, but didn't. Instead, she just hurt. Her chest filled like someone had poured molten metal into her lungs. Squeezing her eyes shut felt like the only way to keep her face from bursting. She wouldn't even know until later how deeply her fingers dug into her palms. Josie shouted, slapped at the steering wheel, threw her head around. And then sat up with her chin on her chest, her hair streaming down and felt like there was nothing she could feel that could make anything better. She looked at her phone.

Texts and calls from her mother. From Matt. Lots from Matt. A text from Jared. The usual patter of texts from Britnee and Ainsley, which had nothing to do with anything. And two from Mikie LaValle. She looked at that one and thought, *what?*

What could he possibly want?

The first text said: I saw your game. You were badass. Damn, girl.

The second text, sent just five minutes before, said: I acted bad. I'm sorry. wish I could talk to u.

And just because, just because there was no other reason not to, just because she was so far out at the end of her rope, Josie texted back: what would u say?

The reply was almost instant: I'm sorry. I don't always do the right thing. But I always wish I could do the right thing 4 u.

Josie didn't answer that for a few minutes. Another text came through: I just like talking to u. my favorite thing about this town. Wish it was ok.

Josie texted back: Always ok to talk.

Mikie: Not really.

Josie wrote: Where r u?

Mikie: Home. u?

Josie: Reservoir.

Mikie: y?

Josie: Need a place.

Mikie: 4 what?

Josie: Think.

Mikie: r u Ok?

Josie: idk.

Mikie: Can I come?

Josie didn't answer. She put the phone down. More texts were coming in from Matt, and more from Britnee and Ainsley. Her brother. Maybe they'd heard by now that something was going on. She didn't have the heart to respond to any of it. She was done with responding. That was it. Responses had exhausted her.

Reacting was her whole life. She was tired of it. And yet on some level she knew that not responding to Mikie would draw him in. Josie opened the door of her truck and stepped outside into the cold night. She wrapped her arms around herself and took a few steps from the pickup, closed the door to smother the dome light. Even in the dark, the snowed landscape seemed to be receding from her with speed. She looked up at the moonless night sky, at the brilliant spray of stars, so close to so much far away. As hard as she watched, none of them moved. It was the universe in a crystal state. Josie wanted one star to fall for her.

But nothing did. She was standing there still, wrapped in her own arms, dangerously chilled—muscles tense and shivering, jaw clenched enough to hurt—but unwilling, on this night, to give up a possibility on the scale of shooting stars, when headlights bounced along the reservoir road. While she waited for the lights to come clear she kept watching scattering of pinpoints in the dome of night. Whatever came, came.

Josie moved her head and the whole sky twirled over her. It was beautiful, she thought. There were still beautiful things. And then Mikie was walking from his car. The headlights doused, the engine ticked. His feet crunched on the snow.

"Jos, what's up, man?"

"Stars right now," Josie said. She was shivering uncontrollably.

"Are you okay? I'm a little bit worried about you."

"Why would you worry about me?" Josie asked. Maybe it was the cold, she thought. Maybe she had stayed out too long in the cold in sweaty basketball clothes. She felt so strange, though, not a part of herself. Josie was down there shivering and she was a little bit above that, watching, watching this Mikie boy approach her, knowing what Mikie wanted and how he would try to get it. Josie watched it from her detached perspective and didn't have anything to say about any of it.

"Cuz you're acting a little different, and I just want to make sure you're okay," Mikie said.

It was peculiar, Josie thought, watching it all from her perch outside herself. Something was going to happen and the groundwork was being laid for it.

"I'm fine," Josie said. "Can we get in your car?"

"Yeah. God, you're freezing. Come on." He put an arm over her shoulder and led her to the car, put her in the passenger seat. *Why?* her detached self wondered.

"So cold," Josie said.

"Here," Mikie said. He took off his jacket and pulled the warm hoodie from his own body and gave it to her. He put his coat back on over his T-shirt.

"I'm so cold," Josie said. She heard herself say it, knew why she was saying it. Cold, sure, but that was overcomeable. The emptiness . . . who knew? "I'm freezing, Mikie."

He started the engine, left the headlights dark, and cranked the heater so that gouts of hot air burst from the dash.

"Why are you here?" Mikie asked. "Is it him?"

"No," Josie said, "But it's always him, isn't it. My whole life."

Mikie had an *I-told-you-so* look on his face, but to his credit didn't say it. Instead he said, "I was just thinking, I spend so much time thinking about what it's like to be me and how much that sucks, but just lately I've been thinking about what it must be like to be you. I mean, I guess it's not as easy as it looks. I guess there's stuff people don't always know about."

She said, "It's not easy being anybody."

Josie felt so cold. Mikie's hoodie pressed the cold basketball uniform against her skin. She craved warmth. The car heaters felt faint. She wanted something to warm her full body. She tried to focus on what Mikie was saying, which was, "I want to understand you."

Well, hats and horns. She wanted to understand her, too. But it was a sweet gesture. She said, "I'm so cold, Mikie."

And from her distance she saw how nervous he was, how much he wanted but didn't want to mess up. He put his hands out tentatively and when she didn't notice them, he put out his arms. And then he was holding her. They did that for a while. She shivered less, though the two parts of herself did not recombine. A detached her still saw herself wrapped in this kid's arms, still in basketball sweats, hair in a ponytail, sweat dry on her skin. The kid, her detached self could see, had no idea what he was going to do.

But when he kissed her, she let him. And maybe then the two pieces of herself began to recombine because she realized that she could kiss him back much more ardently, but didn't. She didn't know if she didn't want to encourage him or if she just wanted to let whatever was going to happen happen without accelerating it.

He kissed her twice. His tongue felt stubby and unsure, jabbing at her mouth. But she let it happen. It helped calm the shivers. She felt less rigid. It felt so good to be touched tenderly. He kissed her again, hard this time, as if he was seeing how far he could get going. She put up no resistance. This, she knew, was it. She could not do this and ever be with Matt again. This would end everything.

And then he stopped. "Will you get in the back seat with me?" he asked.

"Okay," Josie said.

Mikie went out the driver's side door and came in through the back seat door. Josie just climbed over. She did not want to go outside again. She'd already started to think about how she would get home, how that would mean going outside again to get in her truck. Maybe Mikie could just drive her, she thought, although part of her knew how stupid that sounded. Mikie took a bit of time getting into the back seat and very suddenly Josie understood why. He was holding a joint when he slammed the door behind him.

"Sweetgrass," he said. Josie heard him chuckle at his little Indian joke. She watched him light the joint and take a long drag, close his eyes, let the smoke slide through his nose. He looked like nothing she'd ever seen before.

"You want?" he asked.

Josie didn't answer. She took his hand, moved it to her mouth, let him hold the joint while she breathed it in. The smoke hit her lungs in an acidic splash, and she coughed so hard she gagged. Mikie laughed at her.

But he talked to her. "Why are you here?" he asked.

"It's stupid," she said.

"It's not."

"It's family shit."

"All families are a dark forest," he said. "Russian proverb."

"I don't get it."

"They all look alike from the outside, but inside . . . who knows?"

"How do you know Russian proverbs?"

"Reading," Mikie took another long hit from the spleef, his eyes squinting. He handed it to her again, "This time, go easy. Just a little sip."

Josie took the joint, sucked less, this time noticing the mossy taste, the musky funk in her mouth. She coughed again, coming out.

"What can books tell me about my life?"

"Oh shit, Josie, I don't know. What do you want to know about your life?"

"I want to know what I'm doing. If it's right or if it's wrong. If I'm making good choices."

Mikie laughed. "You're sittin' in a car, with me, smoking dope. You really need someone to tell you if you're making good choices?"

"I don't care about tonight. I mean the rest of my life."

"The rest of your life is a whole string of tonights."

"Tonight's different. I want to know if my life is going the right direction. If I want the right things."

"Well, that much I can tell you straight up—there's no way of knowing what you're doing until it's all done."

Josie made a face to show him he wasn't helping. Mikie shrugged.

"I was waiting for one falling star," she said. "When you came."

"If you want falling stars, man, you gotta look in August. Perseids. Sometimes there's a hundred an hour."

"How do you know?"

"I've seen it."

"How do you even know to look?"

Mikie laughed. "Oh, redskin shit. Old Indian secret. Or eighth grade science class." He laughed again.

Josie was high fast. Five minutes in, she felt like a guitar string that had just been plucked, the edges of herself all tickly vibration. Mikie seemed so confident all of a sudden, so full of whatever he wanted to say. She wanted to go back outside and look at the stars because she knew they'd all be moving now.

She'd find one shooter. But she didn't want to be cold again. She felt warmer now, warming, and she let herself be drawn into Mikie to feel even warmer. She was surprised by the sturdiness of him. He looked so skinny, so bony. He was, in fact, hard and roped with muscle across his chest and shoulders. Pretty quickly she felt that he had a hard-on.

It was weird being high. Something she'd never done. What was weird was doing it without Matt. All of her firsts had been with him. First time, of course, but so many others. First real kiss. First time she drove. First time she got drunk. First time she spent the whole night with a boy.

First boy who came to her family's for Christmas. Any first she could think of, Matt had been with her. And now she was getting stoned in the back seat of a car with a kid she really knew not all that well. He started kissing her again, those strange, tentative kisses, and this time she let herself be part of it and he almost instantly became more confident. Or more insistent. Her detached self split off again enough to watch and think: *How stupid.*

This boy is getting me high so he can have sex with me. And that will be the end of growing up, the end of being Matt's girl, the end of the part of her life that was really over anyway. And the other stupid, stunned, insensate part of herself thinking: *This is a nice thing I'm doing for him.* She didn't need him to tell her that he was a virgin. He was a mad rush of terrified glee. As high as she was, Josie felt a swell of confidence from his fumbling hurry. She understood that every inch of her naked skin made his fingers clumsier and more dumb.

With Matt everything seemed in his hands—the timing, the pace, the decisions about when each article of clothing would come off, and which ones wouldn't be bothered with. Finally, she was doing something different. She let it keep happening fast, let him keep snatching at her clothes, grasping her flesh, thrilling in his rush. She listened to his breathing, a fast, shallow pant. She felt herself breathing faster, felt herself falling in with him, growing giddy and awhirl.

"Condom?" she mumbled at the right time.

Mikie uncorked a gasp of frustration at the sudden need to speak. "Oh god, you're not going to make me stop now, are you?"

"You don't have one?"

"No," he said, "I didn't know this was going to happen. Can't I pull out? I promise to pull out."

"You gotta promise," Josie said, dopey and sated with sensation.

"I promise."

"Mikie," she warned.

"Oh my god, I *promise*," he whined. "Just don't make me stop."

She was not sure he was ever fully in her before he started pulling out. It was over that fast. Josie was not disappointed. She was, instead, pleased by the power she felt to empty this boy of his anger, his fear, his everything. Pleased with being able to cause him to surrender all his neurotic hang-ups in the pursuit—however brief—of pleasure with her body. She had caused him to hold himself now, in his hands, awash in a baffling puddle of embarrassment and gratitude.

He was apologizing, but she shushed him, held his face, pressed his hair to his head with her fingers. She kissed his mouth, holding him to her even as he tried to pull away, until he relaxed and let himself respond to the sensation of her kiss. *There we go*, she thought as his tongue began to meet hers, *now we finally connected.*

Just before Josie left to get back in her truck, Mikie said, "Can you tell me one thing?"

"What?"

"Why?" When she didn't answer, he said, "Why me? Why me now?"

You're not him, she almost said. But, even stoned, she could see how he might take that. So she caught herself and put it this way: "You're different."

* * *

When Tom left Pep's, very shortly after Cal Frehse did, he walked out into the cold and climbed into his pickup. Tom didn't want to go home. He wanted to see Jenny. Her jaw was too long. Her nose was too long. Her smile was too wide. Her forehead was too wide. He loved all of it. Maybe he was going to love her. He remembered what she had said about moving fast and deeply into like, in case love came along. So he called her. She answered. She said yes, she would like for him to come over.

"I've been at the bar for a while," he warned.

"Not my first rodeo," she said.

Tom drove to her house and got out of his truck and, before he went in, tilted his head back to peer up at the starry sky. There was no moon, though the belt of the Milky Way seemed to hold its own incandescence. He couldn't single stars out. There seemed thousands, and on the periphery of his vision they seemed to be swirling. He couldn't make them hold still. Maybe, Tom thought, it was because there were so many.

Or maybe it was because he'd been drinking. When Jenny opened the door wearing a man's long-sleeved shirt over a pair of flimsy cotton sleeping shorts, purple and patterned and edged in lace, he knew he hadn't woke her, and, even intoxicated, he understood that she'd had time to choose what she wore. The problem with being him and knowing the specific collection of women he knew in the order he knew them—the high school sweetie, the challenging college girlfriend, Sophie, the sad lonely hook-ups in Great Falls and Havre—was never understanding whether the signals were archetypical or temporal.

Most signaling systems were designed to be recognizable to all appropriate user groups. Stoplights. Semaphores. Play calls he signaled in from the sidelines. They all held up over time and circumstance. He knew she could sense his confusion, but she didn't do anything to allay it.

"Do you want a drink?" she asked.

"No, I've had enough," he said.

And she walked to the sofa, sat at one end, curled her legs under herself. He sat next to her.

"What," she asked, "would you do if you never got to coach another football game?"

Well, shit, he thought. *Now we're going to just talk about that?*

So he stalled by saying, "What would you do if you could never teach another class?"

"Be a mom," she said right back, and then: "Oh, shit. I'm sorry. I didn't mean to . . . I'm sorry, Tom."

She had shifted and was petting and then holding his upper arm, and looking into his eyes.

"No, it's okay," he said.

"That wasn't what I meant to say . . . or mean . . . I'm not usually a lout."

"It's okay, really," he said. Because it was. He knew she hadn't meant to say anything other than one of her personal truths. He liked that about her.

He liked that every approach funneled into a straightforward path to who she was. She hadn't let go of his arm, and he hadn't moved. But he was looking at her, seeing her face, the openness of it.

"Tom," she said. "I want to tell you this because I really like you."

"I like you, too," he said, thinking it was funny that what they weren't saying was "I love you." Because they were too old. Because if they were younger they would have been in a hurry to say that, and it would have changed what they meant, changed the way they could talk about how they felt, altered their trajectory. He liked the way they were saying this first instead, knowing they'd get to that other soon enough.

"I'm a mom. First, last, and most of the middle," Jenny said. "That's the most important part of who I am, but it's also not all of who I am. It's not all of what I want for myself. I'm not looking for help raising my kids. But I do want help to make my life interesting and complex and fulfilling."

"For a long time," Tom said, because he felt now was the right time to try to explain himself, "my life pointed at one thing. I thought it was everything, and I gave everything to it. While I was doing that, I met my wife. And we had a good thing. We had a great thing. I mean, it's gone now. I've let it go, but I don't want to pretend it was some sort of bad marriage. It wasn't. She was great for me. She changed the way I felt about what I wanted from my life. And then we had our son, and he changed me even more. And then, when I lost all that . . ." Tom stopped and watched himself, waiting to see if he might choke up. He could feel the urge.

But it seemed important to push through. "When I lost all that, I think I just reverted to that first thing, the one I knew best. I sort of sacrificed myself to it again. Burned up all the pain with constant effort. But I didn't pay close enough attention. I didn't notice the flaws all along the way. I just let it subsume me too much."

Jenny didn't hesitate or give him a moment's cushion to hesitate. One moment he was trying to figure out if he had finished his thought, and as soon as he was looking at her eyes, she was kissing him. She slipped her hand around the back of his head and held him so she could kiss him the way she wanted and he felt it as a sweet relief but then noticed the insistence, the duration, the not-going-away sweep and swirl. It felt like a continual rush of warm sugar melting into his mouth.

When she broke it off, slowly, a taper, a fine point, she said, "I really, really like you."

"I really, really like you, too," he said, and this time he led the kiss.

When they stopped she took a long time to let both of her eyes look at each of his. "What happens to you if you don't coach any-more?" she asked, and he understood right away that she was ask-ing about their future, the chance of it, asking to see a glimpse. He could give her that. Why not? She had whole lives to weigh in the balance.

"I've been thinking about it a lot," he said. "I think I could be happy as just a teacher." Then he hurried to say, "Not just a teacher. Not like that's any small thing . . . I mean I think I could be happy without coaching. I could be happy with the interaction I get from teaching. I could try harder. Be better at it. I could see how it would be rewarding on its own."

He let his head nod a little while he paused to warm up to the second thing. "Just in the interest of complete honesty, I think another thing I could be happy doing would be coaching on staff at a bigger school, maybe college. Not head coach. I'm not say-ing that's the way. I just . . . for the longest time there was one way for me. I wanted to run everything my way. It meant a lot of stress, but the feedback was really clean. W and L. And the results were always ownable. They were mine." He saw her eyes change as she followed him, and knew she was trying to understand, to frame things in a way she could empathize with. And that made his night.

That was great. Because nobody had ever done that for him before. There was more time, there on the couch, Jenny with her hand on the back of his head, her face close to his. They kissed more. They talked. Some of the things mattered. Some was the confetti of tiny laughs that made them feel part of the same procession, one they both understood would march toward a bed together.

* * *

It was not a party, really. Just some junior boys with some beer on the night before Thanksgiving and a bonfire down in a coulee. Josie would not have come if she hadn't had sex with Mikie five nights before. That, she understood, was why she went—a need to make something more legitimate, a need to make something not cheap. That and it seemed so obviously someplace Matt Brunner would not be. Because Josie doubted that Mikie LaValle and Arlen Alderdice and Wyatt Aarstad would know enough to invite girls to their gathering, she made Britnee Mattoon come with her, and Britnee brought Ainsley Martin and a sophomore cheerleader, Brailey Ridenour.

Ridenour? the boys always said, *hell, I'll be done in a couple minutes.* But Brailey was a good sport. She was a rodeo girl, pole racing and goat roping. Brailey had punched a boy in the nose at a party her freshman year because he made a joke about goat sex. After that, the ride-an-hour jokes became more a form of tribute than denigration. As it turned out, because the party was on Wyatt's place, his cousin—and Josie's teammate—Jocelyn was also there, and she'd brought a friend.

The girls outnumbered the boys. Josie and Britnee and Ainsley and Brailey drove together in Brailey's pickup. They had bottles of Twisted Tea that Brailey somehow wrangled, and they were singing "Save a Horse, Ride a Cowboy" as loud as they could. For the first time in a while, Josie felt good. Clear, is what she felt. She was with her girls, doing something she wanted to do. Josie was happy that Mikie didn't start the night possessive.

"JoFreeze," Mikie had said, all hip-hop, when she walked up. When she and her friends climbed out of the truck, Josie could see that Wyatt and Arlen were impressed. Four other boys were standing around a fire pit, all sophomores and freshmen.

Behind them a stand of cottonwoods glowed like tall ghosts in the firelight. She knew the other kids, but none of them well. Of course she played volleyball and basketball with Jocelyn Aarstad and they could talk and would. But after some easy hellos, Josie, Britnee, and Brailey knotted up, drinking from their bottles, watching the firelight lick at the darkness around them.

Mikie came over, bumped fists with Josie, said, "You guys need drinks? You have drinks. Tell me when you need drinks."

It got awkward from there. Mikie went back to Arlen and Wyatt. There was no music, just the crackling fire. The sparks shooting into the dark sky. Except where the fire melted in, there was snow on the ground, and the girls all wore Carhartts and mittens. The boys didn't seem to know what to talk about and so made dumb jokes and laughed more than they wanted to. Josie and the girls she came with huddled and talked about why they were there. They all felt cold.

"I promised," Josie said.

"What promise?" Britnee said. "Why Mikie? You're gonna get his ass shattered by your boyfriend."

Britnee didn't know what had happened with Matt. Josie had told nobody. She said, "I don't want to be one of those people."

"You mean people like us?" Britnee said.

"I don't want to be one of those people who don't do things and don't talk to people because certain people say they shouldn't," Josie said. "You're not like that, are you?"

"Don't judge me for my judgments," Britnee said. They laughed and clinked bottle necks.

Nothing changed for a long while. On the ridges above them coyotes yipped, trying to convince other coyotes of something. The smoke rose from the ring of firelight into near-perfect darkness. Probably there were stars overhead but you couldn't tell near the fire.

The boys had piled a stack of wood as big as a boat, and it was dry enough to spit and snap and shoot streamers of wobbly red sparks into the darkness. Josie could see her girls were losing attention. They'd spent so many weekends of their lives at dozens of parties that looked just like this—pickups, a bonfire, dark empty coulees all around—but the boys here were too young. Nobody snagged an interaction. She felt like she'd organized a mercy mission and everybody arrived to find charity work really boring.

Then Mikie wandered over again. "Ladies," he said, "I just want you to know that we're working with shortcuts to mood elevation, if anybody thinks that would be fun." He acted like the emcee of the party, confident and goofily smooth.

"WTF?" Britnee actually said.

"There's pot," Josie said.

"I'm not smoking pot," Ainsley said.

Britnee looked at Josie. "Are you smoking pot?"

Josie smiled, held her hands up, a definite maybe. Britnee slapped her shoulder. "Josie Frehse, are you smoking pot?"

"I'll do it," Brailey Ridenour said.

"What?" Britnee said, that two- or three-syllable, sing-song *are you kidding me* what. "When did all my friends become dope fiends?"

Ainsley said, "What is wrong with you people? What is wrong?" She grabbed Josie by the arm and swung her from that inner circle. "Smoking dope? Really, Jos?"

"Not really," Josie said. She didn't mean that.

"All you girls? Where was I?" Ainsley asked. "When did this happen?"

"Ainsley," Britnee said. "You really need to try this. Just try."

"No!" Ainsley said, and she stomped away to the other side of the fire.

Mikie produced a one-hit pipe and packed it. He lit and hit it. Re-packed. Handed it to Josie. She cocked her head, looked right at Britnee, and put the pipe to her lips. Mikie held the lighter. Josie burned her lungs, showing off with too deep a hit. Gagged up a thick plume of smoke.

Nobody mentioned it. Brailey said again, "I'll do it." She got the next hit. Mikie packed another one for himself and burned it. Then Britnee said, "Good god. Give it to me."

Headlights spilled over the coulee bank and turned into a pickup truck coming to the party. For a while, every fifteen minutes or so, new vehicles arrived. Two hours after Josie arrived, the party had swelled. Her brother was there, though she stayed away from him because she was sure he would know she was high. Josie was standing arms-over-shoulder with Britnee, who was saying, "This from a guy who nine times out of ten people will say the movie is better than the book." She was talking about the guy she met on Tinder, a guy from Spokane. An older guy.

She wasn't saying how much older. Josie would worry, except that Spokane was such an unreachable place. As a really high person, Britnee having a secret lover there seemed fine. There was a lot of talking around the fire. Josie wandered, talked to Jocelyn, made conversation with Wyatt Aarstad. She smoked again with Mikie and Wyatt and Arlen Alderdice in the dark away from everybody else. Britnee spotted them and came straight over, wanting more.

After a little while they were all standing and talking about many things. Wyatt Aarstad was saying, "You think about it, a hundred years ago I would have shot you as soon as looking at you. We wiped all you fuckers out and it was easy."

And then Mikie was saying, "The way it was with the tribes—before all you fuckers ever showed up—they knew the exploits of famous warriors who went out and did brave deeds. They knew who counted coup, who stole horses. They talked about it formally. Now, what do white people know? You know the exploits of famous people who pretend to be people who do brave deeds. Actors. Clint Eastwood."

Josie couldn't disagree, but also couldn't care. She was stumble-around wasted. She looped an arm over Britnee and they stumbled around without going anywhere and laughed at each other.

Then Britnee stumbled with a little purpose away from everybody else and said, "Josie, can I ask you, can I please ask you?"

"You ask me everything," Josie said, maybe jerking the arm around Britnee's neck too hard.

"Are you hooking up with him?" Britnee said. "Because I do not understand. I don't . . . you are the girlfriend of Matt fucking Brunner. Like why—seriously why—would you even thinking about hooking up with Mikie LaValle?"

"I'm not thinking about that," Josie said, because it was the easiest thing to say and, at the moment, completely true. As if to prove Josie had done the right thing, within moments Britnee started breaking down the colors in the fire. And then she started doing what Josie knew she would do—wandering over to Josie's brother and wrapping her arm around Jared's neck and laughing at everything he said. Maybe a half hour later, Josie found herself standing by Mikie. She said, "You guys are throwing a pretty good party."

He didn't say anything.

"This is kind of a coup," Josie said.

"Is that an Indian joke?"

She laughed and he laughed and then she laughed at him laughing and, knowing she was stoned, found a piece of herself that wasn't completely engulfed in the laughing that thought: *he's not being a jerk.* It all seemed to be going easy. And then another set of lights rolled down the gravel road into the coulee and behind the lights she saw Matt Brunner's pickup. The surety hit her like a sharp elbow in the solar plexus. Matt didn't come alone.

Alex Martin and Waylon Edwards swung out of the truck, too. None of them wore coats, though the temperature outside had already dropped into the low twenties. They knew their arrival was a big deal. Alex and Waylon waded right in, but Matt stopped just outside the sphere of firelight, hands stuffed in his front pockets, looking around like he was trying to find something he suspected would be there, like he couldn't go one step further until he verified his hunch. During that time, Josie tried not to look at him.

She was having trouble standing straight. Her throat felt tight from the weed. She stayed close to her friends, an arm around

Britnee, a "don't go" for Brailey. She had tried not to, but eventually Matt caught her looking at him. He let his eyes press her down, let her feel the weight of what he thought about her until she broke it off. Mikie, Josie saw, was in deep conversation with Wyatt Aarstad and Arlen Alderdice. They were, she had no doubt, offering up the voice of reason and he was countering with the voice of stoned.

What Josie would always remember about how things happened next was that everything seemed so far away. The dope was part of it, she would always know that, but she felt so removed in other ways. She watched what happened like she was peering at the scene through the cardboard tube from a roll of paper towels. She never moved to do anything to stop it.

From Matt arriving until the end, she never spoke to Mikie. Josie saw Matt take a stripped-out beer box, turn it upside down, and sprinkle some of the lighter fluid that had been used to start the bonfire on the bottom of it.

Then Matt lit it up, held it above his head, and patted his mouth with the palm of his other hand, high-stepping around in some mockery of an Indian dance.

"I'm on the goddamned warpath," Matt said to Alex Martin. Both giggled and snickered. Then Matt sprinted over as if to plunk the burning cardboard onto Mikie's head. Mikie batted it to the ground, flapping his fingers like he'd burned them.

"You don't like my headdress?" Matt said. "Try to play along with you fucking redskins and look at what I get."

Mikie looked right and left. People clumped and pressed in.

"Bad night to be an Injun, boy," Matt said to Mikie. Matt seemed very pleased. He looked more energized than Josie had seen him in weeks. "Just like the old days," Matt said. "White man gonna kill your ass."

Part of Josie wanted to sacrifice herself to stop what she knew was next. She'd go home with Matt, let him do whatever he wanted to her if it meant the end of what was happening. But another part of her felt like one of those hawks she always saw floating just above the prairie, bumping and dipping over contours, reacting to things she was not touching.

She heard a new voice, Wyatt Aarstad, yelling at Matt. "Back off," Wyatt shouted. "Get out of here. Nobody needs this shit."

"I need this shit," Matt said, and he rushed Wyatt and seemed to blast him to the ground. He looked around until he found Josie and, staring at her, said, "I'm so tired of this. I need to end this little fucker."

Josie could hear the girls calling for Matt to cool out, back off, shut it down. Maybe one was Britnee. She hoped maybe it was Britnee. People seemed to still be saying things when Matt swung and hit Mikie and knocked him down.

"You're so fucking dead," Matt said.

He didn't wait for Mikie to get up, but rushed in, kicking. Mikie twisted to crawl away and got to his knees and Matt stood over him and punched the back of his head. Nobody else moved. The fire licked portraits of all their faces from the dark. Josie would remember shock and surprise on some faces, but acceptance on others and, even worse, hunger. Matt's arms swung in wide arcs, blurred by dark and firelight. He stopped to kick Mikie's face, stomp on the back of his neck.

Mikie scurried like a rodent, flurrying to cover himself, cowered and hunched. Josie saw Matt grinning, his teeth pressing together in a frantic gleam. Matt letting Mikie get to his feet and grinning, if that's what it was. And then two things happening at the same time. Mikie standing, pivoting. Wyatt Aarstad rushing up and grabbing Matt from behind, encumbering his arms for a moment until Matt, furious at the distraction, whipped one arm free. And also at the same time—all of it happening as if each action were layered on top of the other—Mikie looping his arm at Matt's midsection. Matt's face swiped to surprise and then to hurt.

He sank to his knees and cried out one short, sharp bark. Wyatt fell away from him. Mikie stumbled forward, stayed on his feet.

In all her years of knowing him, Josie had never heard Matt cry in pain. At the very end he sounded like a wounded little boy, confused and unbelieving that the world could hold so much hurt. The knife seemed like some tool from a fantasy book, the shiny glint of stainless steel twinned with a dripping red shimmer of dark blood. She saw it only for a moment before Mikie put it back into whichever pocket or secret place it had come from without wiping the blade. She heard Mikie say, in a near mumble, "I gotta get out of here," on his way to his car, which he drove away at what, to Josie, seemed like a remarkably controlled speed. They were a far way out in the country.

It would take volunteer EMTs a while to reach this coulee, this bonfire. The sheriff might be on the other side of the county, one hundred miles away. They would all have to live with this moment for a while until some adults came and lifted it from them. Matt bled onto the snow. Jared Frehse knelt with him, pressing his hand onto the wound, cradling Matt's head. Josie knew she should go to him, too, but she felt frozen, placed. Moving did not feel like an option. Matt had stopped making any noise except heavy breathing.

Then that shuddered and halted and gasped, several breaths cut in half, finished in heaves. Josie could hear the burning wood crackling, popping, hissing, though the sounds seemed to have nothing to do with the shower of sparks pouring skyward. The undulating firelight lit and unlit bare cottonwood trees overhead, making them look like tall, faint figures taking turns leaning in to see what had happened, to see how Matt Brunner had died.

* * *

Caroline Jensen heard Mikie come in like she usually did. She heard the car, no different than any other time. Heard him fumble with the door. Drunk, probably. Stoned, probably. He spent a lot of his time stoned these days. She didn't think any of these things consciously, just registered it all. A teenaged boy. How was she supposed to know how to deal with a teenaged boy? And she heard him in the kitchen, then in his bedroom, and then she was back asleep. It was hours later when the pounding began.

She woke again, the half-light of dawn brightening the square of window in her room. The trailer reverberated with shock and sound, and then somebody was yelling for her to open up or they would break the door down. She sat up in bed startled, could not imagine what the fuck was happening.

"Caroline Jensen, open the door or we'll break it down," a man was shouting. He knew her. How did a man who would break her door down know her? She thought about the gun she kept in the closet, but then realized that if someone wanted to hurt her, they would have just broken the door down or come in through a window. It must be, she realized, police. She rolled from bed, thrust herself into a robe, hurrying out into the hallway as she twisted the belt. She glanced at Mikie's room, saw the door open.

"Wait!" she yelled. "Don't break it! I'm coming! Wait! Wait! Wait!"

Before she reached the door she saw the red and blue pulses of light on the ceiling in the kitchen. *Mikie*, she thought. *An accident. Some kind of accident. But he was home . . .* She unlocked the door and pulled it open to find Sheriff Rue filling the space in front of her. Two squad cars with light bars popping sat in the driveway. She could see men leaning over their hoods, rifles pointed at her.

"Where's your son?" the sheriff asked.

"What happened?" she asked, but Sheriff Rue was by her already, marching down the hall, a deputy right behind him.

"Where's his room?" the sheriff asked, though it was just a trailer and he went right to it. "Where is he?"

"I thought he was here."

"Did he come home last night?"

"I heard him. What's going on?"

"Get everyone in here, search all of it," the sheriff said, then to her, "He killed somebody."

Caroline didn't believe that, because she was in no way equipped to believe that. She had heard something else, she thought. But something was wrong, very wrong, for so many people to be tearing around her house looking for her son. Mikie killed someone? That was not what the sheriff had said. Had someone killed Mikie? The sheriff's breath was terrible—old booze and recent coffee, not enough tooth brushing. Maybe he should drink more water, too. Something rancid in his gut. One side of his mustache had some brownish stain on the tips near his mouth.

"Is Mikie okay?" she asked.

"We need to know where he is," Sheriff Rue said. She saw the way his uniform shirt stretched at the buttons, noticed a dark blotch the shape of Australia just above his belly, saw the tarnish on his badge.

Maybe if she was nice enough to him, he would tell her where Mikie was, if he was all right. "Do you want some coffee?" she asked. "Some muffins?"

He looked at her strangely. "Where's your son, Mrs. Jensen?"

"I thought he was home. I heard him come home last night."

"What time?"

"I don't know. Late. I was sleeping. But I woke up. I always wake up to hear him come in."

"Did you see him? Did you talk to him?"

"No, I just went back to sleep. Once I know he's here, I go right back to sleep."

"We need you to go into his room and tell us if anything is missing. You have to tell us everything."

Well, sure, she thought. *Why wouldn't I?* At least they had stopped with the he-killed-somebody business. "Okay," she said, "I will. But can you please tell me what's happening?"

The men looked around inside the trailer and all around it, which seemed pointless to Caroline because Mikie's car was gone. He was gone. They asked her again what was missing. His coat, his boots, nothing much. Some books, she noticed, and told them that. The books that he always had by his bed, three or four of them. She was going to bet that his little ceramic one-hit pot pipe was gone, and whichever bag of weed he happened to be working through, but she didn't think she needed to tell them that. They asked her where he might go.

The reservoir, she told him. Other than that, she couldn't imagine. Where did he go? Why didn't she know this? When the deputies were all back in their cars, Sheriff Rue stood in her kitchen talking down to her while she sat at the table and held her robe tightly around herself. "If your son comes home, we need you to call us immediately," he told her.

"What is happening? Can't you please tell me what is happening?"

"Mrs. Jensen, your son was involved in an altercation at a party. We believe he stabbed another boy. The other boy is dead."

"No," she said. A long, dubious *nooooo*. "Mikie didn't kill anybody. Who did Mikie kill?"

"Ma'am, this is an active investigation. We'll be able to tell you everything eventually. Right now, it's imperative that we find your boy. I think he's a danger to himself and to others."

"Mike? Mike LaValle? Do you know my son?"

"Ma'am, Caroline. I just left a crime scene where a boy I've known for a long time, a boy I watched grow up, has bled to death in the snow after about twelve different kids say your son stabbed him with a knife. Okay? That's what I know. Nobody told the story a different way. And I also know you had better contact us the minute you hear anything about where he is. Anything at all. If he calls, if he texts, if he shows up."

She said she would, though she wasn't sure that was true. Suddenly there was so much to think about. Mikie had stabbed somebody.

"I know it's hard to hear," Rue said. "I'm sorry. But what's best for your boy is that we find him and get him under control, because he's not under control right now."

"Tell me what they say happened," she said.

"We have to go look for your son," Rue said.

"Who was it?" Caroline asked, though she knew already.

"A classmate," the sheriff said.

"They bully him so hard," she said. "You know that, don't you?" Caroline knew she was saying things to try to make him stay, because if he left her alone here without telling her something different than what he'd already told her, then that would be what had happened. She needed to find a way to make him tell her something else had happened, that it wasn't the way everybody thought, that maybe there had been a mistake. But he was leaving.

His hand twisted the doorknob. She found herself telling stories about things that she had witnessed in the lunchroom, acts of aggression. "They're awful to him. They say hateful, racist things because he's mixed. They say hateful things about me and about him and they push him around. They throw trays of food on him."

The sheriff said nothing to that, just paused in the open doorway, letting the cold bright air pour inside, and looked at her. It was strange, the power of her longing for him to stay—this terrible man who had told her such terrible things. Not because she believed for a moment that Mikie had killed somebody and wanted to help them, but because she did not want to be alone in the trailer on this morning. What if Mikie came home?

What if he didn't? When the squad cars pulled away, she noted how ordinary their tires sounded on the old, dried snow. How the trailer had filled with morning light and looked nothing anymore like the garish scene in the murky dawn when the blue and red lights had washed over the ceiling. You spend your whole life raising a boy—never an easy boy, never a dull moment, but always the great love of your life. You pour all of yourself into that child and the way you live with him and you spend countless hours thinking about what is best for him, whether living here is better than living there and what your TV-watching policy should be and whether you should make him eat things he doesn't like because they're good for him.

Even if he's awkward, you want good things to happen for him and even when he's pursuing things you think might end in heartache, you cheer for his gumption in recognizing what he wants and going after it. None of it is easy, but the loopy grins, the occasional wholehearted hugs, the objective view of him interacting with his peers, finding acceptance in a friend group—they make it all worthwhile. And then one day the sheriff comes and tells you your boy has stabbed somebody to death.

How do you start a morning with that and move through a day? Outside, the sky was huge and pale blue and everything under it looked so ordinary. The leafless cottonwoods stood still, though she didn't have the sense they were waiting for anything. Under them, tall spears of dry, yellow prairie grass poked through the snow. The huge fields of yellow wheat stubble stretched empty and motionless, unchanging. A hundred yards away in the creek bottom three mule deer does switched their tails and gnawed at the frozen ground.

Nothing about the way they acted indicated a change in the world. Could Mikie really have killed Matt Brunner? If she was honest there were plenty of days she felt mad enough to kill Matt Brunner. But not really. Swat him. She'd wished she could clout him across the mouth on a few days.

How badly had he pushed Mikie this time? Mikie would have had to be pushed. It would have to be extreme circumstances. Something extreme. And then an accident. Defending himself and . . . what? Trying too hard. That was what she would be able to hold onto, how she would find a way forward into the day. But then she thought of how scared Mikie must have been to do something like this. How scared he must be now, going who knew where.

* * *

Tom woke with the light and knew nothing more than he had known when he went to bed the night before. Winter. Cold. Except he was in Jenny's bed. He turned his head and looked out the window—second story, a new vantage point at this time of day. But even from here, the land tilted toward an unbelievable horizon, beautiful and immense, the distance even in early hours so very far away. It was Thanksgiving. He turned back to Jenny, could feel the warmth of her legs tangled with his, felt her hair cool on his cheek. He kissed her forehead and started to gently slide his arm out from under her body. She woke.

She pulled him to her. "Shhhhh," he said. "The dog. I have to let her out. I'll come back." They had until afternoon together and alone—she had, the night before, delivered her kids to their father for his family's Thanksgiving gathering near Chinook. Jenny made a not-really-awake sound of acceptance, and he slid from the bed. He drove through the silent streets of town and then to his farmhouse. Scout was scratching at the door when he stepped up to it. He let her out and started walking across the fields, his legs light, the crunch of frozen snow under each step. Scout was such a busy little girl, so different when he didn't bring his shotgun.

She made up her own mind. Far to the south, somewhere down south of the Missouri probably, somewhere a hundred miles away, Tom saw a line of clouds sketched along the horizon, purpled along the bottom, definitive and solid enough to be a front. Maybe it would affect them. But the west looked clear, a curve of bending light, hundreds of miles of land between him and the edge of the earth. He had read that, at sea, you can see seven miles to the horizon, and on land, without elevation, it was much, much closer. But he didn't believe that. Some days he saw the faded blue serrations of mountains he knew were a hundred miles away.

Some days he saw the weather in Canada. He walked a half mile along the top of the coulee, seeing bird tracks but no birds. A group of pronghorns seemed to float across the wheat fields several hundred yards away, their tight, fast footwork not evident from this distance. A rough-legged hawk wheeled overhead. When it was time to turn around, Tom felt himself walking a little faster.

He was looking forward to crawling back into Jenny's bed, to her warmth. He was excited about her waking to him. Back at the house, his cell phone on the kitchen counter had a notification on the screen. One missed call. Jenny. *Why Jenny?* She should be sleeping still. He called her right back.

"Hey," she said. That's what she said to him now when he called. "Hey." A warm invite into whatever conversation might follow. A rest before beginning. A moment of connection. But this one was quicker. "Hey."

"Did you hear what happened?" she said then.

"About what?"

"You didn't," she said. "Sit down, Tom. It's bad."

"Are you okay?" he asked.

"It's not about me. It's about Matt Brunner. He was stabbed to death last night."

"Are you . . ." and he stopped because he was going to say "fucking shitting me."

"It was Mikie LaValle. There was a party or something and a fight and Matt got stabbed, and he died before the ambulance could get there."

"Holy . . ."

"I was thinking," she said, "maybe I could come over there." But it wasn't really a question.

Tom couldn't imagine how that might help anything. What he needed to do was get into town and start talking to people. He needed to see David Cates. He needed to see the Brunners. He needed to talk to Caroline Jensen. He wanted to hear what Krock O' knew. But then he listened to that inner scrambling and compared it to the voice on the other end of the phone and what she was really saying. *I can be with you. I want to be with you.* He said, "I wish you would."

Tom would never understand how they wound up in bed so quickly after she arrived. She had come through the door, thrown her arms around him, hugged him so close.

"This is Dumont," she had said. "This doesn't happen here."

He had held onto her and felt her diminishment. He had long before grown tired of comforting people when the world did not meet their petty expectations—of big screen TVs and late model pickups and not enough playing time—but the story Jenny's body told him was about bewilderment.

The only thing he could reciprocate with was physical surety. *I'm here*, was all he could say that made sense. In that way they wound up in his bed at 10:00 a.m. on Thanksgiving morning, Tom elevated by her need for reassurance—and by this sudden release for his own tricky thinking. Jenny was new to him this way. Her body felt long and lean and useful, more responsive in the uneven sighs and peaked cries than even the night before.

When they were done, he wanted to say something about the way he felt. But she seemed past that. She seemed to accept already everything he would struggle to say. Which left him dwelling on Matt Brunner.

"I know," she said. "I've never known anybody who was killed. And by somebody we know."

But that wasn't it. Tom was focused on where he'd gone wrong with Matt—and with Mikie. If he had not fallen asleep on that team bus, if he had not been distracted by Sophie—*I feel bad about so many things*—if he had been able to build a better team, better young men. If he had engaged with Matt Brunner and directed his development—instead of just using him to run an offense. Shit, if he had *liked* him more. And Mikie LaValle. Why hadn't he followed through more? The workouts, the books he borrowed, the lessons. There was so much to feel bad about he didn't know where to get started.

"I know you want to blame yourself . . ." Jenny started. "But Matt wasn't just a quarterback. I had him in classes—he was a lot of things and there were dozens of places where someone could have tried to help him see things."

"Who was closer to him than me? Who spent more time with that kid than I did? And in all those teachable moments? What did I teach him, how to get yourself killed in high school?"

"He seemed in control. Who seemed more in control of his life than Matt Brunner?"

"LaValle came to me, more than once. He wanted to learn more about his heritage. Metis, mixed blood. I think he's Blackfeet, not Metis, but he was interested in the history. I gave him books, we talked after class sometimes. I gave him a workout to do. Tried to get him to quit smoking and start running. He wanted more. I blew it. I had a huge chance and I didn't follow through."

"A kid who's troubled enough to stab another kid to death, there's maybe not much people like you and me can do to save that kid."

"But it's all the steps along the way. It's all the touchpoints where people can make a little difference here and a little differ-ence here and change the way a kid turns out. You have to believe that or you wouldn't be the teacher you are."

"It's hard to know when you can make a difference or not."

"In this case it seems so easy."

"It's hard to know how much time you have. You thought you were connecting with Mike. You thought you had time to let that develop. He's a junior. You thought you had all that time. You didn't know he was going to stab someone the night before Thanksgiving."

They got out of bed around noon, Jenny starting to be con-cerned about being home when her kids came back, her own Thanksgiving treats ready for them. Tom had some places he needed to go. He drove first to the Brunner farm. He'd hunted there for years, felt familiar with every dip and roll in the land. All of it lay there, where it always was, when he pulled into the drive. Gary Brunner came out of the house to meet him before he could even get out of his pickup.

"I know you mean good," Gary said, "But it's not a good time. There's nothing good to talk about here."

"I just want to offer my help," Tom said. "If there's anything I can do."

"You gonna bring my boy back?" Gary asked. He cried openly while he spoke.

Tom didn't answer.

"Then there's nothing you can do."

"I'm so sorry," Tom said.

"Everybody's sorry," Gary said. "Everybody's so goddamned sorry they don't know what to do with themselves."

He turned and walked back in the house, waving his arm in a gesture for Tom to go.

So he went to Caroline Jensen's trailer. He thought he would be one among many people at her home, trying to help. He was surprised to find her alone. She came to the door, wrapped in a robe.

"Did I wake you? I'm sorry."

"No," she said. "No, no. No. They came so early. Still asleep. And now."

They stood, Caroline leaning on the arm that held the screen door open against the spring, Tom half leaning in. She seemed feeble in a way that he pitied.

"I know I don't know you very well," he said. "But I had some interaction with Mike. I liked him a lot. He was an interesting boy."

"He's not dead yet, is he?" she asked. She seemed to be asking if there was news she hadn't heard yet. Tom felt stumped until he realized what he'd said.

"I want to help however I can," he said.

"They say he stabbed that boy. They said he bit that boy. That boy took his truck."

Oooh, he thought, not tracking. He thought to ask something concrete. "Do you know where he is?"

"He's afraid. He is so afraid. Can you imagine having a son who is so afraid?"

For a moment, just a flash, Tom wanted to tell her about what it was like to watch a son die, to be there and see it and know that the boy knew he was dying. A thirteen-year old kid who had lived just enough for Tom to understand how much he hadn't lived yet, cold and bleeding on the pavement, knowing that what he saw, his father's face, was the last thing he was ever going to see.

The cold, livid fear in that boy's eyes. Yes, he wanted to say, I can imagine that. But she seemed so feeble, so unanchored. He wanted to put an arm around her and pull her in. Give her some-place to feel sturdy. But she offered no opportunity.

"I think Mike needs someone to talk to," Tom said. "I want to help if I can."

"If I talk to him, I'll tell him to call you."

And shit, Tom thought, because Mikie's actions had collapsed this woman's life, too. "Can I make you some coffee?" Tom asked her.

"The coffee's in the fridge."

"Okay, I'll get you a cup."

Normality, he thought. Everybody hates it until they need it, and then they grasp at every piece of it. He stayed with Caroline for two hours and eventually sussed out, because he felt the mob roil of hunger in his own gut, that she hadn't eaten a thing since the day before.

"How about I order a pizza and go pick it up?" he said.

"I can make something," Caroline said, churning at a higher level all at once. "I have cherry Pop Tarts. He loves cherry Pop Tarts. I always have those for him."

"Um, I like those too, but you know what I really like? Pep's pizza."

"Oh, my god. He loves Pep's. But it's too far. Stay here. I have coffee and Pop Tarts and mac and cheese. I have so much mac and cheese."

Tom understood that she was unhinged. He knew why she didn't want to be alone, though he didn't know if he would be much help. Maybe he could bring Jenny back here.

"I have my dog at my house," he said. "She's a wonderful little dog. I need to feed her and let her out. Why don't I go get some pizza from Pep's and get my dog and I'll bring them both back here? You're going to need to eat, too."

He could see her working that out, understood how it could feel both comforting and threatening to her.

"I'll be back in less than an hour," he said.

"What will I do?" she asked.

"Hm," Tom said. "Well, can you think about where Mikie might be. You could take a shower . . ."

"My baby's running for his life, and you're talking to me about a shower," she said. Tom noticed how close she had come to wailing it.

"It might just feel comforting. Hot water." He could see that register.

"I'll be back in less than an hour," he said.

But he wasn't.

He called in the pizza order while he drove home. He wanted to get Scout out, maybe bring her with him. It might be a long evening of not being home. He turned into his drive and crested the small rise, seeing the landscape fall away beyond, fall into sky and white distance. When he topped the rise and could see his house, he saw a car already there, a car he didn't immediately know.

Tom drove slowly down the drive. Such a strange day, such strange things happening. The car was a low-slung sedan, not exactly useful for the kind of life most people led around Dumont. He saw the shape of the driver hunched in the seat. A young man-sized shape. He rolled slowly beside the vehicle.

Tom parked beside the car, looked over. The dark shape turned and had a face. Mike LaValle. It was impossible to think of him now as Mikie. Tom couldn't help but wonder, how does one act in this situation? He thought about how much danger he might be sitting next to. Mike could have a gun. He had a knife. He couldn't be too stable. It was possible he was unraveling, that he associated Tom with Matt, that he had an agenda. Which led to questions about how to act next. He could just drive away. Shift into reverse, turn around, drive fast out the driveway.

Call the sheriff, tell them to come get the kid. He had seen Mike's eyes. Something made him not want to. He wanted to look away, like you do when you see a bear out in the woods, or a mean drunk in a bar. But right when Tom had been trying to figure out who it was, Mike had turned his face and looked right at Tom and their eyes had met. He couldn't unsee those eyes.

They held defeat. Tom opened his door, stepped out and stood. He walked around the front of the truck and said, "Mike. How are you?"

Mike looked at the horizon, scratched the back of his head, and answered a different question. "I have these books," he said. "Your books. I want to give them back to you."

"Oh," Tom said, "I'm in no hurry to get them back. You can keep them as long as you're getting something out of them."

Mike opened his car door, lifted up a brick of books, four of them. "Here," he said. "I don't think I'm going to get anything out of them anymore."

"Okay," Tom said. He didn't want to move any closer, but he did. He took the books like it was no big deal, tucked them under his arm, gave Mike a searching look. "You wanna come in? I have to let my dog out."

"Sure," Mike said, "I guess." Like he had nothing better to do. Like he wasn't on the run in a way Tom could not imagine.

"Come on," Tom said.

At the door, Tom could feel Mike at his back while he fumbled with the handle. Mike had come up fast and close. Tom thought maybe this was a huge mistake. Maybe Mike was only coming in to make sure he didn't call the sheriff. But Mike didn't seem that predatory. He didn't seem to be hunting. He walked into Tom's house and obviously wanted to see it. He peered around. First he petted Scout, who acted as if the floor was electrified and stepping on it for even fractions of a second sparked unbearable agony.

Tom held the door open and called Scout out. He was standing inches from the boy. He waved at his bookshelf. "There might be something there you find interesting. If there is, just grab it." What he was thinking was: *You're going to have a lot of time to read in prison.*

They spent some long, nervous moments with Mikie scanning the spines, pulling some books out and reading the backs or inside covers. He put them all back. Tom could tell he wished he didn't have to. He stood and watched and pretended to watch Scout while she sniffed the aromatic news of what had happened in her yard since the last time she had been out.

"Did you ever do that workout, Mike? That one I gave you?" He knew Mike had—Caroline had told him—but wanted the boy to stay aware of connections.

"Yeah," Mike said. "Shit, yeah. I've been doing it every day for a while."

"That's great," Tom said. "Great."

Tom opened the door again, looked out into the snow for Scout. It's funny, he thought, being at home on a cold and bright sunny day with a kid who killed somebody last night.

Mike stopped looking at the books, walked across Tom's living room and sat on the couch. Which surprised Tom. What came next didn't surprise him at all, but the deliberate gesture of comfort that set it up set him off guard. Tom sat in his armchair.

"You know what happened," Mike said.

Tom wanted to be careful here. "I heard something happened. Everybody has heard different things. But I don't know what actually happened."

Mike slump on the couch and blew a huge sigh. He put his elbow on the couch arm and his hand came to his face and his fingers touched his lips gently, almost preciously.

"Do you want to tell me what happened?" Tom asked.

Mike cut a glance at him, looked away, stared out the window. His tone grew sleepy. "It's prolly like they say."

"I don't know," Tom said. "I haven't heard anything from any-body who was there. Most of what I heard was from your mom, and even she doesn't know much."

"You talked to my mom?"

"I went to your house, yes."

"Why would you do that?"

"I," Tom said, stretching it out, "thought she might need some-one to talk to. She's worried. She would really like to hear from you."

"I can't believe you went out there." Tom couldn't figure out if Mike was angry or impressed. The boy's voice seemed to swerve between disinterest in everything around him to a pierc-ing ferocity.

"I'm not trying to tell you what to do, but you would be doing a great thing for your mom if you just call her and let her know you're alright."

"You can let her know I'm alright."

"I can. But it won't be the same. She wants to hear your voice," Tom said, and then thought to try, "like I would if you were my son."

Maybe it was his thoughtful reckoning. Maybe they'd run out of things to say. A silence pervaded for the next little while, and Tom didn't try to prick it. He kept looking at the kid on his couch, a pile of long bones leveraged in strange angles, a sharp, fierce face even in its obvious despair. But Tom couldn't imagine this kid ending the undeniable, gonna-win, gonna-beat-you, gonna-star vitality that had been Matt Brunner. At every moment, Tom knew he should probably be calling the sheriff.

He would, when Mike left. Maybe right away, maybe a couple hours after the kid had a chance to get going. It occurred to him that he didn't actually want Mike to be caught, to go into the system, though he supposed it was an eventuality and probably best for everybody. Even Mike. Between now and then there were spaces. The space between sympathy and kindness.

Between vindictive and shamed. Between what he knew everybody else would think and what he could live with. None of this would make him feel righteous, or even right. He'd already failed this boy so much. Why had they not sat like this months ago, sat and talked about books and history and heritage and hunting and girls and trouble and what was worth celebrating? Mike wiped the back of his hand across his face.

"I did it," Mike said. "I'm not going to pretend I didn't. It was different than I thought it would be."

Tom sat in silence, hearing the confession. It was what he'd always heard, the guilty always want to tell their story to someone.

"He was going to hurt me," Mike said. "He was always going to hurt me."

In his head, Tom was making the distinction between hurt and kill.

"I can go to Canada," Mike said. "You can tell the cops or not. It doesn't matter. I know so many little ranch roads that cross the border. They got Blackfeet reservations there, Peigans and Bloods. U.S. rules don't matter."

Tom pressed his lips together, nodded as if he were weighing the plan.

"Mike, why did you come here?"

"I don't know. Bring your books back."

"I'm going to ask again, because it matters. Why did you come here?"

"I don't know. You always treated me nice. Better than most people."

"Do you trust me?"

"Not really."

"Okay," Tom said, accepting the honesty.

"You knew him. You know what he's like."

"Yeah," Tom said.

"I just wanted him to stop fucking with me. He was always fucking with me. I just wanted him to leave me alone and leave Josie alone."

Tom's first reaction was to say something about finding other ways to do that, but he was stuck with his own question. Why was Mike here? The enormity of what had happened meant the past was scorched earth. There was only next. Whether he could say it out loud, Mike must have come to him for help in figuring out how to get through the next part.

"Canada," Tom said. "I can see why that sounds good. But that life, always running. Never seeing people you care about. Your mother. Josie . . ."

"Or I see them on visiting days, with handcuffs and all the shit?"

"Running is a dream, but it won't be better," Tom said.

"I've been having dreams about running," Mike said. "About horses with white manes, running and running over the prairie and there's never anywhere they're going."

Tom stood and peered around at his surroundings. He was going to let the dog in, he'd decided. He could hear her whining at the door. He wanted to give the boy some space. He didn't know what Mike would do with it, though.

Mike sat up, scooted to the edge of the couch, propped his elbows on his thighs. His fingers seemed to be working out some intricate puzzle between his knees and he watched that process. Then he looked up, out the window, his eyes suddenly full of something, looking as if there were something to see out there instead of distance, something he might find right over the other side of those long horizon lines. Tom stood, stepped over to the couch, let his hand touch Mike's shoulder. Mike didn't acknowledge it.

"Your life won't let you go, Mike. I can tell you have an idea of how it will be, but it won't be that way. Even if you break clean, you have to live with you. You wake up every morning knowing everything you know about yourself. There's no avoiding that. I

can't tell you what to do," Tom said, "but I can tell you that sometimes the only way around the hardest parts is right through the
middle of them."

He patted Mike's shoulder twice, then moved away, went to
the door, let the dog in. Scout dashed for the boy but seemed to
sense a trouble and veered instead to Tom. He scratched her ears,
the back of her head, and then went into the kitchen and got her
food from the pantry, filled her bowl. Scout ate every day like she
was afraid he might pull the bowl away forever. Tom dumped her
water bowl in the sink, then refilled it from the faucet. He spilled
a little putting it back on the floor and got a towel to mop up the
water. He didn't hear the door open and close. He looked up when
the engine started.

He watched through the window as Mike LaValle pulled out of
his driveway. His eyes followed the car up the rise and he thought,
I've failed again. He thought he should call the sheriff. First, he
called Caroline Jensen.

* * *

On the Monday after Thanksgiving, Josie was walking from
the high school to Pep's after school, because they always did.
Ainsley and Britnee always had cheese fries, though that seemed
impossible in the days just after Matt Brunner had been stabbed
to death. Impossible. But it was what they always did after school,
before basketball practice, and she needed these girls now. She
needed their physical presence, needed to know they were
talking and thinking about the thing she couldn't stop thinking
about. Nothing they could do would ever change the things she
knew, but she needed them with her to remind her of who she
was. The car cruised up fast and halted, parked in front of them.

Ainsley let out a small scream. The day was sunny and bright in
the way that only extreme cold can be bright—hard tight bands of
pastel blues and whites stretching for endless miles in the sky, sun

glittering on old snow. Josie knew he'd be slumped in the driver's seat. Britnee grabbed her triceps and yanked her toward the bar, but Josie whirled her arm like a fencer and broke the grip.

"I have to . . ." Josie said.

"You don't," Britnee said, then to Ainsley, "Call 911."

"He killed Matt," Ainsley said. "What if he kills you?"

Ainsley tried to grab her, too, but Josie easily sidestepped and trotted the few steps to the car. Ainsley and Britnee both dug cell phones from their pockets. Mikie rolled the window down. He didn't open the door. Josie did. She pulled the door open, leaned in and hugged him. He twisted and tried to return the embrace. He wound up hugging her arm.

"What did you do, Mikie?" she said into his neck. "What did you do?"

"I had to see you," he whispered.

"They're calling the sheriff," she said.

"I don't care. I'm not going to run away."

She pulled back, her hands still on his shoulders, and squatted down in the open door space. She realized that part of her wanted to be hidden, though she knew she wasn't.

"What did you do, Mikie?" she asked again, not a question in search of an answer, but an acknowledgment that a huge and permanent thing had occurred.

"It was gonna happen," Mikie said.

Josie moved her hands, held his face. She wasn't hearing what he was saying. Still squatting, she looked at Mikie, tried to remember a different version than this gaunt, exhausted boy with sinkhole eyes. She tried to remember him on top of her, the way he looked and felt to her in the backseat of this same car, by the reservoir that night.

But she failed, and she found herself holding his face and asking, *Who is this boy?* She felt so afraid for him. She knew what would come next would be horrible. She reached into the car, let her fingers run through his hair. She liked the feeling of his hair, the glossy strands falling over each other in her fingers like they were liquid.

"You're turning yourself in," she said.

"It was self-defense. Anybody who was there could see it. You could see it."

Josie nodded, not sure of what she could see, not wanting to be told what she should see.

"Everybody saw it," Mikie said. "He said he was going to kill me."

Josie was glad she got to see him one more time. She was glad he wasn't going to try to run anymore. She didn't want to be part of any alibis. She didn't want him to ask her that. Whatever happened to him would happen without her. Down the street she could see two sheriff's deputies rush out of their headquarters and start running toward them.

Maybe it was that she didn't have anything else to say. Or maybe it was that the deputies ran fast. Either way, nothing more was said before the two men crossed her vision at the hood of the car, and she stepped back suddenly to leave them a clear path to Mikie. She stood a few feet away as they tore him from the car, whipped him over the hood, slamming his head and wrenching his hands behind his back for the handcuffs.

And then Mikie was just walking down the street, right past Pep's and the IGA and the abandoned real estate office like it was any other day—except he was walking fast, jostled, his hands cuffed behind his back and men holding onto each arm.

* * *

The trial happened quickly, less than three months later. There seemed no reason to delay. The courts had an opening for murder. The lawyers couldn't come up with requests that would delay. There was no countervailing evidence. Tom had no desire to see the trial, but he'd been told he might be called as a character witness, and so he had to drive to Great Falls. Jenny wanted to go, too, but too many other people would be missing from school, she thought. She should stay and try to add to the normalcy. Tom drove by himself. He had never been to a trial. He'd been called for jury duty, but never asked to serve. He walked into the lobby of the La Quinta in Great Falls and saw Cal and Judy Frehse walking out. Of course Josie would be a witness, but he hadn't thought about her being here. It seemed like too much to ask.

Cal greeted him a little too loudly, said, "Never thought we'd run into each other for this."

"I don't think this is good for Josie," Judy said, letting that linger long enough for Tom to agree. When he didn't, Judy said, "She's obsessing over it. She needs to move on. This isn't helping."

"Maybe there can be some closure here."

"I can't imagine he'll get off," she said.

Tom made a face to say he couldn't imagine it either, but who knew? "He never said he didn't do it."

Cal shook his head at his feet. "How the hell did this all happen, Tom?"

"I just can't imagine," Tom said. He really couldn't. Six months ago he'd been looking forward to coaching the most talented football team he'd ever had. He'd felt excited after long years of not feeling excited. Six months ago.

"I thought for a long time that boy would be my son-in-law," Cal said. "I thought I knew all about him. Then he jumped the rails. Maybe this Indian kid had something to do with that."

"I wonder about that," Tom said.

That night, Tom lay on the strange bed, a foam mattress that wanted to mold to the shape of his body. Nothing about that idea made it easy to sleep. He didn't want to be called as a witness, by either side. Both attorneys had taken statements from him. Mike LaValle's lawyer, a public defender in his mid-forties named Chris Gossens, sounded passionately perfunctory. From behind, you wouldn't have to know he was a fat guy. Almost all the questions were leading, which was fine, he supposed in a deposition, but so obvious that Tom doubted the man's cleverness. Still, Tom thought, if you were in your forties and still a public defender, you were either an ideologue or a failure, both of which were equally problematic. The prosecutor was pure prick.

He had come on as a ranch boy working in the law to keep the home place afloat. His parents, he was quick to tell Tom, still had the homestead out near Dutton. Mostly he was sharp and quick and every question made Tom felt like he'd just stolen something. Nothing was on offer. It was all clever tricks. Spenser MacDonald was there to expose you and beat your brains out for having the gall to pull it off.

Even Tom's most honest responses felt dirty in MacDonald's rephrasing. Though at home he slept naked, he lay in the hotel bed in his boxers and a T-shirt. He left the TV on to mask the disconcerting city sounds—the CMT channel, as loud as he thought Brad Paisley could be without bothering people in adjoining rooms. For a minute he thought about Marlo Stark, somewhere out among the lights of this city. For a minute he wondered if she'd come to the trial.

She must be aware of it. The thought made him remember that small wrinkle in the fabric of his world, the brief awareness of something different. A curtain pulled aside momentarily to reveal a peek down a corridor into a world that seemed bright and colorful, though he could make out no permanent objects. But that was just a tiny shadow behind him now. In the morning he woke at five and showered and realized he had almost three hours to do nothing in.

* * *

Josie opened her eyes at 6:30 a.m., fully awake, her gut electric with anxiety. She'd been dreaming about anxiety, her body already juiced up in flight-or-fight for no apparent reason. She had been thinking so much about what she would have to do today. She knew things that nobody else did.

She wouldn't be able to talk about those things—wouldn't even if she was asked, not today, but she wanted to guard her secret and she feared so much that somehow, some way, the lawyers would make her say something about it in front of everyone. In the shower, she thought about the times she had been alone with Mike. The first night at the reservoir, when he had appeared so sneakily, the things he had prompted her to talk about. She liked Mike. She wanted to like Mike.

She wanted to like him more. Now there was an imperative. Now they were linked in a way she'd never been linked to anyone before. Josie showered and went with her parents to breakfast. She ate a spinach and cheese omelet. Her father seemed so far away, baffled more than distant, but out of reach in any case. And her mother.

Her mother was driving her insane. She actually ordered Josie coffee. Josie never drank coffee. It was as if her mother was trying to make up for sixteen years of neglect in one day—but her mother had never been neglectful. That's what made it feel so crazy. Her mother wanted to talk.

A lot. Josie went into snail mode. Up into the shell. She offered almost no conversations. She had decided to wear a church outfit, a navy dress that reached below her knees. The courtroom was already filling when they arrived. It didn't look like the TV courtrooms. This was benches and cheap carpet and stained plywood everywhere. She could feel the floorboards bounce under her feet as she walked down the aisle to where they chose to sit. Coach Warner was there.

Arlen Alderdice was there. Wyatt Aarstad. Britnee came in with her mother—they'd stayed at a different hotel to save money. Ainsley and her parents had stayed at the Hilton Garden Inn, and they were already seated when she walked in. Ainsley apparently decided the occasion was worthy of formal wear. She wore a dress

Josie had never seen before—royal blue with spaghetti straps. The judge arrived and sat up on a dais that was smaller than what Josie had thought.

Then Mike came in, a guard grasping his arm above the elbow and jerking him into place. Mike looked around, seeing who he knew. Josie saw his glance elicit a tighter lip set, a higher chin angle from his mother, on the other side of the courtroom. He looked at Josie longer than anyone, long enough that she had a moment of panic that he knew what she was hiding.

But he couldn't. Josie had no idea how boring a trial could be. The first hours were spent going through motions, introducing evidence, officers on the stand talking about what they saw. None of them had been there. None of them knew anything about it. It struck her as ridiculous that these people, so far away from where she and Mike and Matt lived, how they interacted and moved through their days, should have anything to say about what happened in Dumont.

But they would have everything to say about it. Ainsley was called first. Josie felt her gut clench when she heard Ainsley's name—for hours, there had been a litany of nothing, words and terms and people who didn't matter, and then Ainsley Martin. Ainsley sat in the chair and raised her hand and told the story pretty much the way Josie remembered it. There was no cross examination.

Arlen Alderdice came next. He told the same story Ainsley did, although he remembered more about the burning beer box, about the exact words Matt had said. Mike's lawyer, the skinny guy with the fold-over gut, asked him a lot of questions. What were the exact words? Did Matt say "kill"? Did Matt threaten injury? Tell us again, what Matt said when Michael took the burning beer box off his head . . .

Then it was Britnee's turn. What she remembered was the arrival, Matt holding back, searching, it seemed to her when she was prompted.

"Did Matt Brunner appear to you like he might do serious bodily harm to Michael La Valle?" Mike's lawyer, Gossens, asked.

"He was definitely going to hurt him," Britnee said.

"Objection!" from Spenser MacDonald.

"We're going there," Gossens said.

"Get there," the judge said.

"Had you ever seen Matt Brunner hurt somebody in the past?" Gossens asked Britnee.

Britnee looked at Josie and seemed to be asking for help, though Josie didn't know what to offer.

"I know Matt beat up some boys before. I saw it a couple of times."

"When you were there, when you saw Matt Brunner about to beat up other boys, did you know it was going to happen?"

"Well, yeah," Britnee said.

"How?"

"He kind of said so. He was always pretty clear about, 'I'm going to kick your a-s-s,'" Britnee said.

"And when he kicked somebody's a-s-s, did he stop when the fight was over?"

"What do you mean?"

"Well, when it was obvious that he had won, did he stop?"

"Okay, I see what you mean. No. Matt was—the couple times I saw it happen, when Matt won the fight he kept on beating the other guy."

The prosecuting attorney asked Britnee if the people she saw get beat up were ever seriously hurt, and she started to say she didn't think so before Mike's lawyer jumped in to object that she was not a medical expert. The court recessed for lunch with Josie knowing she was next or soon.

* * *

Josie Frehse broke Tom's heart on the stand. Both attorneys wanted to use her. Gossens wanted to show what an awful, abusive partner Matt Brunner had been, and he wasn't wrong. Except for years, he wasn't wrong. In moments Matt had treated Josie unacceptably and those moments escalated in recent time and could be a pattern. Tom watched Josie sit in front of several dozen people—many she knew, many she didn't—and tell the story that nobody was telling that night in Pep's.

The pulling of her by her hair from the truck—Gossens, the attorney, got it all out of her—the punch, the kicks, and the tears pouring down her face while she told it. And then it was MacDonald's turn to rip from her what she knew of Mike LaValle, his possessiveness, his talk of killing and hurting. He made her admit, in front of her mother and father and many people they knew well, that she had had sex with Mike LaValle. It all seemed so teenaged to Tom, though it was easy to see how a skilled attorney could turn it into plot.

Mike LaValle's time on the stand was much briefer than Josie's. Gossens built up a long trail of confrontation and threat. He crafted a story that ended at a bonfire with flames on a kid's head and death threats.

"I thought he was going to kill me," Mike said. "I thought a lot of times he was going to kill me, but this time he said he was going to kill me, and I thought he would."

"If you thought that a lot," Spenser MacDonald queried him on cross, "and you're still alive, wouldn't that suggest that your assessment of when somebody really means they're going to kill you isn't very accurate?"

Sitting and watching, Tom hated both of the attorneys for not trying to reach a truth. They were, he realized, trying to be right, which was such a different thing. He thought about how many times had he exhorted high school boys to kill someone, or some team.

Nobody took that literally. He knew Mike LaValle's circumstances and he knew Matt Brunner bullied the kid. He knew Matt Brunner. He knew about the hazing that . . . dissolved everything he had been building. Mike spent most of the time looking dead ahead, but on a couple of occasions he turned to see the crowd and at least twice he caught Tom's eye.

The kid was terrified, clearly, but what Tom took away was acknowledgment. Thank you for bearing witness. There was not much else. Tom was never called as a witness. The closing arguments came at the end of the day.

"Michael LaValle provoked Matthew Brunner at every level," MacDonald, the prosecutor, opened with. "He ignored early warnings. He pursued Matthew's long-time girlfriend until he actually slept with her. He threatened Matthew's social status. And when it came time for Mr. LaValle to account for his continual impositions, he elevated the response beyond any reasonable norm.

"This is Montana," MacDonald said, standing at the jury box, looking them each in their sincere eyes. "This is Montana. This is a place where hard work and waking up early and busting your gut is just a way to get by. It doesn't make you special, it makes you one of us. You know what it's like. I don't have to tell you. I can tell you what it's not like here. It's not like New York or California where people bring lawsuits over hangnails and hot coffee and want to protect murderers and rapists. In those places, juries don't seem to understand what happens in real life. But that's not Montana. Wherever you're from in Montana, you know what life is like.

"If you're really from Montana, you know this case. This case is simple. A high school boy with an eye for trouble moved in on another high school boy's girlfriend. The boyfriend, an enormously popular kid, a great athlete, the quarterback on the football team, the leading scorer on the basketball team, a kid with a bright future, an unlimited future, he reacts.

"Well, who wouldn't? Maybe he says some things. Are the things he says real? Does he carry a gun? A knife? Or is 'I'm going to kill you' something he says with his friends when he plays video games? When they play basketball. 'I'm going to slaughter you.' 'I'm going to crush you.' Isn't that how boys talk? But what happened with this boy, this mixed-blood boy, is he got paranoid. And he brought a knife to a fistfight.

"I want all of you," MacDonald said, sweeping his arm across the jury box, "to think about this. Michael LaValle could have gone another route. He was sleeping with Matthew Brunner's girlfriend. He deserved a beating for that, and Matthew told him he'd get one. For Montana boys, there are times when people act badly and other people can sort it out. It costs society nothing. People get corrected when they're behaving badly. There are lesson to be learned. You take your beating and you go on. You do not thrust a seven-inch blade into someone's guts and watch them bleed out in the snow."

The moment MacDonald stopped talking, Gossens popped up. "Your honor, I have a motion."

The judge indicated he should go on, though she seemed dubious. "I would like to enter a motion that this case be settled by fistfight."

That sparked a sizzling hum in the courtroom. The judge squinted to figure out how to not be outrun on this. The prosecutor's table was a huddle of heads.

Gossens went on: "The prosecutor's closing argument suggests that my client deserved a beating and that, being a Montana boy, he should have taken it like a man. If that's the way we do justice here in Montana, then I am filing a settlement motion. If the prosecutor can knock me out in a fistfight, he wins and my client goes to jail for a long as he likes. If I win, my client goes free."

"That's the stupidest thing I've ever heard," the judge said.

"But it's exactly what the prosecutor is trying to sell the jury on. And here in Montana, there's no legal precedent to preclude it. I'm happy to risk my face against his."

That's how it all starts, Tom thought. As long as every affront deserved a stolid, physical response, nobody had a chance. The day took a long pause while legal issues were pursued. In the end, the prosecutor risked censure. None of Mike's witnesses were impugned. When they all filtered out of the courtroom, which felt more like a room where you might go to earn your driver's license,

Tom stood in the parking lot and remembered Josie on the stand. She would at least get out, he hoped.

That afternoon, all the people summoned as potential witnesses got in their vehicles and drove back home to Dumont. The following day, the only Dumont people left in that room to hear Mike LaValle found guilty of manslaughter were the Brunners, Caroline Jensen, and Tom Warner.

* * *

The prison did not look the way she had imagined it, not like on TV, though it was dirtier and more demeaning than she had imagined. She was X-rayed and searched, and they opened the zucchini muffins she had made, poking through them with wire probes. The disdain of the guards shocked her. Josie couldn't imagine being so unfriendly to people she didn't know. Pretty-little-white-girl-from-Dumont point of view, she thought then.

That's why the world is different than I think it is. She sat at a table. There was no thick, distorting plexiglass, no speaker to talk into, just a table with cold, metal bench seats. Several other tables in the room were already filled with inmates and their visitors. Except for the jumpsuits, they looked like people she had seen all her life. Mikie came in escorted by a guard. He wore a beige jumpsuit, but he was not handcuffed or chained. He wore his mean, misunderstood look, the same one, she thought, he'd had when he walked away from stabbing Matt. He had an oval bruise under his left eye, and when he drew closer she could see swelling all along that cheekbone. She had been warned not to hug him.

He must have been warned of the same, because he sat right down across from her. And his face changed. He stared at her, searching, and smiled right away. It was not a huge smile, but it radiated the relief he was feeling, as if there was somebody in front of him who could finally see him. That made her happy. Even knowing the things she had come to tell him, it felt good to know she brought him back to himself.

"Are you okay?" was the first thing she asked him.

He nodded.

"What's it . . . like?"

"Pretty awful."

Josie didn't know what to say to that, and knew that where he was and where he was going was not the territory of the conversation she'd come to map out.

"Is there anything I can send you? I made these myself," she said, nodding at the muffins on the table.

"The food here is worse than school," Mikie said. He huffed a little laugh.

"No way."

"Dude, way. So way."

"That's awful."

Josie desperately wanted to avoid silences, so she lifted her chin, a gesture toward the swelling on his face. "What happened?"

She saw the change, the curtain come over his eyes, closing off the view into that part of him. He shrugged. "Things happen here."

For a moment she wished he wouldn't try to show her how tough he was. She didn't like people showing her they were tough anymore. But then she understood that it wasn't for her. He would need that to survive now. "Have you talked to your lawyer about your appeal?"

Mikie lifted a smaller shrug as if nothing could be less consequential. Which prompted Josie to think about what was consequential, about why she was there.

"I came here because I wanted to see you," Josie said.

"Thank you, Josie. I mean that. I know it's not, like, where you'd want to hang out."

"But also because I have something to tell you."

She could see that whatever she said next would come as a total surprise, so she said it.

"I'm pregnant. The baby's yours. There's no doubt."

Josie had thought about how it would happen for the entire four-hour drive here. It was true, she knew. She'd had a period between when she last been with Matt and when she was with Mike. And then she didn't have periods anymore. All the way here, she had thought about the different ways to say it, the different things she might say about it. It made her feel so old, so much older than him. She had imagined all the ways he might respond. *What are you going to do? Are you going to keep it? Are you sure it's mine? What do you want me to do? What will we name it? Oh my god, a baby?*

Why are you telling me this? If he reacted badly, she had told herself, it might be just him being furious that life had given him something he was so ill-equipped to deal with, and it would have nothing to do with her or the baby. If he tried to tell her what to do, she would shut him down.

She'd already decided that. She had talked to her mother for a long time about it, tried to tell her everything she knew about Mike, tried to think about anything he might say.

But he said something she hadn't anticipated: "They have to let me marry you. We can do it in here if we have to. They have to let me."

"We're not going to get married," she said. "My first marriage isn't going to happen inside a prison." That felt reasonable. She couldn't tell if he liked her answer, but the certainty with which she'd said it snuffed out immediate feedback.

So he said, "Wow." And then, "Shit."

"I don't expect anything," she said. "I just thought—knew—you had to know."

"You're going to keep it?"

"Yes," she said, firmly enough.

"How are you going to raise it? What about college?"

"My family will help. My mom. She raised me. She did a pretty good job."

"I thought you wanted to go to college and play basketball."

"I guess we don't always get everything we want."

He considered his surroundings before saying, "I guess not."

"It's a girl. I know that already. I don't think there's any reason to make a big mystery out of it."

"Wow. A baby. A daughter. Holy shit. You're blowing my mind, Jos." She thought, though, that he was speaking with the energy of a blown-out mind.

"I know. It's a lot. And you already have a lot."

"I want to be there. I want to be there when you have her."

Josie nodded several times fast. Of course he would. But nobody was going to let him.

"We're going to have a baby," Mike said. "Shit. When will I be able to see her? How old will she have to be before you can bring her here?"

Here was another of those things that made Josie feel so old. She looked at Mike, listened to him talk about his blown mind and his baby coming to prison, though she knew perfectly well that was not what would happen. For so long Josie had so many ideas about how her life would be, so many plans—so many of them hatched during the long, lonely hours driving a grain truck. She had been working from happiness then, working hard in the moment and imagining futures and how they would play out for her.

What life would be like once it got started. Now she was willing to admit that she had no idea how her life would happen. She was going to have a baby girl. She was going to try to raise a child. So many things about what that was like couldn't even occur to her yet. She was smart enough to know that.

She was decisive enough to accept enormous chunks of uncertainty as an outlook for her future. Not-knowing. But to offset the grinding anxiety not-knowing caused, she would choose whenever she could. And she had chosen something she felt she owed it to Mike to share.

"I'm not going to tell my baby her daddy is in prison," she said. "Maybe later, when she's older. A lot. Older. And maybe later, when you're finished here, if you want to come and meet her, then I think it's right for you to know her, and if you can be part of our lives somehow, okay. But I don't want you to think or hope that that means we're going to be a couple, or a family."

She paused to let him absorb that and saw from the inward turn of his face that he wasn't really, that he was opting for outrage and insecurity. Same old thing that put him here.

"Mike, it's such a long, long time from now, you getting out of here, and I'm going to live my life however it happens, and I want to try to be happy and hope for good things for me and this little girl. And I really want you, like, someday if not now, to be able to hope for good things for me and for her.

"And I understand if you can't right now, because I know what you're going through is really hard—really, really hard—but I'm still going to try to find those good things. And if I meet somebody, I want my child to know what it's like to have a father who can be in her life. And if I ever am lucky enough, I want her to see what it's like for her mother to know real love in her life."

"I love you, Josie," he said, scalded by affront. "I know I do."

This was what Josie had come to say. Keeping cool was what she had come to do. She said, "You don't know anything, Mike. You're seventeen and you killed . . . a terrible thing happened that must be so hard for you to come to grips with—so hard I can't even imagine—but you're going . . . you're going to be away from me and from us for a long, long time—most of this little girl's growing-up life. And you're terrified, and who wouldn't be? But the whole real truth is, we were never a couple. You don't love me. You barely even know me."

She could see the angry bafflement, could see he was going to argue the moment she stopped to take a deep breath, so she didn't.

"You don't know when my birthday is, or what I got my mom for Christmas last year, or the music I listen to when I'm driving the grain truck, or who my favorite basketball players are, or what I like to do on rainy days, and you're going to be away from me for so long and there will be so many other things that come up in my life that you won't know about me. You don't love me, Mike. Maybe you love the idea of me. But you don't love *me*. And you can't, not now. Even if you wanted to, you can't for a long, long time."

"God, I do love you, Josie. I have loved you for a long time. You're just too stupid to see it."

She had anticipated this stridence and returned a firm, collected cool. "You wanted me. And you got me. For a minute. But that's not love."

His outrage reduced him to the simplest ember of him she'd ever seen, and she could see something beautiful in that burning purity. A glimpse of his essence, the hot white torch that kept Michael LaValle alight. Josie noted that the nearest guard was suddenly paying attention. She looked across the table at the skinny boy in the jumpsuit, at his wild, fiery eyes intent on burning understanding into her.

He was a kid, she saw, just a kid with two or three ideas about who he was. Although his present circumstances meant he was done being a kid about now. Josie felt like the way adults must feel when they told her things they knew she couldn't possibly see yet. She felt like she knew so many things Mike couldn't understand. She had felt that way before she came here, though the reassurance she saw in front of her was in no way comforting

"I know this isn't fair," she said. "But right now everything I have to think about is this baby. I hope she's as smart as you are, and I hope she's as fierce as you are. I hope she's that willing to fight for herself, to get what she thinks she deserves, like you do. And I hope, Michael, that someday you know her. I'm going to go now."

Mike was scrunching even further forward to protest, but Josie stood and signaled to the guard who had been watching them. When the guard stepped forward, Mike blasted himself backward in the chair, exasperated, arms akimbo, eyes askance. Behind her,

Mike was shouting, "I want to name her! I want to name her!" But Josie was leaving.

She felt awful about what his next days and nights would be like, already here in this awful place and now knowing he would have a daughter in the world and no idea about how she was living for years and years to come. She knew Mike would have a million questions, a million desires and impulses. But, Josie thought, his having them didn't mean she needed to absorb them. She was finished letting other people's desires map her life. She was leaving with her baby girl and going back home to figure out how next would happen.

* * *

August. Harvest. Josie's favorite time. Walking between the pickup and the combine, birdsong ran by her like a current, trickling and eddying away, ringing and pouring away. It was funny to think of a year, what could happen in twelve short months. A year ago at this time everybody had been gearing up for what was surely going to be a state championship run for the football team. Her brother had been a star about to become a bigger star. Her boyfriend had been the quarterback. They were all gone, now.

Twelve months. Coach Warner, the most important person in town, it had seemed back then, was gone. Off to Missoula to be an assistant for the Grizzlies, coaching running backs—coincidentally he would be coaching Jared there. Jared, who Coach Warner talked the Montana staff into giving a scholarship. Jared who, for the first time in his life, would be a benchwarmer. Jenny Calhoun gone, too, gone with Coach Warner and her kids to Missoula. Two people Josie had thought of as fixtures, people she couldn't for the longest time imagine the town without. But there were no fixtures. Only the people you share with friends when you are young.

Matt Brunner.

He had chosen her when she was too young to know what it meant to choose. He became so much to her, more than she could possibly have known while she was in the middle of it. And then he was gone, the first person to be murdered in Dumont in over forty years.

Gone.

Killed by the father of her child.

And now that child. A daughter. A few more weeks and she would have a daughter. She had already decided to name the girl Elle, and call her Ellie. Her mother thought she should not work harvest, that she was too far along, that the heat and dust and stress would be bad for the baby.

But Josie wanted her daughter to know what this life was like, to feel it in her blood. And there was still grain to be harvested and trucks to fill and trips to make to the elevator. Only now Josie was not alone and she wasn't driving trucks. With Jared in Missoula and Matt gone, Cal Frehse needed combine drivers. He hired help, mostly old-timers who'd given up on their own farms. But he knew where to trust. Now Josie drove a combine and the help drove the trucks that she offloaded grain into.

One new hand was a young man from Fort Benton, just a couple years out of high school, a lean, quiet, and tanned boy with an easy smile. In the combine, she could sing to somebody. She had the kicks and twists and hiccups of a living person within her while she bounced along the field. And when it was time to unload? Nobody dates a girl who's nine months pregnant, but she could imagine how a cute boy with an easy smile might like a curvy young single mom one day. There was nothing wrong with imagining that.

How somebody might meet little Ellie and be as charmed by her as Josie already was, might want to bring a lovely young daughter into his own life. If that didn't happen, it was okay. Already Dotty Lantner had committed her own teenaged daughter to babysitting Josie's if Josie promised to play basketball her senior year. Hal Hartack had told her she would never pay for another meal at Pep's. Brad Martin offered her a part-time job, flexible hours, the same work Ainsley did now for almost free. Britnee was some days moving to Great Falls when they graduated and some days moving to Billings, but all the days in between she and Josie talked about how they were going to dress Josie's child and the things they were going to teach her about being a girl. There was still her senior basketball season.

She'd be a mother, but that didn't seem a reason to lose a step. She wouldn't be the first. And other Dumont girls had gone to Missoula and Bozeman to play basketball in college. Her mother had already said she would help with Ellie, and other people would help with Ellie, would make sure that Ellie had everything Dumont could give—and that Ellie had everything that Josie didn't know how to give. Maybe it was all just dreams and the details wouldn't work out.

But maybe was still worth having in mind on a stifling August day with so much hot blue sky overhead. Josie looked at the fields of waving wheat stretching unbroken in front of her. The combine was easy to drive. Staying straight was no problem. She loved where she was. She hoped she could love where she would get to. Behind her, where she'd already cut, straight lines of fresh-cut stubble mapped exactly where she'd been, parallel lines scoring the contours of the earth. If she looked far enough back, near the horizon those rows seemed to angle into each other. The difference between them touching and not touching would be imperceptible.

And she knew that if she were far, far away from here, standing on that distant, unfinished horizon, those same lines might seem to come together on her.